## Reviews from Secrets Volume 4

"*Secrets, Volume 4*, has something to satisfy every erotic fantasy...
simply sexsational!"

— Virginia Henley, *New York Times* Best Selling Author

"Provocative...seductive...a must read!" **4 Stars**

— *Romantic Times*

"These are the kind of stories that romance readers that 'want a little
more' have been looking for all their lives without crossing over into
the adult genre. Keep these stories coming, Red Sage, the world needs
them!"

— Lani Roberts, *Affaire de Coeur*

"If you're interested in exploring erotica, or reading farther than the
sexual passages of your favorite steamy reads, the *Secret* series is well
worth checking out."

— *Writers Club Romance Group* on AOL

## Reviews from Secrets Volume 5

"*Secrets, Volume 5*, is a collage of lucious sensuality. Any woman who
reads *Secrets* is in for an awakening!"

— **Virginia Henley,** *New York Times* Best Selling Author

"Hot, hot, hot! Not for the faint-hearted!"

— *Romantic Times*

"As you make your way through the stories, you will find yourself becoming hotter and hotter. *Secrets* just keeps getting better and better."

— *Affaire de Coeur*

## Reviews from Secrets Volume 6

"*Secrets, Volume 6* satisfies every female fantasy: the Bodyguard, the Tutor, the Werewolf, and the Vampire. I give it Six Stars!"
— Virginia Henley, *New York Times* Best Selling Author

"*Secrets, Volume 6* is the best of *Secrets* yet. ...four of the most erotic stories in one volume than this reader has yet to see anywhere else. ... These stories are full of erotica at its best and you'll definitely want to keep it handy for lots of re-reading!"
— *Affaire de Coeur*

## Reviews from Secrets Volume 7

### Winner of the Venus Book Club Best Book of the Year

"...sensual, sexy, steamy fun. A perfect read!"
— Virginia Henley, *New York Times* Best Selling Author

"Intensely provocative and disarmingly romantic, Secrets Volume 7 is a romance reader's paradise that will take you beyond your wildest dreams!"
— *Ballston Book House* Review

"Erotic romance is at the sensual core of Red Sage's latest collection of short, red hot novels, *Secrets, Volume 7.*"
— *Writers Club Romance Group* on AOL

## Reviews from Secrets Volume 8

### Winner of the Venus Book Club Best Book of the Year

"*Secrets Volume 8* is simply sensational!"
— Virginia Henley, *New York Times* Best Selling Author

"*Secrets Volume 8* is an amazing compilation of sexy stories discovering a wide range of subjects, all designed to titillate the senses."
— Lani Roberts, *Affaire de Coeur*

"All four tales are well written and fun to read because even the sexiest scenes are not written for shock value, but interwoven smoothly and realistically into the plots. This quartet contains strong storylines and solid lead characters, but then again what else would one expect from the no longer *Secrets* anthologies."

— Harriet Klausner

"Once again, Red Sage Publishing takes you on a journey of sexual delight, teasing and pleasing the reader with a bit of something to appeal to everyone."

— Michelle Houston, *Courtesy Sensual Romance*

"In this sizzling volume, four authors offer short stories in four different sub-genres: contemporary, paranormal, historical, and futuristic. These ladies' assignments are to dazzle, tantalize, amaze, and entice. Your assignment, as the reader, is to sit back and enjoy. Just have a fan and some ice water at your side."

— Amy Cunningham

## Reviews from Secrets Volume 9

"Everyone should expect only the most erotic stories in a *Secrets* book. ...if you like your stories full of hot sexual scenes, then this is for you!"

— Donna Doyle, *Romance Reviews*

"*Secrets 9*...is sinfully delicious, highly arousing, and hotter than hot as the pages practically burn up as you turn them."

— Suzanne Coleburn, *Reader To Reader Reviews/ Belles & Beaux of Romance*

"Treat yourself to well-written fictionthat's hot, hotter, and hottest!"

— Virginia Henley, *New York Times* Best Selling Author

## Reviews from Secrets Volume 10

"*Secrets Volume 10*, an erotic dance through medieval castles, sultan's palaces, the English countryside and expensive hotel suites, explodes with passion-filled pages."

— *Romantic Times BOOKclub*

"Having read the previous nine volumes, this one fulfills the expectations of what is expected in a *Secrets* book: romance and eroticism at its best!!"
— *Fallen Angel Reviews*

"All are hot steamy romances so if you enjoy erotica romance, you are sure to enjoy *Secrets, Volume 10*. All this reviewer can say is WOW!!"
— *The Best Reviews*

## Reviews from Secrets Volume 11

"*Secrets Volume 11* delivers once again with storylines that include erotic masquerades, ancient curses, modern-day betrayal and a prince charming looking for a kiss. Scorching tales filled with humor, passion and love." **4 Stars**
— *Romantic Times BOOKclub*

"The *Secrets* books published by Red Sage Publishing are well known for their excellent writing and highly erotic stories and *Secrets, Volume 11* will not disappoint. "
— *The Road to Romance*

"*Secrets 11* quite honestly is my favorite anthology from Red Sage so far. All four novellas had me glued to their stories until the very end. I was just disappointed that these talented ladies novellas weren't longer."
— *The Best Reviews*

"Indulge yourself with this erotic treat and join the thousands of readers who just can't get enough. Be forewarned that *Secrets 11* will whet your appetite for more, but will offer you the ultimate in pleasurable erotic literature."
— *Ballston Book House Review*

## Reviews from Secrets Volume 12

"*Secrets Volume 12*, turns on the heat with a seductive encounter inside a bookstore, a temple of naughty and sensual delight, a galactic inferno that thaws ice, and a lightening storm that lights up the English shoreline. Tales of looking for love in all the right places with a heat rating out the charts." **4½ Stars**
— *Romantic Times BOOKclub*

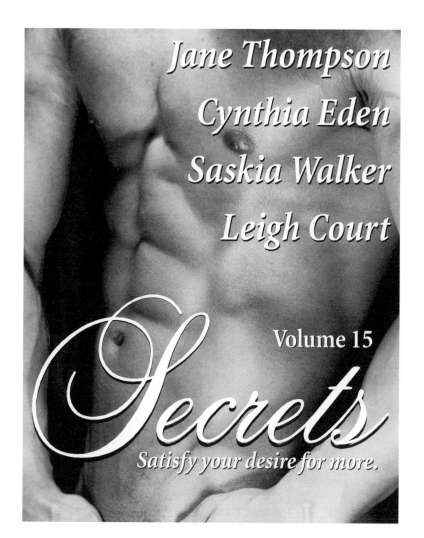

Jane Thompson

Cynthia Eden

Saskia Walker

Leigh Court

Volume 15

*Secrets*

*Satisfy your desire for more.*

SECRETS Volume 15
This is an original publication of Red Sage Publishing and each individual story herein has never before appeared in print. These stories are a collection of fiction and any similarity to actual persons or events is purely coincidental.

Red Sage Publishing, Inc.
P.O. Box 4844
Seminole, FL 33775
727-391-3847
www.redsagepub.com

SECRETS Volume 15
A Red Sage Publishing book
All Rights Reserved/December 2005
Copyright © 2005 by Red Sage Publishing, Inc.

❥ ISBN 0-9754516-5-0

Published by arrangement with the authors and copyright holders of the individual works as follows:

**SIMON SAYS**
Copyright © 2005 by Jane Thompson

**BITE OF THE WOLF**
Copyright © 2005 by Cynthia Eden

**FALLING FOR TROUBLE**
Copyright © 2005 by Saskia Walker

**THE DISPLINARIAN**
Copyright © 2005 by Leigh Court

Photographs:
Cover © 2005 by Tara Kearney; www.tarakearney.com
**Cover Models:** Diana Peterfreund and Will Scheid
Setback cover © 2000 by Greg P. Willis; email: GgnYbr@aol.com

Printed in the U.S.A.

Book typesetting by:

Quill & Mouse Studios, Inc.
www.quillandmouse.com

# Contents

# Simon Says

*by Jane Thompson*

### To My Reader:

Want to hear something it has taken me most of my life to figure out? Perfection is in the eye of the beholder.

# *Chapter One*

*Simon Says* column, Wednesday, June 16<sup>th</sup>

*Nothing makes sense anymore.*

*The Red Sox won the World Series.*

*Arnold Schwarzenegger is still governor of California.*

*Another one of my brothers is getting married.*

*What the hell is going on? The divorce rate is high enough in this country without my family throwing in, state government is already in the toilet and, come on... the Red Sox? I am up a Major League creek without a paddle.*

*Don't get me wrong, I'm all about rooting for the underdog but the Red Sox taking the pennant was nothing less than a harbinger of weird things to come. Case in point, the Terminator is a public servant that just happens to call his opponents 'girlie-men'. This is worse than when Jesse Ventura took over the helm of the great state of Minnesota (let's all take a moment to remember how well that turned out) and, to top it all off, my mom is still mad at me about my drunken best man speech from the last family wedding I had to endure. There's only one thing to do...*

*Vote? Admit that organized sports are no substitute for meaningful interpersonal relationships? Spend some time investigating my knee-jerk aversion to the institution of marriage?*

*Not in this lifetime.*

*I have formulated a three-prong attack (why don't we just call it a fork-attack and be done with it?). Free booze, easy women and access to the beach. Yes, idiot reader, yours truly is looking at three alcohol-soaked days of sun, sand and sex to obliterate reality, gratis a friend of mine whose name and/or address I am not at liberty to divulge (so don't bother asking). It's enough for you to know that my host is in possession of a monstrous beachfront estate, complete with a full bar in his living room.*

*It'll take me weeks to recover from the hangover, and then there will be lawyers to contact, medical bills to expense and letters of apology to compose. In short, there will be a variety of charges.*

*Things are looking up my friend... up, up and away.*

Friday

The first night of Simon Campbell's much anticipated three days of sun, sand and sex found the man himself leaning against the bar in his host's vast living room, a drink in one hand, a blond in the other, and so bored he was seriously entertaining the idea of ditching the blond, keeping the drink, and going upstairs to see what was on TV. It was a sad state of affairs when a man, surrounded as he was by a veritable smorgasbord of beautiful women, found himself wishing for nothing more than a comfortable chair and the remote.

There goes my career.

"Nah," Simon muttered, nudging the blond off his side with an impatient flick of his arm. She teetered back with a giggle, then began flirting with the bartender.

The TV urge was a momentary glitch, nothing to worry about. He was just tired... as in *sleep-deprived*, not tired as in the idea of living through one more weekend like this was starting to feel like one of life's have-tos, on a par with flossing and voting and...

And this train of thought was getting him nowhere.

Simon turned towards the bar to order another Chivas over ice. Maybe booze would help.

As he waited for the bartender to notice him, Simon glanced up at the large wall of glass behind the bar and saw, not the majesty of the Pacific Ocean at night as he had expected, but rather the room reflected back at him. It felt as if he was looking into an old mirror that had gone hazy and dim. Simon studied the collection of laughing, beautiful people spread out behind him. There wasn't a hair out of place or an unsightly bulge among them. With the muted, recessed lighting, the minimalist beige décor and all these beautiful people, Simon felt like he was in an up-scale bar rather than the living room of a private home.

Checking out the faces in the crowd, Simon had to admit that the turn-out tonight was impressive. This being L.A., most of the guests were either household names or grasping after that same dubious distinction, blindly following the New American Dream to the movies, TV or a lucrative re-cording deal.

Simon wasn't interested in having his face on every billboard between Santa Monica and Times Square but that was only because he preferred the writing life... his version of it, anyway. Every Wednesday, his byline appeared in newspapers across the country and below it followed a report from the front lines of what every desk-locked, thirty-something Ameri-can male considered a fantasy life: free tickets to every sports arena and nightclub in the Los Angeles area, invites to record launches and movie premieres and, to his readers' endless delight, an ever growing parade of young women eager to get naked for a chance to appear in print as another one of *Simon Says'* conquests.

Lately, Simon had been tossing in a few political comments but he was going to have to stop doing that. His editor was making just a little too much noise about them, saying that the comments had the flavor of a possible new direction, and if Simon was in any way interested in broadening his horizons, the powers-that-be would have no problem with it.

Yeah, right. The second *Simon Says'* readership fell off, the powers-that-be would fire his ass and he'd be back to writing obituaries. Simon would rather write his own obituary, then shoot himself, than go back to that.

Returning his attention to the wall of glass behind the bar, Simon narrowed his eyes, looking past the frolicsome guests to the serene ocean beyond. He searched for the horizon, that hard, dark line where ocean gave way to sky. Strangely enough, when he found it, there appeared to be someone standing on it.

Huh?

*Must be someone lurking up in the gallery*, Simon realized. Turning around, he looked up towards the second story gallery, a narrow promenade that jutted out over the crowd. There in the shadows, with her hands gripping the wrought-iron railing, stood the one, and thank you Jesus for small favors, *only*, Ms. Georgina Abigail Kennedy.

Early thirties, slender, brunette, and almost as tall as him, Georgina was an annoying spinster-librarian with a hooker's mouth and a snotty, holier-than-thou attitude that made Simon want to mess up her hair and take a bite out of that mouth just to see her react with something more than polite disdain when she looked at him.

"What the *hell* is she doing here?" Simon asked, too shocked by her presence to keep his voice down.

The blond next to him, who had been blithely blathering on about God-knew-what for the past ten minutes, followed his gaze and said, "Oh, I heard she was going to be here."

Simon looked down at… Cherry… no… Sherry… no, wait; what was this woman's *name*… Cheryl, that was it… and watched as she waved towards the balcony. He turned back in time to see Georgina wave back, a serene, All Hail the Queen look on her face.

"You know her?" Simon sputtered.

"I had lunch with her and Valerie last week. Do you know Valerie Kennedy?" Cheryl asked.

"Yeah," Simon said. He and Valerie had been friends for years, but if she had something to do with Georgina's presence here tonight…

"Oh, that's right. You went to Valerie's birthday party last month. I couldn't go, I was in Vegas. And we had sooo much fun."

Something in Simon's expression must have clued Cheryl into the fact he didn't give a rip about her trip to Vegas. After floundering for a second, Cheryl picked up the thread of conversation having to do with Georgina and ran with it.

"Georgina is Valerie's cousin. I was surprised that she was so nice, Georgina, not Valerie. By the look of her, I thought she would be a bitch but she wasn't. Come to find out, she's a librarian and, get this, Valerie told me that our host hired her to organize his library this weekend. Kind of weird timing but…" Cheryl giggled and then waved her hand listlessly in Georgina's general direction, the gesture apparently completing her thought.

"Jerome's having his library organized the same weekend he's hosting this party?" Simon asked. Their host for the weekend, Jerome Vance, was an odd one but shit, this took the keg. "Well, that explains Miss Perfect's presence here tonight."

"Yeah, it sure does… Wait, don't tell me that *you've* met her," Cheryl gasped.

"Yeah," Simon said, glancing back towards the gallery. Georgina had stepped away from the railing and Simon sincerely hoped she wasn't on her way down here. The last thing he needed was another run-in with her high-and-mighty-ness. He was still reeling from his first encounter with her three weeks ago at his friend Valerie's thirtieth birthday party. After Valerie had introduced them, Georgina had gifted him with a thin-lipped smile, a cool 'How do you do' and then spent the rest of the party looking through him rather than at him, quickly changing direction when their paths were about to cross. Basically behaving as if he was something she had scraped off her shoe earlier in the evening and was determined to stay clear of until such time as she could leave the premises altogether.

Simon was usually immune to the scorn ladled out to him by the good women of the world, and he wouldn't have given her a second thought if she hadn't been so damn nice to everyone else. She'd treated every flighty party girl and hard-eyed womanizer to a kind smile, a little chit-chat and an offer to refill their drink. Valerie had stuck by her cousin all night, acting as a buffer between Georgina and the raunchier advances of some of the guests, frustrating Simon's urge to take the librarian down a peg or two by informing her that a few of the men she was being so nice to were thousands of times sleazier than he was.

Simon again felt the need to ruffle Georgina's feathers and get back a little of his own, mostly to make up for the fact that he still remembered the sinking feeling he had gotten every time she'd turned her nose up at him.

No longer the least bit bored, and with the hint of an evil smile playing around the corners of his mouth, Simon excused himself, picked up his drink and made his way toward the narrow staircase that led up to the gallery.

Topping the stairs, Simon paused to allow his eyes to adjust to the darkness. He saw Georgina, a lone woman in a loose-fitting brown dress, slowly making her way deeper into the shadows, eschewing the confusion of light and noise below in favor of this dark gallery, lined by empty bookshelves. She paused to run her finger along a shelf, allowing him a clear view of her face in profile. With her hair resting at the nape of her neck in an intricately formed knot, she appeared a porcelain cameo, cool and finely drawn, above all the messy emotions that plagued normal human beings. When her mouth came to life in a close-lipped, wistful little grin, Simon lost his breath.

*Tell me what you're thinking, share yourself with me.*

Stunned by the depth of longing behind that wholly unwelcome thought, Simon turned to leave her to her solitary wanderings. He'd come up here to mess with her, not yearn for a clue into what had brought on that sad smile. But then she turned her head, aware that she was no longer alone, and he hated her response when she realized who had joined her. The way she stiffened and drew back, crossed her arms over her chest and tipped her nose into the air, all of it shoved him forward, each reaction moving him one step closer until he was nearly on top of her.

She didn't so much as flinch. Instead, she looked him up and down, as if she couldn't quite believe he would dare approach her.

Without saying a word, Simon waited until her eyes met his. Then he pushed forward, breaching that invisible line people set up between themselves and the unknown, barging into her personal space. That got her. She backed up with a soft gasp and a small, stumbling step that left her trapped between the bookshelves and his body. He felt a rush of triumph at having shaken her reserve, but it wasn't nearly enough. He lifted his arm, set his drink on the shelf next to her head and then gripped the edge of that same shelf, caging her on one side.

She didn't like that. Her eyes widened and she drew in her breath. Simon thoroughly enjoyed the tremulous sound as he let his gaze roam over her face.

Large, dark eyes, smooth pale skin and a gorgeous mouth he hated to admit he'd entertained a few fantasies about since the last time he'd seen her. Wide and soft and gently curved, her mouth was the one sensuous aspect of her appearance she couldn't downplay or hide altogether. It probably drove her nuts that she had a mouth any man would pay good money to use. He smiled, a nasty grin fueled by a recurring fantasy he'd had of her, down on her knees before him, her lips wrapped around his cock, his hands buried in her hair, both of them collaborating on the full-scale destruction of her prim façade.

Georgina flushed, as if she knew what he was thinking, as if she could see herself as he did, allowing him to slowly push his cock into her mouth, one of her hands caressing his hip, the other buried under the full skirt of her dress, languidly strumming her clit in time to his thrusts. Simon abruptly lost his sly amusement on a dizzying rush of pure lust.

He licked his bottom lip, peeked down her dress and saw that her nipples had drawn up into tight, hard peaks against her thin white cotton bra.

"Well, well, well… what *have* we here?" he murmured, thinking maybe he'd misjudged her, maybe she was here to do more than organize books, maybe…

Expecting a slap, Simon was shocked by the feather-light touch of her fingertips against his jaw. The gentle touch scrambled his thoughts into a low-level babble that ceased altogether when she leaned forward and gently licked his bottom lip, exactly where he just had. And then she paused, her top lip barely brushing his as her eyes closed and she inhaled, the sound going through him like lightening. That split second of anticipation hung between them, turning him on more than anything that had happened to him in the past… God, how many years?

Then she kissed him and he could taste her, feel her gently sucking his tongue into her mouth, and it felt as if she was savoring him. She slowly upped the pressure, slid her fingers into his hair, turning his head as she deepened the kiss, practically eating at his mouth. Someone moaned, a broken, desperate sound Simon hoped to hell hadn't come from him. It was one of the hottest kisses he had ever received, and he just stood there, hands fisted at his sides, his body so tense he was vibrating, his mind in a whirl, down-shifting from disliking her into a frightening, Holy-Jesus-what-took-you-so-long-to-find-me babble that sounded eerily like the love-struck ramblings his brothers engaged in when talking about the first time they'd met their wives.

The heat and mind-bending skill of her mouth combined with the horrifying wrongness of that thought were too much, and he pulled back, needing a second to calm down and decide exactly what the hell he wanted from her before he either attacked her or ran screaming for the hills. But she stole that second, took that momentary distance and used it to escape down the corridor, leaving him furiously aroused, thoroughly confused and wondering who had just gotten the better of whom.

As he watched her leave him, all he could think was that he'd just been sideswiped by a librarian.

*Forget that, you moron! She's getting away.*

But Simon let her go, forcing his body to turn towards the stairs that led back to the party rather than rushing after her and begging for another shot at that world-class mouth.

A man had his pride, and his revolted at the idea of panting after a thirty-something spinster librarian. And that whole where-have-you-been-all-my-life... that was a load of crap. He hadn't believed it when his brothers spouted it, and he sure as hell wasn't buying it now, not when it was attached to a living, breathing cliché of what most people thought librarians were supposed to be.

Well, at least he'd gotten one thing out of this whole fiasco; his libido was back in full swing. Hell, he was so hard he could go after Cherry... Sherry... um... whatever the hell her name was... without a qualm.

*No, no, no... not what's her name,* his mind screamed. *The other one, the tall one, with the soft hands and delicious mouth.*

"No," Simon said, finishing his drink in one swallow.

Georgina was the last woman in the world that would want anything to do with him, she was...

*Getting away. Go after her.*

"Shut. Up," Simon hissed.

Most people would be alarmed at the idea of arguing with their inner voice but Simon was used to it. Apparently it was normal for someone in his line of work to have a sort of split personality thing going on.

As a licensed psychologist had so eloquently put it, "It's your inner self arguing for a life of its own, trying to remind you that you're more than the dead-brained caveman you pretend to be for that stupid column of yours."

Simon grinned. His professional opinion had come from his sister-in-law, Sylvia, and she hadn't felt the need to refrain from making judgment calls about his chosen profession. No matter, getting a clean bill of mental health had been a relief because having a voice in his head urging him to spend more time at home or with his family, including his niece and four nephews, was kind of scary, as if his brain had been hijacked by Mr. Rogers.

*You're starting to piss me off here. Go after her. She's probably in the attic... alone. Go apologize, be charming, do whatever it takes, just get her under you.*

Whoa, his formerly home and hearth inner voice was starting to sound like General Patton... and no one argued with Patton.

"Fine," Simon muttered, setting his glass down on one of the empty shelves. "But if she slaps me with a restraining order, I'm getting a lobotomy."

Georgina Kennedy knew she should have stayed at home *way* before Simon Campbell pinned her against a bookshelf and peeked down her dress.

"Lured into temptation by books," Georgina muttered as she ran back up the stairs that led to the attic library. "How very fitting."

Georgia should have known this job was too good to be true. Her cousin Valerie was personal assistant to Jerome Vance, an obscenely rich man known for both his extensive personal library as well as the raunchy house parties he liked to host. Unfortunately, it had never occurred to Georgina to ask Valerie if this job coincided with one of those house parties. When she found out that it did, she should have packed up her stuff and gone home. Instead, Georgina had convinced herself that she could easily ignore the shenanigans going on downstairs because she was an adult and in control of her baser nature.

*Riiiiiight...* she'd lasted all of two hours before sneaking down to have a peek at what was going on in the living room. And that's when she'd seen Simon Campbell, slouched against the bar, lazily flirting with every woman that caught his eye. His long, lean body wrapped in a wrinkled, long sleeve white oxford-cloth shirt and broken down jeans, he'd looked as if he'd rolled out of bed an hour ago and was contemplating returning there with a few of the female guests in tow.

Any female guest, apparently, but her.

Which was *just fine* by Georgina because Simon Campbell was a golden haired, black-eyed menace to her mental well-being, a man she had vastly underestimated, based on the persona he had created for his column, *Simon Says*.

For years, and despite Valerie's insistence to the contrary, Georgina had believed that Simon was nothing but an over-indulged, empty-headed play-boy wasting his life on a trivial career scribbling about his useless existence. She had dismissed him as a consummate womanizer, suave and shallow, the kind of guy that spent most of his time with a surfboard between his legs, proudly admitted he read Playboy for the pictures and called every woman he dated 'babe' based solely on the fact that he couldn't remember their names. It hadn't helped that every word and photograph ever printed about the man backed up her assessment.

And then she'd met him at Valerie's party, taken one look at him, up close and in the flesh, and instantly realized her mistake. Everything she had thought about him was indeed true, except for the part about him being shallow and empty-headed. There had been something unnerving in the way he had looked her over, his eyes so dark they appeared black above a long, thin blade of a nose. The man had a cruelly sensual mouth, a mouth that had given Georgina salacious thoughts even as it tipped up at one corner in a bored smirk. He hadn't been charming or flirtatious; oh no, *that* would have been easy enough to deal with. After studying her face for one endless moment, he'd lost his smirk and he'd suddenly looked...

hungry, like a predator calculating whether or not the creature before him could assuage his need.

Her body had reacted before her brain could interfere, softening, heating and for a split second, she'd swayed towards him, wanting him so much she'd almost reached out and grabbed fistfuls of his shirt so she could yank his body flush with hers. That immediate, visceral reaction had scared her so badly she'd done the absolute opposite.

She'd ducked behind a cool façade of polite indifference and, after Valerie finished introducing them, she'd walked away... before she gave into her body's demand that she lunge for his mouth.

Tonight, watching him move towards her through the shadowed gallery, had been just as nerve-wracking as three weeks ago, more so without a crowd of people around to act as a buffer, and she'd wanted nothing more than to take him up on his threat of hard-edged, sensual satisfaction. But she'd held firm, until he'd licked his bottom lip, peeked down her dress and practically purred in her ear. If he'd kept that mouth of his shut, she might have gotten away with her dignity intact. But he'd spoken, his voice pitched so low it had felt like a caress.

And so she'd kissed him.

Okay, she'd practically devoured him but, damn it, she was only human and he...

Georgina stopped her headlong dash up the stairs, bowed her head and covered her face with shaking hands. The look on his face the second after he'd pulled away from her was one she would never forget.

"Abject horror," she muttered, lifting her face out of her hands with a snort. "How very flattering."

With a sigh, Georgina opened the door to the library and slipped inside. Located on the fourth floor of the house, in a large, rectangular attic, complete with a pitched ceiling, the library was so different from that bland, minimalist living room it wasn't hard for Georgina to pretend that she was in a different house altogether. The décor was aristocratically shabby and comfortable, the wood floor covered by a crazy quilt of threadbare Turkish carpets, their wild patterns and jewel-toned colors muted by age. Little bean-pot lamps sat on a variety of low, antique wooden end tables, shedding a soft, golden light from under their linen shades. There was even an old brass bed, wide and long, buried under a mound of pillows and draped with a velvet comforter the color of a summer sky at dusk. The bed was shoved in a corner with an unobstructed view of the ocean outside a row of tall, French doors that led out to a widow's walk. The narrow balcony ran the length of the beachfront side of the house, providing a view of where the ocean gently lapped at the private stretch of silvery sand four floors below. And, best of all, piled on couches, stacked on the floor or shoved haphazardly into the built-in shelves were books. Hundreds upon hundreds of books. From the latest glossy jacketed bestsellers to tattered, clothbound volumes of seventeenth-century poetry, they were everywhere and in no particular order. At least Valerie hadn't lied about this place being in desperate need of a librarian.

*DUN-DUN-DUUUUNNNN!!! Super Librarian to the rescue! By day, a mild-mannered librarian, by night... uh... pretty much the same.*

Georgina pushed away from the door, walking slowly through the dimly lit attic. She trailed her fingers over the satiny surface of a narrow desk set against the back of one of the couches. Pausing, she picked up the book she had been looking through before she'd snuck down to spy on the guests in the living room. Cradling the volume close to her chest, Georgina kept walking until she stopped in front of one of the French doors. Leaning her forehead against the cool glass she wondered why, after a lifetime of behaving herself, had she so utterly lost control with Simon?

*Because, he'd felt like every daydream I've ever had, all wrapped up in soft, white oxford cloth and broken in jeans. Because his hair was golden even in the shadows, and his mouth had been so close, his breath sweet from whatever he'd been drinking. He'd been so warm and smelled so good, it had made me light-headed with wanting him.*

"Oh God," Georgina whispered, closing her eyes, allowing herself to remember what it had felt like to reach for him, to cradle his jaw in the palm of her hand, and she experienced again that instant of anticipation, when their breath had mingled and she had breathed him in. Then she was licking his bottom lip, mimicking the gesture meant to mock and intimidate, tasting him on her tongue and... well, she didn't remember specifics after that, not until he'd wrenched away and she'd realized what she'd done.

Then she'd run off and she hadn't even apologized. What was the etiquette for apologizing for such an indiscretion? A note? Flowers? A potted palm?

Georgina bit her lip to keep from laughing, then jumped when the door behind her opened. Thinking it was Valerie, Georgina didn't bother turning around when she said, "I hope you brought me a drink."

"No, but I could be persuaded to fetch one, if you want."

Georgina literally froze, clutching the book to her chest.

*Oh, Holy Jesus... I so should have stayed at home.*

"Mr. Campbell," Georgina said, keeping her tone even and polite, acting as if he wasn't the last person she wanted showing up.

"Simon," he corrected, shutting the door after him. He walked towards her, looking oddly at home in this shabby, book filled room. "I didn't come up here to annoy you, so drop the act."

"Act?" Georgina asked, startled by his perception.

"Yeah," he said, this time stopping a respectful distance from her. "Act. I saw the way you treated every other person at Valerie's party..."

"Except you," Georgina said, supplying the two words he had left out. So he had noticed that. Damn.

"Except me," he said, tilting his head a little to the side. "Why was that?"

"What does it matter? I can't imagine you lost any sleep over it," Georgina replied, trying not to fidget under his unflinching gaze.

"Humor me."

"Humor you?" Georgina repeated, initially at a loss for words of her own. "Don't you have something better to do?"

"Nope," he said, crossing his arms over his chest then leaning his hip against a leather club chair. In this light he looked tawny and fierce, his face all sharp angles and planes, his dark eyes promising... oh, the things those eyes promised. Did he force women to look into his eyes as he drove them wild? Hard and fast, no quarter, no hiding, stripped bare, until he could see down into their very souls?

*Stop looking at him!*

Georgina cleared her throat as she turned away. "I thought you said you hadn't come up here to annoy me."

"I lied."

Georgina smothered a startled laugh behind her hand.

Simon shrugged then said, "Come on, Georgina. Just tell me why you singled me out and I'll leave you alone."

"Why I singled you out," Georgina hedged, trying to think up a lie that wouldn't hurt his feelings. "Uh..."

"Now, now, no lying. I was honest with you. Come on, Georgina, give me your best shot. I can take it."

"Are you so very used to people insulting you?"

"Yup."

"That's awful," Georgina said, taking a step closer to him, amazed that he didn't seem to mind people disparaging him on a regular basis. Georgina had a tendency to get snippy when people put her down, especially when she deserved it.

"All in a day's work," he said with a shrug.

"You need a new job."

"Tell me about it."

Georgina smiled, and he returned the favor, grinning at her, utterly charming, laid-back...

*He's conning me, luring me in with this easy banter so I'll tell him what he wants to know.*

"And you talk about me putting on an act," Georgina muttered, stiffening her spine, mentally putting some distance between them.

Simon eyes narrowed as he dropped his casual pose, moving towards her with that same stalking gait he had used in the gallery. Georgina knew she was in over her head with this man, even as another part of her experienced a deep-seated, intensely feminine welcome of the 'Oh baby, come to mama' variety. Simon stopped his advance, thank God, when the door suddenly opened and Valerie poked her head inside.

"Hello, Simon. What are you doing up here?" Valerie asked, then before Simon could respond, she turned to Georgina and smiled. Valerie was pretty, petite and had inherited every single ounce of sex appeal their twig of the Kennedy family tree had to offer. Completely unfair that she was also whip smart, had a sparkling personality and possessed a free and easy attitude towards life that not one of their stuffy family members had managed to subdue. As far as getting her fair share of the good genes had gone, Georgina was convinced that she'd been royally shafted.

Valerie waved Georgina towards her and said, "Cheryl and a few of the people you met at my party are on the beach, and they wanted to know if you would come down and—"

"Yes," Georgina said, the word out of her mouth before Valerie had even finished talking, ignoring Simon's knowing chuckle. Yes, she was running from him and no, she wasn't going to look over and see the light of triumph glowing in his eyes. She wasn't up to drinks and chitchat but she was less up to sparring with Simon alone here in the attic.

"You coming?" Valerie asked Simon, holding the door open wider as Georgina scurried out into the hall.

"Absolutely," Simon drawled. Georgina didn't have to see his face to know that he was smirking. Apparently, he was still determined to make her pay. For a man that didn't mind being insulted, he was being awfully thin-skinned about the way she had treated him.

Valerie led them down the hall to the old cage-style elevator Georgina had avoided on her earlier trip downstairs. The thing was original to the house and since the house had been built in the early thirties, possibly before the advent of building codes, Georgina previously had opted for the stairs. Filing into the elevator behind Simon, Georgina strove for calm. She could do this, have a drink, a friendly chat with a few of the guests she knew and then, when no one was looking, she could retreat back to the attic, lock the door and get back to work.

"I see you brought some reading material," Simon said, pointing at her chest. "Is that in case we bore you to death?"

"Huh?" Georgina asked, stumbling a little when the elevator lurched into motion. Looking down, Georgina saw that she was still clutching her book.

Valerie peeked at the spine and giggled.

"Don't say a word," Georgina warned, giving Valerie the death glare. "Not one word or I will hurt you."

Valerie just laughed then shrieked when Georgina raised the book as if to clobber her cousin with it.

"Now ladies," Simon said, snatching the book out of Georgina's hands. "Well, now, what's this?" he asked, squinting at the words printed on the spine. "*The Erotic Short Stories of Abigail Scott.* Well, hello, the mysterious Abigail Scott, huh? I bet her popularity is all about the fact that no one knows who she is. I heard she's actually a middle-aged man living in a hovel in the wilds of Alaska." He looked back down at the book and said, "I didn't know Jerome stocked chick-porn in his library."

Chick-porn?! Of all the nerve! Georgina held out her hand. "Give me that back."

Valerie made a humming noise in the back of her throat.

"Not one word," Georgina hissed.

Valerie, as usual, ignored her and said, "That isn't *exactly* Jerome's book."

Simon frowned, looking between the two women and then down at the book of erotica in his hands. "Then whose is it?"

"It's hers," Valerie said, pointing at Georgina.

Georgina groaned, even as some absurdly proud part of her whispered, "Yes, mine, all mine and I've got the copyright to prove it." Not that she had ever admitted that she was the infamous Abigail Scott in public. Aside from Valerie, there were only a handful of people that knew her secret.

And she wasn't about to tell Simon. Middle-aged man, indeed! Is that what people were saying about her now? The last time she had checked her message board, the rumor was that Abigail Scott lived in a crumbling old manor home, half-mad with grief over a long broken heart, a la Miss Havisham of *Great Expectations* fame.

"You're a fan of Abigail Scott?" Simon asked, his eyes wide in disbelief.

"No," Georgina snapped, annoyed at his reaction. "I most certainly am not a fan. In fact, at the moment, I can't stand the woman. Now give me that book."

The elevator chose that moment to come to a jarring halt, tossing Georgina forward.

Simon reached out to steady her. "Why am I getting the feeling that I'm missing something here?"

"Because you're oblivious to anything that doesn't come easy," Georgina snapped, dancing away from his touch.

"Do you come easy?" Simon asked, his voice dropping an octave.

"No, Mr. Campbell," Georgina purred, snatching the book out of his hands. "I require a tremendous amount of effort."

The elevator door slid open and Georgina sailed out, pleased as punch at the timing.

*Beat that exit line, you hack.*

# *Chapter Two*

Author's preface to *The Erotic Short Stories of Abigail Scott*

*There is something utterly delicious about a handsome stranger dressed in a beautifully tailored suit. He is unknown, possibly unknowable…nothing more than a chance encounter on the street before he is gone. But when he is near, he possesses infinite possibilities… will he be tender, will he be rough, will he go down on me? Que sera sera, eh?*

*I can't help but wonder, was he just another stuffy Wall Street drone or, underneath that layer of fine dark wool, was he in a constant state of excruciating masculine rut, ready at all times with a nice thick cock, tailor-made for me to ride?*

*That is the beauty of a stranger met by chance, then gone forever. I am never subject to the disappointment that invariably comes when a devastatingly handsome man in a Saville Row suit reveals himself to be a crashing bore, more interested in the state of the economy than the juicy peach I've got waiting for him between my legs. It stands to reason that he would be exceedingly interested in money; those yummy suits don't just grow on trees, now do they?*

*The stories that follow are dedicated to every woman who, like me, found the courage to say hello to that dashing stranger… only to end up stuck discussing the Dow Jones Industrial Average at some dreadfully dull cocktail party. It has been my experience, unfortunately, that the fantasy is always better than the reality.*

After sailing out of the elevator, it took Georgina a good two minutes to realize that she had no idea where she was going. Looking back over her shoulder, she saw Simon leaning against a wall, watching her with an amused look on his face.

"Well, are you going to stand there and gloat or are we going down to the beach?" Georgina asked.

Simon rolled his eyes. Then, taking her elbow, he led her down the hall, through the now deserted living room and then out into the night through a set of open French doors. They walked onto a wide stone patio that, similar to the living room, bore all the signs of a fast, mass exodus; full martini glasses clustered in groups on tables, cigarettes still burned in ashtrays, and, out here on the patio, several spindly little bistro style chairs were lying on their sides.

"Where did everybody go?" Georgina asked, picking her way through the fall-out.

"Bonfire on the beach," Simon said, hustling her down a stone staircase that led to a wide stretch of lawn. The serpentine path to the beach was marked by lit tiki torches and littered with shoes, shirts and, most alarmingly, a pair of leather pants. Before Georgina could find a way to stage a hasty, yet hopefully graceful, retreat, Simon was leading her down a rickety flight of wooden stairs. Georgina immediately gave up on the idea of retreat to focus on placing each foot on each tread, breathlessly waiting for a groan, a crack and then a whip-smash trip to the beach below.

Once safely back on solid ground, Simon strode across the sand towards a makeshift bar, set up a forgiving distance from the big pile of flaming railroad ties sitting smack-dab in the middle of the beach. Georgina walked across the sand, squinting against the blazing light from the towering bonfire, trying to make out the faces of the guests. Not watching where she was going, she ran right into Simon's broad back.

"Hey, stop when you get to me," he said as he turned to face her. "So, what's your poison?"

*You*, she thought but instead replied, "Jack and coke and please, Mr. Campbell, make it a double."

"So, Gentleman Jack, eh? I pegged you as more of the white wine type."

"Well, you were wrong."

"So I was," Simon murmured, swiping his thumb across his bottom lip. Georgina narrowed her eyes at the gesture, silently daring him to mention the kiss in the gallery. "Wonder what else I've been wrong about," he said.

"I'm sure the list is simply endless," Georgina drawled.

Instead of being offended, Simon barked out a laugh. "You're probably right."

Then he walked away and, after fanning herself like some faint-hearted heroine, Georgina went back to her former search for a familiar face in the crowd, but for the life of her, she couldn't find one. Not even Valerie.

And then Simon was back, handing off her drink then moving to stand next to her. Georgina had no earthly idea of what to do next. Apparently, the only person she knew down here was standing silently at her side as the other guests went about whipping themselves into a collective frenzy around the bonfire.

There was no way she was going to try and insert herself into that mess and, if she went back up to the attic, she had a feeling Valerie would just find another excuse to drag her back down. Taking a sip of her drink, Georgina decided it was safer to stick with Simon until Valerie reared her meddling head.

*Better the devil you know.*

*You two look like you're waiting for a bus.*

For the first time that night, Simon agreed with his inner voice. He'd been standing there for what seemed an eternity, racking his brain for a topic of conversation. Cookie recipes? Housekeeping tips? The Dewey Decimal System? Christ, what did it say about him that he couldn't think of anything to say to a woman like Georgina?

*Tell her she's pretty.*

"That's lame," Simon argued.

"What's lame?" Georgina asked, glancing around her.

"Me," he said, watching as she fished a slice of lime out of her drink. When she held it to her mouth and sucked on it, he groaned, remembering the way she had sucked on his tongue.

"Are you okay?" Georgina asked as she dropped the slice of lime back into her glass.

"Peachy," Simon mumbled then gritted his teeth as she daintily licked the tip of her index finger. Christ, she was driving him crazy, and she didn't even know it. Or did she? This was one of the *many* reasons he stuck with party-girls. Everything they did was straightforward. There was absolutely no mystery or confusion. If one of them sucked a lime, then licked her fingers, she was asking for sex, end of story. Georgina's intentions couldn't be as easily interpreted; maybe she just liked the taste of lime… on her lip. Oh man, if she needed help getting the lime juice off her lip, he was more than willing to help.

*Okay, if she keeps licking her lip like that, go ahead and lunge for her, if only to stave off a heart-attack.*

That's when it suddenly occurred to Simon to wonder just what in the hell he thought he was doing hanging around this woman. Directives of his inner-voice aside, he was seriously wasting his time chasing after Georgina when what he was supposed to be doing was chasing after professional hot chicks he could write about in his column. His readers sure as shit didn't want to hear about Georgina. According to the reader-mail he received, they were married to women like her. They wanted to hear about women like Cherry-Sherry-Whatever-the-hell-her-name-was, a woman that was easy to impress, screw and then ditch.

*Georgina doesn't fit into that category.*

Simon rolled his eyes and muttered, "Tell me something I don't know."

"Okay," Georgina said. "Uh… did you know that armadillos are the only other mammals, aside from humans, that can contract leprosy?"

"What?" Simon asked on a surprised laugh. "Why in the hell do you even know that?"

Georgina shrugged, even as a smile teased one corner of her mouth. "I'm a reference librarian. I know all sorts of useless stuff."

"Like what?"

"Well," Georgina said, gazing up at the night sky for a second, giving him yet another view of her profile, this time in the flickering light given off by the bonfire. Man, she was pretty. Real pretty. Why hadn't he noticed how pretty she was when he'd first met her?

"Okay," Georgina said. Simon quickly looked back towards the bonfire.

"Did you know that the supercomputer was invented by a man named Seymour Cray?"

"I had no idea," Simon deadpanned.

"Well, did you know that the country now known as Botswana was once called Bechuanaland?"

Simon sent her a wry look out of the corner of his eye. This one he knew. "I'll give you fifty bucks if you can spell that."

"B-e-c-h-u-a-n-a-l-a-n-d."

"Show-off."

"Nope, just smarter than you're used to. Now, where's my fifty bucks?"

"Yeah, yeah, I'll send you a check," Simon said, trying to keep back a smile. Pretty, intelligent and in possession of a smart-mouth. The triple threat. Simon stared down into her dark eyes and felt an almost desperate need to drive her away because he had the sneaking suspicion that there was no way his inner voice was going to give him a moment's peace if he left this woman behind.

*Damn skippy.*

"Why did you single me out at Valerie's party?" he asked, wanting, no, needing to know the truth.

Georgina blinked up at him, surprised by his quick change of subject.

"They say confession is good for the soul," Simon replied, shifting closer, until he was facing her rather than standing at her side.

Georgina rolled her eyes. "Whoever said that never met this priest I knew when I was in high school. He had eyes that made a girl think he knew every deviant thought she'd had for the whole of her life."

"So," Simon said, quickly shifting away from her. "You're Catholic?"

"Cradle," Georgina replied, short-speak for cradle-Catholic, a person born into the faith.

*Your mother will be thrilled. She's always telling you to find a nice Catholic girl and lookie here…*

"Were you a Catholic-school, all-girl-school-girl?" Simon asked.

Georgina groaned as she nodded. "From kindergarten to senior-high."

"Do you still have your high-school uniform?"

Georgina laughed. "Yes and, before you ask, yes, it still fits."

*Now there's an image to take to bed.*

Okay, Georgina Kennedy was beyond the triple threat. She was… Simon couldn't finish that thought because an image of Georgina in a short plaid skirt and little white blouse, unbuttoned to reveal her thin white cotton bra, went parading through his head.

That did it. To hell with his column. He'd make something up and swear to it because there was no way he was leaving this woman alone until he got her under him. Twice. Simon nodded to Georgina's empty glass and asked, "You want another one?"

*Now, if she declines the offer of another drink, at least try to charm her into staying. If that doesn't work, you have my permission to rush her.*

≈ঔ৲(ᴉ᪾)৴ঔ≈

"You know, I really should get back to work," Georgina hedged. She shouldn't spend one more minute in this man's company. He was funny, charming, and sexy as all hell; in short, a total menace to her determination to live a quiet, useful life… even if it killed her. "I have to—"

"Is your whole life one big have to?" Simon interrupted.

"No," Georgina said, insulted at the accusation that she was that dull. Well, actually her life was pretty dull. Except for the whole secret identity thing, but that was pretty boring because she couldn't tell anyone about it.

"Well, mine is and if you have a drink with me, it will relieve the pressure."

"Pressure?"

"Stay with me and I'll explain."

"I *really* shouldn't spend any more time with you."

"I swear I'll behave," he said, laying one long-fingered hand over his heart. "I'll be whatever you want me to be."

*Naked, sweaty and inside me?*

"I seriously doubt that, Mr. Campbell," Georgina choked out, hoping her face wasn't as flushed as it felt.

"You think I can't behave myself? I'll have you know my mother signed me up for dance lessons and a bunch of other boring etiquette crap when I was in junior high."

Georgina laughed, she couldn't help it. "Boring etiquette crap?"

"I'll answer any question you have," Simon said.

"Any question?" Georgina asked, lifting her eyebrows to show she didn't believe him for a second.

"Any question."

There had to be a catch. There always was when she got offers as delicious as this one. "And will you be offering any honest answers to these questions?"

"No."

"Then may I safely assume that that was your only honest answer of the evening?"

"Of the *year*," Simon corrected.

Oh, what the hell. In for a penny, in for a pound.

"I'd love another drink," she said.

*Idiot,* the voice-of-reason hissed as soon as Simon ambled away. *Don't spend any more time with him. He's too charming by half and...*

"Oh, hush up," Georgina muttered, turning to smile up at the stars overhead. She was in that lovely place, just shy of sober, when everything seemed, not so much possible as not worth worrying about. The waves rustled against the shore, the moon turned the sand silver and the guests, well, the guests were getting dangerously close to one another. Since they weren't doing anything that would get them thrown out of a bar, Georgina went back to smiling up at the stars.

"You're not going to start in spouting star facts now are you?" Simon asked a few minutes later as he handed off her second drink.

"No," Georgina said around a smile, looking up at him. In that moment, their gazes locked and something frighteningly intimate passed between them, something she couldn't brush away with a clever comment or useless fact. Georgina took a quick step back, right into the path of a gaggle of howling, shouting male guests, one of whom had the audacity to goose her.

Georgina flinched, a full body ruckus that sent her arms out in front of her. She dropped her drink as well as her book and grabbed for Simon, an instinctual reaction she was too off-balance to question.

"Whoa," Simon soothed, wrapping one arm around her shoulders. "You okay? What happened?"

"Someone just goosed me!" Georgina huffed.

"Goosed?" Simon asked.

"Grabbed my ass," Georgina said, and then realizing that she had once again taken liberties with Simon's person, quickly backed away.

"I'm so sorry." Flustered, she looked down and saw that they had both dropped their drinks. The glasses were lying on their sides, the sand under them dark and wet. Her book was between them, on its back, pages lazily turning in the breeze.

Before Georgina could lean down and pick up the mess she had made, a waiter rushed over. He gathered up the glasses, handed Georgina her book, then sort of hung there, waiting to see what she wanted to do with it. The cover was soaked and covered in sand.

Georgina handed it back to him. "Just toss it."

"You're pretty free with Jerome's books," Simon said, watching as the waiter hurried away.

Using the skirt of her dress to wipe the wet sand off her hands, Georgina replied, "It's my book."

"All yours?" Simon teased.

Georgina, distracted, embarrassed and not a little drunk, replied without thinking, "Yup, and I've got the copyright to prove it."

꙳ᘓ(ᗡᗡ)ᘔ꙳

For the second time that night, Simon literally lost his breath. He hadn't been wasting his time after all. Georgina Kennedy was a former Catholic schoolgirl turned uptight librarian that wrote porn under an assumed name. Christ, she was *exactly* what his readers wanted to hear about. If she had a twin sister she was willing to kiss, he would end up on the short list for a Pulitzer.

How could he have missed this? Granted, ever since she'd laid that kiss on him in the gallery, he'd been playing catch-up but this...

"You're Abigail Scott," he breathed, suddenly remembering that odd scene in the elevator.

Georgina nodded, once, almost imperceptibly.

"You're Abigail Scott!" Simon repeated, his voice rising on each word, until he was yelling at the end. Hearing what he had said, several guests drifted closer. Simon glared them away.

Georgina hunched her shoulders as she hissed, "Would you please keep your voice down?"

"No! Holy hell, Georgina," Simon practically yelled as he raked his hands through his hair.

"What? What's the big deal?"

"What's the big... oh, that's rich. Hey," Simon snapped, grabbing her arm when she tried to dart around him. "Where do you think you're going?"

"Back to the attic," she said, pulling against his hold. "Where I should have stayed but *no*... Let go of me."

"Not in this lifetime," Simon hissed, grabbing for her other arm. His readers were going to go ape-shit when they heard about her.

Before she could take a swing at his head, Simon got both her wrists under control. She muttered something under her breath.

"What was that?" he asked, hoping it was a string of stupendously foul swear words.

"I said, 'Jesus, Mary and Joseph'," she snapped, glaring up at him.

"Amen," he muttered. "But, unless those three owe you a big cosmic favor, you aren't going anywhere... *Abby*."

Abby?

Cheeky, gorgeous bastard. Out here in the firelight his black eyed gaze bored into hers. He was unnerving in his intensity, magnetic.

However, her inconvenient attraction to him did not change the fact that her days of blissful anonymity were over. Half a dozen people had heard Simon shouting that she was Abigail Scott. People were whispering her and Abigail's names in the same sentence. Georgina had worked very hard to keep those two names separated, only to be outed by *Simon Says* at a raunchy house party by the sea.

Georgina had always feared that this day would come, that at some point she would slip up and tell someone about Abby... uh, Abigail Scott. But this was Simon Campbell.

She was willing to bet he hadn't become famous by letting opportunity pass him by, and outing Abigail Scott as nothing but a former Catholic school-girl turned frigid librarian was a humdinger. Add to that the shabby way she'd treated him at Valerie's party and, well, if she was in his place, she wouldn't let her go either.

"You aren't going to let this drop," Georgina asked, her gaze focused on the hand he had wrapped around her wrists. "Are you?"

"Nope. Spill it. You're going to tell me everything about Abby, and you're going to do it right now."

Fine, she'd made her bed, but she wasn't going to lie down in it alone. She wanted something in return, some piece of him he didn't hand out to the general public. Maybe it was the firelight or maybe it was the booze, but somehow Georgina found the courage to say, "I'll tell you about Abby if you tell me something not everyone knows about you."

"There isn't much to tell. My life is an open book. What you read is what you get," Simon replied with a smug grin she was coming to know and loathe.

"Yeah, right. Tell me another one," Georgina said, annoyed that he would try to evade her. "Something really personal or no go."

"Okay… you're on. I'll show you mine if you'll show me yours."

"After a fashion," Georgina hedged. What did he mean, he would show her his?

And then he let go of her wrists and, before she could even think about bolting, began unbuttoning his shirt.

"Where did Abby come from?" he asked, sliding buttons free of their holes with quick, impersonal efficiency.

"Why are you unbuttoning your shirt?" Georgina squeaked, taking a quick step back.

"I'm asking the questions here. Tell me about Abby."

The phrase *Keep your shirt on* popped into Georgina's head but she shook it off and tried to give him the shortest, most impersonal answer she could think of.

"Uh… I… um… sublimate all my sexual energy into my writing," Georgina said, trying desperately not to peek at the thin strip of chest revealed by his now open shirt.

"Duh," Simon said. Shrugging out of his shirt, he balled it up and tossed it over his shoulder. "I could have told you that."

Georgina nodded but she wasn't really listening.

*Oh my, will you get a look at that.*

⚜

Simon had a rope tattooed on his body. It started at his wrists, twined up both arms, thickening as it went then draped across his back in an elegant sweep, giving the impression that, should the mood strike him, he could simply lift the rope away and be done with it.

Simon hated it, wished he'd never gotten the stupid thing and kept it hidden as much as possible under long-sleeved shirts.

"Stunning," Georgina murmured as she approached him. "What does it symbolize?"

"Nothing but a guy that had way too much money and free time," Simon replied, giving her the same pat answer he gave everyone.

Georgina rolled her eyes. "That's worse than my answer. Come on, did you go through a martyr phase or something?"

"Hardly. It's just a tattoo. I got it when I was twenty-five, which, before you ask, was seven years ago. It means nothing. I'd just signed a lucrative syndication deal and I was flush with cash. That's it."

"If you say so," she murmured, taking a step closer to him, studying him as if he were a painting rather than a living breathing man.

"When did you write your first story?" Simon asked. She was almost too close now, and he was having trouble distracting himself from the feel of her breath fanning across his bare chest.

"In college. I was twenty-one," she replied, gently tracing the strip of black that crossed over the inside of his elbow.

Simon sucked in his breath at the contact. Who knew that patch of skin was so sensitive?

"Why erotica?" he asked, even as he clenched his hands into fists at his sides.

"Because good girls don't go out and have sweaty, steamy sex with strangers. According to my Psych 101 class, reading and eventually writing erotica acted as a safe outlet for my decidedly un-ladylike urges."

"You aren't a virgin, are you?" Simon asked, hoping she didn't notice that his voice went up about three octaves.

*Please say no, please say no, please say no.*

"No. Nice girls can have sex."

Simon let out his breath in a relieved rush as Georgina muttered something under her breath.

"What was that?" he asked.

"They just can't have good sex," Georgina replied but she didn't look up from his shoulder as she said it.

"That's because you've been having sex with guys that think you're a nice girl."

"If you say so."

Simon recognized a brick wall when he ran into it. Georgina wasn't going to tell him anything else about her sexual history, not that she needed to. He'd heard it before. She'd probably had a few fumbling sexual encounters with a few shy, nice young men that believed her too respectable for the dirty stuff. Based on that small and limited sample, she had judged the experience wanting. He'd read Abigail Scott and knew her famous refrain. 'The fantasy is always better than the reality.'

If he had his way, he'd show her that his reality was better than any fantasy.

"When did you first publish?"

"Three years later. Valerie and I had too much to drink one night, to celebrate something or other, I can't remember anymore, and I showed her some of my work and she dared me to send it to an editor."

"And you did?" Simon asked, surprised.

"I have trouble saying no to a dare," Georgina said, sliding just the tips of her fingers up his arm to rest on his shoulder. "Especially when I've had too much to drink."

"I'll have to remember that," Simon murmured, losing sight of her as she slipped behind him.

Georgina hummed absently in response, and Simon realized she was so absorbed in studying his tattoo that she wasn't paying attention to their conversation. He was used to his tattoo getting a lot of attention from women. Some of them even traced the line but it never felt like this, as if they weren't aware of the man wearing it. From Georgina there was none of the usual coy eye contact and little oohs and aahs about how much it must have hurt.

No shit, it had hurt but never like this, a dull ache where she'd touched and a prickling anticipation where she hadn't.

"Uh...would you say that your stories are your fantasies?" Simon asked, hoping she didn't notice that he again sounded like Peter Brady.

"Absolutely," she said, as she came around from behind him. "Not that anyone will believe it. I only ever told one man I was dating about Abby and he automatically assumed that my work was autobiographical. Before I could assure him that he couldn't be more mistaken, he was crossing himself and calling me a modern day Jezebel. Needless to say, I've never made that mistake again."

"That guy was beyond gay," Simon muttered.

Georgina shrugged. "Not necessarily. The men that are attracted to me are really conservative, and they're pretty up-front about the fact that they're looking for a woman that won't embarrass them in front of their boss or their mother. I figure it's obvious that they'll be horrified when they find out about Abby so I just sort of gently hint that things aren't going to work out between us and—"

"So basically, you drop them before they can dump you," Simon surmised, frankly amazed that some guy had yet to call her bluff, chase her down and sit on her until she coughed up exactly why things weren't 'working out'. And the guy that had crossed himself and labeled Georgina a Jezebel had been gay or crazy. What man wouldn't get down on his knees and thank God that his girlfriend wrote erotica?

*An insecure moron that you should be grateful for. If that guy had been thrilled about Georgina's secret career, she might not be here with you tonight. She might be happily married with two kids and a mortgage, spinning her raunchy tales in private for a grateful audience of one.*

Simon silently gave thanks for all the uptight morons Georgina had dated over the years then gently cupped the side of her face in his hand, his thumb caressing the underside of her jaw. Her skin was unbelievably soft, warm, vibrant with her accelerated pulse.

"What are you doing?" Georgina asked, shying away.

"Touching you."

Georgina shivered, wrapping her hand around his wrist. "Please don't."

"Why not?"

"Because I am fairly certain you are not prepared to deal with the consequences of your actions."

Simon lowered his head until his lips barely brushed the side of her neck. Oh, he was more than prepared to deal with the consequences. The scent of her skin alone was enough to make him dizzy.

"Mr. Campbell," she breathed. "I will answer any question you have. It is no longer necessary for you to *torture* me."

"So," Simon hissed, wrapping one arm securely around her waist. "You can't stand me touching you. That kiss in the gallery was—"

"An honest reaction to a wholly false seduction," Georgina said, shoving at his chest.

"Honest my ass," Simon grunted. "At least I admitted I'm a liar but you—"

"What do you want from me?" she whispered.

"A little *honesty* would be nice."

"Honesty? You want honesty? Fine! I should have *slapped* you up in that gallery. That would have made sense *and* it would have given you the revenge you'd so obviously come looking for. Admit it, that's exactly what all of this is about, revenge for the awful way I treated you at Valerie's party."

Simon clenched his back teeth together to keep his jaw from dropping open. Magnificent didn't even *begin* to describe Georgina Kennedy in a rage. Her eyes flashed, her pale cheeks flushed and her mouth, that lush sensuous mouth… was still moving.

"Stupid, clueless man, thinking to use that body and that voice as weapons of revenge, trying to goad me into reacting like the frigid, judgmental bitch you believed me to be. Thinking I would scold and reject you," Georgina pointed at him. They were so close the tip of her finger nearly poked out his eye. "Or, and this is more likely, given the way you crowded me, fall into a fit of the vapors and faint dead away at having all that lovely male flesh shoved so near to my own, so close I could almost taste your intent, dark and rich, intoxicating…"

꙳ᗷᑕᘉᑐᗱᣔ꙳

Simon made a strangled sound of disbelief and let her go. Georgina stumbled back, feeling the fight drain out of her. He was disgusted to discover that she was so twisted as to find his version of revenge a turn-on. And how could she blame him since she was pretty much disgusted herself?

It was probably pointless to go on but if she told him everything maybe he would let go of his petty revenge/investigative report and leave her in peace. "You wanted to know why I singled you out at Valerie's party. Well, the truth is I wanted you from the second I saw you, wanted you under me, over me, however I could get you as long as it ended with you inside me and it scared me so badly," Georgina laughed, a dry, self-deprecating sound, "Shocked the hell out of me so completely that I drove you away to keep from lunging at you and embarrassing us both in the process."

Simon's mouth fell open. More abject horror.

"Apparently, my efforts were in vain," Georgina said, rubbing her forehead. "I have to get back to work. Enjoy the rest of your evening, Mr. Campbell."

Georgina turned and walked back over the unforgiving sand towards the stairs, dodging clutches of party-guests as she went.

"What a disaster," she mumbled.

*Yeah, but at least you got to see Simon with his shirt off.*

"Ah... the voice of reason returns. Where the hell did you go off to? I could have used you back there."

*He took his shirt off.*

Remembering the sight of Simon without his shirt, looking way better than any man that made his living sitting at a computer had a right to, Georgina couldn't argue. "Fair enough. What next?"

*First, find a camera. Then, go back to the beach and take a picture of Simon without his shirt so that when you include him in your next story and your editor says to tone him down because no one man is that delicious, you can hand her proof.*

"If you don't have anything useful to add just pipe down," Georgina muttered but she was smiling when she said it. A camera... Ha! As if she would ever forget what he had looked like in the firelight, with those elegant black lines snaking across his skin, shifting and slithering like a living thing when he had reached for her. Not that he'd ever be reaching for her ever...hang on a second. Now that she thought about it, writing a story about Simon was an excellent way to work out the frustrations of this evening. She'd come up with some scenario where Simon was the one out of his mind for her rather than the other way around and then *she* would be the one that mocked and teased, using his passion against him until he was willing to do just about anything to have her.

And when she finally gave in and let him have her, she could add in all the delicious details she had learned about him tonight. The intoxicating taste of him, the firm texture of his skin as she'd traced those sinister black lines, the feel of his body heat penetrating the fabric of her dress as his mouth barely brushed her neck. As those thoughts tumbled through her mind, a wave of heat swept over her skin, tightening her nipples as it moved between her legs, creating a sharp, prickling need that caused her pussy to throb once, a slow, deep pulse. Georgina stumbled, shocked by the strength of her reaction.

*You might want to stop thinking about this until you're alone and can, you know, do something constructive about it.*

Oh, there was no two ways about it, she was so going upstairs to *do something*. And then she was going to sit down and write out a story starring an intelligent librarian and an empty-headed playboy but, in Abby's world, the playboy was going to be doing a lot of begging.

Georgina snickered.

*And groveling, don't forget the groveling.*

Georgina giggled. By the time she'd reached the foot of the stairs, she was laughing so hard she had to hold onto the banister to keep from falling over into the sand.

༝ઽ✿১ঔ✸

And that was how Simon found her a few minutes after she had struck him speechless and left his ass...again. After a few failed attempts, he'd managed to get his feet moving and staggered after her.

Simon came to an abrupt halt at her side. Her head was bowed, her shoulders shaking.

*Aww, hell... is she crying? Make her stop, say something nice...pat her shoulder. That always works in the movies.*

Georgina turned, saw him standing there and laughed.

Right in his face.

*Yikes! Even you don't deserve this.*

"Yes, I do," Simon muttered.

Georgina got herself under control enough to say, "Would you like to know what I am going to do when I get upstairs? Well, more like what Abby is going to do. I think your readers will be impressed, it'll definitely make a good ending for your expose about Abigail Scott."

"Sure, let me have it," Simon replied, expecting her to say something along the lines of 'Call everyone I know and tell them what an asshole you are' so he was wholly unprepared when she said, "Masturbate."

Simon damn near swallowed his tongue.

"Oh, I'm sorry," Georgina said, sounding anything but. "Has my clinical language offended you? Should I have gone for something more delicate? Let me see...how about take matters into my own hands? Self-gratification, that's a good one. I had a college roommate that called it relieving her private urges. Doing something constructive, that's my personal favorite. What says you, Mr. Campbell?"

Simon blurted out the first thing that came to mind. "Can I watch?"

Georgina rolled her eyes. "Sure, why not? You can even take notes."

Completely ignoring both the eye-roll and acid tone Simon followed her as she climbed the stairs.

"Now, where the hell is the elevator," he heard her mutter when she walked in the deserted living room.

"To the right," Simon replied.

Georgina shrieked and whirled to face him. "What..."

"You said I could watch."

"I was being sarcastic."

"I wasn't. Lead on."

"You know what, Simon? I have just about had it with you."

Simon grinned. How many times had he heard that from the women in his life? Not the party girls; he didn't spend enough time with them to get on their nerves. No, she sounded like his sisters-in-law and Valerie, the only female friend he had that wasn't related to him.

But how to get her to do what he wanted? Bullying her didn't work. Seducing her was out of the question. Then inspiration struck.

"I dare you to let Abby decide," Simon whispered.

"Abby?" Georgina asked, taking a step away from him.

"Yeah, Abby. I think she'd accept in a heartbeat."

"Really?" Georgina whispered. It was hard to tell if she was intrigued at the idea or simply stuck dumb and momentarily unable to tell him to go to hell by the gall of his suggestion.

Simon held his breath, deciding that less was more in this delicate negotiation. It was a gamble, challenging her to let her alter ego call the shots, but he'd read her work and there was something of the sexual adventurer in Abby that just might nudge Georgina into letting him have his way.

"Okay," Georgina said, straightening her shoulders as she spoke. "I'm in... I mean, Abby's in. Let's go."

*If you somehow manage to screw this up, you had better get that lobotomy because I will make your life a living hell.*

# Chapter Three

*If you're going to do the wrong thing, do it with conviction. If you can't manage conviction, go for style.* —Simon Says

Georgina was running on nothing but adrenaline and bravado by the time she threw open the attic door and imperiously waved Simon inside.

What the hell he was running on, she couldn't begin to guess.

Pure stubbornness? An idiotic dedication to getting the whole sorry story on Abigail Scott, down to how she got herself off?

She was determined to end this farce once and for all. Simon would get bored after ten minutes. Hell, he'd probably leave before she got her underwear off.

"So," Simon said, coming to a stop in the middle of the library. "Where do you want to do this?"

Studying him in the dim light, watching as his gaze skipped from one corner of the room to the other, Georgina thought he looked different... twitchy. Was he nervous?

Good.

"You decide," Georgina purred, feeling for the first time that evening as if she was in the driver's seat. She'd make him sweat, see how far he was willing to go with this before he backed out. She might be the sexual amateur, and she was definitely the craziest person in the room, but there was no way in hell she was backing off of this. She was Abigail Scott, fer Christ's sake. She could totally do this.

As Georgina watched, Simon continued to look around the room. His gaze lingered on the bed, moved to the couch and finally stopped on one of a pair of wing chairs sitting across from the couch. He turned, giving Georgina a fine view of his bare back.

In the golden light of the attic, his tattoo didn't seem as menacing as it had on the beach. That tattoo was way more than youthful excess but Georgina couldn't imagine what had prompted him to mark his body in such a cruel fashion. Studying him, Georgina felt a ridiculous urge to lift the rope from his shoulders. Impossible, but the urge was so strong Georgina had to curl her hands into fists to keep from reaching for him.

Then he turned to her and said, "The bed."

Georgina nodded. Fine with her, she did some of her best work on her back…as in plotting for Abby's stories. Abby's stories… wasn't that what she was going to do when she got up here, plot out something where Simon was desperate to have her, willing to do anything to get her? She'd just pretend she was in one of her stories.

Before she either came to her senses or lost her nerve, Georgina reached behind her, grabbed the collar of her dress and in one easy, practiced move pulled her loose-fitting dress off over her head. As she tossed it aside, Simon clenched his hands into fists but otherwise remained still as a statue.

"And where will you be sitting?" she asked, planting her hands on her hips, all the while doing a pretty good job convincing herself that she was wearing a bathing suit instead of a thin white cotton bra and a pair of white cotton bikini panties.

Simon pointed to the foot of the bed. He visibly swallowed but his hand was steady. Damn.

Georgina nodded, turned on her heel and crawled onto the bed.

*You aren't wearing a bathing suit.*

"Not now," Georgina hissed as she rolled onto her back, stretched her legs out in front of her and closed her eyes. Taking in a calming breath, Georgina slowly counted to three and then released it.

The foot of the bed dipped as Simon sat down. In the silence of the room, Georgina could hear him breathing, could hear denim rubbing together as he shifted into a more comfortable position. The bottoms of her feet registered the heat of his body.

Georgina took in another deep breath as she frantically searched her mind for a way through this.

"Come on, Abby," Georgina whispered, her lips barely moving as she spoke. "I really need something here. Anything."

*Pretend that he's paying to watch you.*

The idea drifted through her mind and her body heated, instantly responding to the prompt, as it always did when her dirty little mind sent out a scenario that warred with her inner sense of what was right and proper. Nice women didn't let men watch them masturbate for money.

*Yeah, idiot that you are, you're letting him watch for free.*

Georgina grinned. Okay, she could do this. He was paying to watch her make herself come.

Georgina sighed out her breath as she gently arched her lower back, just enough to un-do the kinks that had built up over the day, then let her body relax with another, deeper sigh. When next she inhaled, she slowly allowed her imagination to take over.

He was watching her, his dark eyes taking in her lush figure sprawled out on the bed… her nipples were already hard, pressing against the thin white cotton of her bra. She could feel his gaze there, knew he wanted to touch but couldn't. That hadn't been a part of the deal. She slowly drew the tips of her fingers down the center of her chest, towards the small plastic clasp that held her bra together. Fingering the clasp, she waited until she could hear his breath hitch, until she could feel the bed move as he changed his position and then, when she was sure she had his undivided attention, she flipped the clasp, pleased when the soft cups didn't immediately slide away. She touched the flesh between her breasts, rubbed away the little ache the clasp had created, moaning a little at the feel of her fingers moving on her skin.

"Please," he whispered, his voice low and raw.

"We didn't say there would be talking," she scolded, even as she secretly thrilled at the sound of his voice.

"There's talking."

*That'll be extra*, she thought but decided now was not the time to talk about money. She would tell him after this was over… if he was still speaking to her, if she didn't drive him away by doing something so tawdry and base.

"Georgina…" he breathed.

She tensed at the use of her name, afraid it would draw her out of her fantasy. Before he could do it again, she placed both her hands over her breasts and gently squeezed, amazed that her nipples were already so hard and sensitive. She gasped, pushed the cotton away and pinched her nipples, greedy for the sensation, shocked when she felt the compression deep between her legs.

"Christ," he hissed. His obvious agitation only added to her pleasure.

She played with her breasts, showing him what she liked, showing him how she wanted him to touch her, wishing she had the nerve to ask him to join her but knowing she was already pushing herself farther than she had ever thought possible. So she imagined his mouth on her, imagined she could feel the wet suction of his mouth on her nipple, his tongue lapping at the underside of her breast, skating along the thin, sensitive flesh between her breasts to capture her other nipple in his mouth, his beautiful, cruel mouth…

Heat flared between her legs and she gasped, so close to orgasm she opened her eyes. She caught herself staring at the ceiling and quickly shut her eyes, closing herself back into her fantasy. She slowly stroked her hands down her body, over her ribs until they rested on her stomach. She felt the rapid rise and fall beneath her hands; she had never come so close to orgasm just by touching her breasts.

Was it his presence at the foot of the bed? Was it the deliciously twisted scenario she had unwittingly crafted? Whatever it was she wanted to savor it, build on it...

"Did you just..."

"No," she replied, her lips curving up into what she hoped was a provocative smile. "But I was close."

Then, before he could say anything, she slid just the tips of her fingers under the elastic waistband of her panties. Her stomach muscles contracted and her pussy twitched with anticipation.

"God this is good," she hissed, clenching her thighs together, adding a little more pressure to her outer lips then shivering at the contact.

"Open your legs," he ordered, his voice loud in the quiet room.

She obeyed without hesitation. He was paying, he could have his say. But, just to punish him for thinking he could order her about, she slipped one hand down to cover her mound, going over her panties rather than inside.

"How does it feel?" he asked.

She shook her head, biting her lip against the words.

"Tell me," he demanded.

*It's his dime...* "Warm, soft, damp. I can feel my clit. It's already sensitive but I'm not ready to touch there yet. I like to wait, to draw it out. The anticipation feels so good as the pressure builds, and there's this incredible heat just inside my body that if I press my fingers...there, not inside but almost, yes, right there..." she lifted her hips and came, a short, quick orgasm that robbed her of the breath to speak.

He groaned, the sound reaching out to her across the bed. She ground the heel of her hand against her clit, curled her fingers into her opening, letting the cotton wick up her moisture as she let out a low moan.

"Those panties are so damn sexy," Simon said. "I haven't had a woman all in white cotton since college," he whispered, his voice softened by memory. "There's something to licking a woman through cotton, until she's so wet I can taste her, taste how much she wants me, how much she likes what I'm doing... until she's begging me to remove them, begging me to touch her flesh with my mouth, my tongue..."

Georgina arched her back, pushing her mound more fully against her hand. It wasn't enough anymore. She slipped her hand inside her panties and the feel of flesh against flesh sent a hard shudder through her body. She focused on the feel of her fingers, slick with her own moisture, rubbing over her distended clit. Her hips picked up her rhythm. She spread her legs even wider, bent her knees, planted her feet on the mattress as pleasure, sharp and sweet, coursed through her body. Using her other hand, she went back to playing with her nipples, pinching, squeezing... desperate... two fingers sank deep into her body... she was panting, moaning, making more noise than she ever had before... oh, God, she was so close...

Warm hands skimmed up the outsides of her legs... soft hair trailed over her knee right before a wet, rough tongue scraped over the inside of her thigh.

"Yes," she hissed, pulling her fingers out of her sheath to concentrate on her clit, upping the ache of anticipation by cutting off the onset of orgasm.

Simon's fingers curled around the waistband of her panties and, with one sharp jerk, he pulled her panties all the way down her legs. He could see everything, her wet fingers playing between her legs, her pouting outer lips, her hungry inner lips...

He swiped his tongue across the back of her wrist.

"Yes," she said, a little louder than before.

Blunt, male fingertips skated up the inside of her thighs. His breath feathered the curls between her legs and still she touched herself, not willing to give up her part in this. She was close and he didn't know the first thing about her body. She didn't trust him to do this right, no man ever had. They'd always been so focused on getting her off, not for the pleasure of making her feel good but to stroke their own egos and, somewhere in the middle of it all, she'd sensed that and had always ended up having to fake it. But not tonight.

But she wasn't stupid. She'd let him help. After all, his fingers were thicker than hers and it had been so long since she'd felt a man's hands on her body, between her legs...

"Put your fingers inside me," she ordered, thrilling at the husky tone of authority in her voice.

Simon obeyed, pushing two blunt tipped, deliciously thick male fingers inside her at the same moment his mouth latched onto the soft flesh of her inner thigh.

Her sheath contracted around the invasion, greedily trying to pull his fingers deeper. She lifted her hips, an invitation to thrust that he ignored.

"Come on," she gasped out. "I'm close, please."

He licked where he had been sucking, easing the burning ache of having marked her flesh. "Move," he urged and she understood. He would provide the penetration and she would control the depth and motion.

"Yes," she whispered, pushing with her hips until his fingers were buried deep inside, until his fist pressed against her ass and she ground even farther, rolling her hips up. He crooked his fingers, raked against the soft pad of flesh deep inside.

"God, yes, right there, don't move," she panted, moving her hips against his hand with small, short thrusts. She could hear his labored breathing and, just under that, the soft, wet sound of his fingers moving in and out of her body. Sensation screamed up her spine and quickly sent her over the edge. She came, bearing down on his fingers so hard she screamed at the jarring sensation of all her muscles locking up as one then letting go, flooding her with a mindless pleasure she felt from the top of her head to the soles of her feet and everywhere in between.

As she slowly floated back to earth, she again felt the rough texture of his tongue on the inside of her thigh, his breath warm and fast on her damp skin. Then he slowly straightened his fingers and her inner muscles fluttered once then clamped down hard.

His breath left him in a rush.

"Again," he whispered, coaxing, his fingers scissoring, stretching the tight ring of muscle at her opening.

She flexed her hips and opened her eyes.

And came, staring into Simon's dark eyes. Her fantasy made flesh, sprawled on his stomach between her spread thighs, a hard wine-red flush staining his sharp cheekbones as he slowly pulled his fingers out of her body and languidly, without breaking eye-contact, he licked the taste of her from his skin.

༜ৡ(ʘʘ)ৡ༜

Simon slowly pulled his fingers out of Georgina's body, shuddering when her inner muscles pulsed once, as if in protest. He watched her as he licked his fingers, watched her as her eyes slid closed.

"Tell me what you were thinking," he whispered, his breath stirring the curls covering her mound. She tried to close her legs.

"Too late for that, you already let me in," he said, rubbing his cheek against the satin smooth skin of her inner thigh. She smelled incredible, warm and salty sweet, the wet luscious scent of her arousal streaked through him. "Tell me."

"That wasn't…" she began.

"Part of the deal? Too bad. Tell me," Simon hissed, frustrated that she would share her body but not her thoughts. He was seconds from letting this go and just screwing her senseless but he wanted more. He wanted inside, and not just her body.

Watching Georgina pleasure herself had been the most erotic thing he had ever seen and he'd seen plenty. At the beginning, emotions had flittered across her face, one after the other, embarrassment, frustration, even a small, mocking smile and then she'd settled in with a deep sigh, touching her body with such skillful hands he'd broken out into a sweat even before she'd gotten her bra off. Then bringing herself close to orgasm time and again only to back off, teasing him until it had been reach for her or gnash his teeth into dust.

And here he was, back to that point, his body strung so tight she had to feel it, had to know he was seconds from pouncing on her.

"I was," Georgina paused, cleared her throat and then, so softly he initially thought he hadn't heard her correctly, said, "I was pretending that you were paying to watch me."

Simon's ears might have taken a second to catch what she'd said but his body instantly understood. And approved, so much so Simon figured his brain was never going to function quite so well again. But who cared? He was crawling up her body before he fully realized what he was doing, sliding one hand under her head, settling his hips between hers spread thighs (thankfully he still had his jeans on or he would have been inside her and to hell with the condom). When her eyes flew open, he rolled over onto his back, taking her with him, settling her wide open pussy firmly over his jean clad erection.

"Hey," she breathed, writhing a little in his grip, whether to get away or closer completely beside the point, Simon didn't bother wondering which. She wasn't going anywhere.

"How much do I owe you for the show?" he asked, digging the fingers of one hand into her hair, pulling out pins as he found them.

"I don't know," she said, her gaze dropping to his mouth then skittering away.

"Five hundred seems fair," Simon replied, messing up her hair as he searched for more pins. When he didn't find any, he threw the ones he had off the bed where they landed on the floor with a scattering of faint pings.

"Five hundred, huh?" she asked, settling more fully upon him. "No checks this time. For this, I only accept cash."

"I don't have that much on me," Simon replied, burying both his hands wrist deep in her gorgeous, *curly* hair. "You are such a fraud. Do you iron yourself out every morning or is it an ongoing, all day process?"

"On-going," she replied, never once losing her smile. "And just how are you proposing to pay me, Mr. Campbell?"

Simon grinned. So he was still Mr. Campbell, was he? Damn but he'd had no idea that ruffling her feathers was going to be this much fun.

"Here's the deal," Simon said. "Every time I can get you to say my first name, you knock fifty bucks off my bill."

Georgina's smile turned into a superior smirk. "Sounds fair to me."

"And if you go over the five hundred, then you end up owing me," he said, running the palms of his hands down her back. She arched into his touch, gently biting her full lower lip when he cupped her luscious ass in his hands. "I'm not even going to ask what the hell you were thinking hiding a body like this under that dress. Unless, of course, you'd like to tell me."

Georgina purred under his touch. Leaning forward until her hard little nipples scraped his chest and her lips brushed the shell of his ear, she whispered, "I have no interest in a man that is more interested in the wrapper than the candy."

Simon huffed out a laugh even as he admired her logic. She had a beautiful figure—long legged, full-hipped, a small waist and pretty little breasts with small, gorgeous nipples that she was even now gently brushing over his chest. Shrink-wrapped in modern, come-and-get-it fashions, she would spend half her day beating men off with a stick but, draped in the awful dresses she favored she blithely flew under most men's radar.

Thank God she'd been such a bitch to him. If she hadn't, he might never have noticed her, might never have chased her down tonight and never know what she looked like standing before him wearing nothing but her underwear.

Simon groaned at the thought of missing that.

"What? Am I hurting you?" Georgina asked, rising off of him, until she was crouched over him on her knees, her long curly hair falling over her shoulders. Her head was tilted a little to the side, surveying him through dark eyes lit, not with passion, but concern. He had a beautiful, intelligent, naked woman (that just happened to fantasize about men paying her to get off in front of them) crouched over him and here he was worrying about what might not have been.

"Moron," Simon muttered.

Georgina's eyes widened. "Pardon me?"

"Not you," Simon said, slipping his hand between her legs, his palm resting over her clit as his fingertips flirted with the damp entrance to her body.

"Simon," she hissed.

"I'm down to four-fifty," he said, gently massaging her until she once again whispered out his name.

"Four-hundred."

"No fair."

"Who said anything about fair?" he asked, tangling his fingers in her pubic hair then gently giving a little tug. She arched her neck and moaned.

"Like that?" he asked.

"Yes, oh God, yes," she whispered.

"Then get off me," he said. "If I don't get inside you within the next two seconds..."

Georgina rolled onto her back, pushing her hair out of her face with shaking hands. Simon got his jeans off, the condom on and was back between her thighs so fast he was surprised he hadn't hurt himself. He came down over her by degrees, until they touched from mid-chest to crotch. His cock twitched, thickened...close, he was so goddamn close.

"Oh God," she whispered, a soft sound of despair. "We're actually going to do this, aren't we?"

"Say no and I'm gone," Simon whispered, even as he settled his hips more firmly between her legs, bracing his elbows on either side of her head, careful not to catch her hair too close to her scalp.

"You could have asked," Georgina whispered, curling her hands around his upper arms.

"And risk you laughing in my face?" Simon asked.

Instead of answering, Georgina slipped her hand between their bodies and wrapped her long, cool fingers around his cock. "Under me, over me, however I could get you," she whispered, reaching farther, cupping his balls then scratching back up to the base of his cock, ever so gently, until Simon closed his eyes and groaned.

"Say yes," he ground out, his control slipping. "Goddamn it, just say..."

"Yes," she whispered, hissing out the end of the word as he slowly entered her. The feeling of being enveloped within her by degrees washed over him. Her body yielding to his was a primal surrender Simon had never appreciated until now. The scent of her skin, the feel of her sheath pulsing as he hilted, the glide of her inner thighs against his hips, her breasts soft and giving under him... her breasts...

Simon closed his eyes on a full-body shudder as images of her rose up behind his eyelids, like a slow-motion montage from some crazy, pornographic chick-flick. He saw her as she had been not half an hour ago, teasing out her blood-flushed nipples, biting her lush lower lip as he pulled her panties down her legs to reveal her slick fingers playing between her legs... Then, out on the beach, smiling up at him, charming, pretty, laughing with him, at him... Then, earlier still, up in this same attic, striving for contained politeness, hiding her nerves behind a cool façade. Turning him inside out with one single kiss in the gallery. Turning her nose up at him at Valerie's party...

"Simon..." Georgina moaned his name, half question, half-plea, ripping him back into the moment as her body arched under his. Under him... the annoying spinster-librarian with the hooker's mouth, the long-legged brunette with the dirty mind who had wanted him from the second she'd met him, even as she'd pushed him away... was under him, moaning out his name, digging her nails into his back, silently urging him to move by clenching up, deep inside. He was...

*Inside her... ah, God, yes. Finally.*

Simon let out the breath he'd been holding, drew back his hips and thrust back into her, hard, suddenly angry that she had made him wait so long to have her. Georgina's head went back, exposing her throat to him, another surrender that fired his blood as she slid her leg up his until her knee hooked around his hip, locking him against her.

*Yeah, like he was the one that kept trying to get away.*

At the thought of her leaving him, Simon clutched her even tighter, shoving in high and hard then staying there, trying to calm himself down before he thrust too hard and hurt her.

Georgina groaned and bit his shoulder, sending a bolt of heat from where she'd bit him straight to his dick.

Simon shoved one shaking hand under her head and gripped the back of her neck but Georgina just growled and bit him again, fighting his attempt to subdue her, jamming her hips against his.

"Harder," she demanded, the word going right into his ear and he just lost it. Every last bit of his control spun away and he took her, harder and faster than he had ever taken a woman before, focused on getting as deep inside her as he could, taking everything she offered and then demanding more, his hands rough on her body as he whispered God knew what into her ear.

She was working with him... against him, frustrating his urge to grind her into the bed for making him wait for her, goading him on, writhing and panting, demanding that he make her come with graphic, filthy language that drove him on until they were both sweating and swearing, straining to get as close as possible... it was nothing less than fast and furious sex at its finest and he loved it, loved that she was with him the whole way, their bodies slick with sweat, tendrils of her hair sticking to his shoulders and chest as she met his every thrust until her orgasm ripped through her, stunning him with the force of her response.

Georgina clutched at him with her whole body, arms and thighs as well as deep inside, her pussy clenching tight then milking his cock with long, hard pulls that made him groan. He gave over to the intensity of her response, feeling it firing his own and there was pleasure everywhere, not just in his cock but his head because she was under him... the annoying spinster librarian with a hooker's mouth... Georgina Kennedy, the woman with the soft hands and delicious mouth.

*Where have you been all my life?*

With that truly terrifying thought careening through his mind, Simon rested his forehead against Georgina's and, in what was possibly the least romantic gesture in a life pretty much devoid of them, muttered, "Aw, well... *shit*."

# Chapter Four

*Simon Says* column, Wednesday, February 18<sup>th</sup>

*Have I mentioned that I have six brothers? I do and they're all cursed, to the tune of seven simple words: Where have you been all my life*

*Yup, sad but true and corny, too. My eldest brother started it. He bumped into his future wife at a deli, heard those words whisper through his muddled brain and then spent the next two months talking (stalking?) her into marrying him. Pretty much the same thing has happened to three of my other brothers.*

*Never fear, this curse thing does not apply to yours truly (for reasons that should be obvious). I bring this up not to make you nervous that I am contemplating a trip down the aisle but rather to announce that yet another one of my brothers is getting married. Congratulations, Ryan. You don't deserve her.*

*And here, a reassurance for the bride-to-be: My brother will eventually stop following you around every second of every day. Be patient. He's just concerned that you'll come to your senses and leave his sorry ass before he can get you to say 'I do'. Of course, my brother Steve is still dogging his wife's footsteps and they've been married for two years, but that's only because he is, outside of me, the biggest loser in the family. He has more than one reason to be concerned that, when his wife says she's just going out to get some milk, in reality she's got a one-way ticket to Brazil, her passport and a fortune in traveler's checks tucked away in her purse.*

Saturday

Georgina couldn't say for sure, never having actually *seen* a man with his pants on fire, but she was willing to bet that if Simon's pants had indeed been in flames he couldn't have left her any faster than he did last night. He'd been on his feet, in his pants and out the door before her heart rate had returned to normal.

She would have been insulted if she hadn't, somewhere in the back of her mind, been expecting it. A man like Simon didn't stick around to cuddle after the fact. Nope, he showed a girl a good time then took off, apparently, at warp speed.

"I really hate it when I'm right," Georgina told her reflection. She was standing in the little bathroom connected to the attic attempting, with absolutely no success, to get her hair under control. Only a few hours into the dreaded 'morning-after' and she was already a total wreck. Simon's scramble to the exit had scattered her hairpins and she simply hadn't had the energy to hunt them up. She'd found a pair of chopsticks in the desk drawer and had thought a kicky up-do involving Asian eating implements would make her feel better.

It didn't. Her head looked like Sputnik.

"Oh, who cares? It's not like anyone's going to see me up here," she muttered. She yanked the sticks out of her hair, threw them at the mirror then stomped out of the bathroom, only to be confronted with the bed she and Simon had shared the night before. She'd stripped the sheets at dawn, shoved them under the bed, covered the bare mattress with the comforter, artfully arranged the pillows and then, in a fit of adolescent pique, flipped it the bird.

"You knew he was only good for one night," Georgina said, turning her back on the bed as she yanked a dark blue linen shift on over her head.

And if she'd secretly hoped that he would stay with her, at least until sunrise? Well, silly girl, one-night stands were for clear-eyed realists, not a romantically addled librarian that had spent the remainder of the night crying into her pillow wondering how she was ever going to forget how incredible it had felt to express her sexuality, not in print but rather in glorious flesh. It was something she had never thought she would be able to do. At least, not without freaking out her partner. But she had found that freedom with Simon. Effortlessly, never once telling herself to calm down and let him lead. She had thrown herself into the experience, given herself up to, lost herself in it…

Georgina bit back a sob, clenched her hands together and shoved the memory of last night into the deepest, darkest corner of her mind (right next to all the Algebra she had ever learned and where she'd put the key to her backyard shed). Snatching a short stack of poetry books off the coffee table, Georgina muttered, "Steady on, old girl," and got to work.

Five hours later, the attic door flew open and hit the wall with a crash.

"Valerie," Georgina yelped, grabbing onto the shelf in front of her to keep from falling off the rolling library ladder she was standing on. "Next time knock! You scared the hell out of me."

Valerie kicked the door shut with an unrepentant grin then strolled over and plopped down onto the couch. Georgina hid a smile at her cousin's version of beachwear: a black string bikini top and a vintage gypsy skirt in seventeen different colors.

"How's it going?" Valerie asked, looking around the book-strewn attic.

"It's going. What are you doing up here?"

Valerie shrugged. "Hiding from the guests, wasting your time, I've got a myriad of reasons. Have you eaten today?"

"No, I've been too busy..."

"Avoiding Simon?" Valerie offered.

"Absolutely." Georgina said then snapped her mouth closed, turning a glare on her nosey cousin.

Valerie laughed. "Thought so."

"Don't want to talk about it," Georgina said, resolutely going back to shelving books.

"Wanna talk about the fact that everyone downstairs knows that my mild-mannered cousin is in fact the infamous Abigail Scott?"

"Nope. Go away."

"Wanna tell me why Simon's walking around looking like a kicked dog?"

Georgina bit back a snide snicker at that. "Couldn't care less."

"Did you shamelessly use him for your own pleasure, then kick him out?"

Dropping the books she'd been holding, Georgina whipped around so fast she again had to grab onto the ladder. "No! Valerie, how could you even think that?"

Valerie shrugged. "You wouldn't be the first nice woman that did."

"That stinks."

*Wait, that's exactly what he did to me. No sympathy! No sympathy!*

"Yup. Which is why Simon sticks to professional hot chicks. You know, dingbats with dazzling looks and long legs and not much else."

"That leaves me out," Georgina said, climbing down off the ladder to collect the books she'd dropped.

"Not last night it didn't."

Crouched down on the floor, Georgina glared over at Valerie. Then she sighed. If she didn't throw her cousin a bone, Valerie was going to sit there for the rest of the day badgering her.

"Look, things just got out of hand. I accidentally told him about Abby..."

Valerie's eyebrows shot to her hairline. "Accidentally?"

"I know, hell of a thing, huh? I've never even once come close to letting that slip but I was a little drunk and nervous and it just," Georgina opened her mouth, flicking her fingertips away from her bottom lip, "fell out. And then I, well, um… let him watch me masturbate," Georgina lost her nerve and kind of mumbled the last word.

Valerie shot forward. "You let him watch you do what?!"

"Oh, you heard me," Georgina said, tossing the books onto the coffee table.

"I most certainly did. Why did you let him watch you?"

"Oh, I don't know, because I'm an idiot?" Georgina asked, sitting on the floor.

Valerie just waited.

"Fine… he dared me to let Abby decide whether or not he could watch me… uh… you know."

Valerie snorted. "Tell me another one."

"It's true!"

"Let me get this straight. Simon just, out of the blue, dared you to let Abby decide whether or not to let him watch you masturbate? Come on, even Simon isn't that…"

"Sleazy?"

"I was going to say perceptive. There's no way he could have figured out in such a short period of time that you can't say no to a dare, especially one that would appeal so strongly to your twisted sexuality."

"Hey! I'm not twisted!"

Valerie laughed. "You most certainly are, and I meant that in the best possible way."

"Gee, thanks. I think."

"And then what happened?"

Georgina opened her mouth then quickly shut it. "Surprise, surprise. Here I am talking about something I don't want to discuss. Valerie, just leave it alone, okay?"

"Hey, I just wanted to make sure that you hadn't toyed with then dumped a friend of mine."

"Me! Have you asked your dear friend, Simon about what happened last night?"

"I mentioned your name and he snarled. I was afraid if I pushed it he'd lunge for my throat."

Georgina refused to read anything into that statement.

Instead, she said, "Well, I didn't kick him out. He left."

"Are you sure you didn't ask him to leave?"

"You aren't listening. He. Left! As in man with his pants on fire, *left*! As in 'Oh my God, the building is on fire', *left*! As in the boat is sinking and it's every man for himself…"

"I think I get the picture," Valerie said.

"Left! Fled might actually be a better description, okay? And I wasn't about to try and stop him because, you know what? The saddest words in the English language are not 'if only' but rather '*as if*'."

"Oh, Georgina," Valerie whispered, her expression softening into one of pity.

The last thing Georgina's battered ego needed was pity.

Stiffening her backbone, Georgina rose to her feet then turned to face the shelves she'd been working on. "I have a lot of work left to do, so if you'll excuse me..."

"Georgina, I'm so sorry. It never once occurred to me that you'd become attached to Simon."

"So if you'll excuse me..." Georgina repeated, going a little dizzy as the word *attached* screamed through her brain. She promptly wrested it into the 'shed-key' corner of her brain.

"Okay, I'll leave you to it but I'll bring you up some lunch..."

"I'm not hungry."

"And you'll eat it."

Georgina whirled around at Valerie's tone but her cousin appeared resolute rather than pitying so Georgina caved. "And I'll eat it."

"Good," Valerie said, getting to her feet. She had the door open and was halfway through it when she paused, turned and with one finger in the air, said, "One more thing."

Georgina laughed. "What, are you channeling Colombo?"

"No. Why? Is Peter Falk dead?"

"*Valerie.*"

"Going," Valerie shrieked, slamming the door after her.

Simon was in the living room, trying to enjoy his first drink of the afternoon and failing miserably. All he could think about was that he had finally met the woman he had been waiting over half his life to meet and he couldn't have her.

Simon didn't delude himself into thinking that The Curse was a guarantee of happily-ever-after. Until last night, he hadn't even believed that the damn thing applied to him.

And it didn't, not really. Because how could he expect Georgina to proudly introduce him to her friends and family as her boyfriend, let alone her fiancé? If he had a daughter and she showed up with someone like *Simon Says* for Sunday dinner, he'd drive the little bastard out of his little girl's life with a rusty butcher knife.

Not like any of this was news to him. He had known for years that his reputation as America's favorite perennial frat-boy precluded him from ever having a serious relationship. *Simon Says* might be a character he had created but that character was as much a part of him as the skin on his back. Hence his goddamn tattoo.

He'd gotten it after signing his syndication deal, that much of what he had told Georgina was true. What he hadn't told her was why he'd gotten it.

Sara Goodwin. She'd been a lawyer he'd met while going through the process of hammering out his syndication deal. Intelligent, pretty and in possession of a smart mouth... his own personal kryptonite.

After the deal had been signed, she and Simon had spent the weekend in bed together and Simon had foolishly thought there was more between them than just really hot sex.

He'd been wrong. When he'd asked to see her again, she'd reacted as if he'd asked her to take a piss in church.

"What woman in her right mind would want to date *Simon Says*?" Sara had asked. Then, and this had been the hardest part of the truth to hear, she'd muttered, "Let alone marry the little bastard."

Initially, he'd brushed off Sara's pronouncement as one woman's opinion. Then *Simon Says* had gone national and, as his fame grew, the pool of women outside the party circuit willing to date him (which had never been that deep to begin with) dried up.

And Simon realized that there was a painful kernel of truth in that one woman's opinion.

Shell-shocked and not a little heartsick, his younger self had felt the need to make a grand gesture of it. As if he needed a tattoo to remind him that he didn't have someone to call his own. He had his brothers and their wives as daily reminders of what he was missing.

Running out on Georgina last night had been the mother of all self-defensive moves. Simon knew he didn't have the sense to steer clear of her, and he didn't want to torture himself by hanging around what he could never have. A woman like Georgina would never accept him back after he'd basically screwed her and then ran out on her. Anyway, just because she'd let him touch her didn't mean she wanted anything else. All and all, it had been the best thing for both of them, not that it had been easy.

Not that being separated from her was any picnic.

To make matters worse, all any of the guys in the living room wanted to talk about was the fact that Valerie's plain-Jane cousin was the infamous Abigail Scott.

And they kept using that phrase, 'the infamous Abigail Scott', as if she was an abstract theory rather than a living, breathing woman.

*A living, breathing woman that you ran out on last night. A living, breathing woman that, if you weren't such a big chicken shit, would be writhing*

*and panting under you right this minute rather than shut away up in the
attic, alone. Possibly lonely, possibly thinking that you had neatly lived
down to her worst expectations of you. No wonder she turned her nose up
at you at Valerie's party. She might have been attracted to you but she knew
you weren't capable of handling a woman like her.*

"Would you give it a rest," Simon hissed.

"Hey man," one of the morons said, thinking Simon had been talking
to them. "Give us a break. Not everyone was lucky enough to get a piece
of the infamous Abigail Scott."

*You have my permission to kill him.*

Simon rolled to his feet. Glaring around at the compendium of morons
on hand, he said, in a cold, clear voice, "Her name is Georgina Kennedy,
and she's smarter than all of you combined. If any of you approach her,
hoping to get a piece of the *infamous Abigail Scott,* she will laugh in your
face and then she'll really go to work on you."

One of the guys snickered. "So, she shot you down, eh?"

The other guys hooted.

"Yeah," Simon lied, throwing the word over his shoulder as he walked to
the door, doing exactly what he should have done last night, namely, taking
his drink upstairs to watch TV.

Slamming his way out into the hall, Simon took two steps then reared
back when Valerie came barreling around the corner. She was shouting
into her cell phone, had a plate of food in one hand, a bottle of wine tucked
under her arm and a sobbing waitress trailing behind her.

"Hang on," she yelled into the phone. "Simon, excellent timing. Do me
a favor."

Simon glanced nervously towards the crying waitress.

"No, not her," Valerie said. "What I need you to do is take this food up
to the attic."

Simon staggered back a step, holding up both hands in front of his chest,
sloshing Chivas onto his hand in the process.

"No way," Simon said, the very idea of seeing Georgina enough to make
his blood run cold. "I'll take the waitress."

"Simon, stop annoying me and just do as you're told," Valerie ground
out. She shoved the plate and bottle of wine at him, forcing Simon to juggle
the bottle, his glass and Georgina's lunch.

When he got a handle on everything, Valerie and the crying waitress
were gone.

"Aw, well... *shit.*"

Simon started muttering to himself as he walked up the stairs to the attic.
"Hand her the plate, warn her about the morons, walk away. Hand her the
plate, warn her about the morons, walk away. Walk. Away."

As far as strategies went, Simon believed that his was foolproof. Warning her about the fact that half the male guests would be after her the second she stepped foot outside of the attic…well, that only seemed fair since his big mouth was the reason everyone knew about Abby.

Once he was standing in front of the attic door, Simon inhaled sharply. "Okay. Hand her the plate, warn her about the morons, walk away."

*Please let her be in bed. Preferably naked.*

"You shut up. One peep out of you that doesn't follow the plan and I'll get that lobotomy." With his now empty glass balanced on top of her sandwich, and the bottle of wine tucked under his arm, Simon let himself into the attic.

He was halfway across the room when he saw Georgina standing in a shaft of late afternoon sunlight. Her hair was down around her shoulders, a wild mass of curls she had made no effort to control, her long, gently curved arms bare, her dress, another loose linen affair, matched the velvet comforter on the bed and her lips were full and red, making him wish he had spent more time kissing her last night.

His foot hit a squeaky floorboard. Her head turned, her eyes widened and she stiffened, jerked back.

"What do you want?" she asked, this time making no effort to be polite.

*You.*

Simon growled.

*Fine. Hand her the plate, warn her about the morons, walk away. Happy?*

"Lunch," Simon held up the plate. "Valerie was busy so I'll be your waiter for this afternoon," he said, walking around the back of the couch towards her. She backed up a step as her gaze skittered away.

"Just set it on the coffee table," she said, turning back to putting books on the shelves.

Simon set the plate on the coffee table, plucked his glass off her sandwich and walked back the way he had come. He was reaching for the doorknob when his inner voice piped up.

*Warn her about the morons.*

Simon cleared his throat. "Uh, Georgina…" he began, turning back to see her standing by the coffee table, examining the ring shaped dent in her sandwich.

"Yes?" she asked, glancing up at him. Impatience radiated off her. She looked so much like she had in the gallery last night, it instantly pissed him off.

"Just thought you should know the natives are gunning for a piece of you," he said with a smirk, reverting to full asshole mode to match her frigid librarian act.

Instead of pokering up, she laughed, a soft, mocking sound. "They don't want me. They want Abigail Scott, sex goddess."

"I know how that feels. Women have been chasing after me for years when, all along, I knew all they wanted was a piece of the myth. As if having sex with a pseudo-celebrity would somehow make them famous by association."

"And that bothers you?" she asked, her tone biting.

*Damn right it does. Never knowing if a woman gives a shit about the man behind the myth.*

"Walk away," he muttered, even as he turned to face her, even as he allowed himself to fully appreciate the changes in her appearance. A man could get lost in those flashing eyes, that gorgeous hair, just spend the rest of his life trailing after her, intent on making her smile, laugh, come...

*Where have you been all my life? I've been waiting for you for so long, I thought you'd never show up.*

"Aw, well... *shit*," he muttered, rubbing his forehead as those thoughts rolled through his mind. This was all so damn hopeless, and yet if there was a chance in a million that he could make this work...

"You said that last night," she murmured, narrowing her eyes at him.

"I know and I'm sorry..." Simon ran out of things to say. He couldn't very well tell her that he was going to be chasing her for the rest of their natural lives, until she either gave in and married his sorry ass or took out a restraining order against him.

"Apology accepted," she snapped. "You can go now."

Looking at her, it was the weirdest thing to know that Georgina somehow *belonged* with him. If he somehow managed to make this work, he was going to be dealing with her for the rest of his life... and he knew next to nothing about her. She could be the most annoying person in the world to live with. She could eat nothing but bean-sprouts and tofu. She could be into yoga and pampering her inner child. Oh, God...

"Tell me right now you aren't a Republican!" Simon ordered.

"No!" she squawked. Then, with a little shrug she said, "Well, I do admire John McCain but that hardly..."

Simon waved off her explanation as he walked over to lean his hip on the desk behind the couch. "That's fine. Hard not to admire the man. What's your stand on the designated hitter rule?"

"The what? Simon, what are you after this time?"

Simon. Not Mr. Campbell. He remembered something about her saying his name and owing her five hundred bucks.

"I forgot how much I owe you," he blurted out, referring to their game of the night before.

"You owe me… oh," Georgina blushed as she became terribly interested in the rug beneath her feet. "Forget about it. That was just…"

"Forget about it?" Simon asked, a wicked smile curving his lips at the sight of that blush. Who would have thought that the way to this prickly woman's heart was through kinky sex-games?

*You are one lucky bastard.*

"I would just forget about it but the thing is you might owe me."

She really blushed at that. "Please don't do this."

Simon went on as if he hadn't heard her. "The only way to know what's what and what's fair, is if we agree to a time frame," Simon said, pushing off the desk as he spoke.

Georgina's shoulders tensed but she didn't back away. "Time frame?"

"Yeah, instead of going for a set amount of money, we agree to a set amount of time."

"For what?" she asked, still studying the floor beneath her feet.

"For you to work off the money you owe me," Simon murmured.

Her head snapped up at that. "That I owe you?"

Simon nodded, snaring her gaze with his, willing her not to look away. "Last night, there at the end, I remember you saying my name quite a few times."

A confusion of emotions played themselves out in her gaze until she simply let her eyes slide closed and asked the one question he couldn't answer with total honesty, at least, not without scaring her into calling the Funny Farm to come pick him up, "Why did you leave?"

So he went for a partial truth. "Because I'm an idiot."

That made her laugh but she composed herself quickly enough to ask. "And if you fall prey to another bout of idiocy? What then?"

"I won't." Simon murmured. "Give me this weekend, just until Monday morning."

*Please, oh please oh please oh please…*

"Why?" she asked.

"Why not?"

*Oh, there's a good answer.*

"Okay."

Simon was so surprised by her response he flinched. "Huh?"

"I said okay," Georgina replied, reaching for the bottle of wine Simon had brought.

Simon took it and started opening it before she could, stealing her hope of having something to fiddle with while she absorbed the fact that, swayed by two little words, she had just agreed to spend the rest of the weekend with him.

"Why not?"

His logic had floored her, stripped away every defense she could have thrown at him, leaving only the truth.

With Simon by her side, she had felt more in one night than she had felt in the past how many years of her quiet, useful existence. With Simon, she had felt... free. He didn't expect her to be the cutest, quietest version of herself. He actually seemed to like it when she mouthed off at him. He knew about Abby and yet he still treated her with respect. He hadn't grabbed at her, assuming he could pick up where he had left off the night before. He had asked her to spend the weekend with him by teasing her with her own fantasy.

Taking a steadying breath, Georgina firmly reminded herself that this was no big deal. It was just sex for the fun of it, a casual affair to burn off the inexplicable attraction between them. What was going to happen this weekend wasn't some sex-infused prelude to forever. If she somehow forgot that fact and became attached to him, she had no one to blame but herself. Simon had been very clear about his intentions towards her, going so far as to give their affair an expiration date.

*Never forget that this ends on Monday.*

The worst thing about keeping that knowledge securely in the foreground was that it didn't change what she was about to do. After years of saving herself for Mr. Right, she was entering into a brief affair with the quintessential Mr. Right-Now, and it was *beyond* more than likely that she would regret him later. But that was the beauty of kissing Mr. Right-Now...later simply did not matter.

Simon handed her a glass of wine then looked around the book strewn attic. "This place looks worse than it did last night."

Georgina slapped her forehead and groaned. "What was I thinking? I can't spend the rest of the weekend playing with you. I have to finish this."

Simon snorted. "Buyer's remorse so soon? Well, too bad. You're not getting out of our agreement that easy. What needs doing?"

Georgina blinked at him in confusion. "Pardon?"

"This mess you've got going here, what needs to be done?"

"Well, I've cataloged most everything. All I need to do is shelve accordingly."

"I can put books on shelves," Simon muttered, walking around to see how she had piled books in front of the rows of mostly empty shelves.

"Simon, be serious. You didn't come here to spend your weekend acting as a librarian's assistant."

Simon turned to face her, hands on hips. "We made a deal. You agreed to it and I'm not going anywhere. You finish your sandwich, I'll shelve books... and, while you're at it, how do you feel about the designated hitter rule?"

Georgina just stared at him, flattered that he wanted her enough to spend his afternoon shelving books to get her. Wow, she'd had dates that had cancelled when she'd called to tell them that she might be a few minutes late.

"Designated hitter," Simon repeated, waving his hand in front of her face.

"What?"

"How do you..."

"Feel about the designated hitter. Yes... uh... no real opinion. I don't follow baseball."

Simon snorted. "Now why am I not surprised? Do you follow any sport?"

"Uh, no, not really. But I like to swim and I'm pretty good at tennis."

"Tennis? Shit." Simon shook his head in disgust as he leaned down to scoop up more books.

Georgina sat on the couch with an offended huff. "Well, excuse me. I hadn't realized there was a right answer."

"The only right answer regarding the designated hitter rule is 'I am against it'," Simon said, glancing at her over his shoulder. "Finish your sandwich."

Georgina saluted him with it before taking a bite. Seemingly assured of her compliance, Simon started shelving books at an impressive pace, eclipsed only by the rapidity with which he asked her the most random questions.

Did she eat steak? Did she practice yoga? Did she have any contact with her 'inner child'?

That one made her laugh. "My upbringing precludes me from putting much faith in psychotherapy. One gracefully accepts the cards that one is dealt, then privately deals with them."

Simon nodded. "My family was more, 'You'll get what you get and like it' but the idea's the same."

"Pretty much."

Before she could ask where all this was leading, he asked her another question and another, until she was laughing and answering without thought. The questions weren't invasive and they were easy, even fun, to answer.

Did she prefer Macs or PCs? Coffee or tea? Eggs scrambled, fried or sunny-side up? Did she like black licorice? When she said that she did, he shuddered.

"Nasty stuff," he muttered. "But if you like it..."

Georgina took that moment to ask a question of her own. "Boxers or briefs?"

"Neither," he replied, unfazed by such a personal question. "Do you have any underwear that isn't white cotton?"

"Nope," she lied, thinking that her small collection of 'dress-up' underwear was none of his business.

"That shit's sexy as hell," Simon said, turning then leaning back against the shelves. "I about passed out last night when you whipped your dress off."

Simon's eyes glittered as he took a good look at her. She was stretched out on the couch, her bare feet propped on the coffee table, one arm under her head, the other trailing off the couch, her glass dangling from her fingers.

"What?" she asked when all he did was stare.

"It's the strangest thing but the more I learn about you, the sexier you are."

"Why, thank you."

"Was that a compliment?"

"It most certainly was," Georgina purred, her body warming under both his gaze and his words. "I have always felt that a person must be sexual in both mind and body, one without the other is... oh, not shallow but..." Georgina raised her glass to her lips as she struggled for the words.

"Half-assed?" Simon asked.

"Not how I would have put it but you're right," Georgina murmured, setting her glass on the floor as a gentle sweep of heat rolled over her body. "Come here," she whispered, bravely crooking one finger at him.

Simon grinned, a wicked slide of lips over teeth that kicked Georgina's pulse up another notch. "What's the magic word?"

"Now," Georgina drawled, trailing the tips of her fingers down between her breasts, arching a little, enjoying the sensation, even through the linen of her dress.

Simon rolled his eyes, even as he pushed away from the shelves. "We've really got to do something about your manners."

"And you're going to teach me?" Georgina asked, licking her lips as he settled down at the other end of the couch, one arm draped over the back of the couch, legs sprawled open, suggestive, daring her to keep her gaze on his eyes rather than dipping down between his thighs.

"Now there's an idea," Simon said, narrowing his black eyes at her until she felt a small flutter of unease. "Me teaching you. There are quite a few things I wouldn't mind showing you the finer points of."

"Now, Simon," she soothed, reaching out to smooth just the tips of her fingers over the back of his hand. With a quick flip of his wrist, Simon snagged her hand in his, smiling at her gasp.

"The way I see it," he said, rubbing his thumb over her palm. "What we have here is one helluva of a learning opportunity. You've got an impressively filthy mind but very little hands-on experience." Simon paused.

Georgina nodded. No use lying.

"I, on the other hand, have the experience but my mental game is for shit."

It was Georgina's turn to roll her eyes. "Liar."

"I'll take that as a compliment."

"You would."

Simon snickered. "Damn but playing with you is fun."

Georgina blushed with pleasure.

"When you blush like that, it reminds me of what you look like when you're excited, all pink and pretty, soft..." he murmured the last word, his thumb rubbing the delicate skin at the inside of her wrist. He paused, his gaze tracing the movement of his thumb. "Before we go any further, I want to make something between us very clear."

*This is where he tells you not to get attached, not to expect anything past Monday morning.*

Georgina braced herself accordingly and thus was floored when he said, "I've never met anyone like you and, if I screw up, if I do something you don't like, you have to tell me. No means no and stop means stop. No gray area, no safe-words, none of that, okay?"

Georgina let out the breath she'd been holding on a sigh that sounded perilously close to relief. "Okay and thank you, it hadn't occurred to me to..."

Simon's grin returned as he looked into her eyes. "See, a learning opportunity. I teach you, you teach me."

"I can't imagine what you've got to learn from me."

"You have no idea..." he murmured, pulling her towards him.

## Chapter Five

*I am ever hopeful that a man will turn out to be more than he appears. Unfortunately, I have yet to have that hope fulfilled.* —Abigail Scott

Simon slid down until he was stretched out on his back, his head resting comfortably on the arm of the couch. He slowly brought Georgina down with him as he went, pulling her over him, until her hips were cradled between his thighs, his fingers were sifting through her hair and they were kissing, gently, both of them taking the time to savor the other.

He removed her dress with a minimum of fuss. She helped him off with his t-shirt, then got to her knees and watched as he took off his jeans. He slid his bare legs between her thighs, urging her back towards him, his hands sure and strong on her body, until she was straddling him, waiting, watching as he took his time opening a condom packet then slowly rolled the latex over his erection.

And as she watched, Georgina wondered why some people said that stopping to put on a condom killed the mood. For her, the wait added a whole different level of anticipation. It was an opportunity to once again decide that yes, she wanted this man, wanted what was going to happen between them.

It was also an opportunity to watch Simon as he handled himself, how he enjoyed the feel of his hands on his cock as he smoothed the latex by thrusting into his own fist. He looked up at her as he did it, his eyes narrowed, his color heightened. He tightened his fist once around the base of his cock, the full head pulsed, the tracery of veins bulged, just a little, just enough to let her see that he was enjoying this.

"Tell me what you're thinking," he whispered.

Georgina looked at him lying beneath her, his lips slightly parted, tongue pressing against the backs of his bottom teeth, his neck corded with tension, the black lines of his tattoo like vines, swirling down his arms, taut bronze skin, glimmering with a thin sheen of sweat…

"You are the single most beautiful man I have ever seen," she whispered, feeling once again that glorious freedom to say what she was thinking without fear that he would censure her.

Simon shifted beneath her, one hand still wrapped around his cock, the other moving to her hip, helping her as she positioned herself over him, never once wincing or laughing at her unsure movements. How awkward she must seem to someone like him, someone so used to this complicated dance of aligning bodies for pleasure... and yet, meeting his eyes, she saw only a dark reflection of her own need.

"You with me?" he asked, just as she felt the blunt tip of his cock nudging her moist opening.

"All along the way," she replied, unable to hold back a dreamy smile as she slowly sank onto him, accepting him into her body without reservation or inhibition. "I love the way this feels," she whispered once he was fully seated within her. "The stretch, even that little hitch of pain at the outset, all of it..."

She let her voice trail off. Sensation took over and she could no longer put feeling into words. Swiveling her hips, she took him deep, beginning a slow, languid pace that seemed to match the long, late afternoon shadows stretching across the floor. The distant hum and whisper of the ocean as it crept up the beach then receded acted as a metronome to her movements, taking him deep then slowly receding, only to come back to him, again and again, until she was lost in a haze of pleasure.

Her head felt heavy so she let it drop back, felt the ends of her hair tickling her back. His hands cupped her hips but he didn't try to guide her as she rode him, her pace increasing as her blood rushed through her veins. His hands tightened and he groaned.

"Are you with me?" she asked, teasing him, flexing her hips as she felt her body tighten up. Georgina opened herself to it, ready for a gentle slide into oblivion.

Simon had other plans.

He bucked under her, driving deep, deeper than she had gone and her orgasm coalesced into a blinding flash, harsher than she had expected, radiating out then coming back hard as he pulled her down over him. His mouth latched onto her breast and, with three hard upward thrusts, he sent her spinning into another orgasm, richer and darker than the first.

When she came back to herself, she was breathing so hard she would have been embarrassed if he didn't sound just as winded as she did.

"Christ, Georgina. This gets any better and I'll be in the morgue before Monday," Simon muttered.

Laughing, she sat up and blew her hair out of her face. There followed another awkward sex moment—climbing off him while he held the condom in place. At one point, her foot slipped and she almost fell over onto the coffee table.

"I never put the awkward, undignified stuff in my stories," she muttered with a quick hop and skip that left her standing at the end of the couch, wild haired and blushing.

"You're just new at this," Simon said with a teasing grin. He swung his feet onto the floor, stood up, took two steps then tripped over a book. Georgina giggled as Simon cursed his way to the bathroom to get rid of the condom.

Walking over to the bed, Georgina whisked the comforter off of it, like a magician doing the tablecloth trick, leaving the pillows undisturbed on the bare mattress. Wrapping it around her, she walked over to one of the French doors and let herself out into the early evening.

The sun had set not long ago, the moon had yet to rise, allowing sea and sky a brief opportunity to match their myriad shades of blue, neatly obliterating the line of the horizon in the process. As she let go of her instinctual search for the horizon and simply admired the view, Georgina felt as if she was being slowly drawn out across the surface of the ocean, as if she was the sky, absorbing the motion of the waves, dipping into the valleys of water then rising up on the crests.

And, just for an instant, Georgina felt a part of that ancient, unbroken connection.

"Gorgeous," she whispered, wondering why she had never realized that sky and sea didn't meet only at the horizon, but everywhere and all at once in a seamless, ongoing dance of give and take.

"What are you doing out here?" Simon asked.

Georgina turned to see him, shivering a little in the tangy breeze. He had his jeans back on but hadn't bothered with a shirt.

"I never realized..." she began, then paused and felt foolish.

"You never realized what?" he prompted, moving to stand next to her at the rail.

"That the sea and sky don't meet only at the horizon but all along the way."

"I never thought about it that way," Simon said, his eyes tracking across the view, from left to right then back again, his mouth turned down in a slight frown.

"Me neither," she whispered, watching him until his perusal of the view became easier, less linear. She was suddenly very glad that he was there to share this new view with, glad that he was genuinely interested in what she was showing him. Georgina couldn't remember a time when she had felt so free to say and do whatever she felt in front of a man. She was usually so careful, scared that she would let it slip that she wasn't what she appeared to be. But with Simon, she didn't have to pretend.

Georgina felt a burst of giddy pleasure at that thought. And then the voice of reason reared its practical head.

*Just remember, this ends on Monday.*

*All along the way*, Simon thought, rolling the words around in his head.

Georgina had said that earlier when he had asked if she was with him. But he didn't mention that. It was too soon to start spouting off about how he felt that they were like the ocean and the sky, meeting everywhere and all along the way. How he felt that she fit him in places he had thought were too messy and difficult to ever find a good, lasting fit.

Instead he asked if she was hungry.

"Starved."

Simon went inside and dialed Valerie's cell phone number, hoping she hadn't turned it off for the night.

"Someone had better be dead," Valerie growled.

"I need dinner for two," Simon began.

"Call a restaurant, I'm *busy*."

"Up in the attic for me and George," Simon finished.

Silence, then Valerie hissed, "Hey, Roger... get off me... I know you're close but I need you to get lost for awhile." Simon heard a man groan then Valerie said, "Okay, I'll have it sent up as soon as I can."

Simon hated to interrupt Valerie's fun. He knew he could have called down to the kitchen directly but if he had done that, it would have been all over the party in under three minutes that Abigail Scott was entertaining *Simon Says* up in the attic. It wasn't anyone's business but theirs what was going on up here, and Valerie could be counted on to keep the staff from gossiping.

"Thanks, Valerie," Simon said.

"You're welcome, but Simon."

"Yeah?"

"Hurt her and I will destroy you."

Simon hung up before he could say what he was thinking. Namely, that if he screwed this up, the person that would end up hurt would be him.

If someone ever asked her what she had had for dinner that night, Georgina honestly wouldn't have been able to remember. What she would remember, possibly for the rest of her life, was the way Simon had looked sitting across from her (bare-chested, per her request) smiling and laughing as he told her about what it had been like growing up with six brothers in a three bedroom house in Encino.

"Madhouse does not even begin to describe it," he said. "There was never enough of anything to go around. I got into more fistfights with my brothers over things like who got the last pork chop. Hell, I didn't own a brand-new pair of jeans until the summer I was thirteen. I got a job clearing vacant lots with two of my brothers, and the first thing we did when we got paid was go out and buy clothes that no one else had worn."

"Were you the youngest?" Georgina asked, amazed at his ability to talk easily about a childhood most people would have railed against.

"I should have been so lucky. I'm fourth in line for the throne," Simon joked. "Smack in the middle."

"I don't have any siblings," Georgina said with a sigh. "I remember long, lonely summer days when none of my friends could play. I've always believed that was when I developed my love of books. A book is never too busy to play with you."

"Well, the next time you get bored, call me and I'll send a couple of my brothers over. And don't worry about returning them, I've got plenty to spare."

Georgina laughed, not believing him for a moment. He might be too much of a guy to say it but he loved his brothers. It was there in the way he talked about them, their wives and the ever increasing number of nieces and nephews they were in the process of providing him with. "You'd fight tooth and nail if anyone tried to take one of your brothers away."

"Not when I was thirteen."

"Well, despite what that column of yours says, you're a grown-up now."

Simon fiddled with his fork for a few seconds then said, "About the column. I... that is, my editor has been all over me to broaden my professional horizons."

Georgina sat back, surprised. "Really? I thought *Simon Says* was a cash cow for any paper that carried it."

"Oh, it is but my editor Lillian says, and I'm quoting here, that I'm wasting my talent on titillating the underdeveloped minds of a pack of slavering morons, bless their hearts."

Georgina laughed at Simon's impersonation of his editor.

"Lillian's from Tennessee, and it's good form to tack 'bless their heart' on to the end of an insult. I've probably had my heart blessed more than any man in America, thanks to Lillian." Simon paused then, in a much more serious tone, said, "The thing is, I don't know if it'll fly, going whole hog into politics when all I'm known for is party-girls and organized sports."

"Nonsense, there's room in every career for growth. Maybe your editor thinks your readers are ready to broaden their own horizons and doesn't want them abandoning the paper when they get tired of your shenanigans."

"Shenanigans?" Simon asked.

Georgina demurred from further comment by changing the direction of the subject. "Why politics? Why not go to the sports page?"

Simon shifted in his chair then muttered something she didn't catch.

"Again?"

"I have degrees in both political science and journalism."

Georgina dropped her fork.

"What?" Simon asked, thrusting his chin out.

"Nothing, I just...I mean it never occurred to me that someone like you..."

"Someone like me what?" Simon asked, his voice dropping an octave.

Georgina realized that she was on the verge of insulting him and that was the absolute last thing she wanted to do. Suddenly, struck by inspiration, she said, "It's sort of like when you found out that I'm Abigail Scott. You know, mousy little librarian writes porn. Total shocker."

Simon snorted, shoved his chair back and stood. "Here's the difference, my little mouse. Finding out that you write porn was a total turn-on whereas finding out that brain-dead *Simon Says* has two college degrees that didn't arrive in the mail from 'How to be a Misogynistic Pig University' is the shocker."

Georgina watched helplessly as Simon paced over to the French doors. He shoved his hands in the front pockets of his jeans, the black lines of his tattoo jumping as he tensed his arms and set his shoulders.

"Okay, I am shocked. I made assumptions about you based solely on a...a *character* you've created and I for one should know better, what with Abby hanging over my head. Please don't be mad," she said, walking over to stand next to him.

He just continued staring out at the ocean, his mouth turned down in an angry frown.

"What can I do to make it up to you?" she asked, daring to loop her arm through his.

Simon glanced at her out of the corner of his eye.

"Anything," Georgina said, eager to dispel the tension between them. "Just ask and it's yours."

"Anything?" Simon asked, his mouth hitching up at the corners in a dangerous grin.

Georgina's pulse kicked up as heat flared in his eyes.

"Uh... well..."

Simon started making chicken noises.

"Fine. Anything."

*Man, this is almost too easy.*

Biting back an evil laugh, Simon circled Georgina's velvet comforter draped form. She had left it on, per his request, and he loved the way she looked in it, like a Greek Goddess come to life. A contrite goddess, willing to do anything to get back in his good graces. Well, they'd just see how Georgina defined *anything.*

Clearing his throat, he asked after something that, if she was smart, she would tell him was none of his business. "Would you say that you have an excessive list of sexual hang-ups?"

Georgina narrowed her eyes. "Define excessive."

"Ever been tied up?"

"Nope."

"Ever had group sex?"

"No!"

"Let's try a tamer one. Ever gone bald down below?"

"Ever what?"

"Shaved the kitty. Waxed the peach. Took a blunt to the..."

Georgina shrieked and held up her hands. "I get it, I get it. No, I have never shaved off my pubic hair. Why, does it bother you that I'm not smooth down there?"

"Hell, no. Doesn't matter to me, I'm just grateful you let me down there. I'm not about to get fussy."

"I've thought about doing it but..."

"Afraid of the itchy growing-in stage?" he asked.

"That and well... lots of things about it make me uncomfortable."

"Like what?"

"It just seems wrong, as if I'm regressing to when I was a little girl, before puberty. As if I'm giving up a symbol of my maturity."

Simon raised an eyebrow at that. "Now tell me the real reason you don't go bald."

Georgina snorted. "How annoying to be attracted to a man that reads me so well," she muttered. Simon grinned. So she thought he had her figured out, did she?

*You wish.*

"I think I'd feel vulnerable and exposed, stripped bare like that," Georgina went on.

*Bingo. Get her to give you that one.*

Simon pinned Georgina with a heated look and said, "Here's what's going to happen..."

"Uh-oh," Georgina said, taking a step back.

Simon took her arms and pulled her closer. "You've got an impressive list of hang-ups and that can't be good for your career."

"What do my hang-ups have—?"

"Don't interrupt," Simon said in a mock command.

Georgina saluted him.

"One," Simon said. "I'm going to pick one of your hang-ups and we're going to..."

Georgina tensed. "Nope. Stop right there."

Simon lowered his gaze, letting his lashes hide his eyes as he licked at his bottom lip. "I'm going to shave that gorgeous cunt of yours because I want to see you, bare and vulnerable..."

"Simon," Georgina breathed. "Please don't ask this of me."

"I'm free to ask for what I want, and you're free to refuse. Remember, yes means yes and no means no. I'm not going to force you to do anything you don't want to," Simon reminded her, watching as she bit her bottom lip and struggled with her unruly sexuality. If he was reading her right, the flush that was burning her cheeks and the slow dilation of her pupils, somewhere inside she wanted what he was offering. But he couldn't push too hard... this had to come from her.

Slowly releasing her, Simon took a step back and then another. Her eyes followed him, her expression a little desperate.

"I'll be in the bathroom. You want this, come on in. You don't... well, I could use a shower. And Georgina, this isn't a requirement. If it's a no, we're still on until Monday."

She nodded and Simon felt a slight shift in her, back towards the safe and narrow.

*Oh, what the hell. Just a little push.*

"And, if it's no, I'm fully prepared to spend the rest of the weekend having sex the way a nice woman you want everyone to think you are would, straight missionary with the lights off."

Georgina gasped at his statement, hating it that he could read her so easily. Hating that, given a choice between straight missionary and having him shave her... a jolt of heat seared down her spine at the mere idea of letting him do such a thing. Fortunately, the shaving was tame compared to her other hang-ups. He was again offering her what she wanted, but this time he was tossing in a choice, more of a challenge... almost *daring* her to accept.

"Why, you vile, manipulative..." Georgina seethed.

"That's it, talk dirty to me," Simon said then turned on his heel and strolled towards the bathroom.

The stunning sight of that rope drawn draped over his back is what stopped her from telling him exactly what he could do with his challenge.

He had neatly taken the reins, making this an issue of pride, a sexual game of chicken...who would blink first? Lousy, arrogant male that he was, Simon obviously assumed it would be her. Had last night taught him nothing?

"Oh Simon, simple, simple Simon..." Georgina murmured, letting the comforter slide from her body. "You have no idea who you're dealing with."

ᕼᕼᕼᕼ

Simon sat on the wide edge of the bathtub, his jeans riding low on his hips, his hair falling over his eyes, giving him a boyish appearance at odds with the black ropes wrapped around his arms. He was fiddling with a razor he had found in the medicine cabinet, waiting to see if Georgina was going to decide he was an arrogant asshole and go to bed without him. There was a slight noise from the attic and he glanced up and there she was, standing naked in the doorway.

He said, "Come here," his voice husky and low, relieved that he hadn't driven her away.

Georgina sashayed, there was really no other word for it, towards him, her hair a wild tumble around her shoulders, her eyes heavy-lidded, that gorgeous hooker's mouth soft and slightly open. She stopped a few feet away from him, jutted out her hip, crossed her arms under her breasts and met his gaze, a heated challenge shimmering in her eyes.

"Closer," Simon said, his lips barely moving.

She took one step closer and waited, letting one eyebrow lift, that expression of cool disdain combined with the fact that she was gloriously naked making Simon want to toss the razor, grab her by the hips and bury his face between her thighs. But he didn't. He had a reason for doing this, hell if he could remember it right now, but it had seemed important a few minutes ago.

"Closer," he hissed.

When Georgina was nearly on top of him, he inhaled once through his nose, caught the scent of her arousal and grinned. She had come to him, no more running away, no more hiding. This was going to be good... nerve-wracking but good.

"Put your foot up on the side of the tub," he said, reaching over to turn on the water, giving her a minute to get herself steady as he got the water to a good temperature. Wetting a washcloth, he handed it to her and said,

"Wash yourself. I can't think straight with you smelling like sex."

Instead of blushing or sputtering at his crudeness, she took the cloth and began to gently wipe between her legs, letting her head drop back as she rolled her hips, getting off on the feel of the terrycloth rubbing her sensitive flesh.

"That is so damn sexy," Simon muttered, looking up at her. She met his gaze. "I can't decide whether to shave you or eat you."

Georgina dropped the cloth into the tub. Then she reached up and grabbed the shower-curtain rod with one hand, elongating her torso as her breasts lifted and the tips tightened. She rested her cheek on her upraised arm and let her eyes slide closed.

"This is your game," she purred. "It doesn't matter to me what you do."

*Yeah, right... shave her and then eat her and we'll see who's able to play casual by the end.*

He handled her carefully, slowly, drawing out the intimacy of the moment, the bathroom still and silent around them. When he was satisfied with the results, Simon rinsed the razor for the last time and turned off the water. Georgina looked down at the small patch of hair Simon had left her. She frowned, confused. "You're done?"

Simon glanced up at her and shrugged. "I liked that thing you said about being a grown woman and not a little girl. As far as excuses go, it has merit. Women have hair down there, little girl's don't. And if I know anything about you, you are not a little girl."

Georgina lost her detached, sex goddess mien and asked, "Then why did we do this?"

"To see if you trusted me," Simon replied, remembering why he had started all this.

She chewed on her bottom lip for a second then asked, "Does this mean we're done with the hang-ups for tonight?"

"Yeah," Simon said. He was rewarded with a wide smile of relief. This was more than enough for tonight. Tomorrow maybe he'd push her again, but for now he just wanted to spread her out on that big bed in the attic and take his sweet ass time driving her as crazy as she made him, by doing nothing more strenuous than standing around converting air into carbon dioxide.

*A definite imbalance of power that needs to be rectified, pronto.*

*To see if you trusted me...*

Georgina would have spent a few minutes, okay hours, mulling over that comment but Simon distracted her by leaning his shoulder into her upraised thigh and kissing her between her legs, a luscious, open-mouthed assault that let her know beyond a shadow of a doubt that this was not something he was doing because it was expected but rather because he wanted to.

She grabbed the shower rod with both hands and hung on for dear life. Simon pushed his tongue so deep into her sex she wondered why his mouth hadn't been included in one those female-centric tour guides as a not-to-be-missed attraction of the Southland.

"Good Lord..." Georgina panted, her knuckles going white as the leg she was standing on began to tremble. Simon had drawn back and was now lapping at the newly bared skin of her outer lips. The sensation was incredible, the skin unbelievably sensitive to the rasp of his tongue. When he slipped two fingers into her sheath, she surprised them both by coming. She grunted, a deep throated, animal sound that reverberated off the tile walls and sent Simon's mouth into overdrive, licking and gently biting until Georgina was sobbing, her orgasm rolling on, an endless, swamping pleasure everywhere.

"The bed," she gasped, knowing she was seconds from falling over into the tub, and she didn't want to end the evening in the ER.

Simon got to his feet and was hustling her out of the bathroom so fast she slipped on the tile and had to grab him to keep from going down. She laughed. He cursed and picked her up, tossed her over his shoulder and walked through the attic with her hanging down his back, laughing even harder at his caveman antics. She was not a small woman by any stretch of the imagination and being carried was something that hadn't happened to her since the third grade.

Simon dumped her onto the bed, shed his jeans and was ripping open a condom packet before she had her hair out of her eyes.

His face was flushed and he was a little wild around the eyes, a man in full rut. If he hadn't had to get the condom on he would have already been inside her. Georgina fell back on the mound of pillows, spread her legs and ran her hands up over her breasts, arching her back in anticipation.

Simon knelt on the bed, one knee between her legs as he looked into her eyes.

"Damn," he breathed, frozen in place, his gaze dropping to where her fingertips were lightly pinching her nipples, then down between her legs, her newly shaved sex wide open and ready for him. "Oh God...Georgina..."

Georgina leaned forward and pulled him over her, like a heavy, living blanket, all hard angles and lean planes, his skin hot and smooth, his muscles tensed and ready.

Simon kissed her, his tongue entering her mouth as his cock penetrated her sex. When he was seated fully within her, he pulled his mouth away and whispered, "I was going to go slow, make you as crazy for me as I am for you but you—"

"Yeah, right," Georgina panted, rolling her hips up to take him even deeper. "Remember what I said last night? If I were any crazier for you, I would have jumped you at Valerie's party."

Simon buried his face against her neck and whispered, "Son of a bitch," as he drew back his hips, leaving her until just the head of his cock was inside her. "It makes me crazy to think I could have had you three weeks ago."

Georgina laughed at his reaction then gasped when he slammed into her, hard.

Again. And again, straightening his arms until he was looming over her, driving into her until she couldn't lift her hips, couldn't match his thrusts, could only wrap her hands around his forearms and accept the pleasure he was giving her. She arched her neck until only the crown of her head was touching the pillows.

"Look at me," Simon ordered, his voice gravely and harsh.

Georgina tensed, remembering that this was what she'd been afraid of, that he used pleasure to strip her bare, until he could see down into her soul, a witness to all her secrets. Every time before, he'd been as lost and dazed as she but this was different. She felt very much at his mercy, open and vulnerable.

"I said look at me," Simon growled, bending his elbows until his chest brushed her breasts, until he stopped moving, holding her there on the edge of completion, and she wanted to come more than she wanted to hide so she opened her eyes and saw him, disheveled, breathing hard through his mouth, his gaze intent on her, his expression almost pleading.

Georgina gently cradled his jaw in her hand and let him look his fill, open and unafraid because he knew about everything she had spent years trying to hide and he had wanted her anyway.

"Simon," she breathed and kissed him, softly, gently, worshipping a mouth that had given her so much pleasure, by word as well as deed. She tightened deep inside, the kiss enough to finish her, sending her into a gentle, rolling orgasm that took him down with her. He shuddered as he buried his hands in her hair, her name coming out of his mouth on a groan, a dying man's last gasp, before he thrust once more and went still, pressing his forehead to hers, jaw clenched, held tight in the sweet agony of completion.

Georgina held him close, absently running her hands up and down his back until he abruptly pulled away and disappeared into the bathroom.

Oh God, if he ran away tonight… Georgina closed her eyes and rolled onto her side, her back to the door. She'd made the mistake of watching him leave her last night and she wasn't about to do it again.

"Where the hell are the sheets," Simon grumbled a few minutes later.

"You came back," she murmured, rolling onto her back. "Oh, the sheets… I sort of…"

Simon just grunted as he crawled into bed next to her. "Forget the sheets, move over, you're on my side."

"Oh… sorry."

Settling down next to her, Simon paused halfway through getting the comforter over them and asked, "What side do you sleep on, anyway?"

"The side you're on."

"Can you live with that side?"

"Uh… sure." Georgina would have made some blasé comment about how it didn't really matter, since they only had tonight and tomorrow night to worry about, but Simon rolled her onto her side and wrapped his long, warm body around hers. He was asleep within two minutes.

Georgina frowned. She didn't want to go to sleep. There was so much more she wanted to do with him and there was only so much time.

Simon snuffled out a soft snore into her ear.

Georgina giggled.

Simon snored. Were fantasy men allowed to snore? Apparently hers was.

Georgina lay there in the dark, allowing her mind to wander until it stumbled over something Simon had said earlier that evening.

"I have degrees in both political science and journalism."

She had reacted so poorly he hadn't had the chance to tell her where he had earned those degrees.

Georgina snorted. Simon had probably gone to some beer soaked campus where they gave out grades during toga parties and…She caught herself before she went any further. There was something about her assumption that felt mean and, oddly enough, disloyal.

"Simon," Georgina whispered, gently shaking the arm he had wrapped around her waist.

"Gluh?"

"Where did you go to college?"

Simon propped himself up on one elbow and stared down at her as if she had lost her mind. "Come again?"

"I asked where you went to college."

"And this is important at two in the morning because?"

"Just answer the question."

"Harvard," he muttered then flopped over onto his back with a tortured groan. "Bad enough you keep me up all hours fulfilling your voracious sexual appetites and now this."

Georgina stared sightlessly up at the ceiling, only half-listening to Simon's bitching.

"Hey," Simon said, waving his hand in front of her face. "You okay over there?"

"Harvard?!" Georgina asked, turning her head on the pillow to glare at him.

"Yeah, so what's the big deal? Lots of people went to Harvard."

"People like former Vice-President Al Gore went to Harvard!"

"Yeah and Tommy Lee Jones was his roommate. What's your problem?"

"You! You are my problem!" Georgina said, clambering over him to get out of bed. "You tell me about your childhood, about the hand-me-down clothes and the fist-fights over who got the last pork-chop and then you think it's no big deal that you went to Harvard?"

Simon sat up, his brow creased as he watched her furiously pacing back and force next to the bed. "Lots of poor kids go to Harvard," he said. "They have these things called scholarships and…"

"Yes!" Georgina yelled, stopping to point emphatically at him. "And do you have any idea how brilliant a person has to be to qualify for one? Do you?"

Simon scratched his bare chest and frowned. "Are you mad at me because I'm smart?"

"No, Simon. I am furious with you because you are brilliant and wasting it on Simon freaking Says."

Simon flopped back onto the bed. Throwing his hands in the air he groaned. "Christ, you sound just like Lillian and Sylvia and Julie and Mary and Maddie and …"

"Spare me the roll-call of your former girlfriends, Simon," Georgina growled.

Simon lurched into a sitting position and hissed, "They aren't my former anything. Lillian is my editor and the other four are my sisters-in-law." Simon stopped, then said in a much calmer voice, "Well, Maddie isn't technically my sister-in-law but she will be once Ian comes to his senses and…"

Georgina wildly waved her hands at him. "Stop right there. Don't you dare try to change the subject!"

Simon leaned forward and said, in a cutting tone, "I hadn't realized we had a subject going that was any of your business. What I choose to do with my degree is my business, not yours, so just lay off."

Georgina felt as if he had slapped her. She was scolding him about squandering his education, acting like she was someone whose opinion mattered to him when the truth was… the truth was…

She was just another in a long line of women he had slept with.

"You're right," Georgina said, smoothing her hands down her bare thighs, suddenly a little embarrassed to be standing before him naked. "What you choose to do with your education is most certainly none of my business."

Simon scooted toward the edge of the bed, his expression softening. "George, I'm sorry, I didn't mean..."

"Oh, please don't apologize," Georgina said as she oh-so-casually swiped Simon's t-shirt off the back of the couch. After she pulled it on, she gave an airy wave of her hand and said, "I was just being silly. Ignore me."

Georgina dug a clean pair of underwear out of her bag then went to wash her face, brush her teeth and braid her hair. By the time she climbed back into bed, Simon was asleep and Georgina had managed to shove every single one of her inappropriately complicated emotions regarding Simon, his past and especially his future into the deepest, darkest corner of her mind where they belonged.

*Just remember, this ends on Monday.*

"As if I could forget," Georgina whispered into the dark stillness of the attic.

*Chapter Six*

*What's the harm of a little light bondage between friends?* —Abigail Scott

Sunday

Simon glanced over to where Georgina was curled up on the couch, slogging through the Sunday crossword puzzle and nibbling on a scone left over from breakfast. Her unruly curls were piled on top of her head, held in place by two chopsticks that stuck out from her head at weird angles and made her look as if she had had an unfortunate accident at a Chinese restaurant. She was wearing one of his rattiest t-shirts, a pair of faded black sweat pants and she had cotton balls shoved between her toes to keep her freshly painted toenails from getting smudged before they had a chance to dry.

All in all, she looked like a woman that had about zero interest in the idea of impressing the man she was with.

And Simon couldn't have been happier. Sprawled out on his end of the couch, only half-listening to the end of a Dodger game on the radio, Simon felt as if he had stumbled into another man's life. And the thing of it was, he liked it. A lot.

If anyone had told him on Friday afternoon that he would be happily spending his Sunday afternoon helping a woman shelve books and paint her toenails (and, at the risk of sounding vain, Simon felt he had done a damn fine job on Georgina's toenails, considering that stupid little brush he'd had to work with and the fact that Georgina's feet were insanely ticklish) he would have called that person a liar.

Not that he wasn't chomping at the bit to pick up where they had left off last night. Far from it. But Simon felt as if he was walking a tightrope. Too much sex and he'd be reinforcing her assumption that he was just in it for the sex. Not enough and she'd think he had lost interest.

Women. A man couldn't win for losing with 'em but Simon wasn't about to let that stop him.

Georgina belonged with him. All he had to do was convince her of that. He'd flirted with the idea of telling her about The Curse but had immediately nixed it as insufficient evidence. For her, it would be nothing but a bit of kooky family folklore.

He needed to hand her proof that he wanted her to become a permanent part of his life. Unfortunately, he had blown a golden opportunity last night by shutting her down on the subject of his education and subsequent career choices.

Defending himself by saying that what he did with his education was no one's business but his own was a knee-jerk response he gave everyone that went after him for squandering his hard-won Harvard education. Simon wanted to think that, if she hadn't sprung that conversation on him at two in the morning, he would have handled it better. He'd tried to reopen the subject a few times today but she'd acted as if she had no idea what he was talking about.

He knew *Simon Says* was an enormous hurdle between him and happily-ever-after, especially with a woman that craved a façade of respectability. He'd spent half the night tossing and turning, trying to come up with a solution that would allow him to keep both his column and Georgina...

No go. *Simon Says* had to die.

This morning, with Georgina immersed in her initial attempt to solve the Sunday crossword, Simon had called his editor and told her that he was beyond open to the idea of broadening his horizons. Lillian had about jumped through the phone, telling him she would contact the proper authorities and have an answer for him by Thursday, Friday at the latest.

"I need to know if this is going to happen by Monday morning," Simon had replied, casting a furtive look towards where Georgina was chewing on the end of her pencil and glaring at the crossword.

"Monday?! Simon, you've been dragging your feet on this for months and now you..."

"Please, Lillian. I'm on my knees here."

That had gotten her. Without further comment, Lillian had promised that she would try.

Simon wasn't sure what he could offer Georgina as proof of his good intentions but the body of *Simon Says* seemed like an excellent place to start. Strangely enough, now that he had ordered the execution, Simon was actually looking forward to burying the little bastard.

It had reminded him that *Simon Says* had started out as a joke, a composite sketch of the idiotic frat-boys he'd run across during his undergraduate years at Harvard. The fact that *Simon Says* had made his first appearance in *The Harvard Lampoon* should have tipped people off to the fact that the character had been a joke.

Instead, Simon had received an offer to bring *Simon Says* to Los Angeles. Simon had just graduated, he'd been broke and looking for a job that would take him back home to the Southland. And so he had accepted, with the intent of using *Simon Says* as a stopgap measure between college and a real job.

Unfortunately for that plan, the money had rolled in almost from the beginning and, to a young man used to pinching every penny until it screamed, living the high life had been more of a seduction than he could resist. The rest, unfortunately, was history. Eight years later, Simon finally admitted the awful truth. He had become that which he had initially set out to make fun of, a snide empty-headed playboy.

"Well, that was stupid," Simon muttered, rubbing his forehead.

"What was stupid?" Georgina asked, looking up from her crossword.

"Me," Simon said. He would have told Georgina about his little epiphany but his cell phone rang. Simon reached over the back of the couch and snatched the phone off the desk. Seeing Lillian's number on the display, he quickly excused himself and went out to the balcony.

"Lillian?" he asked, gripping the phone.

*"Simon Says* is officially dead and you owe me big."

"I know. I'll do whatever you want, just name it."

"Invite me to your wedding."

"How did you…"

"A woman knows these things. *Vaya con Dios*, you big dumbass and kiss her once for me."

Simon walked (floated would have been a better word but Simon refused to apply such a pansy-ass description to his actions) back into the attic at the exact same moment Georgina threw her pencil across the room and yelled, "What normal human being knows the name of Jimmy Carter's National Security Advisor right off the top of their head?"

"Brzezinski," Simon replied.

"Bless you."

"No, that's the name of Carter's National Security Advisor. Zbigniew Brzezinski."

"I'll give you fifty bucks if you can spell that," Georgina teased.

Eager to show off the fact that he had a fully functioning brain, Simon did.

⁂

Georgina quickly looked up Simon's answer, making him spell the name twice before she conceded that he was right. Slamming the biography of Jimmy Carter closed, Georgina just stared at him.

"What?" Simon asked.

"And you talk about me," she muttered, tossing the book onto the coffee table.

"About you what?" Simon asked, stretching his arms over his head. He looked like nothing more than a beautiful, muscular bona-fide bad boy... that just happened to know the name of a man most Americans hadn't even heard of.

"You talk about me being a fraud," Georgina said. "You're just as bad as me, if not worse."

"How do you figure?" Simon asked, slouching down onto the couch.

"List the member states of the European Union."

"Huh?"

"Just do it."

And he did, throwing in the fact that Turkey was trying to become a member but their harsh legal system and dicey human rights record were holding them up.

When he wound down, Georgina threw up her hands in disgust.

How had she managed to so grossly underestimate him? If Simon Campbell was nothing but a spoiled, shallow playboy, then she was the freaking Queen of Sheba.

Simon had been peeling off layers since the moment she had agreed to spend the weekend with him, revealing more and more of himself. After more than twenty-four hours of this, Georgina was in an almost constant state of panicked anticipation of what fascinating, wholly unexpected thing he was going to reveal next.

"Do you like opera?" Georgina demanded.

Simon jerked back as if she had slapped him. "Hell, no."

"Well, that's too bad because I love it! I've seen every production the Los Angeles Opera has performed for the past six years."

Simon looked as if he was going to be sick.

"I'm going to take a bath," she said, mad at herself for childishly playing up one of the few differences between them. It wasn't his fault. He couldn't help who he was, just like she couldn't seem to help liking him, not because he was her fantasy-man come to life but because he was just... well... him. Simon.

"Uh, George?" Simon asked.

"What?"

"Are you mad?"

"No, I'm not mad... I'm furious. But not with you."

After a long soak in the tub, Georgina got dressed then looked at herself in the mirror and tried to be objective.

"I don't look like too much of a slut," she murmured, smoothing her hands over her bare stomach.

The woman in the mirror did not agree. She thought she looked like a total slut and her expression showed her disgust.

"What? I have to do this," Georgina whispered to her reflection. "I have to get back on track here. Sweaty monkey sex is all I can afford. If I go back out there in my regular clothes, Simon and I might spend the rest of the evening getting to know each other even more, and I'll be in love with him before dessert. I tried to put him off today but he didn't seem to mind the 'boring Sunday afternoon' version of me. He actually seemed to like it... what's that all about? Never mind. Doesn't matter.

*Coward.*

"Damn straight I'm a coward," Georgina hissed, piling her hair on top of her head in a loose, sexy up-do. Simon had said he liked her hair like this, so she shoved the chopsticks back into it then pulled a few curls down to rest against her neck.

Perfect. If Simon wasn't up for some mindless sex the second he laid eyes on her, well, she didn't know what she was going to do.

However, considering the fact she was wearing black silk stockings, a black lace thong and the short black silk robe Valerie had given her for Christmas three years ago, Georgina was thinking Simon wasn't going to do anything but crawl all over her.

How exactly these articles of clothing had ended up in the bottom of her suitcase was something Georgina was going to have to bring up with Valerie the next time she saw the meddling little brat, but for now Georgina was a woman with a mission.

She had to protect her heart from her over-active imagination. Spinning fairy tales around Simon Campbell was a heartbreak waiting to happen. Simon had set the time-line for their affair and she had agreed to it. He'd given no indication that he wanted to extent their time together. This was sex just for the fun of it. Nothing more.

*You keep telling yourself that.*

"Oh, shut up."

When Georgina walked out of the bathroom, Simon knew something had changed. It wasn't just her outfit, which was doing a really good job of short-circuiting his thought process. It was more the determined glint in her eye. He had seen that same glint in his mother's eye when she geared up to clean out his father's garage, a sort of 'my-way-or-the-highway' expression Simon wasn't so sure should ever be worn by a woman in the bedroom.

"I was just thinking," she began, her clear, crisp voice startling in the quiet room. "We talked about my hang-ups but we never got around to yours."

Simon shrugged. "I don't really have any, what you read is—"

Georgina cut him off. "You honestly expect me to believe that whole what-you-read-is-what-you-get is business? Do I look like a fool?"

Georgina's robe had slipped open, revealing what she wasn't wearing beneath it.

"Holy God in heaven," Simon whispered, the sight of her pale skin against all that sinful black clouding his mind. The edges of her robe were caught on her distended nipples, taunting him, daring him to get up and set them free.

"I'll be generous," Georgina purred. "Just one little ol' hang-up is all I'm asking for." Noticing the direction of his gaze, she smoothed her fingers down the open edges of her robe, right over her nipples, arching her back a little, hitting him where he was most vulnerable... his obsession with getting her under him.

"Hang-ups..." Simon mumbled, his tongue suddenly feeling too thick for his mouth.

Georgina nodded, her smile of the come-hither variety.

"Bondage," Simon said, slowly getting to his feet.

"Oh, so you don't like to tie women up?"

Was that relief he heard in her tone?

"Nope, I like tying the ladies as much as the next guy. Hell, probably a little more if I'm being honest."

Georgina's eyes widened as a flush spread up her chest to blossom across her cheeks. "Well... uh... then I must assume that you don't like being tied up."

"It's just not something I feel comfortable letting someone do to me," Simon said.

Georgina considered him a moment and Simon cursed at the light that came into her eyes. Here it came. If she asked this of him, could he do it? Could he allow her that kind of control over him?

Georgina pushed away from the desk and approached him, slowly, hips swaying, sloe-eyed and dangerously arousing.

"What?" Simon asked, backing up a step. She kept walking and he kept backing up until the backs of his knees hit the edge of the bed.

"I want you to let me tie you up," she murmured, her lips barely moving as she spoke.

Simon's entire body broke out in a light sweat at her words. His knees sort of gave out. He sat down on the bed but he tried to make it look as if he had planned it by casually leaning back and bracing his weight on his arms.

She kneeled down before him, placed her hands on his spread knees and practically purred, "I want to make you come."

*Holy Christ!*

"Will you let me?" she asked.

"Oh, yeah," Simon breathed, the words escaping him before he could think through the consequences.

Georgina smiled, a little grin that would have done the Mona Lisa proud.

So this was love, doing things that scared you, handing yourself over to someone and trusting that they would take care of you. Forget handing her the body of *Simon Says*, he was going to give her his own.

If this didn't convince her that he was in this for more than just a weekend fling...

❧⟨♋⟩❦

A little light bondage was more than she had bargained for this evening, but since Simon was offering her something he had never offered anyone else, she wanted it.

*Maybe now he'll remember me past Monday morning.*

"Undress," Georgina said, rising to her feet in one graceful movement.

With a nod, Simon got up and started to disrobe, his gaze never leaving hers, until he stood before her without a stitch on, hands at his sides, easy in his nudity rather than arrogant. Not that he didn't have a lot to brag about. Tall and lean and tawny skinned, she knew every inch of him, had reveled in him. Even the black tracks of his tattoo had become familiar, but they had yet to lose their ability to intimidate. She knew that they were more than the result of youthful excess but she wasn't about to ask. This was all about the present.

"Tell me what you're thinking," Georgina murmured as she slowly walked around him.

"I can't," he said, his voice low and strained. "Not now."

Georgina nodded. Fair enough. Let him keep his secrets, all she wanted was his body.

"Please lie down," she said, gesturing towards the bed.

He obeyed, inclining his head as he went, infusing the respectful action with a narrowed-eyed look that said he was going to do this but that there would be consequences.

Georgina shivered at the thought of what Simon would consider turn about for this. He had to know she'd let him tie her in a heartbeat, that she would let him do pretty much whatever he wanted without much resistance on her part.

Not that it mattered. When she was done with him, he would be too tired to come after her tonight and tomorrow...

Never mind tomorrow, Georgina thought, propping her foot on the bed once Simon was settled. This was all about the present.

"You're going to love this," she purred, slowly pushing her robe off her knee and across her thigh, watching as Simon shifted down so he could peek at her panties. He inhaled sharply.

"You said you only wore white cotton," he said, his gaze fixed on the thin strip of black lace between her legs.

Georgina shrugged and rolled down her thigh-high black stocking, watching him, waiting for him to figure out that she intended to tie him with them.

Comprehension dawned, followed by a hard flush that streaked across his cheekbones.

"Oh, shit," he murmured, watching as she tossed one stocking on the bed then went to work on the other.

Georgina pulled the second stocking from her foot then, picking up the first, she ran both of them through her fingers. Simon struggled into a sitting position, tension radiating off him.

"Georgina..." he said, rubbing one of his wrists. Georgina wondered if he knew how clearly that gesture communicated his fear. She was willing to bet that if he did, he would stop it immediately.

"Simon."

He swallowed, his throat working, his eyes moving between her face and the stockings dangling from her hand. He went down, one vertebra at a time, still watching her, still unsure.

"Lift your arms over your head and..." she didn't have to finish. He did as he was told, wrapping both hands around the curling brass that formed the headboard.

He was so tense his body had picked up a slight, under-the-skin vibration. With his arms stretched above his head, the black lines of his tattoo looked amazing. She thought about tying him face down so she could see the entire tattoo but it would have been too much. She didn't want him to fall out of the sensual haze she was trying to blanket over him.

Georgina sat down next to him and, pulling one chopstick out of her hair she used the tip to tilt his chin up until he met her eyes. "If, for one second, you don't like what I'm doing, you tell me to stop and I will. No safe words, no games. Stop means stop and no means no and..."

"Suck my dick means suck my dick," he finished, his tone loaded with false bravado as he jerked his chin off the point of the stick. She poked the chopstick back into her hair and made a soft tsking noise.

"Poor Simon," she whispered. Using one of her silk stockings, still warm from her body, she tied one of his wrists to the bed. His wrist flexed under her hands but he remained silent as she worked. When she was done with that one, she crawled onto the bed and then straddled him. He inhaled sharply as she settled over him, turning his head towards the wall.

She quickly tied his other wrist before she lost her nerve. The longer this went on, the more she craved having him like this, contained and at her mercy. But it was an enormous risk. What if she couldn't satisfy him? What if everything she did he'd had done to him many times before, by women who knew what they were doing.

Well, no woman had ever tied him up. She had that in her favor at least.

"Kiss me, Georgina," he whispered. He turned and looked up at her, his black eyes intense.

She shivered at his plea, uncertain whether to give in to his request.

"I'm not going anywhere so kiss me, touch me, do something because I don't know how long I can stay this way."

Georgina leaned down, sliding her body along his until she was nose to nose with him. Then she licked the side of his neck. The muscles under his skin jumped, from his neck all the way down to his abdomen and she grinned and did it again. And again, until he was arching under her, his erection hard and urgent against her stomach.

She slowly moved down his body, kissing and licking, rubbing, touching, stopping here and there when the mood took her, forgetting for a few minutes her fear of not being able to satisfy him. She had never explored a man's body before and it was a revelation. Simon was strong and firm in so many places that it made the tender, almost delicate spots all the more fascinating. The concave depression where his arms met his torso, the hollow at the base of his throat, his lips, the backs of his knees, the insides of his elbows... but nothing came close to the seemingly fragile fall of his scrotum. She'd done nothing more than exhale over that part of him when he groaned.

"You are going to be the death of me," he muttered, twisting one of his wrists against the ties.

"Stop doing that, you'll hurt yourself," she said, meeting his gaze. Hoping to distract him from trying to get loose, she said, "I have read that some men like it when a woman licks and nuzzles their balls."

Simon's hips twitched, his cock swelled just a bit more as he literally choked out his response. "Holy Christ."

"I'll take that as a yes," Georgina murmured, once again studying the soft fall of his scrotum. Reaching out to cup him in her palm, Georgina was amazed. It was as if God had made this part of a man vulnerable on purpose, to remind him that, no matter what he told himself, he wasn't invincible.

"I'm going to come if you don't stop..." Simon lost the last of those words on a guttural moan as Georgina licked him with long, flat strokes of her tongue, like a big cat giving comfort.

"Where did you learn to do this?" Simon gasped, his thighs tensing as she inhaled his scent. He smelled rich and musky, overheated and intensely male.

Her body reacted to the scent of his arousal, softening in anticipation of having him. She reached down between her legs but Simon stopped her by growling and bucking his hips, throwing her off him. She reached up and gently raked her nails down the insides of his thighs for thwarting her.

Simon howled at that, his back arching off the bed. "Heartless, torturous bitch," he ground out, lifting his head to glare at her.

"That's it," Georgina muttered, crawling up his body. "Talk dirty to me."

Simon snorted but his gaze was between her legs, zeroed in on the thin strip of black silk she had yet to remove. "Please tell me you're going to punish my bad behavior by forcing me to lick between your legs."

"You wish," Georgina said, adding in a little sneer to keep the excitement out of her voice. The idea of having him service her while tied helplessly to the bed was tempting but this was about him, not her.

Simon speared her with a contemptuous look. "Scared?" he asked, his lips twisting into a smirk.

*Terrified.*

"Of you? Hardly," Georgina sniffed. "And stop trying to get what you want. You'll get what you get and be grateful."

Simon gave a heartfelt sigh. "Damn. Well, can't blame a guy for trying."

Georgina laughed, she couldn't help it. The man was a menace, pure and simple.

Leaning down so that their foreheads touched, Georgina wrapped her hands around his upper arms and said, "What am I going to do with you?"

"Anything, everything…" Simon whispered, rolling his hips between her spread thighs, letting go with a wicked laugh when she hitched in her breath and ground down on his cock. "Whatever you want, whatever you need…" he went on, his breath coming hard and fast as she countered his movements, welcoming the pressure between her legs.

"You," Georgina admitted, knowing she was admitting to needs he'd never agreed to fill. But he didn't know that she was speaking of needs beyond the physical and she said it again. "I need you."

"Then *take* me."

Pulling back, Georgina found a condom in the bedside drawer. She carefully rolled the latex over his erection, thoughtlessly mimicking his habit of

running his fist down his cock to smooth the latex then squeezing once.
Simon jerked and swore. "How did you know..."

"That you like a little squeeze before the main event?" Georgina asked,
meeting his gaze from under lowered brows.

"Yes," he breathed. Georgina felt a surge of power the likes of which
she had never known.

He was thoroughly hers, to do with as she wished. She swiped her tongue
down his shaft before taking him in her mouth, as deep as she could, pulling on him as hard as she dared, using her hands and mouth and tongue,
feeling his shocked pleasure in how he swelled and pulsed in her mouth. He
moaned, a helpless sound at odds with the way he thrust his cock farther
down her throat, an aggressive, instinctive demand that she take everything
he had to offer.

And take him she did. She was now almost desperate to make him come,
to have him know what it felt like to be at the mercy of another, to be unable
to even ask them to stop, let alone mean it. Just this once she wanted him
to know how it felt when he touched her.

"Georgina," he panted, trying to hold back even though they both knew
he was seconds away from orgasm. "Please... not without you... ah, God...
*please...*"

If he managed to choke out the word stop, Georgina knew she was honor-
bound to respect that but he was too far gone. She felt the first surge and
focused the efforts of her tongue on the sensitive ridge just under the head
of his penis. Seconds later he came, swearing and shaking apart under her.
She quickly looked up at his face, pulled tight with the glorious tension of
release, teeth bared, eyes squeezed shut, his mouth open on a prolonged,
silent wail of surrender.

Gorgeous.

Georgina knelt beside him, carefully removing the condom before unty-
ing his wrists, waiting for him to open his eyes and look at her. When he
did, Georgina drew back. The intensity of his gaze was unnerving.

"My turn," he said, his voice a hoarse rasp.

"Don't even think about it," Georgina said.

"Oh, you wouldn't believe the things I've been thinking on this weekend," Simon drawled.

"Now, Simon..." Georgina said.

"Oh come on," he said, his tone coaxing. "You'll love it."

"Just as long as I don't end up loving you," Georgina muttered then froze
when her mind retorted, *Too late...but nice try.*

# Chapter Seven

*Despite having zero experience with either, I imagine love and quicksand have one thing in common; once you realized you've stepped in it, it's too late to kick free. —Simon Says*

"What did you just say?" Simon whispered.

Georgina slapped her hand over her mouth as every thought she'd ever had about Simon (that hadn't fit in with her theory that her attraction to him was based solely on the physical) came rushing out of the shed-key corner of her brain.

"I said I have to use the facilities," Georgina mumbled as she scrambled off the bed and made a beeline to the bathroom. After making sure that the door was locked, she sat down on the cool wide edge of the tub and burst into tears.

She loved him. Despite all of her efforts to remain detached, she had somehow managed to fall head over heels (or, as her Uncle Lenny liked to say, ass over elbows) in love with Mr. Right-Now. And, just to add insult to injury, she had agreed to an expiration date for their affair!

"What am I going to do?" Georgina whispered, getting up to look at her reflection in the mirror. "I can't go out there and act like nothing's changed. Anyway, since I have no ability to keep my mouth shut around him, I give myself about three seconds before I'm blurting out that I love him and just think about how much fun that conversation is going to be. I bet he has a set speech he gives women that end up falling in love with him."

*If he even suggests the idea of being friends, hit him.*

"Oh, I plan on it," Georgina muttered, crossing her arms over her chest. "In fact, I plan on putting a lot of the blame for this right on his shoulders. 'What you read is what you get.' Ha! He should come with a warning sticker 'Caution: This man is more than he appears.' The nerve, suckering me into agreeing to a happy little fling and then turning into this fascinating, funny...*nice* man!'"

Georgina turned on the cold water and splashed her face. Her righteous indignation grew so strong it propelled her out of the bathroom before she had really thought through what she was going to say to the man that was waiting for her.

She got halfway across the attic before she noticed that Simon wasn't where she'd left him. In fact, he wasn't anywhere in the attic.

"Oh, that's just great!" Georgina railed, snatching her black robe off the floor. "I come out here to lambaste him for his part in my emotional debacle and he doesn't even have the grace to..." Georgina stopped raging when she noticed that one of the French doors was ajar.

Walking over, she pulled the door open and there was Simon, fully dressed and leaning against the railing, the breeze off the ocean rifling his hair as he stared out at the expanse of sea and sky spread out before him. At the sight of him, her righteous indignation sputtered once and then died, leaving her feeling shy, defenseless and hopelessly in love.

*Not a good combination.*

"Damn," Georgina muttered.

Hearing her, Simon turned and straightened up, crossing his arms over his chest. "What, were you hoping I had conveniently disappeared?"

"Huh?" Georgina asked, surprised by his cool tone.

"I thought about doing the polite fade, most nice women prefer that route but since you're a special case I've decided to stick it out."

Georgina shook her head, confused not only by his words but also by his almost combative stance, shoulders back, spine erect, chin up... uh-oh, he looked as if he'd been taking 'disapproving librarian' posture lessons from her.

Simon blew out a breath and then said, "I love you. I should have told you earlier but I was afraid that you'd run screaming at the idea of a guy like me being in love with you, so I bargained for some more time together, hoping that you would get to know me and... shit, I don't know... realize that I'm not a total loss situation but, since you bolted for the bathroom looking as if the hounds of hell were after you I'm guessing—"

"That I love you, too?" Georgina asked, shivering from more than the cold.

"What?" Simon whispered, losing both his mocking tone and the 'up-yours' stance.

Instead of replying, Georgina walked over to him and wrapped her arms around him, holding him close, savoring the solid feel of him next to her body. After he put his arms around her and squeezed so hard she yelped, he took one step back and looked down at her, as serious as she had never seen him.

"You love me?" he asked.

"Yes," Georgina whispered, almost afraid to say it too loudly, as if any sharp noise would destroy the moment.

"Even though I'm *Simon Says*."

Georgina reached up and gently smoothed the wrinkle of worry from between his eyebrows. "Simon, you are so much more than *Simon Says*, but you know what, I love him, too. One of the reasons I love you is that you've made me feel like it's okay to be myself, all of myself, even the parts of me that I've kept hidden for fear of what other people would think. How could I expect you to accept all of me without being willing to do the same?" Georgina bit her lip and sighed. "Of course, I don't know how I'm going to handle the party-girls but I think we can work something out."

"What, are you going to be my chaperone when I go out?" Simon teased.

"I was thinking more along the lines of a bodyguard," Georgina replied. "I could carry a tire-iron and whack them on the head if they got too close."

Simon laughed, pulling her tight against him. "What would you say if I told you I'm retired?"

"Retired? When?"

"Today. I called my editor and she helped me deep-six the column."

"When?"

"This morning."

"And you didn't say anything?" Georgina asked, a little of her former righteous indignation sparking to life.

"As I said, I wasn't sure how you would react to my loving you so I thought I could get you some proof of my intentions and killing off *Simon Says* seemed a good place to... Hey! Your nails are sharp, stop digging them into my arm!"

"This morning! You knew you loved me this morning and you didn't say anything? I've been a mess all day and you... you... get back here, where do you think you're going?"

Simon ignored her as he slipped back into the attic, calling out as he went, "Actually, I've known that I loved you since Friday night!"

"What? Oh, that's it!" Georgina yelled, dashing back into the attic. "Get undressed, you are so getting tied to the bed again."

"Wait," Simon laughed, capturing her hands in his after she'd managed to get his t-shirt off without his help. "There's a lot more we have to discuss"

Ignoring him, Georgina leaned forward and swiped her tongue across his chest, teasingly catching just the edge of his nipple.

Simon sucked in a delightfully unsteady breath, even as he tried to keep the conversation going. "There are going to be a lot of people that are going to say that you're crazy for getting involved with me and... Hey! Stop trying to distract me, this is important."

Georgina grinned as he tried to scoot away but she followed. He was still valiantly trying to make a point but she no longer cared about it. He said he loved her, she loved him and that was all that mattered. While that might sound naïve to most people, Georgina no longer cared what most people thought. From what she'd seen and just recently done herself, most people discounted happiness in pursuit of more "serious" emotions. Like misery. If she had stayed with her initial conclusion that there was nothing between her and Simon but sexual attraction, she would have missed out on the chance to be happy.

Well, most people could take their opinions and shove them.

"Georgina," Simon panted, wrapping his fist in her hair. "We need to talk and I can't think straight when you do that."

Georgina delicately licked her way up his neck, gently kissed his mouth and said, "I've never felt more alive in my life than I have with you. If people say disparaging things about us, let them. Given a choice between going back to what I was and going forward with you, I choose you."

Simon looked into her eyes and whispered, "Do you mean that? Those are brave words but—"

Georgina silenced him by gently running the pad of her thumb along his bottom lip. "It's always easier being brave when you don't have to do it alone. I can be as brave as I need to be, if you're with me."

"All along the way," Simon whispered. "When you said that thing about the ocean meeting the sky all along the way, I felt like you were talking about us, about how we blended together, especially in places that I always feared were too difficult to ever find a good, lasting fit."

"Well, what do you know," Georgina said, blinking back tears as she brushed her lips across his. "This *is* some sex-infused prelude to happily-ever-after."

Simon barked out a surprised laugh. "Not how I would have put it but you're right."

With Simon smiling at her, his love for her so clearly evident in his eyes, Georgina felt so giddy she thought about breaking out into song, or something else equally silly. But then Simon reached for one of the silk stockings that were still attached to the headboard and her urge to warble turned into something else entirely.

Simon's dark eyes flicked between Georgina's flushed face and the length of silk he now had gripped in his hand. His lips slid against his teeth in a grin of the 'all-the-better-to-eat-you-with' variety.

"Now that that's all settled," he drawled. "I do believe that it's your turn to be tied to the bed."

# *Epilogue*

*Simon Says* column dated July 7th

*By the time you bozos read this, I will be married.*

*Is that shocked silence I hear? Well, no matter. I love my wife and, here's the shocker, she loves me. However, I think she's in a mild state of shock at finding herself married. That's mostly because I initially told her I wasn't rushing her into anything; then whined and moaned about her unwillingness to commit. After three weeks of this she broke down, drove me to Vegas and finally made an honest man of me. She's now set herself the monstrous task of turning what was once my house into our home. She's thrown out half my stuff, unearthed about 9,000 paperclips I didn't know I had and gently, but firmly, talked my dog out of sitting on the kitchen counter. She's still got a lot of work ahead of her, but all in all, I think both the house and I are coming along nicely.*

*Now that I am a happily (read as smugly) married man, this will be my final column as America's favorite perennial frat-boy. Ah yes, dear idiot readers, this is indeed the end of an era.*

*If you're wondering what I'm going to do with the rest of my life well, your guess is as good as mine. I think I'll take a few weeks off and chase my wife around the house and then maybe I'll get a job writing about politics.*

*Things are definitely looking up my friend... up, up and away!*

## *About the Author:*

*Jane Thompson is the pseudonym of a fabulously wealthy, stunningly beautiful New York socialite who spends her days shopping, having lunch with her scores of equally fabulous friends and dodging marriage proposals from tall, dark and sinfully handsome men.*

*Ah, the joy of fantasy, eh?*

*I'm actually a housewife and mother who spends a ridiculous amount of my time either standing in line at the supermarket or peeling my cats off my furniture.*

*I'd love to hear from you, so e-mail me at* janethompson@earthlink. net.

# Bite of the Wolf

~✦~

## by Cynthia Eden

## *To My Reader:*

Have you ever wondered… what if? What if monsters are real? Vampires, werewolves, all of those creatures that stalk the night—what if they really exist? What would they be like?

In *Bite of the Wolf,* I took one of my favorite night creatures, the werewolf, and I gave him life in the 21$^{st}$ century.

Gareth Morlet is an alpha wolf, the unquestioned leader of his pack. And now, he must face the greatest challenge of his life… he must claim his mate.

I hope you enjoy reading Gareth's story. Please feel free to visit my website at www.cynthiaeden.com or send an email to info@cynthiaeden.com to let me know what you think of my werewolf tale.

# Prologue

Gareth Morlet had finally found his mate. The beast within him roared in triumph, while the man smiled in grim satisfaction.

He'd finally found her. After years of searching, she was within his grasp.

His fingers tightened around the color photograph. The young woman with the wide smile and sparkling blue eyes stared back at him.

"Get the men ready," he ordered, his voice a low growl. His gaze never left the photograph. "We leave at dusk."

Alerac, his second-in-command, hesitated. "Will she come willingly?"

Gareth's heart pounded. The thrill of the hunt was already coursing through him. "Does it matter?" She was *his*. And he would have her, one way or another.

"*He'll* be looking for her, too," Alerac warned.

Gareth nodded grimly. He was aware of the threat to his future mate. "Then I'll just have to make certain that I get to her first." The words were a vow.

No other would have her. She was his.

# Chapter One

Trinity Martin had the uncomfortable feeling she was being watched.

Her gaze scanned the dark street as she jogged. She didn't see anyone. She didn't hear anyone, but she felt—

Stalked.

Hunted.

She'd felt that way often in the last week. She picked up her pace, wanting to get back to her tidy little house. Wanting to run inside and lock the door behind her. The sooner she got home, the better she would feel. She would—

A loud, triumphant howl split the night.

She froze, every muscle in her body tightening. What the hell was that?

The howl echoed again, and this time, it seemed closer. Much, much closer. Too damn close.

She broke into a full run. She wanted to get off that road. And away from whatever was waiting in the darkness, howling at her.

The sun had long since set, but the night sky was full of stars, and the moon hung, heavy and full, in the sky. She could see easily in front of her. If she could just get home—

A long black limousine rounded the curve up ahead. It drove toward her, slowing as it approached.

She stumbled to a halt, her tennis shoes sliding against the pavement. The door opened and a man stepped out. Trinity's jaw dropped. *Damn.* She blinked, certain her eyes were playing tricks on her. But no, he was still there.

He was gorgeous. Absolutely gorgeous. From the top of his thick, midnight black hair to the bottom of his black boots. He. Was. Perfect.

His features were classically handsome. He had high, strong cheekbones and a straight, elegant nose. His jaw was firm, and his mouth… she swallowed… the man had the most deliciously sinful mouth she'd ever seen.

What would that mouth taste like?

She blinked, wondering where that thought had come from. She wasn't

the type to lust after strange men. Hell, she was hardly the type to lust at
all. But there was something about this man...

He walked toward her and she realized then that she'd been staring at
him, her mouth hanging wide open. She snapped her lips closed and backed
up a quick step. "Uh... can I help you?" God, the man was tall. He had to
be at least six foot three, maybe four. He definitely towered over her own
five foot five frame.

He was dressed casually, in a pair of jeans and a white tee shirt. She could
see the hard line of his chest beneath the shirt, see his sculpted muscles.
His straining biceps...

*Down, girl.*

He smiled at her, flashing a dimple. "*Oui*, I'm afraid that my companions
and I are a bit lost." He spoke with a faint French accent. "We are looking
for Maple Lane."

She lived on Maple Lane. 104 Maple Lane. Third house on the left.
Lifting her hand, she pointed to the street just up ahead, the street the limo
had passed right by. "It's... ah... right there."

The man didn't look toward the street. Instead, his gaze swept over her.
The moonlight shone down on them, and she realized he had golden eyes,
dark, molten gold. His gaze drifted over her, lingering on the tips of her
breasts and the bare expanse of her legs. She shivered, feeling the weight
of that stare as if it were a physical touch.

His gaze lifted. "You shouldn't be out here... alone." He motioned toward
the limo. "Come with us, and I'll take you home."

She shook her head. Sexy or not, there was no way she was going to get
into the car with him. She watched the news. She knew all about the horror
stories. Take a ride with a handsome stranger... end up dead. "Thanks, but
I can make it home on my own. My... um... my house isn't that far from
here." She forced a smile to her lips, shivering slightly as she felt the sweat
drying on her skin.

He frowned and glanced behind her at the dark, empty road.

The howl split the night once again.

Her stomach clenched. "Look, I've really got to go—"

He grabbed her arm, pulling her against his chest. His arms felt like
steel bands around her.

"What the hell are you doing?" she screeched, struggling against his
hold.

His arms tightened. His gaze was locked on the darkness behind her.
"You're too late," he muttered.

"What?" What was he talking about? "Too late for what?" She jerked
against him, but his hold was unbreakable. "Listen, buddy, I want you to
let me go, *now*!"

Two other men climbed from the limousine, both tall and well-muscled. And absolutely freaking gorgeous.

"You have to come with me," her captor said, turning the full force of his golden stare on her. "It's not safe here for you."

Yeah, she was really starting to get that impression. Three really big men were surrounding her, and some kind of dog was howling in the distance.

"Let me go," she snapped.

He shook his head.

She kicked him in the shin as hard as she could.

He grunted in surprise and released her.

She spun around and took off running.

"Trinity, stop!"

She glanced back, her eyes widening. How the hell did he know her name?

He was running after her, his features locked and tense.

Real fear lashed through her. She kept running as fast as she could until her thighs burned and her breath panted out. She could see the line of houses, could see the cheerful lights. Her neighbors were up there. If she could just get their attention—

She opened her mouth to scream.

He tackled her to the ground.

The beast within Gareth growled as he looked down at the sprawled form of his soon-to-be mate.

He fought the urge to strip her. To yank the running shorts off her long, shapely legs and to thrust deep, deep inside of her.

When she'd run from him, she'd aroused all of his primal hunting instincts. Now that he'd caught her, he wanted to claim her. To sink into her moist warmth and lose himself in the promise of her body.

He shifted, rolling her beneath him so that she faced him. Her chest was heaving, her limbs shaking. Her body was trapped beneath his now. Her breasts, high, firm breasts, were pushing against his chest, and her thighs were trapped between his legs. He'd never seen a more beautiful woman. A wealth of raven black hair framed her heart-shaped face. She had high, delicate cheekbones, and a small, straight little nose. Her lips were full, tempting. He couldn't wait to kiss those lips.

And her scent... God, her scent was wrapping around him, seducing him. Driving him crazy. He lowered his head toward her neck, his nostrils flaring. She smelled like flowers, like the night.

Like woman.

He growled. He'd been waiting for her for so very long. He opened his mouth, needing to taste her. Just one taste.

She screamed, bucking her body beneath his. His head jerked back, and he stared down at her in confusion.

"Get. Off. Me. You. Psycho." She gritted the words from between clenched teeth.

He frowned.

"Gareth." Alerac hurried toward them. His blond hair seemed to shine in the night. "We have to go."

He didn't want to go. He wanted to take his mate. There, beneath the night sky. Wanted to claim her and hear the sound of her moans filling the air.

"It's not safe for her," Alerac said, carefully averting his gaze from their bodies.

Gareth clenched his jaw, knowing that Alerac spoke the truth. He'd heard the howl earlier. He knew the rogue wolf was in the area. He had to take Trinity away from there.

He rose, pulling her to her feet, his fingers locked around her wrist. "You have to come with me," he told her, casting an glance toward the row of houses. Had anyone heard her scream?

"I don't have to do anything," his mate snapped, tugging on her arm. "Now let me go!" She aimed another kick at his shin.

Gareth jerked her toward him, trapping her against his chest. His arms tightened around her. "I don't think you understand what's happening," he said, the words almost a growl.

"Oh, yeah, I do." She glared up at him, her stare fierce. "You and your boys are trying to attack me!"

He shook his head. "No, we're trying to protect you."

Her lip curled, showing a hint of her sharp, white teeth. "Right."

Anger flashed through him. No one had ever doubted his word before. No one. And to find that the woman he would bond with dared to question him...

He felt his control begin to slip.

"Now let me go!" She was squirming against him, pressing her breasts against his chest, rubbing her body against his.

He captured her pointed little chin, forcing her to look up at him. "I'm here to protect you. You're my mate." It was his duty, his right, to protect her.

Her eyes widened. "I'm your what?" She swallowed, and he saw the quick movement of her throat. "Listen, buddy, I don't even *know* you."

"You will," he promised, his gaze dropping to her lips. "You'll know me very well." And then, because he couldn't stop himself, because he didn't want to stop himself, he lowered his head, and he kissed her. His lips pressed against hers, his tongue sweeping against her mouth. She gasped, and her lips, those soft, luscious lips, parted for him. He growled low in his throat, the sound one of triumph, of satisfaction.

He thrust his tongue into her mouth, eagerly claiming the sweetness that waited for him. She tasted so good. Like innocence. Like sin.

She wasn't fighting him; instead, she was leaning toward him, her mouth meeting his in wild abandon.

He'd wanted this, wanted her, for so long. Now she was within his grasp. His to take.

He could feel her breasts, feel the sharp points of her nipples pressing against his chest. He wanted to taste those nipples. Wanted to lick them, suck them. Wanted to feel them in his mouth, against his tongue.

Trinity jerked her head back, staring at him with wide eyes. Her lips were moist, glistening, and he lowered his head, wanting to taste them again.

"Stop!" She strained against him. "Let me go!"

*Never.* He shook his head.

"Gareth..." There was a definite warning edge to Alerac's voice.

He swallowed and nodded. They had to leave. He had to get his mate to safety. He lifted her up, easily hoisting her over his shoulder.

She screamed again and pounded her fists against his back. "Put me down, you bastard!"

He ignored her. He tightened his arm around her legs when she tried to kick him and headed toward the waiting limo.

Alerac followed at his heels.

"Let me go!" she screeched, jerking hard against his hold.

Michael, Gareth's cousin and trusted friend, had stayed by the car. When he saw their approach, he hurriedly opened the back door. A smile curved his lips. "Your mate has spirit." There was admiration in his voice.

Trinity froze. "What? What did he just say?"

Gareth eased her off his back and let her feet touch the pavement. She immediately tried to sprint away from him.

Michael caught her, locking his arm around her waist. "Sorry, *mademoiselle*, but I can't let you leave."

Her eyes widened as she looked at him. "What the hell is this?" Her gaze darted between the men. "Am I being kidnapped by male models?"

A quick bark of laughter slid past Alerac's lips.

Gareth frowned at him, then directed his attention back to Trinity. "Get into the car."

She didn't budge. "Who are you?"

*Your mate.* Gareth had to bite back the instinctive response. "My name is Gareth Morlet." He bowed to her.

She looked at him as if he were crazy. "Look, Frenchie, get the hell out of my way, and I won't call the cops on you when I get home."

He shook his head. She really didn't understand, and time was running out. He could feel the call of the moon. "Don't make me force you," he said.

"Now, I'll tell you one more time. Get in the car." His voice was hard, cold. No one had ever refused his orders.

She shook back her glorious mane of hair, looked him straight in the eyes, and said, "Make me."

He wrapped his hands around her neck and felt her stiffen, saw the sudden fear that flashed across her lovely face. Good. She should be afraid. He wasn't someone that she could play with. She would have to come to understand that.

"Gareth..." She breathed his name on a whisper.

"Shh..." He leaned forward and kissed her sweet lips. *Sleep, my one. Sleep.*

Her eyes widened, went blank and glassy. Then her lashes fell, and she slumped against him.

He lifted her and climbed inside the limousine. Michael and Alerac quickly followed him. Within moments, they were on their way, speeding away from the darkened road, away from Maple Lane.

Gareth looked up, feeling the weight of Michael's stare.

"Is she what you expected?"

He glanced back at the sleeping woman. His gaze swept down her body, and hunger stirred within him. "No," he whispered, the word almost a growl. "She's more."

# Chapter Two

Trinity opened her eyes and discovered two very important facts. First, she was naked.

Second, she wasn't alone.

She was in a king-sized bed, covered only by a black silk sheet, and *he* was with her.

Gareth. The too-sexy to be real man who'd kidnapped her. The psycho.

He was watching her, his golden stare intent upon her face. A small frown marred his otherwise perfect brow.

"What did you do to me?" she asked, pushing herself up, carefully keeping the sheet over her breasts.

He blinked, then a smile stretched across his face. "Nothing… yet."

Her eyes narrowed. "Why am I naked?" Her gaze darted around the room. "And where am I?" The last thing she remembered was Gareth kissing her. His lips had been so warm against hers. And then—

She frowned, trying to remember.

"You're in my home." He raised his hand and stroked the skin of her upper arm.

Goosebumps rose along her flesh. She swallowed and felt heat begin to rise in her belly even as a dark suspicion burned in her mind. "You kidnapped me, didn't you?"

He shrugged and slid closer to her. "I don't think of it as kidnapping."

"No?" Oh, damn, but he smelled good. Her heart was pounding like crazy in her chest. "Wh-what would you call it then?" The sheet was covering him, but it pooled around his waist. His chest, his thickly muscled chest, was completely bare.

One black brow lifted. "Retrieving something that was lost?"

She blinked, not understanding. "I don't—"

His hand was on her breast, lightly stroking the nipple through the thin barrier of the sheet.

"You've got the most beautiful breasts," he muttered, his burning gaze locked upon her. "I watched them while you slept. And I wanted to touch them, to taste them." His thumb slipped across the taut nipple and she bit back a moan.

"Don't touch me," she ordered, but her voice was weak.

His features tensed, but his thumb continued to stroke her.

Oh, God. It felt so good. Her breasts were tight, aching. It had been so long since she'd been with anyone, since she'd—

She jumped from the bed. "Look, Mister—"

"Gareth," he said, his voice soft and his gaze locked on her naked body. "I'm Gareth."

She knew that, but she didn't want to call him by name. He was her kidnapper, for goodness sake! Not her buddy. "I don't know what you did to me or how you got me here, but I want to leave." She took a breath, tried to calm her racing heart, and said, "Now."

He shook his head. "I can't allow you to leave. It's far too dangerous." His gaze was locked on her breasts. He licked his lips. "I hope you taste as good as you look."

The man had a serious one track mind. She crossed her arms over her breasts. "Where are my clothes?"

He shook his head and rose slowly from the bed. "You don't need them right now."

He walked toward her and her gaze fell, dropping to stare at the long, thick length of his dick that rose, hard and hungry, from the cradle of his thighs.

"I've been waiting a long time for you," he whispered, his voice like rough velvet. "Don't make me wait any longer."

She shook her head and jerked her gaze up. His golden eyes seemed overly bright, almost feverishly so, and his face had a stark, feral look. "I just want to leave, okay?" She stepped back, moving slowly. She had the feeling that he would pounce on her at any moment.

"I told you. It's too dangerous. If I let you leave, *he'll* take you." He shook his head once, a quick, negative shake. "That's not going to happen." His gaze trapped her. "*You're mine.*"

"Look, I don't know who 'he' is," she muttered, taking another small step back. There was a door behind her; she'd seen it when she'd jumped from the bed. If she could just get through that door—

His nostrils flared. "I can smell you, smell the scent of your sex." His cock swelled even more.

Okay, time to give up playing it cool. Trinity turned on her heel and ran. A low growl rumbled behind her.

Her fingers latched onto the door knob and she jerked the door open. She fled down the hall, her bare feet pounding against the hardwood floor. She could hear him behind her, hear the thudding of his footsteps, the harsh rumble of his breath.

She rounded the corner—

And stumbled to a halt when she saw the other two men. The men who'd helped Gareth kidnap her. Their eyes widened when they saw her naked body.

Gareth roared, grabbing her by the arms and jerking her behind him. His body shielded her from the other two men, and he kept an unbreakable hold on her wrist.

"Leave!" He snarled, his shoulders stiff with rage.

The other two men lowered their heads and instantly left the room.

She stood behind him, shaking, embarrassment sweeping through her. Who was Gareth? What did he want from her?

He turned slowly to face her, and Trinity's eyes widened at the sight of him.

His cheeks were hollow, his eyes blazing. And his teeth—

She swallowed, fear pounding through her. His teeth, his canines, were sharp. Long.

Too sharp. Too long.

He lifted his hand, and she saw that his nails had grown, had changed. Claws grew from the ends of his fingertips.

She could only stare up at him, stunned, terrified, and she knew, with utter certainly, that she was in danger. Mortal danger.

Because Gareth Morlet wasn't a man.

The eyes that stared at her were those of a beast.

He could smell her fear.

And her lingering arousal. The two scents wrapped around him, fed his hunger, and he knew that he was going to take her. Knew that he had to take her.

The others had seen her. They'd seen her naked body, seen the pink-tipped breasts, the soft thatch of black hair at the cradle of her thighs.

He wanted to kill them. They were his friends, his packmates, but that didn't matter. They had seen Trinity's body. And he wanted to kill them.

His control was razor thin. He needed her, needed to bury himself in her tight heat, and he needed to do it *now*.

"Get on the table," he growled, jerking his head toward the center of the room. Trinity had fled to the kitchen, and while he would have preferred that their first mating be in a bed, he didn't have the strength to wait until they went back to his room.

She lifted her chin, and for a moment, he thought she would deny him, but then she stepped forward, and moved slowly toward the table.

He wanted to howl in triumph.

His gaze dropped to the curves of her ass. He needed to touch her, to slide his hand over the smooth globes.

Trinity stopped at the table, glancing back over her shoulder. There was fear in her gaze. And, beneath the fear, hunger. A hunger to match his.

"Get on the table," he repeated, stepping toward her. His balls were tight against his body, and his dick felt like it would burst. His mate had the most perfect little body. Soft, smooth skin and slender legs. Those beautiful breasts.

She climbed onto the table and lay down on her back. Her legs were locked together, and her arms were positioned stiffly at her sides.

He licked his lips, already tasting her.

He took a quick breath, and yanked the leash on the beast within him. He felt the change in his bones as he fought back the driving hunger. His claws disappeared, but his incisors stayed strong and hard in his mouth.

He leaned over her, bracing his hands on the table. Her gaze, so bright and so blue, met his. "You're not a... man... are you, Gareth?"

He shook his head. No, he wasn't a man. He wasn't human, not really. But there would be time later to tell her. Now... now he needed his mate.

His head lowered toward her breast. He couldn't wait to pull her nipple into his mouth. To suckle her and hear her cries of need fill the air.

"Don't..." she licked her lips, her small, pink tongue flashing out, "don't hurt me."

He stilled. His hand lifted, caressed her cheek in a feather light touch. "You'll know nothing but pleasure, *ma petite*," he promised. There was no way he would hurt her. He couldn't hurt his mate.

She seemed to relax at his words.

He lowered his head and closed his lips around the tip of her breast. She tasted as good as he'd thought she would. Better.

His mouth widened as he suckled her, trying to taste more of her. His hand came up and began to rub her other breast, his fingers plucking the nipple. She was laid out for him on the table, and he intended to make a complete meal of her.

He heard her gasps, and the rich scent of her arousal flooded his nostrils. His little mate wanted him; he could smell her need, could feel it. Her nipples were tight, and he bit down against her, gently, and his fingers squeezed her breasts. She moaned, tilting back her head. Her hips began to move, rocking against the table.

He lifted his head and stared down at her. Her nipple gleamed, the moisture from his mouth shining against the tight peak. The beast within him raged. Demanded that he thrust into her now, hard and deep.

His gaze drifted down her body, past the smooth expanse of her stomach, past the flat plane of her abdomen, down to the dark hair that covered her tender flesh. He slid his hand over her body, marveling at the softness of her skin. He could feel the weight of her stare upon him, and it heightened his desire, his need.

"Spread your legs," he ordered, and after a small hesitation, Trinity obeyed. She opened herself to him, and the sight of her spread thighs nearly brought him to his knees.

He parted her soft flesh with his fingers. She was hot, and wet. The proof of her need was plain to see in the cream that coated his fingers as he stroked her.

He couldn't wait to thrust inside of her. To bury himself balls deep in her snug warmth. A growl rumbled in the base of his throat.

He pulled his hand away from her and moved to the edge of the table. He locked his hands around her thighs and pulled her toward him, not stopping until her legs dangled over the side of the wooden table. He stepped between her spread legs, his hands gripping her thighs. Staring into her blue eyes, he pushed her thighs farther apart, leaving her completely open to him.

He could see the pulse pounding at the base of her throat. He could hear the sound of her ragged breathing. And he could smell the thick aroused scent of her cream.

He stroked her inner thighs, slowly working up to the center of her need. Her pussy was open to him, the folds a dark, flushed pink.

He slipped a finger inside of her, marveling at the tight feel of her. She arched her back, moaning softly.

He pressed his finger deeper into her. She was so tight and hot, she was going to feel like heaven around his dick.

He worked another finger up into her warmth, pushing down hard. Her breasts pointed into the air, her nipples tight.

"Gareth!" His name was a desperate cry upon her lips. Her face was flushed and her hips bucked against him.

He leaned forward, capturing a breast in the heat of his mouth, while he continued to thrust his fingers into her pussy. Deep and hard. Her inner muscles were clamped around him, holding him tight, and her cream coated him.

Her moans were driving him crazy. Her body was twisting, undulating against his as hungry need swept through her. Her fingers were on his back, digging into his skin. With a flash of pleasure, he realized that his mate was marking him. Marking his flesh.

Good. Because he sure as hell intended to mark her. She would wear his mark for all to see.

He lifted his head and gazed down at Trinity's glorious body. She was

perfect. Those breasts, those thighs—God, he could come just from looking at her.

His dick was swollen. Hard, hungry. It was time, time for him to take
his mate. He pulled his fingers from the hot cradle of her pussy and brought
them to his lips. Her gaze, bright, dazed, locked on him.

He lifted his fingers to his lips and licked her cream, his lips curving
at the tangy taste. "I knew you'd taste good," he whispered. And he knew
that later, he would have to have more of her, taste more, that he would
taste all of her.

He positioned his dick against her opening, feeling her wet heat coat
the broad head of his shaft. He knew once he thrust inside of her that his
control would be shot. He prayed that he'd aroused her enough so that she
would be ready for him.

"Gareth!" Her voice was a breath of sound. Her hips arched against
him. "I need you!"

He thrust deep, burying himself to the hilt. Her pussy locked around
him, holding him tight.

So. Damn. Tight.

"I claim you," he gritted, as he pulled almost out of her hot warmth and
then thrust back, hard and strong, into her. "I claim you as my mate. I bind
you to me. I give you my protection, my vow."

He thrust again. Deeper. Harder. "You are mine. My mate, my woman!"
His hips pistoned against her, thrusting in a frenzy. Again and again he
buried himself in her warmth.

His orgasm was pressing on him. His balls tightened and a tingling
began at the base of his spine.

He bent over her, his mouth fastening on the tender curve of her throat.
His fangs scraped against her skin. He could feel her pulse, could feel the
frantic pounding of her blood.

"Trinity..."

He felt her body tighten around him, felt the shuddering grasp of her
delicate muscles as her climax ripped through her. He thrust into her, burying
himself in her over and over again, and he knew he could wait no longer.

He buried his teeth in her throat, piercing her skin. Her blood flowed
over his tongue. The taste was rich, sweet, and he drank from her, taking
her very life essence into his body and creating a link between them, a link
that would hold until the final mating ritual had been completed.

He felt another climax rip through her. He heard the choked cry that
was his name slip from her lips.

And then his own orgasm swept through him. He jerked his head away
from her, howling as the pleasure snapped through him. His body shuddered,
emptying itself deep into the core of Trinity's body. Black lights danced

before his eyes. His arms tightened around her, pressing her against him in an unbreakable hold.

As the last tremor swept over him, his body collapsed against her, crushing her against the hard table. Her body was a soft cushion for him, warm, welcoming. And the soft echoes of her climax still shook her pussy, sending pleasant ripples over his cock.

Her hands were on his back, stroking lightly. He liked her touch, and he licked the curve of her breast to show his appreciation.

Her heart was still pounding, but its rate was slowing. He stretched, enjoying the feel of his body rubbing against hers. He'd never felt—

Trinity stiffened beneath him.

He sighed and lifted his head from the soft pillow of her breast.

She stared up at him, the passion gone from her wide blue eyes. Her hand lifted, touched the curve of her neck, and her fingers came away bright with blood.

Horror filled her gaze.

So much for soft words from his mate. Gareth locked his jaw, knowing what was coming.

"What," she enunciated slowly, "in the hell are you?"

# Chapter Three

What had just happened? Trinity lay on the table, ripples from her orgasm still moving through her, and wondered if she'd gone crazy. Absolutely freaking crazy.

Because, after all, she'd just made love with a monster.

She stared at the drops of blood coating her fingertips.

A *biting* monster.

And she'd loved it. Every single second of it.

She was crazy. Had to be.

She shoved against his chest, feeling trapped on the table, trapped beneath the solid weight of his body.

Gareth moved back slowly, pulling his still erect cock from her body. She glanced up at him, enormously relieved to note that his fangs were gone.

*Fangs.* Jesus. What had she done? Gone and found herself some kind of vampire boyfriend? As if her life weren't already screwed up enough. For the last five years of her life, she'd lived like an old spinster. Then, when she'd just hit thirty, she'd gone and slept with the undead!

"Trinity..." His lips pressed together and turmoil seemed to swirl in his gaze. "Don't be afraid of me."

She scooted across the table and stood on trembling legs. "Yeah, well, don't bite me."

His hands clenched. "I couldn't control myself. I had to taste you. It was the bonding."

Her eyes narrowed. "The what?" She glanced around the room, searching for something to cover her body. She couldn't stand being there, stark naked. What if his two friends came back?

Spotting a hand towel on the counter top, she grabbed it and held it in front of her waist. It was better than nothing.

"You're my mate," Gareth said, staring into her eyes. "I had to bond with you, to link your blood to me so that no other could claim you."

She didn't like the sound of that, not at all. "Look, Frenchie," she muttered, "don't get me wrong. I had a good time." An absolutely, mind-blowing orgasm of a good time. "But I think you're confused. I'm not your mate.

You don't even *know* me."

"I know everything about you." His gaze swept over her. His pupils flared as he stared at the tips of her breasts. "Everything. I've spent my life waiting to claim you. And now that I have, you'll be with me, forever."

She shook her head. "I'm… uh… not really looking for commitment right now, you know?" What she was looking for was a way out of this nuthouse.

A low growl rumbled in his throat. "There is no choice," he snarled. "Not for either of us. We are bound. Bound by the blood!"

"Are you a vampire?" she asked him, her voice hushed. She really had to know. Because if he was, she thought she would have to scream.

He threw back his thick mane of hair and laughed. Actually roared with laughter.

Trinity clutched the small towel tighter and stared at him. Was laughter a good sign?

"A vampire?" A tear streaked from the corner of his eye. "Certainly not." There was a touch of disdain in his voice.

Her shoulders relaxed. Maybe she'd just imagined the teeth, maybe—

"I'm a wolf. A werewolf."

She blinked, and her heart seemed to stop. "A what?"

He smiled, his dimple flashing. "And you, my lovely, are my mate." A hint of fang appeared.

She tried to sound reasonable. "Werewolves aren't real."

A faint line appeared between his brows. "But vampires are?"

Okay, he had her there. "Look, I just want to leave, all right?" She hated the weak, almost pleading sound of her voice, but she really had to get out of there.

He shook his head. "No, I told you before. It's not safe."

Like it was safe to be in the house with a guy claiming to be a werewolf.

"At least…" she swallowed and tried for what she hoped was a placating smile. "At least let me get dressed."

His gaze drifted over her body. "But you're so lovely," he breathed. "Your breasts are so full and pretty." His cheeks were flushed. "I could stare at you all day long."

A curl of warmth spread through her. *Lovely.* She'd never been called that before.

His head jerked back, and his eyes took on a distant look. "The others are returning."

What? How did he know that—

"Go." He pointed back down the hallway, toward the room she'd fled earlier. "Your clothes are in the closet."

She turned, quickly positioning the cloth over her backside. He laughed softly at her gesture.

"It's too late for that, you know." His voice was a silken purr. "I've already seen every part of your delectable little body."

She stiffened and glanced back at him. "I'm not like this," she whispered. "Not usually."

One black brow arched.

She licked her lips. "I- I don't sleep with strangers. I mean, strange men. I mean—" Hell, he wasn't even a man. But she wanted him to understand. She didn't make a habit out of having sex with men she'd just met. It was just that with him, well, she'd lost control. Hunger had burned through her, and all she'd wanted was... him.

He smiled at her, his face softening. "I know. And I'm glad."

"But don't get the idea that it's gonna be happening again," she told him and saw the smile disappear from his face. "Cause I just want to get out of here, back to my home." My life. *A life that doesn't include a werewolf.*

His eyes shimmered, actually shimmered, as the gold started to glow. "Oh, my mate, there is one thing that you can be sure of." His fangs flashed. "It will most definitely happen again."

At the sight of the blatant hunger on his face, Trinity fled down the hall, running as if a beast were on her trail.

Because he was.

She tugged on her clothes in record time. They'd been exactly where he'd said, folded all nice and neat in the closet. After she dressed, Trinity paced the room, wondering what her next move should be. She could hear the faint rumble of voices and knew that Gareth's friends had returned to the house just as he'd warned.

The house. Gareth's house. She moved to the window and peered outside. It was still night. The moon shone down on the area, illuminating a thick forest.

She blinked. A forest? Where the hell was she? And how was she going to get out of there?

She fumbled with the latch and forced the window open. Cool night air swept inside. She could smell fresh pine and the scent of leaves.

A knock sounded at the door.

"Trinity?"

It was him. Gareth.

The man she'd just had mind-numbing sex with.

The werewolf.

The knob rattled. "Trinity? Are you finished?"

Good thing she'd locked the door. She took a deep breath, and said, "Not yet. Give me just a few minutes."

A pause, then, "I know you're scared, Trinity. But I can explain everything to you, if you just give me the chance."

He could explain everything? She glanced up at the full moon. She was trapped in the woods with a man who claimed to be a werewolf, a werewolf that she was pretty sure had used some kind of mind control whammy on her earlier. How else had he managed to get her into that limo and out to this godforsaken cabin?

"Trinity!" There was a demand in his voice this time.

"I'll be right out," she called, knowing the words were an absolute lie.

He didn't respond.

She took a deep breath. It was now or never. She lifted her tennis shoe up and crawled through the narrow window, landing with a soft thud on the other side.

Crouching on the ground, she wondered which way she should go. Wondered where—

The door crashed open. *"Trinity!"*

*Damn.* She sprang to her feet and headed straight for the line of trees in front of her.

"No, don't run from me!" His bellow followed her. "It's not safe!"

She didn't stop. She ran as fast as she could, her heart pounding, her tennis shoes slapping against the rough earth. Fear filled her as she fled, but she had to get away from Gareth before she did something that she would regret.

Like beg him to take her again.

Because she couldn't shake the memory of having him in her body, of having him thrust deep into her. She couldn't forget the strong, thick feel of his cock, the explosion of feeling that had rocked through her at his touch.

And that terrified her.

She jumped over a fallen limb, and kept running, her legs moving in a quick rhythm. Maybe she could find another cabin, find someone to help her—

A long howl split the night.

She froze.

Her chest was heaving, her calves aching. She didn't know how far she'd run, but that howl had been close.

Was that Gareth? Or—

Just ahead, the bushes began to shake.

A large, white wolf jumped from the brush, its mouth open in a hideous snarl that revealed dozens of sharp teeth. The animal growled at her, advancing slowly.

Trinity couldn't move. She could only stand there, stunned, staring at the beast. It was huge. Thick with bulging muscles. Its coat gleamed in the night. And its teeth—

Oh, my, what big teeth you have...

The better to eat me with...

"G-Gareth?" Was that him? Because it sure as hell wasn't an ordinary wolf. She'd bet her life on it. "I-Is that you?" She held out her hand.

The beast's jaws snapped, and she jerked her hand back, narrowly avoiding the loss of her fingers.

A cold chill swept through her. The wolf had black eyes. Dark, merciless eyes.

"Y-you're not Gareth, are you?" She whispered, taking a tentative step back.

A low, fierce growl was her only answer. The creature's muscles bunched as it prepared to lunge at her.

She opened her mouth to scream—

And a large, black wolf jumped in front of her, its fangs bared.

The white wolf snarled, then turned and ran, disappearing into the night.

Trinity lifted a trembling hand to her throat as the black wolf turned toward her. Its golden eyes met hers.

"G-Gareth?"

It threw back its head and howled. The sound seemed to rip through the night.

The wolf padded toward her. Its head bumped against her thigh.

She stared down at the beast, shaking. It was even bigger than the white wolf. And its teeth—

Its head nudged her again, and the wolf looked up at her, watching her with a steady golden stare.

She lifted her hand, reaching slowly outward, terrified that it would snap at her, but feeling drawn, almost compelled, to reach for it.

The wolf didn't move.

Her fingers sank into its thick fur.

Its golden stare never wavered. The wolf crowded against her, pushing her body back against a tree, but it made no move to attack her.

The wolf padded away from her and threw back its magnificent head and howled, the eerie, mournful sound sweeping through the forest once again.

As she watched, the wolf changed. Its bones shifted, cracking loudly, terribly, and the hair seemed to melt from its body. She stood there, transfixed, watching the wolf change. Transform.

In seconds, the body of the wolf was gone, and in its place stood a man, a tall, strong, naked man.

Gareth.

He glared at her, his face tight with anger. "Do you want to die?"

She shook her head.

"Then why did you leave me? I told you it wasn't safe. Rafe is hunting you. He wants to take you from me—"

"Rafe?" she whispered in dazed confusion.

His eyes narrowed. "The wolf that almost ripped you to shreds. He knows you're my mate, and he wants to take you, to hurt me."

He stalked toward her, rage apparent in the stiffness of his body. "I won't let you put your life at risk." He grabbed her arms, pulling her toward him. "You're too important."

"I didn't know," she protested. It's not like he'd told her to beware of a rampaging werewolf. "You didn't tell me—"

He kissed her, crashing his mouth down on hers. She tasted the rage in his kiss, the fear.

The hunger.

His cock pressed against her, and she felt the strong, hot heat of his desire.

He tore his mouth from hers. "He would have killed you. Ripped your throat out."

She stared at him, stunned and more than a little sick. She remembered the creature's teeth, and she could still hear its snarl...

He kissed her again, his mouth pressing hotly, angrily against hers. His tongue swept into her mouth, pushing past her teeth, claiming her.

She held her body stiffly in his arms, still frightened and confused, not fighting him, but not embracing him. She didn't understand what was happening between them, didn't understand the feelings he stirred within her.

How could he affect her so easily?

All at once, his mouth gentled on hers, tempted instead of took and she felt herself begin to respond to him.

His head lifted. His eyes blazed. "Don't deny me."

Need was pounding through her body, replacing all other emotions. Her breasts were tight, hard, aching. A heavy, languorous heat flooded her. In that moment, the last thing she thought about doing was denying him.

She gasped as his hands, those large, strong hands, rose and covered her breasts. His fingers stroked her, teasing her nipples. Pinching the tight peaks.

Her thighs clenched.

His mouth lowered toward her, and he kissed her neck, his tongue rubbing wetly against her skin. She could feel the warm stir of his breath, could smell his strong, masculine scent.

The edge of his teeth pressed against her.

She jerked back, her eyes flaring with fast fear.

His golden eyes were locked on her, his face a tight mask of lust.

Her heart pounded. Fear and a dark, desperate desire filled her.

His fingers lifted, threading through her hair, and he pushed against her, pushed her down with a steady, unbreakable hold.

"Gareth—" Her heart was pounding, and she could feel a dampness coating her panties.

"Suck me," he growled, forcing Trinity to her knees. "I want to feel your mouth on me."

Her knees hit the ground, and she felt the cold, slightly damp grass beneath her. She lifted her gaze, licking her lips. His cock was right in front of her. He was hard. Huge. The head seemed to reach toward her, and she trembled with the wave of longing that swept through her.

She wrapped her hands around the thick length. He jerked beneath her touch, a low hiss sliding past his lips. She was amazed by how smooth he felt and how strong.

"Trinity..."

She looked up at him, her fingers slowly stroking his cock. His golden eyes were glowing. A wave of nervousness swept through her. What was she doing? This wasn't her. She didn't—

"I need you." His fingers tightened in her hair. "Suck me, Trinity."

She wanted to. She wanted to taste him, to put her lips on him, and feel his arousal. But... "I-I've never done this," she whispered, lowering her gaze to stare at his thick cock.

He stiffened.

Oh, God. Humiliation burned through her. So much for playing the sophisticated lover. She dropped her hands, and tried to rise, but his hold was unbreakable. "Gareth—"

He thrust his cock toward her. It looked even bigger now, and a faint drop of moisture was on its broad head. "Taste me," he ordered. "Let me be the first, the only."

But what if she did something wrong? What if she—

*"Taste me."*

There was such need in his voice, such hunger. She couldn't deny him. Leaning forward, she opened her mouth and took the tip of his cock inside. Her lips slipped around him, pulling his length deep into her mouth.

He growled.

Her tongue licked his cock, tasting him, tasting the faint saltiness of his pre-cum.

"Oh, that's good, *ma petite*," Gareth muttered. "So good."

He moved against her, thrusting lightly. His hands were locked on her, teaching her how to match his rhythm.

She opened her mouth wider, trying to take more of him. He felt so good, so thick, so—

He jerked away from her, his chest heaving.

She stayed on her knees, staring up at his heavy cock. She could still taste him in her mouth.

"For the record," he said, his voice hoarse and ragged, "you are never, *ever* to do that to another man."

She blinked, raising her gaze to meet his.

"Because if you do," he continued, reaching to pull her up against him. "I'll kill him."

His hands lifted, catching the hem of her shirt. In one quick move, he yanked the tee shirt over her head and tossed it onto the grass.

She was wearing a bra, a small, plain, white bra. He lowered his head, pushed the fabric aside, and licked her.

His hand slipped down her body, curving at the top of her running shorts. His fingers, his nimble fingers, drifted down, down the front of the shorts, and pressed against the juncture of her thighs.

"Spread your legs," he whispered, his tongue snaking out to lick the upper curve of her breast.

Shuddering, she obeyed.

His fingers pressed against her core, rubbing against the fabric of the shorts, teasing her throbbing clit.

She trembled, her body hot, burning hot.

"Are you wet for me?" he asked.

She nodded, not able to speak.

"You know what I am," he muttered, his fingers pressing against her. Teasing. Tormenting.

Tension was building, her climax spinning toward her.

"Do you still want me?" he asked, his words harsh. "Say it. Give me the words."

She licked her lips. "I-I want you." God help her, she was desperate for him.

"Good. Because I'm about to explode for you." His lips curved. He stepped away from her. "Take off your clothes."

She jerked them off in seconds, then reached for him, her fingers closing eagerly around the strong breadth of his shoulders. She rubbed her nipples against his chest, and his cock pressed against her thighs.

His arms locked around her, and he lifted her. "Wrap your legs around me," he said, his golden stare locked on her.

The strength of his body pressed against her. She could feel the solid wall of his chest, feel the corded muscles of his arms.

She wrapped her legs around his hips, instantly feeling the press of his cock against her opening. Her cream drenched the head, coating him. He growled.

"Can you take me this way?" His hands tightened around her hips.

She'd like to see him try to stop her. She licked her lips, nodding.

"Guide me into you," he said, his mouth raining kisses over the curve of her shoulder.

She swallowed, her flesh flushed with desire. She reached for him, stroking the broad length of his erection. With shaking hands, she parted her folds and pressed his cock against the entrance of her body.

"Good. So good." The gold of his eyes seemed to flare ever brighter. "Now take me." He thrust into her.

She gasped, throwing back her head as she was filled with his cock. It felt wonderful. So unbelievably wonderful.

He filled every inch of her with his solid length. And when he began to move...

She shuddered, clenching around him. *Oh, God...*

Her fingers dug into his shoulders. She lifted her body, moving in time with his thrusts. Faster. Deeper. Harder.

"That's it, *ma petite*, move. Yes, yes. So good." His mouth pressed against her neck, and his hips moved, faster, ever faster against hers, as his cock thrust deeply into her body.

Every time he withdrew, his cock slid against her clit, rubbing her, teasing her. Every muscle in her body tightened, yearned.

He sucked the skin of her throat, nibbling softly. She gasped, feeling her climax build. She moved against him, on him. Once. Twice. Deeper.

"Are you close?" He lifted his head. His lips were moist, his eyes glowing. "Will you come for me?" A hard, deep thrust. A slow slide against her clit. "Will you?" His cock buried itself in her core.

Trinity screamed, feeling her orgasm rip through her in a blinding wave.

"*Mon Dieu!*" He threw back his head, his teeth clenched. "I can feel you squeezing me." His eyes closed. "So. Damn. Good." He shuddered, and she felt him pump into her, felt the hot blast of his semen as he came deep within her.

In the moments that followed, they stayed together, locked in each other's arms.

Trinity was loathe to move. Gareth surrounded her. His body. His warmth. His scent. She could feel the pounding of his heart, could feel the slight movement of his chest as he breathed.

In his arms, she felt safe. Secure.

Which had to be crazy, since the man was a werewolf.

Still, she'd never felt so close to another person. Never before actually felt... linked to another.

And she did feel linked. Bound to Gareth.

Bound to a werewolf.

He lifted his head, and his eyes no longer glowed. His mouth twisted in a half-smile.

She flushed, realizing suddenly that her legs still had a death grip around his waist. "I—uh..."

He kissed her, a light, quick kiss on the lips. "Trinity...you understand now, don't you?"

"Understand?" She repeated, blinking. She didn't understand a whole hell of a lot that had happened in the past six hours.

"We're meant to be together," he whispered, his hands anchored at her waist.

She hesitated. "Gareth—"

"Shh..." He kissed her again. "Just give me time, okay? Let me convince you that we're meant to be."

God, he was gorgeous. His eyes were beseeching, his jaw strong and determined. And his mouth...

She took a breath.

"Trinity..." His golden stare was intense. "I promise, you have nothing to fear from me."

She wanted to believe him. Wrapped in his arms, his cock still strong within her depths, she wanted to believe him, but she remembered what the black wolf had looked like when it had jumped in front of her. She remembered the flash of fangs, the snarling growls.

He must have read her fear because his expression darkened. "Give me time," he whispered. "Give me the time to prove what we can have, what we can be." He swallowed. "I'm more than the wolf. I'm a man, too."

Her heart pounded. A part of her wanted to flee, wanted to run from him as far and as fast as she could. But another part of her just wanted to stay here, in his arms. Forever.

"Give me a chance," he whispered, his lips feathering over her neck.

A moan slipped past her lips.

His hips pulled back and thrust against her, the friction of his cock electric.

"Say you'll stay with me," his words were harsh, but his hands were gentle upon her. "Don't leave me."

Her breathing hitched.

His hands lifted her hips. Up. Down. His cock rubbed against her clit. "Say you'll stay." His teeth were clenched. His cheeks flushed. "Stay!" And as hunger ripped through her, she could only nod.

# Chapter Four

His mate was beautiful. Gareth stared at Trinity, marveling at the luminous beauty of her face. They were on the deck of the cabin. Dusk was falling and the golden hues of the sunset seemed to surround Trinity.

She'd been with him in the woods for two days now. She hadn't mentioned wanting to leave again, and he was glad for that small favor.

Rafe was still out there, stalking them through the wilderness. Waiting for his moment to strike.

He'd caught the rogue wolf's scent a few times, but he hadn't been able to track him. In truth, he hadn't wanted to leave his mate's side long enough to track the white wolf.

He inhaled deeply, drawing her sweet scent into his lungs. His cock stirred, and he wondered if he could tempt her into—

"How did you become a werewolf?" Trinity asked, her blue gaze lifting to meet his.

He'd known the question would come, sooner or later. "I didn't become a werewolf," he said, taking a step toward her and enjoying the way the wind lifted her silky hair.

She frowned, her dark brows drawing together with a faint line. "But I saw—"

He touched the skin of her cheek. "Sweet, what I meant was that I didn't *become* a werewolf. I was born one."

Her lips parted in surprise, then she shook her head. "How is that even possible?"

His lips hitched. "Trust me, it's possible." He inhaled again, drinking in her scent. Lilacs. The woman smelled just like lilacs.

"So what, when you were a kid you would run around the house as a wolf?"

He stepped back. It was either put a distance between them or strip her and plunge into her tight sex. "We don't change until adolescence. When we hit puberty, the wolf develops in us. We heed the call of the moon, and we change."

He wanted to answer her questions, but he also wanted, very much, to make love to her. To hear the soft moans that slipped past her lips. To feel the hot, wet clasp of her body around him.

The woman was addictive.

Her gaze drifted to the darkening sky. "But you don't always change."

"No." He shook his head. "The older one gets the more control one develops." He thought he saw a small sigh of relief slip from her lips.

She turned to face him. "That first night, you—you did something to me, didn't you?" Her blue gaze held his. "To make me get into that limo, you did something."

He nodded once.

"What did you do? What did you do to me?"

His heart ached at the pain he heard in her voice. "Trinity…"

"Just tell me."

He took a deep breath. "My kind has many gifts." Some good and some bad. "To a certain extent, we can… influence… the thoughts of others."

"Mind control." Her lip curled in distaste.

"Yes." He wouldn't lie to her. "That was the only time I did it, I swear. I needed to get you out of there, to some place safe." He didn't want her to think that he would use his powers against her.

"How do I know you won't do it again?"

He stiffened. "I won't use that power against you. I don't want you to be with me because I'm controlling you." He wanted her to come to him because *she* wanted him, as much as he wanted her.

She rubbed her arms and walked to the edge of the deck. Her gaze was locked on the woods.

The sound of the encroaching night surrounded them. He could hear the crickets, the rustle of branches.

The soft pad of a wolf's steps, inching closer. Closer.

He stiffened. Michael and Alerac were inside the cabin.

Tilting his head back, he inhaled the night air, inhaled the scents, used the power of the wolf within to sense the creature that stalked him.

That stalked his mate.

His fangs burned, and his nails lengthened into claws.

"That's good to know," Trinity murmured, apparently oblivious to the danger that was surrounding her. She turned slowly to face him. "Because that first night, you scared me—" She broke off, her eyes widening.

His lips curled back, and a growl rumbled in his throat.

"Gareth?" Her voice was a squeak.

He snarled.

She stiffened, and he saw fear flash across her face.

"Get inside." Rafe was close, too close. And the beast within was fighting to get free to kill the wolf who'd dared threaten its mate.

Trinity didn't move.

Behind her, a white wolf crept from the shadows of the forest. Its teeth were bared, dripping blood from a fresh kill.

Gareth had to change, to take the form of the wolf to fight the creature that threatened Trinity.

"Go!" His voice was barely human. It sounded more like the growl of an enraged beast. He heard the popping of bones and felt the burning agony that signaled the change.

He saw Trinity staring at him in horror.

And saw the white wolf inching toward her.

Trinity reached out a hand as if to help him. He snarled at her, his teeth flashing. She didn't understand the danger, didn't know that Rafe stalked her—

With a howl, he shed his human form, emerging fully as the beast. His heart pounded, and he wanted to feel his enemy's throat beneath his teeth. He launched his body into the air, feeling the muscles of his body coil and release.

Trinity screamed, crouching down and covering her face with her hands.

He leapt over her, landing on the lush grass and running toward his prey.

The white wolf was waiting for him, its fangs bared.

Trinity slowly lowered her hands and forced her lashes to lift.

The deck was empty.

Her heart was pounding and she was pretty sure that she'd just lost ten years of her life.

Jesus. She'd thought that Gareth was attacking her. She'd thought those teeth were going to lock around her, tear into her—

Vicious growls echoed through the woods.

She jumped to her feet and spun around. And then she saw them. The two wolves were locked in mortal combat. Biting. Slashing with fangs and claws.

The door behind her slammed open. Michael and Alerac raced to her side.

"Trinity, what's happen—" Michael broke off, his gaze landing on the fighting wolves. "*Rafe.*" There was rage in his voice. Hate. He growled fiercely.

Alerac stiffened and barred his fangs.

Gareth's claws raked the other wolf, and the creature yelped, jerking back.

"Jesus," Trinity breathed, unable to tear her gaze from the sight before her. Gareth was relentless, attacking the wolf over and over. Ripping flesh. Biting.

He was in a killing frenzy.

"Stop him!" She screamed, grabbing Michael's arm. "He's killing him!"

Alerac smiled, his fangs flashing. "Good."

No, it wasn't good. It was horrible. She swallowed back the revulsion that burned in her throat. Gareth was killing that wolf, no, killing that *man*. Slowly and violently. She couldn't stand it, couldn't stand the blood. The howls of pain. She jumped off the deck and ran toward them. "Stop!"

The black wolf lifted its head, its golden eyes locking on her. Its teeth were stained with blood.

She was grabbed from behind and yanked back, her body forced against a solid wall of muscle. "Don't move," Alerac growled into her ear.

She jerked against him, struggling with all her might.

The black wolf stepped toward them, its mouth curled back in a snarl.

Alerac's hold tightened. "Dammit, woman, stop!"

She ignored him, desperate to stop the slaughter that was happening right before her eyes. Her nails scraped against his forearm, and her body twisted like a snake in his arms.

The black wolf snarled, stalking toward them. Behind it, the other wolf staggered to its feet and scampered toward the bushes.

"No!" Alerac's cry lashed out into the night.

The black wolf advanced upon them, its eyes locked on Alerac. A low growl rumbled in its throat.

The wolf was less than a foot away from them now. Trinity could feel the hot touch of its breath against her skin and smell the odor of blood that coated its body. She could see the killing rage in the depths of those shining golden eyes.

"Don't move," Alerac whispered. "Whatever happens, just don't move." He released her and stepped to her side.

The wolf barred its teeth.

Alerac dropped to his knees and bowed his head before the beast. The black wolf stepped forward, its mouth spread wide, its teeth gleaming.

Trinity's heart pounded so hard that her body actually trembled. She stared down at the wolf, at Alerac, and felt terror rip through her.

"Gareth..." She tried to call to the man.

The wolf's head lifted, its mouth curled in a deadly snarl.

"Gareth?" Oh, God, could he even understand her in his wolf form?

The wolf threw back its massive head and howled. As she watched, the wolf's body contorted, bones snapped, and the fur disappeared. In moments, Gareth stood before her. Naked, strong.

Completely enraged.

His eyes blazed with anger. His muscles were tense, his jaw locked. "Just what the hell did you think you were doing?" His voice cut like a whip.

She lifted her chin. Her entire body was shaking now. She'd just seen two wolves, correction, *two werewolves*, almost fight to the death. And now she was being yelled at by her lover.

It was really too much.

"I couldn't let you kill him," she muttered, glaring back at him.

Alerac's head jerked up and he looked at her as if she were crazy. "Why the hell not?"

Gareth immediately turned on the other man, fangs barred. "And don't you *ever* touch her again."

Alerac swallowed. "I didn't want her to come between the two of you. One of you would have killed her."

"I wouldn't harm my mate," Gareth snapped.

"I couldn't take the chance." Alerac glanced toward the dark woods. "The *fureru de la mort* was upon you. I didn't know if you would even recognize her."

"The what was upon him?" She asked blankly.

Alerac's jaw flexed. "The death rage."

"Oh." *The death rage.* Werewolves suffered from a death rage. Just great.

"I would never harm my mate," Gareth snarled.

Alerac rose to his feet. "You haven't completed the bonding. I couldn't risk her—"

"She is not yours to risk. She's mine."

"Actually, she's not," Trinity said quite clearly, tired of the men ignoring her.

Gareth's head jerked toward her. His burning gaze locked on her. "You deny me?"

"I'm not some kind of possession, okay? You don't own me." And she was damn tired of him acting like he did. She raked her hand through her hair.

"I am your mate."

She wet her lips. "I want to go home." She sounded like a whiny six year old, but she didn't care. She needed to get away from him. Needed time to think, to clear her head.

Alerac stepped away, slipping into the house.

Gareth stared down at her, his face twisted in anger. "You can't leave me."

"Yes," she said, clenching her hands into fists. "I can." She took a quick breath. "Look, it has been an... interesting weekend, ok? But I need to get back home now."

He flinched, and for a moment, she saw raw pain in the depths of his eyes. Then his expression closed down, and she saw only stark determination on his face. "You will stay with me."

She locked her jaw. "I need time, Gareth. Time on my own." Time away from werewolves and death rages. She closed her eyes, shuddering. "And what the hell is a death rage, anyway?"

"It is a rage that comes upon my kind when we are locked in battle. If we are pushed too far, if our mates are threatened, we turn fully to the beast. We lose sight of everything, but the desire to kill." Gareth's voice was very quiet.

Her eyes snapped open and she looked at him, horrified. Her knees shook as she realized how close she'd come to injury, to death.

"No," he said, apparently reading her fear. His voice was soft. "I would never hurt you." His hands gripped her shoulders. "I couldn't."

She shook her head, barely hearing his words. "I have to get out of here." Panic was rising in her, hard and fast. It was just too much. Too much to take in. She needed space. Time. She needed to get away from him. She twisted, jerking against him. "Let me go!"

"Never." The word was a vow. "I've searched for you my entire life, I'm not about to let you walk away from me." His mouth crashed down on hers.

She tasted his anger in the kiss, his rage. And his hunger.

Her own hunger rose even as she struggled against him. His body was hard against her, naked. Strong. She felt the stir of his cock against her, felt it brushing against her belly.

He lifted his mouth, a bare inch, and whispered, "Tonight, I'm going to take you in the way of my kind. We'll complete the bonding, and you'll never want to leave me again."

Terror ripped through her at his words.

And she knew that she would have to find a way to leave him.

# Chapter Five

He could smell her fear... and her desire.

His lips curled. "My mate, why do you fight me, when you know that you want our joining as much as I do?" He stroked his hand down the softness of her cheek.

She shivered.

"I'm going to taste you tonight," he whispered, his gaze dropping down her body. "All of you." She was wearing a short skirt, a button-down shirt, and a pair of tiny sandals. He'd bought the clothes for her, arranged to have them brought to the cabin. And now, he couldn't wait to rip them off her.

His hands trailed down her body, stopping to cup the warm weight of her breasts. "I'm going to taste you," he told her, teasing her nipples with his fingers. "I'm going to lick you, taste your cream, and make you come against my mouth while my tongue slides inside your cunt."

She shuddered. "Gareth—"

His right hand slid to the edge of her skirt. His fingers stroked her silken thigh. "Then I'm going to take you, over and over, until I feel you milk my cock, until I spill my seed deep in your body." He was rock hard from wanting her. He couldn't wait to bury his cock in her, to hear the moans that would slip past her lips.

"The others—" She glanced back toward the house, flushing.

"I'll send them away," he promised. He didn't want the others in the house that night. Not when he fully bonded with his mate. "Go to the bedroom," he told her. "Take off your clothes and turn off the lights." He kissed her, because he had to taste her. "Then get on the bed, and wait for me."

"Gareth—" There was still fear in her eyes.

He kissed her again. "Go, my mate." He would prove to her that she had nothing to fear from him. They would bond, and she would stay with him, forever.

She swallowed, a shadow moving in the depths of her eyes. Then she turned, and fled into the house.

He smiled, the smile of a wolf.

He'd been too hard on her. Gareth stood outside Trinity's bedroom, outside *their* bedroom, and he felt a strange hesitancy sweep through him.

He should never have ordered her to the bedroom. He'd seen the fear in her eyes. Hell, she'd been terrified. She'd just watched him nearly kill Rafe. The last thing she'd needed was to be ordered to bed.

He rapped his head against the door. What had he been thinking? What the hell had he been thinking?

Now that the *fureru de la mort* had finally cleared from his mind, he was functioning rationally again. And thinking that he was an idiot.

*Mon Dieu*, had he actually ordered Trinity to go strip for him? Right after she'd seen him nearly rip Rafe apart?

That had certainly been a great way to calm his mate's fear. It was because of the *fureru de la mort*. It had drowned him, swamped him with adrenaline. And then when he'd seen Trinity, seen her wide eyes, her trembling lips, well, fierce lust had been added to his already simmering emotions.

And now, he had to apologize to his mate.

If she would listen to him.

He straightened his shoulders and knocked softly on the door. "Trinity?"

No answer.

He turned the knob and stepped inside. All of the lights were extinguished. Pleasure and anticipation rushed through him. His little mate had done as he'd asked. She'd actually prepared for him, for their joining.

He stepped into the room, lust roaring through him. Soon, soon he would taste her, would plunge deep into her—

He froze, his senses screaming at him.

Something was wrong.

He could smell Trinity. Smell the scent of lilacs, but it was a faint scent.

He couldn't hear her. Not the sound of her breathing, not the rustle of the sheets.

He narrowed his eyes. Thanks to the gift of the wolf, he had excellent night vision. He could easily make out the furniture in the room. The bed. The soft mound in the middle of bed.

The mound that wasn't moving.

He roared as he lunged toward the bed, ripping back the sheets to expose the pillows that had been arranged to fool him.

His body was shaking with anger, with fear. Trinity had left. She'd snuck away from him. She was gone. Alone, in the night.

And Rafe was still out there.

His lips pulled back in a snarl. If the other wolf hurt her, if he so much as laid a finger on her—

He closed his eyes, unable to bear the thought of Trinity in danger. He had to get to her, find her before it was too late.

And he knew, in his heart, that if anything happened to her, it would be his fault. Because she'd run from him. He'd terrorized her, and she'd run.

He spun on his heel, calling for Michael and Alerac.

He had to find her.

Before Rafe did.

It had actually been easy to get back to her house, almost ridiculously easy.

She'd hiked up to the main road and caught a ride with a truck driver. She suspected her mini-skirt had helped her to get the ride. The driver, a balding man in his late fifties, had taken her to a nearby diner, and she'd arranged for a cab to pick her up and take her back to town.

The whole escape took three hours, tops.

She smiled as she walked up her cobble stoned sidewalk. It really had been too easy. She picked up her mat and grabbed her spare key. And she wondered what Gareth was doing.

She hesitated, her hand on the lock. Leaving him had been harder than she'd thought. With every mile that passed, she'd felt an ache inside. An ache for him. *Gareth.* She blinked, realizing that her eyes were watering.

Damn the man. What had he done to her?

She bit her lip and unlocked the door. Being away from Gareth was actually hurting her. Her heart ached and she needed him, needed to see him and hear his voice.

God, the man had really done a number on her.

Why did she miss him so much? And why the hell was she wishing that she was still at that cabin, with him?

She stepped inside, turned on the light—

And was jerked against a heavily muscled chest.

Trinity opened her mouth to scream, but the sound was smothered by a strong hand.

"Shh, *ma petite*. We can't wake the neighbors, now can we?"

At the sound of Gareth's voice, relief snapped through her.

He spun her around, pressing her back against the wall. His hand stayed locked over her mouth. "You've been a very bad girl, Trinity. Very bad."

Her heart pounded.

His right hand went to the top of her shirt. With one quick yank, he ripped the shirt open, sending buttons flying. She gasped.

He smiled, and she saw the hint of a fang. "Do you know what my people do when our mates try to run from us?"

She shook her head, fear and a heavy arousal sweeping through her.

He leaned close, and she saw the flare of his nostrils as he inhaled her scent. "We hunt them down... and then we take them to bed. We make love to them so long and so hard that they never think of leaving again." His hand brushed against the curve of her breast. "That's what I'm going to do to you. I'm going to make love to you, until you never, ever think of leaving me again."

His gaze met hers. Glowing. Hot. "I can't let you leave me." He took a shuddering breath and lifted his hand from her mouth. "I need you too much." His mouth captured hers, his tongue plunging past her lips.

She met him, met his kiss head on. Her tongue thrust against his, rubbed, stroked, and hunger heated her blood. She didn't think about fighting him, about denying him. She just thought of... him.

Gareth. She needed him. Wanted him.

She felt his hand on the waistband of her skirt. She heard the pop of the button as he yanked on the material. And then she felt the skirt fall down her legs, felt the rough brush of the fabric against her thighs.

She stepped out of the skirt, kicking off her sandals at the same time.

His hands, those warm, hard hands, wrapped around her waist. He pushed his leg between hers, pushed his muscular thigh up against the core of her body.

His eyes were glowing as they looked down at her. His breathing was ragged and his cheeks flushed.

He bent his head, and his mouth locked on her breast through the thin fabric of her bra. And he sucked her, hard and deep. She gasped, arching her back and digging her fingers into the strong width of his shoulders.

His head lifted with a growl. "I want to feel your nipple. I want it against my tongue."

Trembling with arousal, she unhooked the bra's clasp. He watched her, a grim smile of satisfaction curling his lips. "Good. That's a good girl."

She dropped the bra. His mouth locked on her nipple, warm and wet. She felt the swirl of his tongue. The light bite of his teeth. She lifted her hips in hungry demand, riding against his thigh.

Her panties were already wet. She could feel them and knew he could feel them, too.

Knew that he could smell her arousal.

"Gareth!" There was need in her voice. Hunger. Her breasts were aching and heat pooled heavily in her core. She wanted him, wanted him to fill her, to thrust deep, deep into her body. She wanted to feel his cock, strong and hard, sliding in and out of her body. Sliding against her clit.

She forgot her fear, forgot everything but him and the hunger that burned through her. A hunger only he could satisfy.

Her fingers fumbled with the buttons of his shirt, pushing the material aside. She stroked his chest, found his small, masculine nipples, and began to tease. To torment. Her fingers plucked against him, rubbed. He growled, his mouth still feasting on her nipple.

Her fingers slipped down his body, down, past the hard plane of his stomach. Her hands found the button at the top of his jeans, and her hands shook as she touched him.

His head lifted. "No." Gareth shook his head. "I'm not done with you yet." He grabbed her, picking her up in one quick move. "Where's your bedroom?"

"D-down the hall. First door on the right." Her heart was pounding, her body felt tight, hungry. And if she didn't feel the strong length of his cock plunging into her soon, she thought she'd go crazy.

Gareth didn't bother turning on the light when he entered the room. He carried her to the bed, dropping her lightly on the soft mattress. "Take off your panties," he ordered, standing at the edge of the bed.

She lifted her hips, sliding down the small scrap of lace. Lace *he'd* bought for her. She stared up at him, barely able to make out the line of his body in the dark room.

But she could see his eyes. Glowing bright gold, burning with lust. For her.

"Spread your legs," he said, his voice guttural.

She bit her lip, staring up into those glowing eyes.

"Trinity, spread your legs for me."

She could hear his hunger, could almost feel it surrounding her. She parted her thighs.

He growled, and she felt his hands lock on her legs, felt him pull her toward the edge of the bed. Then his fingers were trailing up her thighs, moving lightly against the sensitive skin. A gasp slipped past her lips.

A big, strong finger slid into her.

"You're wet." His voice was thick with need. "And hot." A second finger pressed into her.

She moaned, her body tightening around him.

"I'm going to taste you... every bit of you."

His fingers slid out of her, and a cry of protest sprang to her lips.

"Shh..." She could feel his breath against her legs, against her thighs. "Relax, *ma petite*. I'm going to taste your pretty little pussy."

Then his lips were on her. His tongue was thrusting against her clit, sliding. Rubbing.

She closed her eyes, pleasure ripping through her. Oh, God. Her body tightened. Yearned. Needed.

His tongue slid into her, licked.

"Gareth!" Her hips lifted off the bed.

His tongue pushed into her body, rubbing against her sensitive folds. Every muscle in her body tightened, and she could feel her orgasm building.

His tongue swirled around her clit. She screamed as her body erupted. Waves of pleasure pounded through her. She lifted her hips, pressing her body against him, against his tongue.

Then his hands were on her, and he was lifting her, turning her over on the mattress.

"Gareth? What—" Her body trembled. Aftershocks of pleasure hummed through her.

He was positioning her on the bed, moving her with gentle hands. "This time," he murmured, his voice hoarse with hunger, "we'll do it my way."

She was on her knees now. Her hands were braced on the mattress, and she looked at him over her shoulder. His eyes glowed back at her.

The bed dipped beneath his weight. She felt the brush of his bare legs against her and realized that he'd undressed.

"Don't be afraid," he whispered, and his hands wrapped around her waist. He spread her legs apart and his cock pressed against her core.

"I'm not," she whispered, and realized it was the truth. She wasn't afraid. Not of him. Not anymore.

He growled, and his cock thrust into her. A moan slipped past her lips. God, he was thick. Her muscles felt stretched, tight. She arched against him, her body stroking slowly against his.

And then she felt his mouth on her, on her neck. She felt the sting of his teeth.

His cock pulled out, then pounded into her. Hard and deep.

His teeth pressed against her, lightly scoring her flesh.

He felt so huge inside of her. Hot. Thick. His cock moved in and out, faster, harder. His teeth pressed against her neck, not hurting her...

Marking her.

His hand slid around her body, parted her folds, and stroked her clit. "God, you feel good," he whispered. "So tight. *You're so damn tight. And you're mine.*"

His fingers were rubbing her, teasing her, and his cock was sliding deep into her. She could feel her climax building again, coming closer... closer...

She bit her lip, moaning as her orgasm shuddered trough her.

And still he pounded into her. Deeper. Harder.

"Give me your throat," he gritted, his hips pistoning against her.

Dazed, she tilted her head back.

He growled, then his mouth was on her again. His cock pounded into her. His tongue stroked her neck. She felt him explode within her.

And felt the bite of his teeth against her.

# Chapter Six

When she awoke, the morning's light was shining through her window. She winced, trying to turn onto her side, away from the bright sunlight.

Her gaze fell upon Gareth. He was still sleeping, his features relaxed, his body completely nude.

*Gareth.*

What had he done to her? She could feel a difference within her body. She'd felt it last night, felt it when he'd made love to her.

*When he'd bitten her.*

She raised her hand to her throat, lightly touching the still tender flesh. What had he done?

Moving slowly, she rose from the bed, keeping her gaze locked on him. She held her breath, not wanting to wake him.

Because if he woke, she didn't know what she'd say to him.

Maybe something along the lines of *Say, you took a bite out of me last night, and now I feel all weird. Am I going to wake up with fur tomorrow?*

She shuddered. She really didn't want to become furry.

Taking quick steps, she headed away from the bed. She didn't waste time dressing; she just grabbed her clothes and crept out the bedroom door.

*Hell.* Now what was she supposed to do? She had a sleeping werewolf in her bed.

A werewolf who said she was his mate.

And damn if she wasn't starting to see him as *her* mate.

She jerked on her clothes.

A knock sounded at the door.

She frowned.

The knock sounded again, louder this time.

She looked back over her shoulder, wondering if the sound had woken Gareth. Then she paced forward, and glanced through her peep-hole.

A tall, blond man stood on her doorstep. His head was averted, so she couldn't quite make out his features, but… it looked like Alerac.

She pulled open the door. "Look, Gareth's sleeping right—"

The man spun around, his gaze locking on her.

And she realized he wasn't Alerac.

His features were thin, hard. His lips were twisted into a parody of a smile, and his coal black eyes stared mercilessly into hers. And she could see the hint of his fangs.

She swallowed. "Let me guess. You're Rafe."

He nodded.

She thought about screaming, about slamming the door shut in his face, but then he moved in a lightning fast move, grabbing her and shoving his hand over her mouth.

"And you're the little human who's going to die." He dragged her further into the room, and his booted heel flashed out and slammed the door shut.

His left hand stroked down the column of her throat. She could feel the edge of his claws. "Oh, I'm going to enjoy this…"

Her eyes widened. This couldn't be happening! She stared up at him, seeing death.

"Let her go." Gareth stood in the doorway, clad only in a pair of blue jeans.

At the sound of his voice, relief snapped through her. Gareth was there. He'd help her.

Rafe shook his head. "I don't think so." His claws slid down the front of her shirt, pressing against the curve of her breasts. "We haven't got to have any… fun… yet."

Gareth's jaw clenched and his gaze stayed locked on Rafe's. "This isn't about her. This is just between us."

Trinity jabbed an elbow into Rafe's side. He didn't even flinch, but his hand moved from her breasts and locked around her middle, pinning her in place.

"Of course, she doesn't matter," Rafe said, laughing softly. "She's just your little mare."

His what? She stiffened.

Rafe glanced down at her. "Has he told you yet? Told you why he's so desperate to have you as his mate?"

"Rafe." There was a warning edge in Gareth's voice. He took a step forward.

"It's because you can mate with him. You can give him the whelps he wants so badly." His hand lifted from her mouth and he stroked her cheek. "Werewolves can't mate with just anyone. I saw the file Gareth has on you. The doctors he hired say you're the only woman who can bear his children." He looked back at Gareth. "You must have thought it was your lucky day when you found her."

Gareth finally looked at her. "Yes," he said softly, "I did."

"A perfect genetic match," Rafe muttered. "How the hell can a human be a genetic match for a werewolf?"

Gareth didn't respond, but a muscle flexed along the plane of his jaw and his hands fisted.

"Doesn't matter," Rafe said, his hand sliding down to the curve of her neck. "She won't live long enough to give you children."

His claws scored her neck, and Trinity felt a liquid warmth slide down her throat.

"You don't want to hurt her," Gareth growled, taking another step forward.

Rafe blinked. "Of course I do." He spun her around, lifting his claws. "That's why I'm here. To hurt her. And you." He smiled down at her, and she saw his teeth lengthen, sharpen. "Say goodbye, little human."

She kicked him in the balls, as hard as she could. His eyes widened, and his face flashed pure white.

"Good-bye," she muttered, jerking out of his grasp.

Gareth grabbed her arm, shoving her behind him. Then he transformed into the black wolf in a single instant and lunged at Rafe, his jaws snapping and biting.

In a blur, the other man transformed, becoming the huge, white wolf.

Trinity inched back into a corner, unable to tear her gaze away from them. Howls and growls echoed through the room.

Oh, God, there was so much blood. Her furniture was smashed beneath their massive bodies. Her couch ripped to shreds. And still they fought.

She knew that this time, they wouldn't stop, not until one of them was dead.

What would she do if it was Gareth?

The death rage had completely overtaken him. Gareth had one thought, and one thought only.

*Kill.* He had to kill Rafe, kill the bastard who'd dared threaten Trinity.

He tasted Rafe's blood, and howled in victory. He heard a crash behind him, heard the thunder of footsteps, but he didn't bother to look back. He wouldn't let anything stop him this time.

This time, Rafe would die.

He would pay for the lives he'd taken, for the innocents he'd tortured. Pay for daring to touch Trinity.

His claws slashed into Rafe's side. Gareth snarled, tasting victory.

"No!" Trinity's voice.

Rafe fell to his side, blood surrounding him. Gareth stepped closer, opening his mouth, already tasting Rafe's death.

"Dammit, stop him!" Trinity sounded frantic. "Just stop him! Don't let—" She broke off, swearing.

His head turned toward her. Alerac and Michael were there, crowding her against the back wall. Her gaze met Gareth's, frantic, fearful. "Don't," she whispered.

He stepped toward her.

Rafe jumped to his feet and lunged for him.

A shot echoed through the room. Rafe's body trembled, then fell to the floor. The white wolf vanished, its fur fading away. Rafe's body appeared, with a bullet hole in his chest.

Gareth snarled and jumped across the room, landing at Alerac's side.

Alerac dropped the gun and fell to his knees, baring his throat to Gareth.

Gareth shifted back to his human form, glaring down at his friend. "Why? The kill was mine."

Alerac lowered his head.

Gareth's claws flashed, and he grabbed Alerac by the throat, forcing him to meet his gaze. "You took my kill." No wolf was ever allowed to take the leader's kill. Not and live, anyway.

Fear was heavy in Alerac's gaze, but so was satisfaction. "H-he killed Lisa... He killed my Lisa."

Gareth stiffened. *Lisa*. Little Lisa. Alerac's baby sister. She'd been found slaughtered, in the woods near his home in France.

Alerac looked at Rafe's still body. "I suspected it was him, and when he came to the cabin, he left this for me." He lifted his hand, holding up a small locket.

Lisa's locket. Gareth recognized it instantly. Alerac had given the locket to Lisa on her tenth birthday and she'd worn it everywhere...

Alerac lowered his head. "He killed Lisa," he whispered again, his voice thick with grief. "I can face my death now, for I've given her vengeance."

Michael swore softly.

"What?" Trinity's mouth dropped open. "Face your death?" Her gaze flashed up to meet Gareth's. "What is he talking about?"

He sighed. Taking a leader's kill was a crime punishable by death in the pack. How could he make Trinity understand?

"Gareth, he saved your life!" Trinity grabbed his arm. "Why would he think you'd kill him now?"

"Because he took my kill," he told her softly, never taking his gaze off Alerac's form.

"So what?" Her voice was close to a screech. "Gareth, he's your friend!"

Alerac's head was bowed, as he waited for his fate.

"Yes," Gareth whispered, "he is." He reached for Alerac.

The other werewolf bared his throat, acceptance of his fate written on his face.

Gareth's claws flashed toward him, stopping a bare inch from his jugular. "But if you ever take my kill again..." He let the threat hang in the air.

Alerac swallowed, his head moving in a quick nod of understanding. He knew he wouldn't escape punishment a second time.

"Good." His claws disappeared and he pulled Alerac to his feet. "Michael, get rid of the body."

His cousin pulled out his cell phone and made a quick call.

Gareth hesitated, staring at Alerac. "I'm sorry about Lisa. She was... very special." Lisa had been the first female werewolf born in thirty years. When she'd died, the pack had mourned for years.

"Yes." There were tears in his eyes. "She was," Alerac said.

"She was our hope for the future," Gareth continued.

Alerac glanced at Trinity. "But now we have a new hope."

"Yes," he agreed, staring at his mate's confused, and beloved face. "We do."

# Chapter Seven

Within minutes, two black vans pulled up at Trinity's house, and several suit clad men appeared. They bagged Rafe's body and then they yanked her carpet up, taking care to remove all traces of Rafe's blood.

"Trinity."

She tore her horrified gaze away from the men and found Gareth watching her with his steady golden stare.

"Trinity, we need to talk."

She nodded, and turned away from the room, rubbing her chilled arms. She walked down the hall with Gareth following closely behind her.

She knew they needed to get away from the others. Knew they had things to talk about, to settle. *Your little brood mare.* The words still echoed in her mind. Had Rafe been right? Was that truly all she was to Gareth?

She opened her patio door and stepped outside, tilting her head up to feel the sun's warmth, needing the warmth to chase the strange cold from her body.

"I'm sorry." His voice was soft, sincere.

Her eyes widened in surprise, and she glanced back at him. "What did you just say?"

His lips thinned. "I said I was sorry. I exposed you to danger." He drew closer, his hand lifting to stroke her cheek. "Please know that was never my intention."

His hand felt warm against her skin, and she wanted to rub against his touch, but she couldn't do that. Not yet. She had questions to ask him. With an effort, she held her body still. "What was your intention?" she asked, then paused a beat. "To get me pregnant?"

*You can give him the whelps he wants so badly.*

Gareth stiffened, and his hand dropped.

Instantly, she missed his touch.

"Why did you come to find me?" She had to know.

"Because you're my mate," he said, his jaw clenched.

"Did you really get a doctor's report on me?" Had he checked her out? Checked to see that he could breed with her?

He nodded.

Her heart seemed to freeze. "I see." The sunlight wasn't warming her. She just felt cold now.

He pulled her against him. "Let me explain—"

"Explain? Explain what? How you want to breed with me?" All along, he'd just been using her because she could have his children.

"Alerac's sister, Lisa, was the last female werewolf born to our pack. Before her, there hadn't been a female born in thirty years. When she died," he swallowed, "when she died, I thought the pack's future would die with her."

His fingers bit into her flesh. She stared up at him, barely feeling the tears that trickled down her cheeks. God, when had she started caring for him so much? When had she fallen in love with him?

"Without women, without possible mates, my pack was going to die out. My people were going to die." He shook his head. "I couldn't let that happen." He stared down at her, his eyes blazing brighter than the sun. "I found a doctor, one of our kind, and he started doing tests for me."

"Tests?"

"Genetic tests. Tests to see if humans could merge their DNA with my kind." He took a deep breath. "A small group of women were found. Women who would be perfect genetic matches for us."

"So is that all I am?" she asked, jerking away from him. "Some sort of DNA match for you?"

"No." He shook his head. "You're more than that."

She tried to step around him, to run into the house, but he moved, blocking her with the strength of his body.

"Trinity, you're everything to me."

Her breath caught and she stared up at him.

"From the moment that I first saw your picture, I've been obsessed with you." His fingers lifted, tracing the curve of her lips. "I saw your smile in a photograph, and I couldn't wait to see it in reality. To see you."

Her lips parted. She wanted, quite desperately, to believe him. To believe what he was saying. "Gareth…"

"Then I did see you." His hand fell to his side and his mouth curved. "You were strong. And so *alive*. I couldn't take my eyes off you." His voice roughened. "I wanted you, so much. I wanted to touch you. To claim you."

"You kidnapped me," she reminded him, her voice husky.

He winced. "I needed to protect you. Rafe found out about the research. About you. I was afraid that he'd hurt you. I couldn't risk your safety."

"You could have explained. Maybe told me—"

"That a crazy werewolf was on your trail? That he wanted to hurt me by killing my mate?" He shook his head. "You wouldn't have believed me."

He was right. She would have thought he was certifiable. That first night, she *had* thought he was a nutcase.

Then he'd proven to her that monsters were real. That heroes were real.

"Please give me a chance, Trinity. A chance to start over, to show you how good it can be between us."

She wanted to. Trinity stared up at his face, stared into his beautiful golden eyes, and she wanted to give him a chance, wanted to give *them* a chance. But… "Is it just because I can give you children?" she whispered, her heart aching.

He shook his head. Then he kissed her, a hot, long kiss. His tongue slid past her lips, slid into her mouth. Teased her. Stroked her. "No, it's because I love you."

And she believed him, believed the emotion she saw reflected in his golden eyes.

"I love you, and I want to spend the rest of my life with you. You'll be happy with me, Trinity. I swear you will be."

"Gareth—" She broke off, not knowing what to say. "We just met a few days ago—"

"We're mates," he told her, his jaw clenched. "We're meant to be to-gether."

"Will I change?" She asked, her hand lifting to her throat as she remem-bered his bite. They'd bonded last night in the way of his kind. Would she now become… like him?

He shook his head. "No, my love. You're not going to start howling at the moon." His lips twisted in a faint smile. "You'll always be just the woman you are." His smile disappeared. "My Trinity."

"So I'm not going to become all furry?" She really wanted clarification on that point.

"No." He shook his head. "Only those born as werewolves can change." He swallowed. "So our children…"

Would become all furry when they hit puberty. They'd change. They'd have the power of the wolf.

She took a deep breath and stared at him. At his handsome face, his strong body, his warm golden eyes.

And she smiled. "Our children would be just like you." That didn't sound bad to her. No, not bad at all.

He nodded, his face tense as he waited for her answer.

"I think I can live with that," she told him, reaching up to stroke his hard jaw.

Stark relief flashed across his face. "Are you sure?"

Her lips curved as she nodded. "I'm sure." Sure that she couldn't imagine her life without him. Sure that she needed him. Sure that she wanted him...

And, yes, even sure that she loved him.

Fur, fangs, and all.

## *About the Author:*

*I've wanted to be a writer for as long as I can remember. As a child, I wrote short stories all the time for my number one fan—my mother (who, of course, never, ever had anything negative to say about my fabulous misspelled work!). As I grew older, I still wrote, but the stories became longer, more complex.*

*I have long been a fan of the paranormal genre. I just can't ever seem to get my fill of ghosts, werewolves, or vampires! I was thrilled to have the chance to write my paranormal tale for Red Sage.*

*I would love to hear from my readers. Please visit my website at:* www.cynthiaeden.com *or you may send an email to:* info@cynthiaeden.com.

# Falling for Trouble

❧☙

## by Saskia Walker

## *To My Reader:*

Before I became a full time writer, I worked in an office. At the end of the working week we would all wish each other a really wild weekend. Perhaps you do that too.

One Friday evening, Sonia Harmond wonders what it would be like to have a *really* wild weekend. Would it be the kind of weekend that would involve jetting across Europe, defeating an international crime syndicate, being seduced by a gorgeous man… and trying not to fall in love along the way?

Sonia's about to find out… and so are you.

## *Chapter one*

"Here you go ladies, drop number one."

The taxi driver drew the car to a halt. Sonia grabbed her bag and attempted to pull herself into order before the light flashed on. Too late. The cabbie, a cheeky-mouthed Londoner, had flirted with them all the way from the West End, keeping their sprits high, and now he'd turned round and was watching as she struggled to her feet. No matter how big the inside of a London cab was, it was quite impossible to get out of them in a short skirt and high heels with any sense of decorum, especially after a girl's night out in the city.

Somehow she managed to get one stacked heel onto the pavement, then the other, and swung loose of the cab, her trio of workmates cheering as she whipped round and gave them a bow and a wave, before slamming the door.

"See you at work on Monday, girls."

"Hey, Sonia, have a wild weekend," Alison called out of the window as the cab sped off, whooping as her blonde hair flew up in the breeze.

"You, too," she murmured, watching as the lights disappeared into the night. A wild weekend? Her evening out with the girls was probably as wild as it was going to get. Sighing, she walked toward the wide steps that led up to her flat, a conversion on the second floor of a Victorian terrace. She opened up her bag as she went, hunting down her keys.

A sound behind her stopped her in her tracks. She spun on her heel and scanned the bushes that lined the path, her senses suddenly alert and honed, despite the cocktails she'd indulged in over the course of the evening. Someone, or something, was there.

Her hands trembling, she rummaged in her bag for her keys. Her pulse rate picked up, her lungs constricting. The steps to the entrance were a couple of feet away. If she made a dash for it she could get to the door in maybe five seconds.

"Sonia Harmond?"

She jumped at the sound of her name, then swore when she dropped the keys. A figure emerged from the far end of the bushes. He stood just outside the fall of light from the streetlamp, but she could tell it was a man—a tall, well-built man. She didn't recognize his voice, but he knew her name. Caution was in order. Who the hell would hang out in the undergrowth after midnight? Not anyone she knew.

"Who is it?" she asked, playing for time. She stooped down and fumbled on the pavement for the keys. Maybe someone would walk by. Her fingers closed on the key ring. She stood up just as the man stepped forward into the light from the nearby street lamp.

*Wowza.* He was tall, dark and handsome. She'd spent the whole evening hoping to meet a gorgeous guy and then one mysteriously emerges from the bushes when she gets home? *What the hell was in that last cocktail?*

He stepped closer, slowly, so as not to alarm her. She could see him clearly now.

"I'm sorry if I frightened you."

He looked genuine enough. If he'd wanted to mug her he could have done it by now.

"You don't know me, but we should talk."

She stared up into his mesmerizing green eyes, sharp and darkly fringed. Talk? She'd be lucky if she could remember her own name. He was to die for. Just one look at his mouth and all the dormant regions of her body flashed into action. The core of her body hummed with the kind of response only brought on when a really impressive male specimen was on show.

He offered her a friendly smile, and when that sexy mouth moved, so did something inside her. *Oh boy.* She couldn't help returning that kind of a smile.

He obviously wasn't about to attack her. He knew her name. He had to be the new neighbor who'd moved in on the third floor. *Oh, lucky day!* She took a deep breath, trying to regain her equilibrium.

"Let me guess." She eyed him up and down, taking the chance to inspect his black leather jacket and beneath it, the tight white t-shirt that outlined his solid physique. Her gaze dropped lower to his blue jeans, where they were worn and faded over his hips. She forced her gaze down again, to his sturdy boots. *Yum.* He was built, as well as gorgeous. She'd heard from Doreen in flat 5 that the new guy was quite a dreamboat.

Flicking back her hair nonchalantly, she put her hand on her hip, interest and curiosity firing her veins. "You've got to be the new occupant in flat 8?"

"Sorry, but no."

He seemed amused by her attempts to guess his identity and he was eyeing her with as much curiosity—and interest—as she was sending his way. The unexpected encounter was getting more intriguing by the moment.

"I'm a friend of your brother."

"Alec?"

He nodded.

That shed a different light on it. But she'd met most of Alec's friends. Except—she took another look—oh yes, it had to be: tall, sexy, looks to die for. Realizing who he was, she folded her arms across her chest, her smile turning somewhat more wary. "In that case you've got to be the infamous Mr. Oliver Eaglestone."

"Nice work. Ever thought of taking a job with MI5?" He winked at her.

"Very funny, but I thought that was more your line?"

"No, I'm your standard variety Metropolitan Police. I have to say your skills of deduction are pretty good and with your killer looks, MI5 might consider you for undercover work." He gave her a cheery smile.

He was trying to get round her for some reason, but she didn't trust him for a minute. She gave a dismissive laugh. "It wasn't hard. I know most of Alec's friends, and your description has been mentioned."

He raised an eyebrow in query.

"My mother does love to gossip," she added.

Oops. What was she saying? She didn't want him to know she and her mother gossiped about Alec and his friends. "Anyway," she said, quickly changing the subject, "what can I do for you, Mr. Eaglestone, or is it a pastime of yours stalking round bushes in the dead of night, putting the heebie-jeebies into women on their way home?"

"As I said, we should talk." He took another step closer, his expression growing serious again. He put one hand on her shoulder, an action that startled her, not least because it set all her hungry female instincts into overdrive. He seemed to be reaching out to reassure her, but she was responding in a much more basic way. The man was pure sex, and he was touching her. The result was inevitable. Her body was burning up in response.

"I really hate to ruin your evening by telling you this, but Alec called me and asked me to get in touch with you. He's in trouble and I—"

"In trouble?" she interrupted. Her blood froze in a heartbeat. "What kind of trouble?"

"I don't think we should discuss it here."

"Then come inside." She rattled her keys. She was fast growing impatient. Mention of trouble and Alec did that to her. She disliked most of his supposedly recreational activities: mountain climbing, trekking through the Amazonian jungle, womanizing on a grand scale, that kind of thing, and Oliver Eaglestone was the man who encouraged him into it. He was his best mate, his philandering friend, which meant she instinctively thought Oliver was trouble with a capital 'T,' even though she'd never actually met him before.

"No, look, I can't explain right now, but it might not be safe. I know this will sound crazy to you, but Alec's got mixed up in something illegal. He's being used, but you might be implicated as well. I want to get you away from here, then I'll explain everything." He took in the mistrustful look she was giving him and added, "I promise." He indicated a parked car further down the curb, something low slung and black.

"He's not... hurt, is he?" She could barely bring herself to ask. Her stomach had started to churn.

He shook his head and stroked her arm soothingly. Despite the alarm bells he'd set off and the fact her imagination was working overtime on possible 'Alec in trouble' scenarios, his touch sent a flame right through her.

"Come on, please, I'll explain just as soon as we get away from here."

She noticed that he glanced over his shoulder, as if keeping an eye on the street. He was obviously concerned about Alec. She didn't really have a choice if she was going to find out what the hell was going on here, but she was thrown by the riot of conflicting emotions his sudden appearance had brought about. She needed a moment to gather her thoughts.

"Give me a couple of seconds, will you?"

He nodded, his expression watchful.

She took a deep breath, pushed her hair away from her face, closed her eyes and counted to ten. Alec was in trouble. Whatever she thought of Oliver Eaglestone, she had to find out what was going on.

"Okay, lead the way, I'll hear you out."

Oliver watched her climb into the passenger seat of his MG, trying to reconcile the vague, rather uninviting image he had formed of 'Alec's sister' with this total sexbomb diva.

Alec had called her a tough, Home Counties girl with a bright future in government research. He'd pictured a dull scholarly type, the type of woman who thought mucking out the stables on a weekend was good for the soul. *Wrong.*

Then there was Mrs. Harmond, Alec and Sonia's mother. She'd repeatedly mentioned that she couldn't understand why her daughter hadn't settled down with a nice young man yet. He'd pictured a woman dedicated to her career, a serious-faced spinster. *Wrong again.*

He blamed The Widow Harmond—as Alec called her—for misleading him. She'd trapped him using a plate of delectable home-cooked food as bait and then she worked real hard to promote and sell her daughter, Sonia. He'd naturally assumed Sonia was some kind of frump, as any man in that situation would. It was a natural assumption to have made, he reassured himself.

Then there was the fact that it was his friend's sister. You weren't supposed to have instantaneous sexual hankerings toward your friend's sister. It just wasn't done. That was part of The Good Friend Code. As was dropping everything you were doing to help out when the friend was about to be thrown into a foreign jail.

Sonia had confused him and thrown all his previous assumptions out of the window. She wasn't a scholarly type, not to look at, nor was she a hard-faced spinster.

When Alec had called asking for help, he mentioned Sonia usually went out on Friday and so he'd waited in ambush. When he'd first seen those long, sexy legs emerging from the cab, he'd been fascinated. When the entire, luscious woman emerged, his attention was fully engaged. She'd swung out of the cab in a movement that triggered his deeper, more carnal interests; she was sensual, fluid and lissome. His hands had itched to hold her, to touch her. Like the desire to stroke a sleek, wild cat.

Then she had smiled and bowed to her friends and the suggestion of her warm, fun personality immediately made an impression on him. He'd never seen a picture of Sonia so he'd just assumed that she wasn't the target he was awaiting, until her friend had called out Sonia's name.

When he had realized it was her, he'd stalled. It was the smile on her face, the laughter in her voice, the obvious pleasure of a good evening out with her friends. He hadn't wanted to crash her party with the bad news and he'd hesitated. But she'd been aware of him. Classy, sexy *and* bright. He was impressed—he had to admit it.

Settling into the passenger seat, she turned to him and smiled.

"Sexy car."

Her mouth was wide and full, stunningly inviting. Her hair bounced whenever she moved, the mop of black waves invited him to weave his fingers through it. He wanted to tease strands out while he looked into those expressive amber eyes of hers. They sparkled with challenge and more—the hint of sexy thoughts going on in her mind. That did bad things to a man, made a man lose his train of thought.

He turned the key in the ignition, glancing at the clock on the dash. He would have to explain on the way to their destination, but how much could he get away with *not* telling her? She might get difficult. She didn't look like the hysterical type but you never can tell with women. He'd always prided himself that he could cope with just about anything, except a hysterical woman.

He took a deep breath. He had to explain the big picture, win her over, and convince her to break into a government office on a hunt for evidence, and that was just for starters. He also had to do all of that before they arrived at the door of said government building.

He did a quick route map in his head while he assessed the level of traffic. The streets weren't busy, mostly cabs circulating the club routes. Westminster was about eight minutes away from Chelsea, tops, at this time of night. He didn't have long.

"Sonia," he began, as he pulled the car out into the street, "this is probably going to be difficult for you to take in, and I'm going to have to ask you to trust me on what I'm about to tell you."

She folded her arms across her chest, eyes narrowed, a defensive but expectant look on her face. Mistrust poured out of her. She had one eye on the road and his driving. This wasn't going to be easy.

"Alec phoned me from Prague. He was asked to carry and deliver a package of papers—"

"Yes, by Tarquin Smythe, my boss," she interrupted.

He nodded and accelerated, putting his foot down, getting through the Chelsea shopping streets in a matter of seconds, shortcutting through Pimlico and heading for the river.

"So what's the problem? It's just a job. Tarquin overheard me talking about Alec's courier jaunts and when I mentioned he was off to Prague this weekend, Tarquin asked me for his contact number, said he'd give him a job on the side to help fund his trip."

Oliver nodded again. So far so good. She was taking it in, but how would she react when she realized her boss had asked her brother to carry something that wasn't Alec's usual type of document? He sped the car up, taking it outside a double-parked taxi, despite the oncoming traffic. Out of the corner of his vision, he saw her hands grab for the dash. She had fast reactions. That was good news. She might need them.

"Exactly." He scooted the car back into its lane just in the nick of time. "But he's discovered that the papers contain information relating to an illegal arms shipment that's taking place on the Czech border. He wants to turn the documents in, but he's afraid he might be implicated and take the fall for it."

"Wait a minute," she blurted. "There must be some mistake, a misunderstanding."

This was what he was expecting, and he braced himself for worse to come. She was a loyal employee. Her feelings would be divided until she got the full picture.

"Alec's got it wrong," she continued, "Tarquin wouldn't be involved in anything like that. I mean, my opinion of the man isn't particularly high, but he couldn't afford to be involved in anything seriously dodgy. He's a senior European government liaison officer. He'd lose his job if it came out." She shook her head emphatically. "There's got to be some mistake."

"Well, that's what we've got to find out," he said, trying to bring her on board. They'd reached the river and were making time on the dual carriageway. He could see the Tate Gallery spot lit on the opposite bank of the Thames. They weren't far off now. "If Alec's right, he could be in deep trouble. He phoned me because I have experience of surveillance work and data encryption. If we can find a way to anchor this with someone other than Alec, he'll be safe to turn the papers over to the police."

He glanced over. She was staring ahead at the road, her hands twisting in her lap.

"You'd want to help clear his name, if it were true, wouldn't you?"

"Of course I would," she blurted, "I just can't believe what you are saying, I mean—illegal arms!"

"I know." He reached over and patted her arm, then instantly regretted it when he felt the urge to linger and stroke and tease her until she purred. This wasn't the time or the place for thinking about the more pleasurable activities they might enjoy, if things were different.

And if she wasn't Alec's sister.

"Take your time," he added. "I know it's a lot to take on board." Actually, she had less than a minute before they reached the office building, and he still had to convince her to help him break into Tarquin's office. They'd passed Lambeth Bridge. He could see the Houses of Parliament on the opposite side of the river. "I'll do all I can to help. It'll be off the record though. It has to be, and he's laying low until Sunday evening, when he has to do the drop."

"Sunday evening," she repeated, her tone dazed.

They were within sight of the building. "Yes, if we're going to help Alec, we have to start right away, and I think we should start by looking for evidence in Tarquin's office."

Silence.

He could feel her eyes boring into the side of his face as he parked up in the neighboring street to her workplace.

"Excuse me?" Her tone was incredulous.

He switched the engine off, glancing around to make doubly sure he'd picked a reasonably inconspicuous place to park.

"Are you trying to suggest what I think you're trying to suggest?" she demanded. "You want me to snoop in Tarquin's office in the dead of night? You've got to be kidding!"

He smiled. "You know, I like you." He tossed the car keys in his hand while he spoke. "You're attractive, hellish sexy and, for one o' clock in the morning, you're very bright indeed."

"And you're a cheeky so-and-so who has got to be winding me up."

Despite the feisty retort, the expression in her eyes was pleading. She so wanted it not to be true. He couldn't blame her; so did he, but he'd had the chance to come to terms with Alec's predicament.

"Please tell me it's a joke. You and Alec are having a joke at my expense, and you're going to take me home now."

Now she looked like a little lost kitten when a few minutes ago she was a sleek, exotic cat. What a lady. Every new mood she exhibited pushed his curiosity rate up. Man, she was having a weird affect on him. Fascination had got him locked on target and she was it.

"I wish I could, Sonia, I really wish I could."

"This is why you came for me, isn't it? You need me to get in here." Her eyes wandered from the Government building where she worked, across the river to where The Houses of Parliament loomed up. She swallowed and he could see her heart was beating fast, the rise and fall of her breast catching his eye.

He nodded and gave her a moment to take it in. He had the feeling she'd get out of the car and stomp off if he didn't keep her engaged. "I'm afraid I've done a bit of background digging on the trader Alec has to meet. He buys up arms out of the old eastern block. It's his primary source. The documents could be the papers necessary to ship diplomatic baggage."

"What does that mean?"

"It's basically immunity from the usual checks. European customs will let whatever it is through without checking the contents. I imagine that's why Tarquin is trying to pass the papers on via a courier. He wouldn't want to be caught with a forged document of that nature on his person. It's bad news, whatever the shipment is."

"But how did Alec know? He doesn't normally know what's in the documents he carries for people, and it's not like he even reads any other languages outside of French."

Goddammit, she was sharp. He was hoping she wouldn't ask questions like that. He shrugged. "He picked something up about the name of the person he had to meet and decided to look a bit further. Unprecedented, yes, but it was a job on the side, and when he saw what the documents were about, he knew he couldn't just go ahead. He must have got a friend to translate and that's when he got in touch with me for confirmation." He hurried through the last part. He didn't want to tell her who it was that had been translating for Alec in Prague. Let Alec explain that particular gem. "I confirmed the ID of the recipient and said I'd help out."

Her lips were pursed as she thought it through.

"Look," he said, eager to push on, "put yourself in his position. Alec can't go through with it knowing that arms are at stake, possible terrorist activities. In this day and age it doesn't bear thinking about. But if we band together we might be able to help him out *and* stop it going any further."

She gave a small nod, but her expression was still mistrustful. "I see what you're getting at, but why don't you just suggest that Alec turns it over to the appropriate forces, Interpol or whoever deals with stuff like this in the Czech Republic?"

"That might well be the best thing to do," he agreed, "but first I'd like to give Alec something solid to prove his innocence. Tarquin will have his tail covered. He's used a courier, for a start, and Alec could take the fall. We don't want that to happen. That's why we need evidence first."

He took a deep breath. This was when he had to voice Alec's real fears, and when he would come close to scaring her. He didn't really want to do that, but he also needed her to be aware of the danger. "The other thing is that unfortunately you are already involved, whether you like it or not. You provided the link to the courier. We might be covering your back too." In more ways than one if Tarquin turned nasty.

She looked pale, but didn't flinch. "I see. Well, I'm not worried about me, I have nothing to hide, but I am concerned about my brother." After a moments silence, she nodded with slow deliberation. "What do we have to do?"

"I want you to get me into Tarquin's office." He nodded in the direction of the target building. "See what we can find. Have you ever been in there after hours?"

"Not for work, although some people do work into the night. I went back once, when I forgot my mobile phone."

"Good, we can use that excuse if we're questioned, okay?"

"I guess so."

Her expression was daunted, to say the least. But time was pressing on and he'd promised Alec a call back ASAP. The guy was out of his mind with worry and needed reassurance that he was doing the right thing.

"Is there a security guard?"

"Yes, on the main entrance. He covers the building."

"Are there other entrances?"

"I use a side door on Coopers Yard. It opens onto a staircase that goes straight up to our floor."

"And it's a key code entrance?"

"Yes." She turned towards him, her eyes narrowing as she realized he'd done some advance research.

He smiled. "Cameras?"

"No. Well, on the entrance yes, so that the receptionist knows who is approaching. Our offices don't do anything critical. It's *entente cordiale* in the cultural and social agenda. Nothing of any real value is held here."

"Okay, any idea what the guard does? Does he check out the building or stay by his desk?"

She shrugged, looking back at the building, and then her eyes lit. "Wait. Alison, that's Tarquin's PA, she had a thing for him for a while and she works late sometimes. She used to make a joke about him being regular as clockwork, on the hour every hour."

"Excellent." He glanced at his watch. It was 1:25 am. He opened up the glove compartment, retrieved two flashlights and handed her one. "Right then, let's get a move on. We've got a breaking and entering to execute."

She stared at him, aghast. "You have a real way with words, buster," she declared with a decidedly disapproving expression.

He reached for the door handle and smiled to himself when he heard her groan in frustration behind him. She was muttering curses under her breath as she got out of the car to join him.

## *Chapter Two*

Sonia took a deep breath and tried to steady her nerves. Getting into the building had been the easy part. She could always say she had forgotten her phone if she were questioned. But going into Tarquin's office? That would be much harder to explain.

The familiar corridors felt very different compared to the busy hub she was used to frequenting during the day. Heavy with an ominous silence, only the faint gloom of discrete night lighting brightened their way. Punching the four-digit security code into the keypad outside Tarquin's oak-paneled door, she bit her lower lip and held her breath until she heard the lock mechanism activate and click open. She pushed the door open.

Moonlight spilled into the room and over the massive leather-covered desk that stood at its center. Tarquin's desk. She could feel his presence. Through the tall sash windows beyond the desk, The Houses of Parliament stood in stark relief against the skyline.

She shivered. She could picture his glacial eyes scorning her. She could hear the tone of his voice as he fired her for being in his office after hours on a wild hunt for information against him. His potential reaction didn't make for pleasant thoughts. He was an intimidating man at the best of times and right from her first encounter with him, straight out of University, she'd vowed never to wander onto his wrong side.

"How the hell did I get talked into this?"

"Are you okay?" Oliver said from behind her. She swung her torch round and lit up his face. Oliver Eaglestone, the charmer. He'd sold her a cockamamie international arms story and now she was risking her career to follow up what might be a hoax, or—more likely—a misunderstanding.

"No, I'm not okay. This might be just like another day's work to you, but if I get caught, I'm in big trouble."

I'm in big trouble already, she thought, looking up at him. The magnetic pull she'd felt from the moment she'd set eyes on him wasn't helping her concentrate or rationalize. From what her mother told her, women fell for Oliver all the time. She'd said it like that was a good quality in a man, but Sonia didn't agree. She'd vowed not to become another casualty even before she met him, but after being in close proximity with him she could barely keep her mind on the problem at hand. He was good-looking, charismatic and sexy as hell. Was it any wonder he was such a heartbreaker? "We'll just have to make sure you don't get caught." He gave her a reassuring smile, once again dousing her in his trademark charm. "I don't need two of you in trouble."

Mention of her brother helped ground her. According to his message, it was Tarquin who had set him up. Despite her doubts and denials, she knew deep down that Alec wasn't the sort of person who would make a mountain out of a molehill. He was the levelheaded one in the family; there had to be something in it.

She stepped behind the forbidding desk with determination and walked over to the computer table to one side of Tarquin's stronghold.

"Let's just do this and get out." She flicked the computer on. "What is it you want to look at?"

He shrugged. "Let's try the email first."

She nodded and turned back to the computer. The screen was demanding a password. "Damn. It's usually up and running before we all get in to the office," she explained. "I don't know his password."

"Allow me. This is my field."

He hauled the oak and leather studded desk chair over to the computer table and sat down, flexing his fingers as he did so.

What was he going to do, she wondered, her interest piqued, apply some code-busting trickery?

He leaned towards a framed photograph sitting on the desk.

What a time to take an interest in the surroundings!

Pointing at the glamorous woman on Tarquin's arm, he asked, "Right, what's his wife's name?"

"Gloria," she replied, wondering where on earth this was going.

He typed it in.

Now she got it. He was using complete guesswork. Great, they could be here all night.

It bombed. He tried a couple of variations, adding numbers.

"Kids?"

"No… but," she was getting the idea, "hang on, I'm following your train of thought. Try Cassandra."

His fingers flew across the keyboard.

"Bingo." They were in.

"You were made for this type of work." He glanced up at her approvingly.

She tried not to be flattered. "I thought you were going to do something fancy."

"Hey, I told you, standard variety."

"What is that you do? You mentioned data encryption."

He turned back to the computer. "Tracking illegal activities via the net."

"I see." She didn't want to think about what that might mean. People or goods, or people as goods. It made her shudder.

"Who is Cassandra?" he enquired, while he opened up the email program.

"His, um, well, 'mistress' is what you'd call it, I guess."

"Right." An ironic smile crossed his face. "Good call. You really should consider surveillance work for a living."

Despite her vow to ignore his flattery, that tickled her.

"How did you know about her?"

"Oh, it's common knowledge; she's a receptionist in another part of the building. It's quite the hot topic in office gossip. His wife, Gloria, is onto it. She came in here about a week back after a lunch function, all boozed up and bitter, fishing for information. She practically accused me and Alison, his PA, of being the culprit—said she'd name us in the divorce proceedings."

She couldn't help shaking her head. It had certainly livened up events around the office, but she'd also felt terrible for the poor woman. Alison had told her not to waste her sympathy. She said Gloria was itching for divorce and would come out of it well.

"Might be useful," he commented.

Sonia wondered why, but didn't ask because they were into the mailbox and Oliver was scanning the address book.

"Here we go, Jack the lad."

He'd clicked on an address for someone called Jack Rothschild, a name Sonia was unfamiliar with.

"Who is it?"

"This is the man Alec has to meet, or rather it's one of the many names he goes under. His real name is Jack Watson and his more widely known handle is The Gun Runner."

She frowned, her heart sinking. She was hoping he'd find nothing and agree it was all a big mistake, but something bad was happening, her brother was mixed up in it and now so was she and Oliver. There was evidence here and it was getting harder for her to deny it was happening.

"You okay?"

"Yes, just a bit shaken by all this, you know."

"You're doing great," he reassured.

He was looking at her with genuine concern, and for a moment she wondered if she had been mistaken, thinking he was a womanizing laddish type, judging him before she'd met him. He was putting himself on the line too, after all. Maybe he wasn't so bad.

Then again maybe it was her hormones talking.

"Thanks." She gave a weak smile then lost her nerve again, shivered and glanced over her shoulder. "Hurry, I want to get out of here. This all feels so wrong."

"Of course." He clicked through the mail faster than she had time to keep up. "Looks like they might have arranged to meet tomorrow evening for some sort of an exchange. Hmm... as Alec's got the documents, and the 'goods' must be somewhere awaiting shipment, that's got to be about payment."

"Tarquin's due in Paris tomorrow for a hands-of-culture publicity function."

Oliver glanced back at her. "That might well be it."

"How come?"

"Well, Tarquin wants Alec to do the drop on Sunday evening, and he won't want the papers to get to Watson until he's got his cash for the job. Watson works out of a base in Paris. I can't be sure, but it looks as if they plan to meet while Tarquin's over there. The function would be good cover, too. If I can get some shots of them together, it won't do our cause any harm."

She shook her head in disbelief. "Tarquin wouldn't leave email from an arms dealer sitting on his PC, surely?"

"You'd be amazed at what people leave in email. It's fast becoming our best source of information, and it's increasingly used in court cases."

"You'd think that would make Tarquin cover his tracks."

"He has, to quite an extent. He's talking about payment in notes in this mail, so he's evidently not using bank transfers. He's using a fall guy to deliver the documents. Presumably the goods are somewhere close to Prague, possibly shipping to the Middle East."

She couldn't withhold a pained response to that one. The magnitude of the problem was finally hitting her.

"I'm probably the only one of your brother's friends that would know where to look and recognize The Gun Runner's ID, but that's why he rang me." He gave a wry smile. "If you know the right way to trip the servers, you can trace the email right back to the desktop it came from, but we don't have time for that right now." He pulled a disc from his inner pocket and loaded it into the PC, quickly highlighting a bunch of emails to copy.

She was amazed at the way he analyzed and discussed it so calmly, as if it was all just a puzzle to be solved. But that was what he did, and he obviously did it well. She was fast becoming fascinated; Oliver's mind worked in ways hers never could, and despite her desire to flee the building, it was fascinating to follow the way he processed the pieces of information, like being on the set of the latest crime investigation show on TV. She was a sucker for those cheap thrills.

"So, you reckon Tarquin's meeting this guy, The Gun Runner, after his Paris publicity thing?"

"If Alec's been instructed to do the hand over on Sunday night, Tarquin will want payment in advance and to be well clear of the hand over. It's certainly worth taking a look over in Paris, see what he gets up to. What time is his function?"

"Mid afternoon, at the Museum of Modern art in the Pompidou Centre. It's due to last a couple of hours."

"Excellent. I'll have time to get over there and track him down."

As she watched him copying email to the disc, a sense of dread descended on Sonia, and a knot of fear tightened around her heart. This meant she had to take seriously the threat to her brother's safety.

Before she had time to quiz Oliver some more, the sound of whistling rose up from the floor below. "Oh, my god, it's the security guard."

"I thought you said he did his round on the hour." He glanced at the time display on the computer and then passed his torch over his watch. "It's only ten minutes to two."

"He obviously doesn't stick to his schedule," she snapped, panic swamping her. "What are we going to do now?"

He retrieved the disc from the PC and put it back in his pocket, closing down the mail program as he stood up. He gripped her upper arms, forcing her to focus on him.

"Trust me, we can cover up."

"Cover up? *Cover up* a breaking and entering?" Panic had hit her and hit her hard.

"You didn't break and enter, you simply let us in."

*Oh please!* "Don't bloody remind me."

"We just need to find a good excuse to be here." He glanced around the room. "Do you know him?"

"Who?"

"The security guard." He switched the PC off and shifted the chair back into place.

"Yes, I saw him coming on duty as I left the office."

"Good."

*Good? Was he mad?* To her mind, that only made matters worse.

"Does he flirt with you?"

*What?* "I suppose so, but what the hell has that to do with anything?"

He rested his hands on her arms, urging her to move to the end of the desk. She swallowed, the rising tide of physical awareness between them jangling her nerves.

"You're a very sexy woman." He looked her up and down as he said it and winked. "Trust me."

He let her go and she had to grip the edge of the desk for support. That was the second time he'd called her 'sexy.' Sonia just stared at him, confused and nonplussed by his comments and his actions. And now he was shifting objects off Tarquin's desk.

"Take off your jacket."

"*What?*"

"Like I said earlier, you're going to have to trust me."

How could he be so calm? She felt like her emotions were on a crazy roller coaster ride all of their own.

A door slammed down the corridor. Oliver frowned and gestured at her. "Take off your jacket and get on the desk. When he comes in, tell him I'm your boyfriend and we were playing out a fantasy that you've had about having sex on your boss's desk."

She glared at him, her jaw dropping. "You can't be serious?"

He began unbuttoning his shirt, revealing a strong muscular chest and abdomen. In the pit of her belly, an ache of longing sprang up. She tried to ignore it.

"Believe me he'll be so fascinated, he won't question why else we would be here." He winked again. "I'll offer him a bribe to keep quiet. We can't afford to have your boss hear about this."

She could only stare at him, incredulous. Surely this was all some weird nightmare from which she would awake at any moment? But the whistling was getting louder, doors were opening and closing. The guard was getting closer. Her heart beat out a fierce, erratic rhythm.

Sex on Tarquin's desk? He *was* mad! Who would believe that?

She glanced at the door to the corridor. There didn't seem to be any alternative. With shaking hands she pulled off her jacket and dumped it on the floor. Shimmying up onto the end of the desk, she laid back and cursed under her breath.

He loomed over her, pulled open the buckle on his belt and lowered his zipper.

"What are you doing now?" she hissed, her focus shifting.

"Making it look real." He left his jeans hanging open, revealing white jockeys molded to the rather spectacular bulge inside them. She wouldn't have been able to stop staring, had he not shocked her out of that particular line of behavior by manhandling her body closer and pushing her skirt up around her hips with strong, knowing hands.

The soft jersey dress she was wearing had bunched easily at her waist leaving her exposed, all but for her flimsy lace panties. Heat raced through her and her cheeks flamed. *How dare he?*

As if she wasn't exposed enough already, he wrenched her legs apart and she felt the hard pressure of his belt against her inner thigh. That wasn't all. She could feel him. That enticing bulge. She was lying on her boss's desk at two in the morning with Oliver Eaglestone; her skirt was up around her waist and she could feel his cock. She bit her lip in effort to keep a hold onto her sanity.

A door sounded nearby. The guard was getting close. She looked at Oliver, beseechingly. He was eyeing her body, appreciatively. He gave a low sound of approval, almost a growl. The muscles of her sex clenched in response.

"I think you're taking advantage of the situation," she muttered, while trying to ignore her body's reactions to his proximity. Her clit was pounding and his weight against it was only making it worse.

"I think we're going to have to deal with this trust issue you have."

"Trust *issue*?" she blurted, her hands fisting against the desk. The tension was unbearable.

He put one finger against her lips. "Yes, you're going to have to trust me if we're going to get through this." He shrugged off her accusing stare. "Sexy undies," he added, moving his hand to run his finger under the black lace edge of her panties.

Sensation flew out from his fingertips to race across her skin, desire spiraling through her whole body. Her hips moved under his, her body reacting to his touch. She wanted to hold him, wrap herself around him and take him inside.

The expression in his eyes sharpened.

"Oliver Eaglestone, back off!" She glared at him. Another wave of heat spotted her cheeks. He had her compromised and she was on fire, she could die of embarrassment.

But instead of backing off, he bent closer and kissed her neck. The touch of his mouth sent wildfire racing under her skin. Her head rolled on the desk, her hips arching against him. When he cupped her breasts through the soft fabric of her dress, she groaned. Her body had responded all too well to him. Not only that, but he had responded too. She could feel the pressure of his growing erection between her splayed legs, right where her body wanted it. His hands were locked around the soft under sides of her breasts, his thumbs teasing over the material that separated him from the hard, sensitive surface of her nipples. It was sheer torture. She was on fire with need. Her entire body shuddered with it.

His head snapped up. Their eyes locked.

"Oliver, don't…" This time it was a desperate plea. "He's almost here and you're… you're driving me mad."

Their hips were anchored together by the fierce tug of desire between them. Instead of backing off, he drew closer again and brushed his mouth against hers.

She groaned softly when his lips whispered over hers, gently, inquisitively. She felt his breath mingling with hers, the scent of his cologne and his keen maleness engulfing her.

Yearning bit deep into her core. She responded without thought, driven by desire, reaching to press her mouth fully to his.

He took the offering, kissing her deeply, mastering her senses in an instant. He explored her lower lip as if he was claiming it as his territory. While his tongue tasted hers, one strong hand reached behind her neck to lift her toward him, the other moved over the surface of her breast with deliberation.

She lifted her hands from the desk and moved them to his shoulders, her body arching against his. Firm muscle flexed at her touch. His cock was growing harder by the second and she wanted to touch it, wanted to feel it in her hand, wanted to feel it thrusting deep inside her.

A moment later, he drew away. The expression in his eyes was heavy with desire.

"Oliver?"

He didn't respond.

The footsteps in the hallway had stopped. The door clicked open and the light flickered on, but it was several seconds before either of them could break the connection and look toward the stunned guard who stood in the doorway. Something electric had passed between them. Something primal. Something undeniable.

## Chapter Three

She was breathless, startled and she was clearly aroused. Even now. Oliver watched her out of the corner of his eye while the car's courtesy light illuminated her.

What was it about her mouth that made it so desirable? Kissable and more. Her smile was wide and frequent, her lower lip positively biteable. He hadn't wanted to stop kissing her, wanted to drink her in while he'd explored her body with his hands.

"Do you think he believed it?" she asked as she put her seatbelt on and sank her head back against the headrest.

His eyes adjusted to the gloom as the courtesy light faded. "Maybe. Sonia, look I'm going to take you back to my place for the night. I think it would be best."

She turned towards him slowly, her expression curious. The light from a nearby streetlamp glinted off her hair and lips when she moved.

"Should I be asking why?"

He noticed that she didn't argue the point and smiled. She did have the right to question his intentions. Especially after whatever that was that had crept up between them on the desk. Man, there was lust and there was… *that*. Whatever the hell *that* was had completely thrown him.

The chemistry between them was reciprocal, and when it became fully engaged, it was incendiary.

"To be honest, I'm concerned," he continued, "the guard might talk about finding us. If Tarquin hears about it, he might decide to call by your place just to reassure himself about your motivations. I'm not going to put you in that situation." At the heart of it was his fear for her safety. He didn't want to alarm her, but this situation was looking more dangerous the more he discovered.

"I'm going to lose my job over this, aren't I?"

Her expression grew resigned; it made something in his gut ache. He wanted to take her in his arms and give the woman a reassuring hug, melt away her unhappiness… and then? He shoved the key in the ignition and cleared his throat.

"When you have a chance to talk to Alec and all this is resolved, you can see how you feel. It's too early to tell how this is going to pan out."

"I just can't take it all in yet. It just seems to so... so unbelievable." Her head slumped forward into her hands, her hair spilling forward in a tumble of black, her graceful neck exposed.

"I know."

Instinctively he leaned over and put a hand on the tight muscles at her nape, massaging out the kinks. Big mistake. She groaned her pleasure in the most suggestive way.

"God, Oliver, that's so good... Mmm..."

His groin sensed action and stirred. He couldn't keep touching her if she was going to make noises like that. He drew his hand away. "Is there anyone expecting you at home?"

She straightened and shook her head, pushing back her mop of hair.

For some reason it was good to have that qualified, although he was sure he'd have heard from Alec if she had hitched up with someone.

"Good," he said, without thinking, then added, "let's get on our way," and put his hands on the steering wheel, where they were a whole lot safer than touching her. He'd forgotten everything when he had her under him on the desk and now the tension between them was amplified within the confines of the MG. He kept thinking about her body, couldn't seem to keep his mind off it. Having her stay over was going to be interesting, very interesting indeed.

He started the car and pulled his mobile phone out of his pocket, dialed for directory enquires and asked for airport information. By the time they were over the river and headed south, a safe distance from the hub of London's Government buildings, he'd confirmed availability on Paris hopper flights out of City Airport for the next day and was ticking over thoughts on something Sonia had said earlier about Tarquin's wife.

"Isn't that illegal while you're driving?" She nodded at the phone as he scrolled to Alec's number.

"I won't tell if you don't." The phone rang out and was picked up instantly. "Alec, its Oliver."

Sonia's head snapped back. "Alec?"

He nodded. "Okay mate, we've picked up the trail so just sit tight." They had something to go on, so Alec could rest easier. It would also do Sonia good to speak with her brother.

Alec's voice at the other end of the line betrayed his relief. "Excellent, cheers Oliver, knew I could rely on you."

"No worries. You owe me a drink when this is over though. Listen, Sonia's here with me, I'll pass you over."

She grabbed the phone eagerly and started giving her brother the third degree, a combination of telling him off and quizzing him. Oliver couldn't help smiling to himself as he listened to the two siblings working out their feelings of annoyance and concern.

"Yes, okay, I'll tell him and just stay out of trouble until Oliver gets there!"

She turned the phone off and handed it to him. Their fingers met, and instantly, the tension was back, like static crackling in the atmosphere between them.

He dropped the phone into his inner pocket. "We're almost home."

"Good, thanks, and thanks for letting me speak to him, I appreciate that. Oh and he said to tell you he's staying at 'The Candy Store' and that you'd know what he meant."

He nodded but didn't comment. He could feel her staring at him but he wasn't about to explain, so he changed the subject.

"I was thinking back to Tarquin and the wife you mentioned."

"Gloria?"

He nodded. "How badly do you think she wants to find out who Tarquin's mistress is?"

She gave a soft chuckle. It was a warm sound, vibrating through his senses. He wanted to feel that while she was in his arms.

"I'd say pretty keen. She tried threats and allegations. Rumor has it she wants a divorce."

"I was wondering if she might be worth talking to, to see if she knows anything about Tarquin's dealings outside of his general line of duty."

"But why would she talk to me… oh! I follow, like an exchange of information. I tell her something she wants to know, is that what you're saying?"

"It has possibilities. We ought to consider it."

"Do we have time to consider it?"

"We can make time." He glanced over and caught her eye. "We can make time for anything that might be… helpful."

When she smiled in response, the electricity between them flared high. He wanted her and he knew there wasn't any stepping away. Hell, he was the sort of guy who flirted with women easily and never took it seriously, but he wasn't even trying to flirt with Sonia. In fact he had been attempting to avoid it to begin with, but something was happening anyway. It was just… happening. Who was he to argue?

He lived further out of the city center than she did, in a modern apartment on the south side, close to Kingston Upon Thames. Sonia glanced around the place, quickly taking it all in. It was spacious, sparsely furnished and strewn with books and newspapers. It certainly didn't have evidence of a woman's touch, she noticed with a certain sense of satisfaction. All that womanizing and he got no housekeeping out of the deal? He obviously kept his love life well and truly temporary and separate. She wasn't sure why that got her curiosity up. Maybe it was because she was there in his space. Maybe it was because she had admitted to herself that she was attracted to him and she was eager to pick up clues about him from his surroundings. She had to face the fact that, despite her initial caution, she was fast becoming fascinated with the man. He'd more than lived up to his reputation as a charmer, but there was more to him than that. He cared a lot about Alec, and that seemed to extend to include her, too. That kind of attention could make a woman feel good and she wasn't about to deny it.

She watched as he poured out two large Remy Martins and lifted the glasses, nursing them in the palms of his hands as he sauntered back across the room and offered her one. He moved with the sleek precision of a panther. He oozed pure male strength, calm determination and charisma.

Over the course of the last two hours her inclination to mistrust the man had rapidly melted away. How could she resist? He was playing the hero for Alec and motivating her to do the same in ways that made her feel strong yet feminine. It was the way he included her, valued her input, and yet he was protective of her too. It surprised her that she liked that protective aspect. Was she an old-fashioned girl at heart, after all?

No, she was temporarily vulnerable, not weak.

"Thank you." She swirled the liquid in the goblet, inhaling the heady aroma of the rich amber liquid.

"I'm glad you agreed to stay."

She nodded, cautiously amused.

"Whatever we decide to do about Gloria, I'll take you out to The Widow Harmond's in the morning before I leave for Paris."

She smiled fondly. It made her feel safe and familiar when he used Alec's nickname for their mother. At that moment in time, it was a good feeling to have.

"We'll see," she replied and took a sip of her drink. She didn't want to be left behind, and she tried to decide how to convince Oliver of this. She wanted to do her bit, and she wanted to get to know Oliver better. The way he was looking at her right then assured her of that. The heat in the brandy as it hit her throat had nothing on the look in his eyes.

"I'm sorry I had to bring all this to your door tonight."

"Oh, please don't say that. I'm glad you did. I'd hate to think I could've helped and didn't know. What about you and your evening? It's a bit above the call of duty for a friend, all this, isn't it?"

He shrugged. "It doesn't seem that way. I suppose that's because it's what I do for a living. It was just lucky that I'm not working on a case right now.

I had a few days off so this isn't taking time from something else."

She nodded, wondering what he'd normally be doing with time off—some crippling sporting activity, presumably, all done in the name of a worthy challenge.

"You did really well in there," he commented, and took another slug of his brandy before setting the glass down on a table.

Sonia couldn't help smiling. "I didn't have to do much though, did I?"

He moved closer, slow and predatory. The movement of his muscular body sent a jolt through her, a physical memory of how his body had felt moving against her on Quentin's desk. How he'd felt when he'd touched her. Held her. Kissed her. She swallowed, her heart beating loud in her ears. His eyes were questioning her intimately. He was pure male, intoxicating and powerful, and she was thoroughly mesmerized.

He seemed to notice her every reaction, however small. When she swallowed he reached over and traced one finger up the length of her neck, pausing a moment when she trembled under his touch, before lifting away beneath her chin. "No, you didn't have to do much at all."

She remembered the feel of his mouth on hers and struggled to regulate her breathing. Her lips parted in anticipation. The tug of desire between them was so strong. It felt as if a whirlpool of sensation had them locked at its core, the room around them falling away.

"Is illicit sex on the desk an excuse you resort to very often?" Her voice was barely a whisper.

"No, but then I'm not usually accompanied by an attractive woman who makes the story perfectly believable."

Her body was beating out its response to him, her core pulsing with heat.

"Let me take your jacket." He took her glass, setting it down. Taking control, he eased his hands under the lapels of her jacket to slide it off.

She allowed him to follow through, moving up against him, savoring the touch of his hands brushing against her skin. She looked up into his eyes, unable to resist.

"You're such a gentleman, although I have to admit that wasn't what I was thinking earlier when you had my skirt up around my waist."

He paused, the jacket dangling from one hand, his gaze locked with hers.

"You made it very easy for me to forget that it was a set up." His mouth moved in that slow and seductive smile.

Something was urging her on, willing her to find out more about the pull between them. Her heart was pounding. She took a deep breath. "Parts of me forgot too."

"Being sexually aroused when in danger is not an unusual phenomenon."

He laid her jacket over the back of the sofa. He was still smiling in the most devastatingly sexy way.

"It's not?" Her entire body was sizzling, her aroused, restless nerve endings causing a riot beneath the surface of her skin. If she wanted to stop this interaction hurtling along its current path, she had to do it now.

But she didn't want to. She had met him only a few hours ago, she knew he was nothing but trouble, but still she couldn't resist. She wanted to experience the full-on Oliver Eaglestone charm.

"No. Danger inspires desire."

*Too right, it does.* She stared at him, breathless with anticipation, waiting to see what he said or did next.

He stepped closer and reached out to her hair, easing out a tangle with a simple gesture of his hand. "When you were there on the desk, I forgot everything. I could smell your hair, I wanted to touch you and hold you. When I remembered what was going on, I felt like telling the guard to back off and leave us alone."

She about managed to nod.

His hand moved to the curve of her cheek, gently stroking her, encouraging her to respond. Barely contained desire traveled between them, as palpable as electricity crackling across a stormy night sky.

"Yes, that's what I wanted too," she murmured, and her core flared in recognition of the passion they had both acknowledged.

He rested both hands on her hips and pulled her towards him. His face was millimeters from hers. Intensity crackled in his eyes; he was as aroused as she was. He bent his head to kiss her, brushing her lips with his again in that oh-so-seductive way of his.

She responded, returning the contact, tenfold, her body leaning into his, her mouth opening to him.

He moved to rest a kiss on her neck, sending flames over the surface of her skin and into her blood. "I could kiss your beautiful mouth all night," he whispered, as he pulled away, "but I want to kiss every other bit of you as well."

She moaned aloud, her sex clenching, her mind led by his suggestions. She wanted it badly. She wanted to go beyond the point they had reached on the desk. And she wanted it *now*.

He walked her back against the wall, his body hard against hers, stroking his hands over her, claiming her from throat to thigh with deliberation. The rigid outline of his cock pressed itself forcefully against her. He looked into her eyes. "Can I take you to bed?"

She tried to steady her nerves, but her heart thudded out a violent rhythm and her body buzzed with anticipation. "I can't think of any reason why not."

Within a heartbeat he bent and lifted her into his arms, carried her into the hallway and toward the bedroom. He set her down on her feet and turned to her, moving her dress up around her thighs, slowly exposing her body, caressing it with his hands. "I've wanted to see you naked all night, right from when you stepped out of that taxi." When the material gathered above her breasts, she slipped the dress over her head.

"Oh yes, you're even more beautiful than I would have guessed," he whispered, as he carefully molded one naked breast in his hand. With his free hand, he teased along the top of her lace panties, making her shiver with need. He growled his approval and gently slid them down, bending to kiss her belly as he did so. She swayed, clutching at his shoulders, overwhelmed.

He knelt at her feet, lifting each one to remove her underwear, throwing the panties to one side. He removed her sandals, stroking her feet admiringly. He looked up at her. "Magnificent," he murmured, "From head to toe you are a very desirable woman."

And he was all man. Kneeling at her feet like that, looking up at her with desire in his eyes, she felt like she was breathing in pure testosterone. He was irresistible. "Thank you," she replied, flushing with self-awareness, as he stood up.

Again he lifted her easily into his arms and rolled her onto the bed, his white t-shirt stretching tight over his biceps as he moved, his hands stroking down across her stomach. He kissed the inside of her thighs then eased her legs apart, his mouth moving into the source of her heat with direct, knowing movements.

She shivered when she felt his tongue, firm and direct, exploring her clit. His hands stroked her sensitive places, her mons, the crease at the juncture of her thighs, the folds of skin either side of his hungry mouth.

"Oliver," she murmured. Her body arched, her head falling back against the pillows. She moaned and twisted on the bed while his tongue danced with her clit. Waves of pleasure built up and roared through her body. Her release hit her, fast and deep, but he didn't let up, and the combination of his hands and his mouth on her while she trembled with release was too much.

"Please," she cried loudly, between deep breaths. She wanted it all, to feel the touch of his bare skin on hers, his muscular shoulders under her hands and the thrust of his body inside her.

He stood up, eyeing her possessively as he hauled off the t-shirt and threw it on the floor. He undid his jeans and kicked his boots off, climbed out of the jeans. The hair on his chest, dark but sparse, tapered into a distinct line that led her eyes down into his groin. His cock reared up, long and thick, its head beautifully defined and dark with blood. He snatched at a drawer beside the bed and pulled out a condom, ripping it open and rolling it onto the length of his cock. Each and every movement only seemed to confirm his utter masculinity and the magnetic appeal he had to her senses.

When he climbed over her, she reveled in the sensation of his warm muscular body between her thighs, breathed deep in the musk scent of his body, hungry for him, hungry for it all. His cock pressed insistently into her damp folds, where she was oh so sensitive after his tongue had brought her to orgasm. She moaned and writhed under him.

He eased the crown of his cock into her wet sheath, where she gripped at him, hungry for more. He swore low under his breath when he felt her inner muscles tighten around him and drove the full length of his shaft inside, and again. Each thrust was so exquisitely full and yet bordering on too much, her over-aroused sex was a riot of sensation. He had sensitized her with his mouth, and every time his cock crushed against her, deep inside, a sob built at the back of her throat. Her body reached up to him in desperation for release, her legs locked around his hips.

"Good?" he quizzed. "I want you to enjoy every second."

Dear god, what a thing to say right then, when she was busy melting into his bed and almost crying from pleasure. It made her even wetter; her sex was flooded. The man was like a tidal wave, and his charisma flooded through her, inside and out.

He moved in fast, even strokes, pushing them nearer the brink. His tongue plunged into her mouth. She was powerless to do anything but enjoy; she was in ecstasy. The pressure of his hardness inside her spread the heat of imminent climax through her body, where it seemed to burn. They were pacing, ever faster, towards crescendo. His mouth opened and each quick stride drew a harsh breath from him. Sonia reached for him inside, heat welling from the cauldron lodged in her pelvis.

"Oh yes... yes," he urged, his eyes afire with passion when he felt her spasm. She felt his whole body arch and bow against hers and when he came, it was with a mighty roar and a succession of jerks that belted right through him.

Moments later, while she was still gasping and clutching at his shoulders in the aftermath, he leaned back, reached down and began stroking her from shoulder to hip.

"We're not done yet," he whispered and his mouth moved to quell any resistance she might choose to voice with a kiss, melting her into submission all over again.

He kissed her face, her neck and her breasts, grazing the sensitive nipples with his tongue while his cock once again grew hard and insistent against her and his hands roved over her, provoking every nerve ending in her body.

*That*, she thought, her legs trembling and her mind dizzy at the prospect of another bout of intense lovemaking, *is how reputations are built.*

# Chapter Four

Sonia shuffled in the passenger seat of the MG, squinting as she tried to make out any movement from inside Tarquin's Sussex mansion. Home for Tarquin and Gloria was a sprawling country house set in the green belt of London. That part of the countryside was dotted with small towns and villages where the well-off London commuters lived.

It was well over an hour since they'd parked along the street, Oliver's sporty vehicle merging in with the flash cars parked in the affluent neighborhood. They were across the street from Tarquin's home, where one house had too many cars for its driveway and two land rovers were parked out on the street, giving them good cover.

Surely they couldn't have missed him already? He was due at the airport for his flight to Paris so he had to leave soon. His E-type Jag was still parked on the gravel drive, but he could take a taxi and the thought worried her.

She shifted her position. This surveillance business was uncomfortable, to say the least, especially as she was still wearing last night's high heels and a mini dress. After their night of hot action and a mere two hours sleep, they hadn't had time to stop by her flat for a change of clothes before staking out Tarquin's departure.

"So, tell me." She glanced back at Oliver. "What had you planned to do with your time off work, before this came along?"

She watched him smile at her question, although he never lowered the miniature binoculars from his face. He was focused on the front door, watching for movement, leaving her to watch him—a pastime she wasn't adverse to. She enjoyed the riot of sensations his presence set off inside her. They had been stuck inside the car together for some time and it hadn't helped her keep her libido in check. Fear and danger were powerful aphrodisiacs.

"I had appointments to view some country pubs. I'm thinking of investing, a sideline, you know. I don't want to be doing police work forever. I figured I'd have a second career when the time was right, meanwhile, buy a nice little rustic country pub and get a manager in."

Were there hidden depths to the man after all? "Sounds wonderful. I'm surprised though, Mother says you and Alec will never settle down. That doesn't exactly go with the rustic country pub image."

"Are you accusing me of being incapable of change?" He was still smiling and she took the chance to memorize his profile.

"Well, no, but—"

"Here we go," he interrupted, lowering his binoculars. "There's a shadow in the hallway. Are you ready?"

"Yes," she said, pulling herself together and vowing to keep focused, despite the big distraction she had right by her side.

Looking back at the house she saw Tarquin climbing into his Jaguar. Gloria stood in the doorway wearing a red kimono, waving him off without enthusiasm. They watched as the Jaguar purred past their hiding place and turned onto the road.

"I feel like we should be going after him." She nodded after the car that was speeding off into the distance.

"All in good time. Remember, I don't have to tail him until after his Paris function."

He was so methodical. Just as well he was in charge; she'd have them tearing off in the wrong direction in a panic.

He lifted the briefcase housing their recording equipment from the back seat and opened it up, flicking a couple of switches. When he'd pulled it out of the back of his wardrobe she'd been so amazed at the sight of the gadget that she instantly forgot her initial worries about wearing a hidden microphone. He told her it was out-of-date surplus equipment that he'd kept out of interest, but to her it looked very hi-tech indeed.

"Let me just check you out." He gestured that she face him.

"I thought you did that last night." She lifted one eyebrow. She couldn't resist. Her body seemed to be under the impression that last night's passionate encounter was just the beginning; it was hankering after more of him already.

"So I did." He winked at her then pulled his headset into place. He tapped the radio microphone under the collar of her jacket. "That's all in working order. So, remember what I said, just get her reactions and get out. Ready?"

Sonia swallowed. Her doubts were back. Could she really do this? Gloria, Tarquin's pampered wife, had never liked her and now she was about to point out that the woman's husband was involved in illegal operations. Did she really have the confidence and skills to pull this off?

"You'll be fine. Just think about Alec. We're doing this for Alec."

Yes, she was doing it for her brother and he was in this trouble because of her boss. But that wasn't her only motivation.

There was Oliver.

He gave her the confidence to believe she could make a difference. She enjoyed his company, but she wasn't under any illusions about a meaningful relationship. He wasn't the type to commit, but she liked the idea of spending more time with him and doing her bit to help out.

"Oliver, when we're done here, I think we should stop at my flat to pick up a change of clothes and my passport. I am going to Paris and then to Prague with you. I want to help and I want to see Alec. I need to know he's safe."

"No way. It might be dangerous." He stroked his thumb over her lower lip and then lifted an escaped tendril of hair and tucked it behind her ear. "Sonia, before you go, there's something I ought to say."

She put a finger on his lips, pausing while she remembered how that mouth had felt making magic on her body, the night before. "Oliver, I know what you're going to say."

"You do?" His eyes twinkled.

She dropped her gaze. "I know the score. You're going to tell me that what happened between us last night wasn't serious. Right?" She fiddled with the lapel on her jacket and spoke the words with much more conviction than she felt. What had happened between them was so sudden and intense, but she knew she had to try to keep a level head where Oliver Eaglestone was concerned. She was way too clever to find herself falling for trouble. When she looked back up, she noticed that he had developed a slight frown.

"Sure," he said, sounding rather unsure. "As long as you're prepared for a counter attack," he added and the twinkle came back in his eye.

"I'll hold you to that," she replied, as he pulled her over to him for a kiss. Just feeling his hands on her caused her body to respond instantly. She twined her fingers around his neck, drawing him closer. *So much for keeping a level head.*

He kissed her deeply, his tongue teasing against hers. Every move he made sent a whirlwind of awareness through her senses. His closeness, his sheer maleness overwhelmed her.

She sighed when he moved away. "You'd better not kiss me like that again if you expect me to carry out any important tasks afterwards."

He looked pleased with her remark. "I didn't want you to forget me while you're on the job."

"That's not likely, not likely at all."

Their eyes locked and for a long moment neither of them made a move. Then he reached across her and opened her door. "The sooner we get this done..." he paused for effect, "...the sooner we get away."

Despite his instructions, he seemed a bit reluctant to let her go. But it had to be done.

She shook off the spell, saluted and stepped out of the car. Straightening her outfit, she closed the door quietly. When she set off, she glanced back, nodding at his concerned expression, assuring him she was ready.

"Testing, testing," she said as she walked up the gravel drive toward the house. She glanced back and he gave her the thumbs-up. She smiled and continued on her path. "Now that I've got your attention," she whispered into the microphone, "I want you to know that I'm coming with you. No arguments."

She risked another glance. She could just make out that he was shaking his head, but there was a smile on his face. She might win that particular battle yet.

As she reached for the doorbell she lifted her chin and took a deep breath. You can handle this, she told herself. If you can handle an affair with notorious lover-boy back there, you could handle anything.

"Well, if it isn't the pretty little research assistant," Gloria Smythe drawled, pulling her kimono tight across her chest defensively, her gaze raking over Sonia's rather rumpled night-on-the-town outfit with a condescending look. "Let me guess. You're here to tell me you're involved with my husband, and I don't stand a chance of keeping him."

Sonia fought the urge to laugh aloud. It was such an unlikely idea and the fact that Oliver was listening in was like having someone secretly share the joke.

"Not quite, but I might be able to answer some of your questions, if the terms are right."

"Terms?" Gloria folded her arms over her chest, smirking. "Blackmail is it?"

"No. I'd rather not discuss it on your doorstep. May I come in?"

Without answering, Gloria pushed the door wide open.

Sonia stepped inside, shut the door and followed Gloria down the austere hallway, mentally going over the potential areas of discussion she and Oliver had come up with on the way out here.

Gloria led her into a large country style kitchen. Walking over to a coffee percolator, she lifted the pot and gestured at Sonia with it.

"Take a seat. Coffee?"

"Yes, please." She eased up onto a bar stool and watched as Gloria set up cream and sugar on the breakfast bar and poured out two mugs of steaming hot coffee. Sonia spooned sugar into her cup, her stomach growling with approval when Gloria emptied a large patisserie box of Danish pastries onto a plate.

"Help yourself," Gloria said as she sat down on the other side of the bar and snatched up a pastry. "I badly need comfort food."

Sonia noticed the dark shadows under Gloria's eyes. As she had suspected when Gloria had accosted her in the office, she was far from being a content woman. She sank her teeth into the pastry, watching Sonia warily.

"Thanks."

"So, how much do you want and for what?"

"I don't want cash, Gloria. I'm really thinking that we might be able to help each other out."

Gloria took a sip of her coffee and then narrowed her eyes as she looked over the edge of the mug.

"Help each other out? What a novel idea. In my experience you have to take care of yourself in this world because no one else gives a bloody damn."

Sonia felt a wave of pity for her boss's wife and wondered if there was any way to crack Gloria's shell.

"Let me explain. My brother, Alec, is in a spot of bother and it has something to do with a job he's doing for Tarquin, but I'm not sure what. I thought you might be able to help me figure out what's going on, and in return I could maybe help you with the information you've been looking for."

"Why should I help you? All I need is the name of the little tart Tarquin's shagging, and as of last week I've got a private investigator on the case."

*Damn.*She was a tough one all right, but Sonia could see that her comments had stimulated a glint of curiosity. Sonia didn't particularly want to name-and-shame, but if it was Alec's safety up against a divorce-case that was quite obviously going to happen anyway, she had to give it a go. Everybody in the office knew what was going on between Tarquin and Cassandra, and it wouldn't be long before Gloria's investigator had all the details too.

"Well, I could write down the name you need to know and you'll have it right away. All I want to know is whether you are aware of Tarquin doing business outside his official duties."

Gloria shrugged and picked up her cup again, swirling it in her hand. "Tarquin does lots of extra-curricular business but he keeps me in the dark about it. I can't help you there."

"Anything that you think he might be making a lot of cash on?" She swallowed. It was such a direct question, but she didn't think Gloria was the type of woman who would shy away from talking about money.

She was right.

Gloria stared at her and then reached over to a shelf and picked up a pen and paper. "Write the name down."

It was like a game of truth or dare. What guarantee did she have that Gloria would tell her anything and fulfill her part of the bargain? What would Oliver do if he were in the hot seat?

He'd play the game and take the dare.

She wrote the name down and then folded the piece of paper tightly into her hand, resting her arm on the work surface where it could be seen. Her mouth had gone dry. She lifted her cup with her free hand and took another sip of coffee. It occurred to her that Oliver couldn't hear anything and would be wondering what was going on.

"I'll give it to you when I feel the time is right," she said, for his benefit. She hoped he was impressed; she was. 'Cool' wasn't a word she normally associated with herself, but she was taking it steady here and she could see that Gloria was busy eyeing the visible corner of the paper in her hand. "I also want some assurance that you won't tell Tarquin I've been here today."

"I won't tell Tarquin anything, except the name of my solicitor."

Sonia didn't reply, but she moved the piece of paper around in her hand. She could see Gloria had been baited.

"Look, sweetie, I can't tell you much. I don't take that much interest. Tarquin and I have been like two snarling dogs on a bit of rope for months now. However, I overheard him talking about retiring early, moving to the tropics." She gave another dry, humorless laugh. "He'll be going without me. I never could stand the heat and the bloody insects."

Was this what was at the root of Gloria's bitterness? She felt compassion for her. If he had kept those plans from her, it meant her husband didn't want her to go with him.

"He was talking to a friend who has a place out there. He wants to buy property, and I know for sure our stocks and shares wouldn't cover that sort of investment."

That was exactly the sort of thing Oliver had told her to look for.

"He has money coming in from elsewhere?"

"Not that I actually see. What he earns from the government just about covers this place." She gestured toward the house. "Wherever this retirement fund is, I don't see it. Shame, for if it's invisible I don't get to call him on it in the divorce case." She gave a slow, wry smile.

"Does he know you're going for divorce?"

"Oh, yes. He's trying to find a way out of being called on his affair, says it will reflect badly on his career, but it's really about losing out to me. He hasn't been careful enough… not this time around." She gave Sonia a meaningful glance. "He's been using his credit card on little feminine luxuries that definitely weren't for me."

"I'm sorry." Sonia couldn't help herself.

Gloria shrugged. "It's not the first time."

"These early retirement plans, do you think they've got real substance? Do you think he's planning a new life?"

"Yes. He's just playing for time for some reason, money probably." She pushed back her hair, sighing deeply, her gaze still occasionally sliding to the piece of paper in Sonia's hand. "What sort of bother has he got your brother into?"

Sonia was startled, but Oliver had warned her not to share too much information. "I don't know, but I'm desperate not to let him get sucked into something unwittingly, you know."

Gloria nodded. "Have I helped at all?" She gave a sad smile, and yet nothing that had been said had really fazed her. Sonia couldn't imagine being like that; being that jaded with life and its disappointments that nothing seemed to shock or move her. Was this Tarquin's doing?

"Yes, I think you have helped." She stood up. "I hope you get things worked out to your satisfaction." She put the piece of folded paper down on the breakfast bar.

Gloria stared at it, her arms folded tight against her chest, her cup still clutched in one hand. Now that it was there for her, it was as if she didn't want to see it after all. Sonia forced herself to turn away and leave.

As she walked back down the hallway, she began to wonder if this was only the tip of the iceberg with Tarquin. Gifts for other women, early retirement and an overseas hide away? Had he been doing dodgy dealings for a long time? Abusing his government position to produce forged documents for shipments of illegal goods? If it involved weapons, she wondered what manner of atrocities had occurred as a result.

Her desire to put an end to it strengthened. There was enough horror in the world. If she could help stop Tarquin, she would do whatever it took.

When she got outside, it was a relief to feel the fresh air and the sunshine on her face. And it was an even bigger pleasure to see Oliver leaning up against the side of his car, waiting for her, with a big smile and a thumbs-up. He eyed her as she walked closer, a sexy assessment that made her want to shimmy right up against him and demand he kiss her.

"Did I do okay?"

"You did more than okay, you got some good stuff. Very well handled."

"I can't say I enjoyed it." She grimaced. "I feel kind of dirty, you know."

He nodded.

"Will I have time to grab a quick shower at my place before we head to the airport?"

His eyebrows went up. "You're a tenacious sort, aren't you?"

She smiled. "Yes, but seriously, I have to see Alec. I'll go mad sitting at home waiting for news."

He reached over to the door handle and opened it for her. "Okay, you can come with me." He glanced at his watch. "You've got time for a very quick shower. I might even scrub your back to help speed it up."

"If you scrub my back, it won't be a quick shower," she replied, teasingly, and swung into the seat.

As he closed the door, he was shaking his head, but he was smiling.

She was determined to enjoy every moment of this time with Oliver. She just had to remember not to fall for him. That was the hard part.

# Chapter Five

Oliver glanced at his watch and ruffled his fingers through his hair. Scanning the crowds drifting through the departure lounges, he tried to catch sight of Sonia. She'd darted off towards the departure lounge shopping precinct and told him she'd catch him up at the gate. Fifteen minutes he'd given her. The stragglers were in the queue at the boarding gate. The last call had gone out minutes ago. Women and shopping, and at a time like this!

He shook his head, but he couldn't help smiling. She really wasn't like any other woman he'd known, despite the shopping thing. She was fresh and spunky and hellish sexy. He'd had more trouble keeping his mind on the job in the last few hours than he'd had in his whole career as an undercover police officer. Silent determination and unflinching focus were his trademarks. He wasn't used to being distracted by a smile or the way she tucked her hair behind her ear with one finger when she became thoughtful. Then there was the sex…

"For Pete's sake," he muttered, "here I go again." He turned to watch the last few people in the queue filtering past the boarding desk, trying to maintain his focus.

"Oliver, yoo-hoo."

His gaze swerved back. She was racing through the crowds, waving. Relief poured through his body, relief and something much more tangible: lust. He was loaded with the stuff. He'd never had it like this before. What had she done to him?

Just the sight of her jogging through the crowds had sensations flooding through his entire body. Desire, hot and fierce. But it was more than that, because it was combined with a sense of pride at her gutsy approach to supporting her brother, and a growing need to be by her side and hold her, with the promise of physical closeness later.

"I'm here, just in time too, by the looks of it." She nodded at the queue, shifting her shopping bags into one hand.

The blue jeans and black shirt she had changed into were no less sexy than the hot little number she had been wearing the night before. She just looked sexy all the time; he had to face up to it. That was bad news as far as accomplishing any task was concerned. She was breathless too, her cheeks flushed just like they had been last night, after she had melted into a multiple orgasm. *Hell, she was hot.*

She reached up and kissed him, before grabbing his arm and guiding him toward the gate, as if he had been holding her up.

"You okay? You look kind of dazed."

"Just worried that you might have slipped into a shopping frenzy and forgot why we were here."

"Who me?" She chuckled. "Has Alec been telling stories about my shopping addiction?"

Mention of Alec put a minor hitch in the flow of lust through his veins. He wasn't quite sure when he'd forgotten The Good Friend code of conduct, but it had completely slipped his mind somewhere between Tarquin's desk and his apartment, when all he could think about was picking up where they'd left off when the security guard had entered the room.

That's what he'd meant to talk to her about, outside Tarquin's house this morning. He'd wanted to say something about respect, caring about her on another level, but she'd pulled the rug from under him by being flippant about what had happened between them. He'd felt strangely adrift at that point. He blamed that mood for the fact that he'd subsequently agreed to her coming along on the rest of the trip. He was slipping. His parameters weren't functioning normally.

He had the feeling that things were getting complicated. He didn't do complicated. Not with women. Avoided complicated at all costs, and certainly not with his friend's little sister. A powerful force was disorienting his normally sharp mind: pure, undiluted Sonia.

He handed the boarding passes over at the gate and collected her bags into one hand. "Allow me."

She smiled up at him and he gave a sigh and a weak smile before he kissed her forehead and ushered her along. She clung to his arm happily as they made their way on board.

When they got to their seats she only let him stow her backpack and the larger of her shopping bags in the overhead locker. Once they'd got settled into their seats, she started rooting through the small bags that she'd kept on her lap and pulled out various items to show him.

"Scarves, two of, and two pair of sunglasses for different looks and—wait for it—a complete make-over set. I had just enough time to pick up some tips from the make-up girl and I now know how to change my look completely." She smiled at him proudly. "I'm all set for our Paris surveillance work."

"I told you that you could come along. I didn't say you could do the surveillance with me." No way, he wasn't putting her in that situation. Tarquin was a dangerous man, far more dangerous than she realized.

"But Oliver..." Her face fell. She looked like a little kitten, dismayed to be put down at the end of a cuddle-and-play session. He gave an inner groan. She was a dangerous woman. He reached over and kissed her, unable to resist the soft pout of her mouth, the inviting curve of that lush lower lip of hers. It just shouted "sex" at his every atom.

"Tarquin might recognize you," he murmured, as he reluctantly eased back from the kiss.

"I'll be able to help. I'll spot him much quicker than you. I know him."

The seatbelt signs were on, and the hostess has started her take-off routine. He reached over and pulled the belt across Sonia's hips and locked her into place, his hand lingering in against her waist. "I'm not taking any more risks; you've already done enough by confronting Gloria."

She gestured him at her accessories. "He won't recognize me—that's why I bought all this stuff, and wait till you see what I picked up in the lingerie section, for afterwards." She gave the slowest, sexiest wink he'd ever seen.

Lingerie? Bribery more like, he thought to himself, his glance darting down towards her cleavage, where he pictured something black and lacy. His balls tingled, the pulse in his groin thudding insistently.

He shook his head.

This is what the blokes at work were always telling him about, that one day he, too, would be made into an imbecile around some woman, some woman who he'd also totally cease to function without. He had laughed it off, told them he'd follow women's charms only as far as he wanted to be led.

But with Sonia it was different. He was fast growing addicted. He was a lost cause.

The Pompidou Center loomed up like a testament to all that was ugly about modern architecture, an atrocity on the landscape. Whoever thought putting all the plumbing and the escalators on the outside of a building would be an attractive prospect should have his head examined, Sonia mused, eyeing one corner of the building with suspicion. It was a novelty amongst the class architecture around it, although she supposed it gave heaps more space inside, which had to be useful.

Across the busy Plaza, a crocodile of school children meandered by, high and excitable on a day out of the classroom. To her left, a toddler broke free of his mother and ran towards a gaggle of pigeons, chattering at them in French. The birds lifted and swooped overhead. Sonia ducked, protecting the paper-wrapped crepe in her hand from possible falling debris. She darted another glance over her shoulder toward the entrance of the Pompidou Center.

"Hey, I saw that." Oliver glared at her, doing a credible impression of a stern schoolmaster. He'd told her to keep fixed in his direction—which mostly wasn't a problem, she could look at him forever—so that he could photograph the building over her shoulders and they'd looked like two regular tourists.

"The birds," she explained and nibbled on the crepe, her third. They'd been waiting for over an hour for Tarquin to emerge from his official hands-of-culture engagement.

She was edgy with anticipation. The waiting was really getting to her. She stood on one foot, circling the other one and waggling the toes to get the circulation going. Surveillance work was hard on the legs, not to mention the stomach. She was beginning to regret this latest crepe and binned the remainder. Oliver said it was cover. Much more café and crepe and she would be waddling after their target, instead of following him in a suitably covert but speedy manner.

Oliver watched the front entrance, where a few paparazzi types were hanging about, possibly waiting for the hands-of-culture delegates to emerge, maybe waiting for someone from some other event. The Pompidou was huge and ran several events at a time. They couldn't be sure when Tarquin's event would end, so Oliver was doing circuits to keep an eye on the other less conspicuous exits too.

"How's my disguise holding up?"

"Beautifully." He gave her a once over. "You look bohemian, like you should be roaming the Pyrenees with a sketch pad."

"Perfect, that's exactly the look I was going for."

When he'd agreed she could help him spot Tarquin, she'd given the make-over serious attention. Hiding her distinctive mane of hair had been the most obvious way to change her look. She'd donned a soft cotton scarf in red, binding her hair peasant style with the excess scarf knotted loosely at the back of her head and the tasseled corners trailing down her back. She'd stuffed her new sexy undies and make-up into her backpack with her change of clothes for the next day.

Even she was surprised at the alterations she'd been able to achieve with the make-up girl's quick tips. Her make-up was all rich dark colors, not her usual style at all. Soft, smoky kohl outlined her eyes, making them look deeper set and wide apart, and complemented a warm foundation and a rich, ruby lipstick. She felt decidedly European. She'd set it off with a pair of shades with cats-eye frames perched on the end of her nose.

Oliver stared at her silently, as if deep in thought, before he went back to scrolling on her mobile phone. "I've put my number in here so you can call me super quick. I'm going to go round the back of the building and onto the *Rue Beaubourg.* I'll spend a few minutes checking out the vehicles, in case he's got a driver out back."

"Okay."

"You see anything, you call me."

She saluted. He shook his head but smiled as he turned away. She watched as his now familiar figure cut a path through the gaggles of tourists and school parties littering the plaza. He stood out a mile, to her, and she imagined, to any woman with her full quota of faculties. Tall, imposing, sexy and gorgeous.

The way they went from carnal to comfortable so easily was really something. She wondered how they had come to feel so relaxed with each other so quickly. It had to be the way they'd been thrown together, the speed at which they were moving and the nature of the situation. Like he'd said last night. *Danger inspires desire.*

Did that explain it, this need to be close to him, this sense of attachment? Was it just because she was overwrought and anxious about Alec and this situation that she had inadvertently put him in? Was it fear, or had something stronger made her slip under his spell?

All she knew was that she wanted to be by Oliver's side.

Two slow minutes after Oliver had gone, there was movement within the handful of paparazzi gathered at the main entrance. Three suited dignitaries emerged together. Her breath caught when she saw that Tarquin was with them.

She folded the metro map she had in her hand into her pocket and pulled out her mobile phone. Scrolling quickly, her pulse rate rising, she watched in alarm as Tarquin separated out from the group, leaving them to fend off the photographers, and headed across the Plaza at a right angle.

Her hands shook as she called Oliver. "He's here," she announced into the phone when he answered, her blood pumping fast. "He's come out of the building and he's heading onto the *Rue Berger* on foot."

"Okay, stay on the line and stay right there. I'm on my way."

She could hear him gathering speed, but there was no sign of Oliver, and Tarquin was pacing away into the distance. Fear and confusion hit her. If she stayed put, they'd lose him. They'd come all this way and for what? They needed to know if he met The Gun Runner.

There was only one thing to do. She had to go after him herself. Even as the thought gathered conviction, her blood ran cold and her feet froze to the spot.

*Alec needs my help. I have to be brave.*

"Sonia?"

"Oliver, we're going to lose him." She willed herself to move. She took a few cautious steps, barely avoiding a collision with another pedestrian.

"Sonia, I can hear you moving," he declared, his tone disbelieving. "You're going after him."

"I'm keeping tabs on him until you catch up with me." Tarquin was moving ever faster and she had to speed up and jog along to keep up with him. He must be late for his meeting.

Oliver's voice grew overly loud. "I don't want you getting into any trouble. Hang back but keep him in your sights if you can. I'll be there inside a minute. Don't get close to him. Promise?"

"Yes, okay. I'll hang back but keep him in my sights."

"Sonia!" There was a warning note in his voice.

Tarquin disappeared around a corner and she darted after him. "We can't lose him now, after all this. He's moving fast He's just turned onto…" She strained her neck to read the street sign. *"Boulevard Sébastopol."*

She heard him curse under his breath and the echo of his feet pounding the pavements as he raced to catch up with her. The sound of it and his breathing kept her anchored on the task, despite the urge to crumple into the nearest doorway.

Her breath hitched up.

"Shit."

"What? Are you okay?"

Tarquin had stopped almost immediately after he'd turned the corner. He'd turned towards her and he was staring right at her. Her skin crawled. She could see his frown, the white hairs amongst the dark on his temples, the icy splinters in his assessing eyes. He was ten feet away and she was headed straight for him.

"Sonia, talk to me," Oliver urged. He sounded so far away now. She swallowed, her heart thudding hard against the wall of her chest. Every atom of her body told her that Tarquin knew who she was, but a shred of functioning logic reasoned it out. He wouldn't be expecting her to be in Paris. She looked different; she was imagining that he recognized her.

*"Oui,"* she managed to say into the phone.

She stopped to look at a window display, her heart pounding. She made a supreme effort, pushed her sunglasses up onto the bridge of her nose and smiled as if chatting easily into the phone. She forced herself to take a glance. Tarquin was still staring in her direction. Her blood ran cold.

In her ear, she could hear Oliver as he raced toward her. Take action, her inner voice demanded.

*"Ca va?"* she said into the phone, loudly, and as cheerfully as she could manage. She fixed a grin on her face.

"Has he seen you?"

What could she say? Tarquin was on the move and he was stepping closer.

*Oh God.* She stared, unable to look away, as he descended on her. Her smile faded into nothing, and she fought the urge to run. She closed her eyes.

"*Pardon, Mademoiselle.*" Tarquin pushed past her.

Her body jolted from his touch, and a whiff of his cologne lingered in his wake. She wavered, her legs felt weak.

"Sonia, are you still there?" There was a note of desperation in Oliver's voice.

"Yes, I'm here. I'm okay. He looked at me for a minute, came back toward me and I thought..." She glanced back. He was walking slower, looking about. "It's as if he knows he's being followed."

"He's probably checking to make sure he isn't being watched. Now just bloody do as I say and merge into the crowd. Stay focused on something else and keep him in your periphery."

"I am, oh, wait."

Tarquin had stopped in a doorway and was in conversation with another man. "He's met up with someone. The guy was waiting up the street in a doorway. That must have been who he was looking for." Relief drenched her. He hadn't recognized her at all.

"Describe him."

"About 5 feet 6, balding, glasses, gray suit. Looks like an insurance salesman."

"That's our man."

"Really? That's Watson?"

"You sound disappointed. What were you expecting, safari suit and a South African accent?"

Despite the recent shock, she had to laugh, the sudden sense of relief making her feel giddy. "Well, yeah."

"You watch too many movies. This is the real world." His remark was undermined by the fact they were stalking a known gunrunner and a member of the British government on some dodgy arms deal.

As she watched the two men talking, Watson indicated they move on and Tarquin nodded.

"Hey, they're moving again. Where are you?"

"Right behind you, Princess. I can see them now. Turn away, keep them behind you. Kiss me in greeting when I get there and then I'll take some shots over your shoulder. You can hang up now."

*Princess?* That's what Alec called her.

Glancing past Tarquin and his companion, she made eye contact with Oliver as he moved through the crowd, and then turned her back.

"Bonjour, Cherie," he said as he snatched her into his arms, panting. He kissed her on both cheeks.

She latched her hands on his shoulders, unwilling to let go.

"Okay, I've got them," he added in a lower tone, as he pulled out his camera. "You stay right there, and I'll catch some tape."

She resisted the urge to cling to him like a limpet; instead she savored his presence, breathing in his scent and admiring his broad shoulders, wishing for the moment when she might be able to rest easy against them.

"There you go, phase three complete." He snapped the camera shut and pocketed it.

She glanced over her shoulder to find that Tarquin and Watson had gone.

"I can't believe it," she murmured. "We pulled it off." She felt his arm go around her before she realized she'd moved up against him. She was holding on to him for dear life.

"We did, although you pushed your luck there." There was concern and chastisement in his eyes.

"I couldn't let the moment escape, but I'm glad it's over."

"Yes, it's over," he whispered quietly against her hair. "Just relax." He held her firmly and she murmured her pleasure against him. His hands followed with a more direct acknowledgement, holding her closer, drawing her against the hard outline of his body.

That was such good news. They'd done their bit. Very soon Alec would be out of it too.

"I'll call Alec and then we can take some time out." He eased her away with his hands on her shoulders and looked down into her eyes, his concern still tangible. "We have until ten tomorrow morning before we have to check in for our flight to Prague. Paris is ours."

The way he said those last words tugged at her heart. "Paris is ours," she repeated, and accepted the kiss he offered, emotion rising in her chest. She wanted Paris, and more. She wanted him, more of him. She wanted it all.

# Chapter Six

Oliver swore silently, rolling his head against the velvet-padded headboard of the bed, the minutes dragging as he waited for her to rejoin him after a shower and change. They'd already had quick fire sex up against the wall of the hotel room as soon as they had shut the door on the outside world.

He'd knocked a framed print down when he'd ridden her hard up against the wall, and she laughed and caught it in one hand just as her body clenched on his and he'd buried his cock deep inside her, as if his life depended on it.

He looked over at the wall by the door, picturing her as she had looked there in the throws of lovemaking, with her jeans on the floor, her panties round one ankle, otherwise fully dressed. It was then he noticed that the lampshade on the wall light was askew. They must have hit that too. He made a mental note to check for breakables when they went at it like that. He'd convinced her to forgo the sights and get a hotel. He'd had to be inside her. She'd been desperate too.

Adrenaline did that to you.

But he wondered if it was really just the adrenaline. He'd assumed so the night before, but now... He couldn't deny it any longer. He didn't want to just have sex with her, outstanding though it was. He wanted to be with her... cherish her.

He shook his head, and rested back against the headboard. It was like an addiction, he decided, staring at the ornate ceiling rose. Some weird addiction. But addictions were usually selfish things and he wanted her happiness above all, so this had to be something different. He couldn't get enough of Sonia Harmond, and he wasn't entertaining the thought of this ending when they were back in London.

The bathroom door clicked open and Sonia emerged, an absolute vision in her new black lingerie.

She'd piled her hair high and still had her heels on. *What a total fox.* She sashayed over to him with a smile that would melt ice. His brain seized while other parts of his body remained active.

He swallowed. A corset. It wasn't lacy. It was even better than lacy. It was shiny, like a pool of oil on her body, slick and sexy, clinging to her every curve as if it had been painted on. Her tits spilled over the edge, and the built-in garters looked starkly beautiful on her thighs. She wore it with a scrap of silk over her crotch and sheer black stockings that clung to her legs just the way he wanted to. God knows what the corset thing was made of; all he knew was that his brain had turned to mush and his cock was pounding. It was like a heat-seeking device, and she was the hottest thing on the planet.

She reached the end of the bed and put one hand on her hip, smiling while she looked him over with a direct, assessing stare.

*Argh.* A guy could go insane under that kind of sexual scrutiny. His balls were tight, the blood thundering in his loins. The only rational, functioning part of his brain tried to work out how long he might be able to last.

"It looks like you have a situation there." Her gaze flickered over him.

"A situation?"

"A situation that might need some... attention." She nodded toward his erection, one perfectly arched eyebrow lifted in query.

He forced himself to breathe. "Ah, yes, perhaps, although I have to point out that the 'situation' has been brought on by your spectacular appearance, so you are entirely to blame."

She smiled, and for just a moment her poise vanished and he saw the soft, underlying pleasure she took in his remark. How did she do that, and why did it make his chest feel tight?

"I'm very glad you approve, especially because the outfit was bought to reward you for your patience with me." She ran her tongue against her lower lip in the most suggestive way.

His balls were getting tighter all the time. His cock was practically poking through his jockeys.

"My patience with you is under severe strain right now, Sonia," he murmured in a low growl. "It's not entirely unpleasant, but if I don't get you here on the bed with me soon, I might go insane." He reached forward to beckon her closer, but she put up one hand indicating she wanted him to stay right where he was.

"Now, now, don't wish your life away. Good things come to those who wait."

She slid one knee onto the end of the bed, and began to crawl up the length of the bed toward him. The black bands of her stocking tops were just where he'd have his hands when she settled those thighs either side of his hips. He wanted her, now, but she was taking her time. She inched her way up the bed, tendrils of hair framing her face. The look in her eyes was so bloody sexy. As she slowly crept closer, he forgot the stocking tops because he was taken instead by the spectacular view down her cleavage, soft, pale and inviting against the stiff, shiny black enclosure. In the mirror on the wall behind her, he caught sight of her derriere and her thighs as she moved. It was too much stimulation all at once, too much for a man to bear.

He had to close his eyes for a moment. He thought he'd died and gone to heaven.

His eyes snapped open when he felt her hands on the waistband of his jockeys. He glanced down just in time to catch sight of her freeing his cock and taking it into her hand.

He arched his eyebrow at her. It was about the highest level of response he could manage.

"Why, Oliver, you look surprised. What were you expecting me to do?" She moved her hand over the arc of flesh between them.

He lifted one shoulder, attempting a shrug. "I'm in your hands, darling." The tension in his voice was nothing compared to that pounding in his cock. It was rigid, hot and ready.

She bent down and kissed the swollen tip and then tasted him with her tongue, sweeping over the surface of his cock-head in circular movements. She was enjoying it, and that fact all but blew out his circuits. His hands dug into the bed covers.

She reached for his balls and embraced them in her hand as she sucked at the end of his shaft, and then swallowed the shaft of it into her mouth, before returning to the head. Her mouth was working sheer magic. He was aching with restraint, pain and pleasure running together in his blood. When she plunged again, filling her mouth with him, he almost came there and then.

"Sonia?" He breathed out her name, choked with sensation.

She eased off, looking down at the throbbing tip of his cock. He reached out to touch her lips and as she looked up, their eyes met.

"You are so delicious, Oliver," she whispered and her voice was husky.

He groaned his frustration.

She laughed.

"Take those panties off and sit on my cock." He grabbed for the condom he'd left on the nightstand

She shook her head and snatched the packet away from him.

Something in his gut knotted.

"Oh, no, I'm not taking them off, after all, I've just put them on." The look on her face was deadpan, but he knew she had to be kidding. She must be kidding. He had to have her. Now.

A moment later she rose up and straddled his thighs, and as she did so, she pushed two fingers down to her pussy and showed him the open crotch on the panties.

"I see," he murmured, almost unable to breath. "Very clever."

She smiled and then ripped open the condom packet. Incredibly, she bent over his cock, rolling it on with her mouth in the most amazing way.

Dear God in heaven help me.

He thought he was about to embarrass himself and come immediately, when she stopped with that crazy mouth thing, straddled him and took him to her hot pussy.

"I want to show you how much I want your cock inside me," she whispered as she trapped his prone body, pinning him down with her hips, her hot, wet pussy gliding down on him and holding him so very tightly.

"Yes, show me," he encouraged, hoarsely. He wanted that too, more than anything in the world. He'd wanted to be inside her all day. He reached forward to hold her cinched waist in its elegant black enclosure.

She trailed her fingers over the line of his chin and down his throat, stroked her hands over his torso and followed the dark patterns of hair on his chest. Somewhere it registered that he liked the fact she seemed to touch him possessively.

His hands went to her thighs, holding them around the black stocking tops. Her legs tensed and flexed, and she found her rhythm, riding his cock fast and hard. What followed was a blur of exquisite pleasure. Each time she slammed down, his cock wedged hard up against her core. She whimpered and clenched, her entire body shuddering with pleasure while she milked him off to climax.

He was pretty sure he lost contact with the world for a few moments, but his hands locked onto her waist until his vision returned, until the soaring sensation that ripped his body up from the base of his spine leveled off and he regained his faculties. Then he rolled her over onto her back, determined to stay inside her for as long as possible.

He was unwilling to let the afterglow slip away. He rolled his hips against her, the pluck of her damp panties a tickle that brought a smile to his face. When his cock finally gave up the battle to stay inside, his fingers took over. He explored her damp passage, where shivers of delight still sped over the intimate surfaces of her secret places. Then he stroked her clit till she growled and cursed and came all over again, locking her knees over his arm as he worked on her.

She was so beautiful. He loved to see her come. He savored every moment, teasing her with intimate kisses, savoring her every whimper and moan. He simply didn't want it to end. When she pushed him away with feeble hands and truly seemed unable to endure another moment of his attentions, he turned them toward her exquisite underwear.

"You're a cruel man. Doesn't a girl get to rest when she's had a hard day doing surveillance work, hmm?"

He smiled but ignored her accusation. He didn't feel ready to confess he hadn't enough and possibly never would.

"This is totally fabulous," he stroked the surface of her corset, "but I find myself compelled to explore it and discover its mechanics."

She chuckled lazily, her eyes barely open.

"How very like a man."

"Yes," he answered, instantly wondering how many other men there were in her life, and if he could fight them off, one and all, with his bare hands. Instead of quizzing her about it and ruining the moment, he just assumed there were hundreds of the bastards. He couldn't really blame them, but he'd throttle them nonetheless. He sighed into her cleavage, kissing deep in its exquisite shadow, before he undid her.

He couldn't blame them, no, and instead he opened the first hook and eye of the corset with possessive hands, enjoying the sense of power he got when he had to squeeze her breasts together in order to release that lock.

He'd only got half a dozen steps down the ladder of minute hooks and eyes when he decided to roll her onto her back and tackle it from the other side—more to make the moment endure than anything else. He had the feeling that when she was naked, they would meld together and sleep might claim either one of them, or both.

"Laces?" He was surprised. "How in hell's name did you get this on by yourself?"

"It's a woman's secret," she said sleepily into the pillow. "Like the way we can take our bras off without taking our tops off."

He didn't answer, because while he hadn't seen it himself, he had heard of this phenomenon and he was puzzled by the potential mechanics of that too. He stored it away to ask for a demo the next day.

"Can we do that again with you sitting on me but facing away, so I can tug on your laces while you ride my cock?"

"Jesus Christ, Oliver! If I had an ounce of strength," she flashed him a look that made his chest ache, "we'd be doing it now."

He smiled and stored that away too. He was storing lots of plans away. This wasn't going to be over when their joint cause was, oh no. At least, not if he had anything to do with it.

When he finally had her free, he rolled her warm, supine body back into his arms and kissed her face, then kissed her sleepy eyelids, forehead, cheeks, mouth.

"You do realize that it's men who are supposed to fall sleep after sex?"

Her eyes flickered open.

"Yes, but I believe in equality. You did that last night, so now it's my turn. I'm utterly sated."

"And you weren't last night?"

"Yes I was, but this is day two. We women are superior beings but even we are known to fall asleep eventually."

He couldn't help smiling at that. He loved the easy ambience between them, loved the way it flowed from red-hot to this, this glorious after glow. She was beautiful, her hair a black wave against the pillows, her eyelashes dark against her skin. Her expression was edged with humor; she was so much fun to be around. He laughed. He couldn't help it.

"What?"

"Well, when I pictured Alec's sister, I just didn't picture this. I was expecting some tedious frump."

"Oliver!"

"Blame your mother."

"Don't worry, I will. She's got a lot to answer for," she replied, laughing. Then she sighed and a frown appeared on her forehead.

"Please don't worry, Princess, we're winning. Alec's going to be safe now."

"I know." She gave him a warm smile and stroked her hand over his cheek. "I know he's safe. I was just wondering what will happen when it's all done. I will lose my job, I suppose."

He turned his face into her hand, kissing her warm palm. He hated that her worries had intruded, hated that he couldn't wash them all way with a stream of kisses.

She'd done a fair job of hiding how upset she was but after the close shave with Tarquin, he could sense it in her every cell. It wasn't over yet. If Watson got word of any problems, things could turn nasty. All he wanted to do was to protect her from that possibility.

As far as she was concerned they'd done their bit; they just had to meet up with Alec and turn the evidence over. Experience told him it was never that simple, but she didn't have to know that. She also didn't need to know about his concern that Tarquin *had* recognized her or that word had reached him about the guard finding her in his office.

This was a high stakes operation and Tarquin, let alone Watson, would never leave any unresolved issues to chance. There were many reasons why he had to stop the delivery of the documents, not the least being Sonia's safety.

That was why he had hustled them back to the hotel after witnessing the meeting between Watson and Tarquin. Well, that and the fact he had to have Sonia right then, and if they hadn't hurried, he might have taken her right there on the street.

"If Tarquin is exposed, there's no reason for you to be fired. Quite the opposite might happen."

"I guess so," she said thoughtfully. "But the more I think about it, the more I'm not sure I'd want to go back, now. It was a stepping stone anyway." She shrugged. "A place to enhance my research skills when I got out of University."

"What is it you like about your job?"

"The satisfaction of producing information that's a valuable part of important policy making. And working with European counterparts."

"You can use your skills elsewhere, but it may never come to that."

"It all seems very far way. All that's important now is making sure Alec is safe and..." She paused and looked directly at him.

"And?" His chest constricted.

"And... this." She looked unsure.

"This?" He was pushing her, and he had no idea if it was a wise move, but he couldn't help himself.

"The moment, I guess."

"Yes, the moment." Looking deep into her eyes, he ran his thumb over her cheek. He wanted the moment to last, and last.

"Hey." She prodded his shoulder. "If you're on holiday this week, why didn't you go to Prague with Alec? You've been there together before, yes?"

Sheesh, the woman could ask some awkward questions.

"He doesn't want me hanging around all the time," he answered, trying to think of a way to change the subject. Alec certainly didn't want him around when he was visiting Prague, not any more. She'd find out why soon enough.

And Alec would find out about him and Sonia. *Hell.* He didn't want to face up to the repercussions of that particular revelation just yet, although the necessity to do so was almost knocking at the door. "Besides, I needed some time to chill."

She gazed steadily into his eyes, her expression serious. "It must be hard, what you do."

There didn't seem to be any getting away from her difficult questions. "Yes, sometimes, but like I said, I find ways to chill."

Her eyelids lowered. "Like climbing mountains and bungee jumping and seducing hordes of women?"

"Hordes?" Perhaps she had a point, although he hadn't thought about it that way. He grinned and shrugged. "Hey, you said it."

He laughed and grabbed her when she exclaimed and hit out at him playfully. He pulled her close into his arms, kissing her outrage away. "Never one quite as seduce-able as you."

She looked at him as if measuring his seriousness and then, as if somewhat reassured, she snuggled back into his arms.

He realized that he meant what he'd said and that he couldn't quite imagine going after anyone else, not if she was around. Wouldn't life be so much more vibrant with Sonia nearby, someone to really share the everyday things with? Not to mention the other pleasures of having her around. He shook the notion off, suddenly confused over the way his mind was working. He needed to get some sleep.

It was, however, several hours until he achieved that state, and the time in between witnessed a heavy weighing of his heart. Oliver Eaglestone was being subjected to feelings he'd never known before and that kind of thing can keep a man awake.

The recurring dilemma seemed to be whether he was ready for the kind of commitment he was beginning to hanker after, or if he should just stick by his convictions and knock the whole damn thing on the head right now.

# Chapter Seven

Prague was a sparkling jewel of a city, the thriving hub of the Czech republic, with its beautiful old town, the castle, the amazing gothic architecture. It was a sightseers' dream, and it also represented the reunion with Alec and the end of all their troubles. She should have been deliriously happy, but Sonia was feeling an altogether different emotion. She lifted her chin; it was only her stubborn pride that was holding her together.

"Come on, we've just about got time for a drink," Oliver said.

"Nothing for me, thank you."

"Sonia, what's up?"

She swiveled on her bar stool, turning in his direction and stared at him, her lips pursed together, her mind a chaotic torrent of indignant retorts that she barely had in check.

"Despite the fact that I know you and Alec are a couple of no-good womanizers, I find I'm startled that we have to meet him in a place like this." She waved a dismissive hand around the exotic dancing club he'd taken her to.

Humor danced over his face.

How could he? He was laughing at her! Yeah, real funny. They were surrounded by beautiful, scantily clad women—so much for her little underwear fest of the night before.

Was this his way of showing her that he wasn't the sort of guy she should be falling for? And she was falling for him. Her heart hurt like hell and her emotions were tight with disappointment.

"*Alec* is here, that is why *we* are here."

"This is where Alec is holed up?" she blurted. "This is The Candy Store?" *Of course it bloody is, you stupid woman.* She could have kicked herself. She should have known.

"Sonia, I didn't want to stress the point but Alec is still in danger. He's been safe here, trust me. It's good cover and we need that right now. The scheduled drop with Watson is only three hours away.

"The papers Alec was meant to deliver to him are worth a hell of a lot. Watson always covers his back; he may have had Alec followed from the moment he left London. Being in a crowded place like this is a good idea…

for all of us. I don't like the fact you were that close to Tarquin in Paris. You say he didn't recognize you, but neither he nor Watson is a fool. They haven't survived this long without being vigilant."

It had never occurred to her that Alec might have been followed, that they all could be in danger. This morning Oliver had encouraged her to wear another disguise. She thought he'd been humoring her, going along with the fun of it all. Had he been shielding her from the worst of this, letting her think it was all done and dusted after Paris? Sonia swallowed. Her heart skipped a beat as realization set in.

Oliver gave her a moment and then continued. "If Tarquin recognized you in Paris, he might even have had you followed. I haven't seen any trace of a trail, but we need to be careful, just in case."

"Above all, if Watson doesn't get the papers on time he'll realize his cover is at risk. He's mercenary. He won't go down without a fight."

Sonia's blood froze. Could Tarquin have identified her as well as Alec to Watson? Was Oliver just trying to frighten her into playing along now? If so, it was working. "You told me it was over, in Paris."

"It was, for the time being." He squeezed her hand.

Her mind began to race, her eyes scanning the men standing at the bar. Were they being watched? Had they been followed? "What are we going to do? How are we going to contact Alec without attracting attention? You may look right at home here, but don't you think I stand out like a sore thumb?"

He smiled. "Only in a good way. There are other women around." He nodded his head at the mirror behind the bar, the one that she had fastidiously ignored.

"I didn't mean them." She glanced at the two blonde nymphettes cavorting round the metal poles on the elevated walkway down the center of the club.

"There are other women in the audience." He turned to survey the place.

All she could see were the two cloned nymphets, now down to silver panties, and a large group of men who were obviously on a stag party and clearly thought it was still Saturday night, despite the fact it was well into Sunday afternoon.

Sunday afternoon! She had imagined they'd have already met up with Alec, sorted everything out and they would now be dining at a pavement café, admiring the sights and soaking up the ambience of Prague. Instead it looked as if things were far from over.

"I'm going to try to make contact with Alec, but I need you to stay here and keep out of trouble." His expression was concerned but it softened when he leaned over to give her a kiss on the cheek

"Sometime *trouble* just seems to step into my path." She gave him her best admonishing glance but before she had time to ask anything else, he glanced at his watch and turned back to the stage where some sort of a changeover was taking place.

"Stay put for a few minutes. You'll be safe as long as you stay here. You trust me, don't you?" He waited for some sort of response. "Sonia?"

Her heart ached. "I trust you when it comes to dealing with Alec. Anything else I'm not so sure about."

He smiled as he got up and then leaned over to the barman. "Jacques, could you look after the lady for me and get her a drink?"

The barman nodded and Oliver laid down some cash on the bar.

"Oliver." She reached over and grabbed his leather jacket, easing one hand inside to rest against his chest. "Be careful."

He covered her hand with his own, squeezing her fingers. "You too," he whispered. His glance darted away from her and around the club.

The serious expression in his eyes made her stomach churn. "Kiss me properly before you go," she demanded.

He obliged, swooping in to kiss her deep and hard.

Oh, the feel and taste of him. She'd never get enough of that. When he walked away a moment later, she felt as if part of her had gone.

"What can I get you?" The barman observed her with an amused expression. Was it because she had demanded a kiss, or was it that he'd never seen Oliver *arrive* with a woman before? Was he more used to seeing him *leave* with them?

She attempted a pleasant smile. "A very large gin and tonic, please."

When the drink arrived she knocked it back quickly and tried to act as nonchalantly as she could. She straightened her skirt—something she'd chosen to wear as part of a new look because it was much shorter and more trashy than she'd usually wear, but ironically fit her into the current surroundings rather well—swiveled on the stool and tossed her hair back. If she had to wait here to meet Alec, she bloody well would. And not act as if she were a cringing prude.

She looked around the place, doing a slow circuit of the occupants, wondering if there was anyone there watching them, keeping tags on who they talked to. The idea of it made her feel very uneasy, but she tried to act cool, as if she were nothing but an everyday tourist.

Oliver was right, there *were* other women here. There was a large mixed group partying on the far side of the club. There were also two couples at separate tables, and the women seemed to be enjoying the view as much as the men. She wondered if it was a cultural thing, or if couples went to lap dancing clubs in England too. It wasn't something she had any experience of, but she was experiencing plenty of things with Oliver she'd never experienced before.

The piped music was upbeat and sexy, and the ambience of the place was more fun than she might have expected. One table appeared to be having a business meeting. Others were canoodling with each other while watching the show.

Just then she noticed that Oliver was standing near some sort of doorway, an exit presumably, where she supposed Alec might come in. Oliver was watching her and when he caught her eye, she felt the heat of his gaze. She smiled his way and he nodded at her approvingly.

That made her feel a bit more confident and she leaned one elbow up against the bar, resting back against it. As she did she noticed two men standing down the bar from her. One of them was looking at her with an assessing frown while flipping a mobile phone in his hand. His eyes narrowed as he looked from Oliver to her, and then whispered something to his companion.

Sonia swallowed and looked away quickly, her gaze swerving back towards Oliver. Were they here on Alec's tail? Had they noticed Oliver's movements? Could she somehow warn him?

A new act had arrived on stage and try as she might Oliver seemed more interested in watching the woman on the stage than communicating with anyone else. Sonia swore low under her breath and sat upright on her stool, her fingers knotting together to keep from leaping up and waving at him to attract his attention.

The dancer was a raven-haired beauty in khaki hot pants and a matching shirt knotted at her impressive cleavage. She had a bullet belt slung real low on her hips, like some kind of cross between Lara Croft and Warrior Princess Xena, all power and beauty. Her face was stunning, with Slavic bone structure and gleaming green eyes. The men were cheering her on and throwing cash as she sashayed down the walkway. She stopped walking and then cartwheeled to the end of the stage, where she swung round a pole as if her body were melting into it. Sonia noticed that all the men were all agog. All of them. Including Oliver!

Frustration and an underlying sense of disappointment hit her. Seeing him watching the dancer like that hurt like hell, yet she couldn't drag her eyes away. Each time the dancer looked his way he smiled and waved money at her. At the end of the dance, the woman sidled over to Oliver and slid to the floor into the splits, right in front of him, before rolling onto her back so he could tuck the note down her cleavage.

*That should be my cleavage he's playing with.* Envy gripped her and then, as if that wasn't enough, Oliver spoke to the dancer and nodded over in her direction. She swore aloud when the woman jumped off the catwalk and walked toward her, hips swaying in time to the music. Oliver was watching, his hands in his pocket and he actually looked at her then, finally, and winked at her. What the hell was this about?

The dancer stopped in front of her.

"You are Sonia?" Without waiting for her to answer, the woman grabbed her hand and nodded over at a low sofa set to one side of the bar. "Your boyfriend has paid me to dance for you."

"He *what*?" She threw an amazed look in his direction. Was *this* his idea of good cover and merging with the surroundings or did he want to play out some fantasy? What about Alec? What about the danger they were supposed to be in?

He grinned at her when she glared at him.

"He's not my boyfriend." Denial of her growing attachment to Oliver was her foremost instinct in that moment. Seeing him flirt so easily with the dancer had kicked her emotions into turmoil. She felt like an idiot. Hadn't she warned herself about a guy like him? When had she forgotten that particular point?

"Come on, just give me two minutes of your time. You'll be glad you did, I promise." The dancer held Sonia's wrist and urged her off her perch. Sonia staggered behind her, then straightened up and bit her lip when she realized several heads had turned to watch the warrior princess and her latest lucky customer adjourning into the dark corner.

She sank into the sofa that the dancer nudged her toward. Glancing around she saw that pretty much everybody, including the two guys at the bar, was now watching them.

The dancer began to move to the sound of the piped music with all the sensuous fluidity of a snake being charmed. Sonia couldn't help staring. It was sexy all right and made her wonder if she could learn to move like that. *Maybe that's how you kept a guy like Oliver,* she taunted herself.

"Honey," the woman said, "Oliver has gone backstage to see Alec, and I'll take you there soon. He's fine and he's waiting for the evidence you have brought. Oliver thought the best way to keep you safe while he was backstage was to keep you very visible. That's why I'm dancing for you."

Sonia gaped up at her.

"We called the Czech police when you arrived and the British consulate representative is also on his way," the dancer whispered. "My name is Anja, and I'm a friend of your brother."

A friend of Alec's?

As realization slowly dawned, Sonia glanced back and saw that Oliver had indeed disappeared from his earlier spot.

She looked back at the beautiful dancer in front of her and forced a weak smile. Anja winked. At the other side of the bar, the stag party cheered and waved, clearly even more wired by the sight of the girl-on-girl action than by the earlier more public dance.

Sonia closed her eyes and counted to ten. Was this really happening? The surreal nature of the situation finally hit home and a disbelieving laugh escaped her. She surely had got the wild weekend Alison had wished her on Friday evening. From cavorting on her boss's desk to incendiary sex in London and Paris to lap dancing in Prague, no, this was no ordinary weekend.

And they weren't out of danger yet. She had to let the woman know about the guys at the bar.

When she moved closer, Sonia grabbed her wrist. "There are two men over at the bar. I think they were watching us," she blurted.

Without batting an eyelid the woman nodded and leaned closer, fetching Sonia up off the sofa into her arms. "Dance with me," she instructed, glancing over Sonia's shoulder toward the bar as she rose. "Yes, I see them."

Sonia moved awkwardly, fear and self awareness hampering her every move. Her legs felt leaden, her head dizzy with everything that was going on. In the background she heard a cheer from the stag party. Anja laughed and moved against her, flaunting them both, making them the spectacle of everybody's attention.

"We go backstage together like you are one of the girls, okay?"

Sonia nodded. When the track changed Anja gestured at her to follow and danced her across the club and through the stage door. She took a deep breath, relieved to get away from those prying eyes. They passed along a narrow corridor past open dressing room doors where she saw the blonde nymphettes and other women, and finally into a room where Oliver was waiting.

"Are you okay?" He rose from a chair and took her into his arms.

"What do you think? That was awful." The public display, the two suspicious men at the bar breathing down her neck. She glanced over her shoulder as Anja disappeared back down the corridor.

His eyebrows lifted in a sign of gentle chastisement. Stepping back, he folded his arms over his chest, lounging easily on the arm of a chair. "Anja gave you cover to come backstage. I'm sure you realize that now." His eyes flickered with humor. She could tell he was holding back his amusement.

"It's you that I'm annoyed with. You could have warned me."

"Fair enough." He smiled, calmly.

God, sometimes he was insufferably self-assured. "Why didn't you tell me what you were planning? That you were sending some dancer over to give me cover?"

"Sonia, Anja's not just 'some dancer,' she's the reason your brother's been visiting Prague so often. She's a PhD politics student and does this to fund her studies. Apparently exotic dancing is a flexible sideline that pays well and the girls here are well protected. He's been seeing her for months. He's pretty stuck on her and well... you might be hearing wedding bells soon."

Sonia swallowed, color rising in her face. Shocked wasn't the word.

"I'm only telling you because I don't want you to say anything inappropriate about the club when Alec gets here."

She nodded, and then a wave of indignation rose inside her. All thoughts of telling him about the two men in the audience fled from her mind.

"Well, why the hell didn't you just explain? Then I wouldn't have felt such a fool." She glared at him.

"You didn't give me much of a chance." He laughed. "Anyway, you look even more sexy than usual when you're angry." His gaze swept up and down as if her whole body was on fire. "Like now. I could just eat you up when you're like this."

Despite the nature of his comment, and the effect it had on certain nether regions of her body, she still felt indignant. "Of course I was angry," she retorted. "I was angry as hell. I thought we had something special and there you were, flirting with her in front of me. Tossing me off in the most cowardly way imaginable." The words were out before she'd had a chance to think it through.

"Sonia! Oliver…"

Turning toward Alec's voice, she saw him standing in the doorway to the dressing room. She stood up, breaking into a weak smile, her eyes growing damp as she took in the sight of her darling brother. He looked stressed, his normally relaxed expression haggard. There were dark shadows under his eyes and stubble on his usually clean-shaven chin.

He hugged her, then reached out and put his hand on Oliver's shoulder. Her eyes filled with tears and she felt a weight lifting off her. She'd been desperately in need to see Alec, to help get him out of this mess and make sure Tarquin paid for setting him up. She didn't care what happened to her along the way. She wanted Alec safe.

*And Oliver.*

The police officer was a crumpled-suit, unshakable type who grasped very quickly the meat of the case. His sidekick, a skinny studious type, started by taking notes then got engrossed in what was being said and just listened. Anja, who had changed into jeans and a sweatshirt, translated fast and clear, never struggling for words as she alternated between languages.

Alec sat strained and tense until the officer made contact with his HQ and it became clear action was being taken at a higher level.

The British Consulate had sent a young officer who'd arrived straight from a function and stood around looking awkward in his evening suit. He was clearly overwhelmed by the situation and kept leaving the room to relay what was happening to the consulate general via his mobile phone.

Oliver watched the drama unfold, but he was distracted. He was interested in the way the Czech police and the British Consulate handled the case, especially with its international repercussions, but he was much more interested in watching Sonia, beautiful, strong and feisty Sonia.

That morning she had changed into a denim mini skirt and a black slash-neck, long-sleeved top, and tied her hair into a loose knot. She looked subtly sophisticated, even when she was all hot and bothered about the lap dance. At first, after her outburst, she avoided eye contact with him, then she began to meet his stare, her expression direct, serious.

Now, he had to make a move and respond to her, say something, or she might just walk away. They needed to talk and it had to happen soon. God, he wanted her. The thought that she might just walk away when this was done made his gut twist into knots.

"Okay." Anja stood up, redirecting his attention, and looked around to include them all. "The inspector wants us all to go the station to be interviewed properly and give statements."

"If we've got that far along," Oliver commented, reaching into his pocket to retrieve the plastic zipped bag with the various evidence they had procured, "it'll be safe to hand these over."

Anja nodded and explained to the inspector, who passed the bag to his sidekick.

"Oh God!" Sonia suddenly declared, her eyes wide. "The men at the bar."

"Yes," Anja nodded. "It could be important." She turned back to the police man and again spoke rapidly in Czech. The police man turned and spoke to his sidekick, who stood up. "Dark haired in denim, blond in suit, yes?" she asked Sonia.

Sonia nodded.

The sidekick left the room.

Oliver frowned. He moved and was about to go take a look for himself when the police man put his hand up and blocked his passage.

"He's going to get his men to deal with it. He's called for a police car to take us," Anja explained. "He'll have it brought to the back entrance." She broke into a wide, relieved smile. "We'll be safe now."

Alec hugged her to him. "Thanks, guys, all of you," he said as they followed the police officer down the corridor.

"Just wait till our mother hears," Sonia said and she shook her head disbelievingly while Alec grimaced. "It will be great to get all this sorted out," she added, with a sigh, as the four of them walked to the police car.

Oliver put his arm around her and drew her close. "And I intend to sort *you* out, Madame, just as soon as we are alone," he whispered.

## Chapter Eight

Forty-eight hours, three countries, two flights and God knows how many revelations since that first meeting with Oliver, and Sonia felt giddy with relief about what they had managed to achieve.

Now she wanted to move into Oliver's arms, where she just longed to be held. It was a long wait for that moment though and all the while his male power reached out across the waiting areas and the interview rooms they shunted around throughout that evening. He watched her the whole time, and she felt as if he had her pinned by the strength of his will, as if she would be unable to move away from him, even if she wanted to.

He'd said he was going to sort her out. What did he mean by that? The silent tension between them was stretched during the lengthy statements they had to give to the police. The waiting was unbearable.

Finally, after they'd all been interviewed, they were left alone in a waiting room, gratefully indulging in steaming mugs of tea and crusty bread stuffed with flavorsome ham and cheese that had been brought for them. After they'd eaten, Anja was explaining some of what had been said by the policeman when the door opened and a new face entered the room, a mature man in a neat suit.

"Charlie Douglas," Oliver exclaimed, his tone surprised and he stood to greet the man.

"What is it with you, Oliver? Can't you ever keep away from trouble?"

Oliver put up his hands. "Hey, I'm on holiday, just here to support my friends." He nodded over at the three of them.

Sonia glanced at Alec in query, but he shrugged his shoulders.

Charlie shook Oliver's hand. "The minute I heard your name was involved I said I'd come down myself."

Oliver made the introductions. "Charlie Douglas," he explained, "an old friend of mine from the force. He's working with Interpol these days."

"You'll be pleased to know the Czech police have just picked up Jack Watson not far from the meeting point location you gave them. Two further arrests were made at the club, both known associates of Watson with outstanding warrants in three countries."

Sonia breathed a sigh of relief and Alec got up to shake hands with the man who'd delivered the good news.

"And Tarquin Smythe?" Oliver asked.

"Soon," Charlie replied with a serious tone. "His wife was having him followed, which was useful. She put us in touch with her PI, and Scotland Yard are on their way to pick him up from the flat he shares with his bit of fluff."

Poor Gloria, Sonia reflected. At least she'd forewarned her of trouble and she had the feeling Tarquin's wife might relish public humiliation for her errant husband.

Shortly afterwards they were told they could leave the station, but not to leave the country for another twenty-four hours. It was late when the four of them finally stepped outside the police station. The streets were dark and almost empty but for a few stragglers on their way home.

"I'm exhausted." Alec rubbed his forehead distractedly.

"He hasn't slept in three days," Anja explained.

"Thanks to you two, I had the nerve to put a stop to this. I can't thank you enough."

"It's Sonia who got the evidence." Oliver put his arm around her shoulder fondly.

"It's me who got him into this," she declared, "I had to do something." She leaned into Oliver's embrace, her arm going round him readily.

"Hmm." Alec's eyes narrowed. "I might be exhausted but I'm not brain dead, so would you kindly explain what the hell's going on between you two?"

Sonia stared at him, surprised. She hadn't thought about how Alec would react about her and Oliver.

Silence followed. Then Oliver's hand tightened on her shoulder and he drew her closer against him.

"Sonia and I finally got to meet, and, well, I think I can safely say we enjoyed each other's company."

She nodded her agreement and he smiled down at her.

"I hope you don't object, Alec."

Silence struck again. Sonia was stunned into it. The two men were eyeing each other like territorial big cats. It never would have occurred to her that they would be that way over her.

Alec shook his head. "I should give you a good pasting." His expression was deadpan. "But you're lucky that I'm too knackered to do anything." He laughed. "In fact, all I can think of is how made up The Widow Harmond will be by the news."

Sonia groaned then laughed. "We can use it to take the attention off your run-in with the police."

As the tension broke, the men shook hands and the women hugged.

"I'm sorry I have no room for you to stay over with us, but my flat is so small," Anja said. "I feel so bad."

Sonia shook her head. "Please, don't. We'll find a hotel."

"Oh no. I'll tell the taxi driver the address of my uncle's hotel. I'll give you a note for him and you will have a free room."

Sonia caught a few glimpses of the woman her brother had fallen for, strong, beautiful and friendly—and a doctorate in politics. The Widow Harmond was going to be in for quite a few shocks pretty soon. She looked at Oliver. Would they really be one of them?

They climbed into the first taxi that pulled up. Alec and Anja waved them off, and the driver sped away, following the directions Anja had given him, past the Charles Bridge that led from the old town to the area called the lesser town, passing the moonlit gothic buildings lining the riverbank.

She rested against Oliver in the dark interior of the taxi, and his fingers stroked the back of her neck. She savored the feeling, savored the very outline of his thigh as it pressed against hers and his arms wrapped around her. She stroked her fingers up his shirt, searching for his body beneath, feeling the firm muscle that moved under her hands, his body as responsive to hers as she was to him. She breathed his scent, the fragrance that whispered passion to her body.

"You feel so good," she whispered as she rested her head on his chest.

He squeezed her and kissed the top of her head.

She glanced out at the passing streets. The lights blurred into one another as the car sped past, a streak of orange, green, blue light. Too bright. She wanted intimacy.

His hand stirred on her hip, and she looked up at him. The lights flickered on his face and showed the intensity in his eyes. What would happen between them when they were alone? What would be said?

The hotel was in a cramped side street and they rang the bell three times as Anja had instructed. A light flicked on over the doorway and a tall, sleepy-faced man appeared a minute later. He rubbed at his stubbly beard while he read the note and then broke into a grin, nodding.

"English, like Alec, yes?"

That touched her so much she felt like crying. "Yes," she smiled. "Like Alec."

"Welcome, welcome, English-like-Alec." He led them inside, bolting the outside door and plucking a key from a row of hooks nearby, he led the way up the narrow staircase to their room.

Then, finally, they were alone.

Oliver stood in the doorway, watching her. She walked into the room looking at the furnishings to distract herself from the intensity of his stare.

Sparsely furnished, the room was decorated in bright sunflower yellow paint, with a high ceiling and an old stone dado rail running around the wall. The bed was high and plump with sky-blue quilts and pillows. She stared at it, picturing them there. Would this be their last night together? Would he want to be with her afterwards, or had this only been a fling during this investigation? Was there more to it for him too?

He still stood at the door, looking only at her. She could hear her heart rushing in her ears, the tension between them palpable. She walked over to the window, looking down at the street with its haphazard leaning buildings outlined in the moonlight, and set her bag down on the wooden cabinet.

When she heard him finally click the door shut, she turned to face him. What was he going to say? Did sorting it out between them mean he'd tell her it was goodbye after tonight? If so, could she hold it together?

He sighed. "I want to hold you in my arms, desperately want to make love to you, but we need to get a few things straightened out." He threw the keys onto the bed. "Sonia, I wasn't trying to push you away when I took you to the club." He closed on her, his hands reaching for her arms. "I might not have been what you call a reliable sort up to now, but I'm disappointed you thought I was that shallow."

She shrugged, somehow stripped defenseless. Things between them had become naked and real.

"Okay, I jumped to conclusions, but I was kind of.. hurt." She was falling fast more like. Just looking into Oliver's sharp green eyes could make her heart miss a beat. "I was wrong about you and I apologize."

She knew he felt something for her, after that thing with Alec where he claimed her, no matter what the consequences. She just didn't know how deeply he cared or what she meant to him. "I just wondered if I was another challenge to you, like your other more challenging leisure activities."

He walked her back against the wall, his hands planted on either side of her head.

"You're not like any challenge I've ever experienced, Sonia Harmond." He bent and kissed her neck hungrily, his teeth marking her skin. He was taut with sexual tension. He was exuding testosterone. "I want you. I want more time with you. I want more than this."

Her body gave a great pang of longing, her heart brimming with hope. "I do too." Her hands were on his chest, her body beginning to melt. The need was so strong, so reciprocal.

"I don't think I'll ever get enough of you." His voice was hoarse with emotion. He kissed her, his mouth hungry and demanding, grazing her lips with his. "I want you, Sonia," he murmured. He kissed her face and her neck, his hands roving over her, clutching desperately at her body as if he'd never let her go.

She took a deep, trembling breath. Through his jeans, his cock was large and hard. The tension between them was unbearably high, so much need to give and to take.

She wanted to wrap herself around him and take him deep inside.

He tore his mouth away from her neck. "*Now*," he demanded. "I have to be inside you, right now."

She heard him unzip his jeans. He pulled his cock free and ran his hand over the length of it as she watched, his free hand urgently plucking a condom from his pocket.

"Oh, yes," she whispered, and the emotional and physical need pumped right through her. After what he'd said, she needed him to fuse with her there, deep in her essential womanhood. She was racked with desire for that connection.

He moved his fist on his cock, his jaw tight with restraint. "Pull up your skirt," he whispered. The look he gave her was dark with lust. "I want you right here, against the wall."

Spellbound, she moved slowly, pulling up her skirt, her lips slightly parted in anticipation.

His hands smoothed over her hair and roved down into the niche of her waist, around her hips, to her bottom. He stripped her panties down her thighs. With one mighty arm, he grabbed and lifted her, and she wrapped her legs around his waist.

"I'm going to show you exactly how much I want you," he said, the shaft of his erection hard against her sex.

She leaned her shoulders back against the wall and squirmed and whimpered, pushing against him. He pinned her body with his hands on her hips, lifting her onto his cock. He eased inside her, her hips angled to take him in, her flesh melting onto the hard shaft.

"You're so hot," he uttered, and eased deeper, her body anchored on his cock.

He was so deep inside her, she was thoroughly possessed. She hummed her pleasure aloud, her head falling back against the wall. He arched against her, kissing her face, his hands on her buttocks holding her locked into place.

"I want you so much." He thrust deep and hard.

She moaned, her entire core on fire with sensation, her sex pounding its response.

He thrust again, harder, deeper, his cock huge and demanding. "Do you know now? Do you know how much? Can you feel it?"

"Yes," she managed, her head rolling, her sex clutching at him, over and over. "Yes, Oliver."

"I don't want to be with anyone else, only you," he said through gritted teeth as he thrust again, "and I want to make love to you all the time, so you better be ready for more of this."

Her body was shuddering on the brink of orgasm, her strength and self-control submerged into his will, his words sending her closer to the dizzy edge. "Oliver," she murmured, "I'm coming."

He reacted. He rammed her up against the wall, thrusting faster, his cock fit to burst. She latched her legs around his hips and he rode her hard. Her fingernails dug into his shoulders, her hair tumbling down. Her sex was awash, her thighs wet, her core in spasm. When Oliver came, his cock churning up inside her sensitive flesh, she all but passed out, her body adrift in tidal waves of intense pleasure.

❧✿❧

She peered at herself in the bathroom mirror. It seemed far too early in the morning to be up, after everything that had happened, but she wanted to phone Alison at her office and explain everything herself. The British Consulate rep had promised her he would contact the office on her behalf, but she felt she owed Alison a call.

What would she say? *Hey, I did have a wild weekend. And oh, by the way, our boss is part of an international crime syndicate and I have just helped to bring him down.*

She stared at her reflection. "Who'd have thought it?" she murmured to herself, trying to put some order into her hair with her fingers.

"Sonia, you might want to see this," Oliver called from the bed, where she'd had immense difficulty extracting herself from his arms.

She wandered back to find him propped up against the pillows, the sheet strewn lazily across his hips. He looked both languorous and dangerous, like a lion about to stretch and pounce. He gestured at the TV with the remote.

"Breaking news."

She saw that he'd found the BBC world service news. Her jaw dropped. There on the screen behind the newscasters head was Tarquin's publicity photo. She was so shocked, she could hardly take in what the newscaster was saying.

"A large quantity of automatic weapons has been seized at an abandoned warehouse on the Czech border and further locations are under investigation. A Scotland Yard spokesman has informed us that the haul is part of a multi-million pound arms trade, and that a senior British Government Officer, Tarquin Smythe, may have been involved. Mr. Smythe, a chief European liaison officer, is being questioned regarding involvement in a European crime syndicate working to sell illegal arms overseas. Arrests have made in three countries. We will have more news on this story as it breaks."

They cut to the weather and Oliver flicked off the TV and patted the bed. "I think you're too late. Your friend, Alison, will be far too busy following the news to answer your call."

"I can't believe it," she whispered, the immensity of what they'd been part of hitting her. "The whole thing was much bigger than I realized."

"I know." He looked at her with a serious expression. He'd been protecting her all along—she realized that now. To him, it may have been like the everyday, but to her it was like the unimaginable. He'd guided her through it without making her feel naïve or silly, and that, together with what had developed between them, meant the world to her.

"I thought it would be finished and gone, when we handed over the evidence. Silly of me, I guess?"

He sat up and reached for her. "Big problems tend to have a few aftershocks, you know, like when a pebble hits a pond."

She swallowed. He was still leading her, gently, but leading her to an understanding of the situation. "Are you trying to tell me that it's not over yet?"

"In essence it is, but there will be more stuff to deal with soon." There was a dark shadow at the back of his eyes. "More interviews when we get home, maybe the media to deal with as well, when it all comes out."

She gave a weak laugh. "I have to admit the thought of another day like yesterday makes me want to stay in Prague and hide away here forever."

"Don't worry, I'll be with you for as long as you want me to be. I promise."

Her breath caught in her throat. To hear him say that meant so much. She lifted his hand and kissed his palm. "Thank you," she whispered, and climbed back into bed beside him. She knew how hard it was for him to give her that promise, that commitment, and she wanted to show him how much it meant to her. Climbing over him, she moved her body against his until he groaned with need, then she made slow, sweet love to him, body, heart and soul.

## *Chapter Nine*

The taxi slowed to a halt. "Avenue Court, Western Avenue, yes?"

"Yes, thank you," Alison replied to the cabbie when he put the light on. "Just give us a minute." She turned back to Sonia. "Are you going to be okay? Would you like me to come in with you for a while?"

Sonia looked at the front door. A week had gone by since they had last pulled up in a taxi here together, and what a week it had been. This would be her first night in her own bed. She'd stayed at Oliver's place for the rest of the week, but it was time to get things back to some semblance of normality, despite the news that Tarquin had been granted bail the day before.

"I'll be fine. You just get yourself home."

Alison had been there for her all week, when Oliver couldn't be present, and she'd needed it. Today's debriefing with Tarquin's senior manager had been more harrowing than all the other interviews put together. But she'd come through it, and as Oliver had predicted, she'd gained a lot of respect and a possible promotion out of the matter, if she wanted it.

"I just want life to get back to normal, put it all behind me."

"Not altogether, surely?" Alison winked.

Sonia smiled. "No, not altogether, not the part about Oliver. I wouldn't change that for the world." She glanced at her watch then looked over at the front door again. "Oliver will be here soon but it's been such a hell of a week, I just wanted to go home."

"Call me if you need anything. I can be back here in five minutes."

They hugged goodbye and Sonia waved her off before pulling her jacket closer around her shoulders. The evening was getting cool; the sun was low in the sky. She turned towards her flat, hitching her bag up onto her shoulder.

She heard the figure step out behind her, emerging from the bushes and her blood froze. She yelped when her right arm was seized behind her back.

"Keep quiet, bitch."

Pain ripped through her shoulder. She turned her head fractionally and met his glacial eyes, his mouth tight with resentment. It was Tarquin, and he had a gun wedged into her back.

"Don't even think about it."

"What the hell do you want?"

"Make one more sound and you'll give me a good excuse to use this. Get inside." He nudged her in the direction of the building with the gun.

Her heart was racing, her mind ablaze. She staggered towards the steps. As she did, her bag slipped off her shoulder and before she knew what she was doing she'd instinctively twisted and hurled it around to hit him on the head.

She overbalanced and fell. A gunshot rang out. Blinded by fear, she felt him grab for her and he hauled her back to her feet. She saw that her bag had hit the pavement, her stuff spilling out. And next to it was his gun.

She wrenched free and darted away but he grabbed her by her hair, twisting it in one hand, while the other covered her mouth, forcing her to swallow her scream. When he jerked on her hair, she used the pain to help her fight, to defend herself. She thrashed her arms and legs, making it as difficult as possible for him to keep a grip on her. Tarquin wasn't going to win; he was never going to win this battle.

"You bloody bitch," he said as he struggled to keep her under control.

In the distance she heard shouts, an alarm being raised. A figure racing toward them caught her eye, *a familiar figure*. She bit hard onto Tarquin's fingers then twisted round and kicked him in the groin and watched as he crumpled. Oliver raced over, ducked down and grabbed his arms, pulling them behind his back, a pair of handcuffs locking them into place.

"Nice move, Tarquin, your bail is over as of now."

Holding tightly onto Tarquin, Oliver looked at her briefly, as if reassuring himself she was okay, then pulled his phone out of his pocket to call for assistance.

She panted, catching her breath then rubbed her head.

Tarquin was splayed on his knees, staring up at her with wild eyes. "Bitch," he muttered again.

He was thoroughly evil. She could see it all too clearly now. He'd been willing to get involved in the sale of arms and he'd used her brother as a shield for his criminal actions. All for money.

And she'd got in the way of his plans. His expression was filled with venom. There was madness there in his eyes too, and she knew she should have been afraid. But this wasn't the same Sonia Harmond that had stood in this spot the week before. This was a very different Sonia Harmond.

Was there anything as richly pleasurable as this, she wondered as she lay in Oliver's arms, soaking up every drop of love he offered her, every ounce of the blissful afterglow that surrounded them.

He raised his head from her neck where he'd been planting gentle kisses, and propped himself on one elbow wedged into the pillows.

"Are you feeling okay now?"

"Oh, yes, more than okay, blissfully happy and... well, I know we've got the court case and all, but it feels like it's over now."

"Yes, I know what you mean." He was stroking her, his fingers trailing from her neck to waist, circling her breasts, teasing her taut nipples before passing on again.

"Deep down, I think I had to see him in the flesh. It's weird, but I'm kind of glad it happened."

"The result is he won't be able to bother us again."

The dark shadow at the back of his eyes had gone. It had been there all week, and she had finally worked out what it meant. "You knew that was going to happen, didn't you?"

"I didn't know, but it was a possibility. Anger and the need for revenge do strange, irrational things to people. He's made it worse for himself, much worse, but he couldn't resist the temptation to regain control in some small way."

"Why didn't you tell me?"

"Because it might not have happened, and you didn't need any more stress."

"Sometimes sharing information is necessary."

Silence followed. This wasn't just about Tarquin; they both knew that. This was about what was happening between them.

"Do you always work alone?" she added.

He considered his reply carefully. "No, I work in a team of people working alone." He sighed. "You've got me there, love. I'm sorry. It's just the way it's always been." He shrugged one shoulder.

She laughed, pushing her head back into the pillows, languorous with love even now. "And you say I'm the one with the trust issue."

"I know. It's hard to make changes to accommodate this..." His voice trailed off.

"This? What is 'this,' Oliver?"

He meshed his fingers in her hair. "Our relationship. How I feel about you is a big change for me. I'm not used to being part of a couple. I love you Sonia Harmond and I want to be with you."

She knew that and that's what made her brave, in every way. "I love you too, Oliver Eaglestone. I want all that as well, but we have to start out right. Share with me, share your life with me, your thoughts. Share what's in your mind and heart."

He took a deep breath. "I'll try, right now." He stared at her silently for an age. "Sonia, I want you to be mine. I want you to be my wife."

She couldn't help smiling. "Oliver, is that a proposal?"

"Yes, I guess it is." He tugged her closer, his hands prying her thighs open. "Was it too soon to ask, do you think?" His fingers slid into her hot, wet niche, where she was still fluttering with sensation from their recent lovemaking.

"No, I don't think so." She could see her own pleasure reflected in his eyes. She loved him so much that her heart was brimming.

"So, what's your answer?" he urged as he climbed over her.

"Hmm, well, I don't know," she mused, teasingly. "Unlike you, I am a team player by nature, so I should check with my team."

"Your team?" He drew back, startled.

She chuckled. "Yes, my girlfriends, Alec, The Widow Harmond—"

"Say 'yes' to me and say it right now." He nudged open her thighs, settling between them. "I am part of your team now and I…" He paused while he eased his cock inside her, rolling his hips back and forth fractionally, baiting her for more. "…I insist."

She moaned softly, then bit her lip and locked her legs around him, drawing him deeper with a quick upward movement of her hips.

He groaned deeply. "Please say yes," he whispered as he moved against her, riding her to the hilt.

"Yes, Oliver, I'll marry you." She grabbed the struts on the headboard and began to work her hips against his.

He closed his eyes for a moment. "That sounds so good, and *that* feels so good." His eyes flashed open and his smile was triumphant.

"You see, isn't everything better when you work in a team?" She laughed with pleasure when their hips moved together again.

"Oh God, yes," he replied and when he met and matched her move for move, she was filled with sheer joy.

She couldn't have been happier. In fact, falling for trouble had turned out to be the best thing that had ever happened to her.

## *About the Author:*

*Saskia Walker is a British writer who lives with her real life hero, Mark, and their big black cat in the north of England, close to the beautiful landscape of the Yorkshire moors. Because of her parents' nomadic tendencies, Saskia grew up traveling the globe—an only child with a serious book habit. She dreamed of being a writer when she first read romance at the age of 12 and finally began writing seriously in the late 1990s. Since then she's had short fiction published on both sides of the pond and is thrilled to be the first British author writing for Red Sage. She also writes erotic romance for loose-id.com.*

# The Disciplinarian

*by Leigh Court*

## *To My Reader:*

What happens when a headstrong young Victorian wife is sent to London's notorious Disciplinarian for instructions in wifely obedience? His surprising lessons soon have her writhing in pleasure instead of pain! Enjoy!

# Chapter One

"Clarissa, I'm sending you to The Disciplinarian."

From the doorway of the sitting room in their London townhouse, Clarissa Babcock stared in surprise at her husband. *The Disciplinarian?* Surely Charles couldn't be talking about the notorious legend who was said to turn difficult wives into dutiful spouses using whatever means necessary? No. Charles was reading the paper, so she must simply have misheard him from behind the voluminous pages of newsprint. "I'm sorry, Charles. What did you say?"

"I said I'm sending you to The Disciplinarian."

Clarissa gasped. It couldn't be true! If anyone was the *difficult* partner in this marriage, it was Charles. A seed of worry planted itself in her stomach. The Disciplinarian was a man universally feared by all Victorian women. She took a step into the room. "Charles—"

"Good," he interrupted, putting down the paper. "I see you're dressed."

"What?" Clarissa glanced distractedly at her serviceable grey carriage dress and reached up to finger the brim of her peacock-feathered hat.

Of course she was dressed! Charles had made plans for them for the weekend. "I'm dressed for our trip to the country," she said, then hesitated as a note of uncertainty crept into her voice. "For the Smithson's house party."

"There is no house party, Clarissa. That was simply a ruse to make sure you'd be ready to travel this morning. You may be going somewhere in the country, but I myself will be spending the weekend in town. With my mistress."

"Charles!"

He stood and crossed to the window, parting the curtain an inch to look out onto the street. He obviously saw something there beyond the glass, because he nodded in approval. "In point of fact, I don't know exactly *where* you're going, Clarissa. Nor do I care, so long as you come back biddable."

*Biddable?* Clarissa swallowed hard. Theirs had always been a difficult marriage. It had been arranged by her father, who'd traded Clarissa's substantial dowry in return for Charles's minor title, and who never tired of reminding Clarissa that she had *married up*.

Unfortunately, Clarissa didn't discover until *after* her wedding vows that Charles was a hard, dictatorial man with a quick temper. Over the last two years, his bullying ways had turned her from a young girl who had innocently expected to find love in marriage, into a woman who'd learned that wedding vows did not necessarily guarantee a happy-ever-after. But this? This was too much. "Charles, please be serious. You can't mean—"

"Enough!" He turned from the window, and there was a dangerous look on his face as he strode purposely across the room to her. "You see? This is exactly the reason. Your obstinacy. Your intractability. I am your husband, and you will do as I say! Come with me." He gripped her hard by the upper arm and began to drag her toward the sitting room door.

Fear now bloomed riotously in Clarissa's stomach. It took all her courage—and all her strength—to dig in her heels. "Wait, please, let's discuss this—"

Charles abruptly let go of her arm, drew back his hand and slapped her right across the face. It was the first time in their marriage that he had actually struck her, and she was so stunned that before she realized it, Charles had succeeded in dragging her out of the room, across the townhouse foyer, past their gaping butler, Hawkins, and down the front steps toward a waiting coach.

Clarissa ignored both her stinging cheek and the look of pity from the servant, and tried her best to hold her head up and back erect as Charles resolutely forced her forward. He had never been able to break her spirit, despite his verbal—and now his physical—abuse. She wouldn't let his malice break her now.

He may have crushed her girlish dreams, but no one could take her pride away from her.

As they approached the street, Clarissa saw a coat of arms gracing the side of a shiny black carriage and a man standing next to it. Surely this couldn't be the mysterious *Disciplinarian!* Not only was he taking no pains to hide his identity—a crest of two swords entwined by a single white rose was in plain view—but he was also an obvious gentleman. In fact, Clarissa realized with some surprise that he was the handsomest man she had ever seen. Tall, black haired and blue-eyed, he was elegantly dressed in a dark blue morning coat, paisley waistcoat, black trousers and polished black boots.

And he seemed to be frowning at Charles's rough treatment of her. She began to breathe a little easier, then nearly choked on her husband's next words.

"Clarissa," Charles said acidly, drawing her to an abrupt halt and indicating the handsome stranger. "Allow me to introduce you to The Disciplinarian."

*The Disciplinarian.*

Jared Ashworth saw Clarissa Babcock's reaction reflected in her huge eyes as she stared at him. He saw her shock, then her fear, then her rage. But he was used to all those reactions, and it was easy to keep his own face carefully blank, because he knew by the time he was through with her he would see yet another look in her eyes.

*Gratitude.*

"Get into his carriage, Clarissa," Babcock ordered.

She gasped and her gaze swung around to her husband. "Charles, please—"

"Get in the carriage, woman!" Babcock roared, forcibly dragging her toward Jared's waiting coach. She was struggling outright now, her eyes frantically searching for something, someone, even a passer-by who might help her. Jared was disgusted by Charles Babcock's use of brute force, but he knew that even though people might stop to stare at this little drama, not one of them would come to Clarissa's aid, since Charles Babcock had every right to treat his wife as he saw fit.

It was, unfortunately, the way of things.

Jared's team of horses stamped and nickered nervously in their harnesses, sensing Clarissa's fear as her husband shoved her up the carriage steps. "How long will this take?" Babcock demanded of him.

"The four days we discussed," Jared answered calmly. "She will be sent back to you when she's ready."

"Just send her back biddable," he growled. "I want a proper wife. I've had enough of her recalcitrance."

That obviously was too much for the woman in the carriage. Her cheeks flamed with anger. "You hit me and you're surprised that I'm recalcitrant?"

"Enough!" Babcock roared at her. "You have the gall to defy me even now, when you see where your defiance has led you? Stubborn, willful woman! Obstinate chit!"

His complexion turned an unhealthy shade of red as he jerked his head toward Jared and took three strides away from the carriage. Jared followed him, out of earshot of the woman in the coach.

"I've changed my mind," Babcock growled.

Jared's eyebrow shot up in surprise. He'd never had a client back out of a case before. "You no longer want me to instruct her?"

Babcock's voice dropped to a dangerous hiss. "Oh, I want you to instruct her all right," he said. "I want you to teach her one particular lesson. Cold as ice she is, the frigid bitch. Two years of marriage and still no children. A man shouldn't have to work so hard to get an heir on his own wife!"

It took all Jared's control to cover his shock as he shook his head. "That's impossible. I don't *sexually* instruct—"

"You do now." Charles Babcock grabbed him by the lapels of his morning coat. "Either you warm her up so that I can plant my seed and be done with my duty, or I just may kill her with my own hands and find another, more *agreeable* wife. Is that understood?"

Jared stared at the dangerous look in Babcock's eye. He meant what he'd said. Clarissa Babcock's life was literally in Jared's hands. He couldn't possibly leave her to the mercy of her husband's anger. "Take your hands off me, sir," Jared said coldly.

Babcock gave him a final shake before abruptly releasing him. "I'll be spending the weekend with my mistress in town. At least there I know I'll have a warm reception! You have four days. I'll expect her home Tuesday next."

## Chapter Two

Jared climbed into his carriage, dropped heavily onto the padded bench seat, and slammed the coach door. He was furious. Furious at Charles Babcock's outrageous demand, furious at himself for not outright refusing it, and furious at the woman seated across from him for putting him in this difficult position.

He knocked hard on the carriage roof and the driver started off.

He needed to think.

Charles Babcock was a brute of a man, and probably worse as a husband, but Jared had dealt with boorish husbands countless times before. So why hadn't he patently refused Babcock's shocking order to *warm up* his wife?

Jared knew full well why he hadn't. He'd seen that look in a man's eye once before. Jared's own sister had been beaten to death by her husband in a domestic rage. He couldn't have left Clarissa to the same possible fate.

How in blazes was he going to deal with this new twist to his already scandalous profession?

"Where are we going?" Clarissa demanded.

Jared heard the edge of fear in her voice. Worry had replaced the fury that had been on her face a moment ago. But he was in no mood to assuage her fear; he was just as worried over how he was going to deal with this impossible situation. "You know I can't tell you that."

She looked frantically out the window, studying the passing scenery. "I can clearly see we're on the south road, headed in the direction of Kent."

She was clever, this one. No one knew the true identity of The Disciplinarian. He'd worked very hard these last three years to keep it that way. The crest on his carriage assisted with his guise of The Disciplinarian. And his students were always picked up at their homes, so no one knew where he practiced his particular *lessons.*

He leaned over and silently pulled the shades down over both carriage windows. "And now you see nothing."

She lunged suddenly for the lever on the carriage door, but Jared didn't even bother to react. The far one she found solidly locked, and the door handle next to him he knew she wouldn't dare try for.

She looked at him and swallowed hard. "Are you truly The Disciplinarian?"

He studied her for a moment. She was spirited, clever and obviously brave, but he had a job to do and he needed time to think through his options, to determine how he was going to deal with this particular case. "Yes, I am. So I would highly recommend you sit quietly and not make this harder on yourself than it need be."

She gasped at that. "Harder on myself? What could be worse than to be given over into the hands of a perfect stranger in order to be taught a lesson in how to be a proper, biddable wife?"

His effort to silence her had obviously failed miserably. "Madam," he snapped, "if I'm to obey your husband, you can be certain I will be using more than just my hands!"

By the stunned look in her eye, he knew she envisioned that he meant to beat her, break her spirit, and send her back to her husband a meek, submissive spouse. Thank goodness she hadn't overheard what her husband had *actually* asked him to do.

If this had been one of his usual cases, he would immediately deny that he'd beat her. He could truthfully assure her that The Disciplinarian had never yet laid a hand in anger on any woman. But he didn't know what he'd have to do to Clarissa Babcock in order to satisfy her husband's outrageous demand, so he offered her no words of assurance.

"Move to the center of the seat," he said.

"Excuse me?"

"Slide to your left, to the middle of the bench."

She frowned at the request, but did as he asked.

"Good. Now spread the skirts of your gown out across the seat."

Her back straightened in obvious indignation. "I beg your pardon!"

"Spread the skirts of your gown wide," he repeated slowly. The words were low and sweet, stern but honeyed; an order meant to let her know there was no room for disobedience. It was his *Disciplinarian* voice. "Fan your skirt out over the bench."

She hesitated, but she obviously heard the tone of command in his voice. And the set of his face should tell her that he was not used to being disobeyed. He saw her swallow, and then she slowly spread her skirts, her hands shaking slightly. He quickly put one booted foot on each side of her, trapping her skirts against the padded wooden seat, so that if she tried to move, he would wake. With that, he pulled his hat down over his eyes. "It's a long ride to where we're going. I recommend you get some sleep."

Clarissa Babcock didn't know whether to scream in outrage or shrink in abject terror.

*She was a prisoner of The Disciplinarian.*

The mysterious man seated across from her had been given free rein by her husband to use whatever means necessary to mold her into Charles's image of a dutiful wife. *Whatever means necessary...*

She could only wonder at the awful tools The Disciplinarian must employ. She glanced at him across the carriage. Damn the man! How could he possibly be sleeping, after essentially kidnapping someone against her will?

She looked down at the booted male feet that trapped her skirts and held her captive. His black polished Hessians bespoke a man of wealth and class, as did the rest of his clothing. Such a dichotomy to his base profession.

She and every other Victorian woman had heard of The Disciplinarian. She had to admit, though, that whispered rumors and wild innuendo were the basis of her knowledge, since she had never actually met a woman who had been subject to his lessons. But the charges laid at his feet were shocking and scandalous nonetheless.

He was the perfect threat used by husbands to keep their wives in line. So much so, in fact, that she hadn't believed The Disciplinarian really existed until this moment.

She watched as his head bobbed gently with the rhythm of the carriage. It seemed he truly was asleep. She waited another long minute to be sure, and then glanced cautiously toward the window. Slowly, carefully, she reached out her left arm as far as it would go, keeping one wary eye on The Disciplinarian's sleeping form. She extended her hand toward the carriage shade, but it was just beyond her grasp. She wiggled her fingers, as if that might give her the extra inch she needed, but to no avail. Damn! She couldn't even peek from behind the window shade to catch a glimpse of their route, to watch for a familiar landmark. And she was too aware that leaning toward the shade even slightly would pull on the skirts trapped beneath his boot and risk waking him.

She realized suddenly that he'd known she would attempt this. It was why he'd made her move to the center of the seat.

Her arm fell back to her side in defeat. She was well and truly trapped.

Desperately, her eyes darted around the inside of the carriage. Besides the flimsy reticule attached to her wrist, she had nothing she could use as a weapon against him. One of her hatpins? Her fingernails, perhaps? Pathetic! He could easily overpower her. And it seemed the horrible man didn't even carry a cane that she might turn on him!

With the carriage doors locked, the blinds beyond her reach, and no chance of overpowering him, she had nothing else to keep her from dissolving into true hysteria but to study the sleeping form across from her and look for a weakness there.

She found none.

His muscled legs were long and lean, outlined clearly beneath trousers that were stretched tight in his awkward position. There was strength and power in those legs, and she swallowed hard as her eyes noted how closely his calves and booted feet were positioned next to her upper thighs. Their bodies were almost touching. Scandalous!

Her eyes traveled farther up, quickly moving along his legs and past his groin to settle on his chest. His arms were folded tightly across it, but she could still see how his broad chest filled out the paisley waistcoat, and how his biceps strained beneath his coat sleeves. This was a body built for force, for power. He was pure, masculine strength.

This was no London dandy, despite the stylish cut of his clothes.

He had stood his ground with Charles earlier, an explicit warning in his cold words, even though the two men had kept their voices too low for her to hear most of their conversation. She knew there were few men who dared to stand up to Charles when he was in a rage, but looking at The Disciplinarian, Clarissa did not doubt that this man was one of them.

Her gaze slid up to his face.

She thought back to her first impression of him, how she'd thought him so handsome with his thick black hair and sculpted, aristocratic features. Even with his eyes now closed, she could remember what a deep, ocean blue they were. And his mouth, which earlier had been pulled down into a frown, was relaxed now in sleep. His lips were full. Inviting, almost. Yes, he was a terribly handsome man.

But there was no sign of weakness in him.

So she desperately prayed he was not as terrible as his reputation implied.

With a ragged sigh, she leaned back against the carriage seat and closed her eyes.

Jared took the opportunity to watch Clarissa Babcock through his thick lashes.

She'd wisely given up on trying to look out the carriage window and had spent the last few minutes looking at him instead. *Intimately* looking. He'd found it hard to control the reaction of his male body as her eyes started with his legs and moved slowly up the length of him in a brazen inspection of his form. Thank goodness she hadn't paused at his groin; he would have had to call a quick halt to her little scrutiny if she had. No, she hadn't paused there, but she'd blatantly lingered in her examination of his legs and chest, and when her eyes finally came up to sweep his face he felt sure she would realize he was awake, even through his thick lashes and under the shadowed brim of his hat. But instead, she'd continued to stare at him, with all the gall and curiosity of a child.

Bloody hell, even a whore didn't assess a man's body so boldly!

What did she find so fascinating? Or was she simply sizing up her opponent?

Ironically, her lingering inspection of him gave him a certain hope. Perhaps she was not lacking sexual feelings after all. Perhaps she was only unresponsive to her husband's variety of it. The brute force kind.

Maybe there *was* a way to instruct her that would not involve coercion.

As a test, he moved his booted feet closer until his calves were actually touching her upper thighs, hard muscle against soft flesh, capturing her in a suggestive grip.

She gasped and her eyes flew open. She stared at his face, as if trying to determine if he had simply shifted in his sleep. Then her gaze dropped anxiously to his calves, and he saw her breasts rise and fall with her agitated breathing as she stared at their intimate contact. But after a while, as if convinced he'd settled back into sleep—or trying desperately to convince *herself* of it—she closed her eyes and leaned back again against the carriage seat.

*His touch had affected her.* She was not immune to physical contact. That would bode well for his lessons.

He took a moment to study her face. She might actually be pretty if she would relax that pinched expression she wore, ease up on the scowl that made her lips too thin, and maybe wear her hair in a style that was less severe than that tight bun. Certainly her pale blue eyes were a dramatic contrast to those waves of black hair.

In the end, it didn't matter what she looked like. Or what any of the women sent to him looked like. He had a job to do and he always did it to the best of his ability. But he would try especially hard with this one, since he knew what was at stake for her.

Her very life.

It had been a lucky thing he'd come himself today, and seen first-hand the full extent of the threat that Charles Babcock posed. Jared almost never went in person to pick up the women sent to The Disciplinarian. There was always the chance he'd be recognized, even this far from home. Then, there was always an embarrassing scene at the handover, with the women screaming or crying. Or shouting, as Clarissa Babcock had done. Though he hated the traumatic event, it helped him in planning his lessons to know how each woman reacted.

Only his work was greatly different this time. There was nothing else to be done but to tell Clarissa what her husband wanted The Disciplinarian to do to her.

*Sexually warm her up.*

It was late afternoon when the carriage finally came to a halt. Clarissa had no idea how many hours had passed or how many miles they'd eventually traveled. All her attention during the trip had been focused on trying to stay calm, fighting the rising panic over what she feared was in store for her.

The sun was low in the sky when The Disciplinarian handed her down out of the carriage in front of a lovely manor house. She frowned, thinking it an incongruous setting for a house of horrors. The picturesque, two story structure was nearly covered with climbing ivy, and the heady scent of blooming roses filled her nostrils. Set in a lush, green glen, the house looked peaceful, serene, perfectly at ease out here in the country.

For in the country they most certainly were—Clarissa could not see another house within eyeshot. Certainly not within screaming distance.

"Rose Cottage," The Disciplinarian offered.

Clarissa's eyebrows shot up in surprise. The grand manor house was the farthest thing from a *cottage,* but its name made her look back at the coat of arms adorning the carriage.

Two crossed swords entwined by a single white rose.

"Yes," he acknowledged. "That rose is famous in these parts."

"What parts would that be?" she asked, trying to sound innocent.

The Disciplinarian gave her a wry smile and a shake of his head. "This is my man, Soames," he said with a wave of his hand, indicating an older man who was coming down the front stairs to meet them. "He will take you to your chamber. I'll give you an hour to freshen up, and then we'll have an early dinner. You must be starving, since we didn't stop for luncheon. And exhausted, too, after today's—*activity.* I'll go speak with the cook."

He gave her a short, solicitous bow and took the stairs two at a time, disappearing into the house with an energy that belied his having spent the last few hours in a cramped and uncomfortable carriage. She was left to stand with the servant Soames, having no luggage and knowing full well that the man knew exactly why she was here.

"Good day, ma'am," he said, giving her a polite nod. "This way if you please, ma'am." He turned to lead the way up the stairs.

Clarissa hesitated. This was the perfect moment to run, if she planned to run. But she saw that the carriage driver was watching her closely, and she knew she wouldn't get far. So with the same determined resolve she had called on during Charles's tirade this morning, she took a deep breath, picked up her skirts, and followed Soames into the house.

To her utter amazement, he led her to a charming bedroom on the second floor.

It was a perfect room, with a four-poster bed tucked snugly into a far corner, a small dining table near the door, bookshelves lining three walls, and an armoire with a full-length looking glass set next to a dressing table by the bed. Even her own room in London wasn't nearly as comfortably laid out as this.

She threw a confused look at Soames. She had been treated with every courtesy so far: The Disciplinarian, despite his intimate brush against her in the carriage, had been a perfect gentleman; his servant couldn't be more solicitous in his attentions; and the room she'd been brought to was not the hideous torture chamber she'd expected.

What was going on here?

But suddenly Soames bowed and backed out of the room, and she clearly heard the lock turn in the door.

She took two quick steps and rattled the knob, but the door was secure.

So. Whether by silken ties or by harsh rope, she was still a prisoner.

She fought to keep her panic down as she turned to examine the room more closely. The Disciplinarian had said she'd have an hour of privacy to 'freshen up' before he came with dinner. Perhaps in that hour she could find a way to escape. Or possibly not. Others before her must certainly have tried. She imagined that The Disciplinarian would not still be in business if he let hysterical wives flee without the *instruction* he'd been paid to give them.

Still, she had to try. She crossed to the window near the bed, surprised to find that the window rose easily. She'd half expected it to be nailed shut. But when she leaned her head out and looked down, she knew the reason. Any leap from this height was sure to cause injury—a broken leg or ankle at the very least.

With a sigh, she closed the window and paced the edges of the room. There was no poker for the fireplace, nothing obvious that she could use as a weapon. She walked past the bed, testing the mattress absently, noted the water closet—which was a surprise way out here in the country—and stopped at the small dining table, set with two high-backed chairs. The arms of the chairs sported four-inch high pineapple carvings, in the French style, at the ends of the armrests.

Everything in this room said the Disciplinarian was a man of wealth and taste. What, then, had driven him to such an unsavory profession? Was he simply a rogue, a bounder, a cad?

Whatever he was, he would be coming to her in less than an hour. She took off her hat and laid it gently on the dressing table next to the bed. Her gloves and reticule joined it. She visited the water closet to 'freshen up' as he had suggested, and then turned her attention to the books on the shelves. None of them was weighty enough to tempt her to consider throwing them at his head, but the titles amazed her in their depth and breadth of topics. History, geography, biography, social commentary, classical fiction.

No, there was nothing here she could use as a weapon, so she would just have to keep her eyes open for any opportunity that might present itself. But now more than ever, the man who imprisoned her was a puzzle. An enigma.

The sharp rap on the door, followed by the scrape of a key in the lock, set her heart hammering.

The Disciplinarian opened the door himself, followed closely by his man, Soames, who wheeled in a tray of covered platters. Despite her nerves, Clarissa took a breath, raised her chin, and crossed the room to meet him.

"Supper," was all he said.

Soames laid out both places, and The Disciplinarian came around the table to politely hold out her chair. Clarissa hesitated but then sat, the tantalizing aroma of the food calling to her rumbling stomach.

Soames bowed his way out of the room, and the two of them were alone.

"I hope you find the room comfortable," The Disciplinarian inquired.

Again, Clarissa couldn't stop the confusion from crossing her face. "Very comfortable. Thank you."

He nodded and lifted one of the silver covers. "May I?"

She looked at the steaming platter of veal smothered in a delicate brown sauce, and nodded. "Yes, please."

He helped them both to the meat, and then served out a generous portion of boiled potatoes and vegetables. He solicitously poured red wine into her glass and his own, and then dug into his meal.

She was amazed at his attempt at dinner conversation. He drew her into a discussion about politics, the new railway system, the plight of the working classes. He couldn't have been more attentive, treating her with surprising respect. If she had met him under different circumstances, she would have enjoyed his company. Found him very engaging. Very attractive.

At last, finished with his meal, he leaned back in his chair and studied her intently.

She swallowed hard at the look on his face. This was more what she expected. Supper was over, but he was staring at her as if she might be dessert, looking at her like a predator regards its prey. Had he just fattened her up for the kill?

"That will be all for tonight," he said, surprising her once again. He rose abruptly from the table. "You've had a long day. Your lessons will begin tomorrow."

As if on cue, there was a small knock on her door and Soames silently entered the room.

"How..." Clarissa said, standing up as the servant approached the table, "how on earth did he possibly know we were done?"

"I never allow more than an hour for dinner," was the odd reply. They watched as Soames cleared the dinner things off the table and onto the wheeled trolley, but The Disciplinarian put a hand on the man's shoulder as the servant made ready to roll the serving tray away. "Wait," he said, then turned to her and held out his hand. "The knife, Clarissa."

She looked at him, almost as shocked that he had taken the liberty to call her by her Christian name as by what he'd said. "I beg your pardon?"

"The dinner knife, please."

She bristled in outrage, but he calmly raised one eyebrow in question, daring her to deny it.

Reluctantly, Clarissa brought the knife out from between the folds of her skirt and bit her lower lip. Damn. She'd thought herself so clever! He hadn't even looked twice when she'd picked the knife up earlier to carve her veal. How could he possibly have noticed her hide it between the folds of her gown as she'd stood up when Soames had entered the room?

She grudgingly put it into his palm.

"Thank you," he said.

She watched as The Disciplinarian deposited the knife onto the trolley, and then held the door for Soames, who quickly exited the room.

The Disciplinarian crossed back over to her, and the unreadable look on his face made her pulse race. Had she angered him enough to make him change his mind? Would he beat her now after all?

"You said we were done for tonight," she reminded him, taking a small step back.

"We are," he agreed. "Would you like me to help you undress?"

She gasped at the outrageous comment. "*I beg your pardon!*"

"Calm yourself, Clarissa," he assured her in a low, soothing tone. "There is no lady's maid here to help you. I am simply offering to unhook or unlace or untie that which you cannot reach."

"I would rather sleep in my clothes!"

"For four days?" he said reasonably. "Come. There's a night rail in the armoire. Have I been anything but a gentleman today?"

"There's no one at all who can help me?" She looked at him with narrowed eyes, trying to figure out his intentions.

He put up his hands as if to reassure her. "I give you my word—"

"The word of a kidnapper... a, a cad!"

He looked at her pointedly. "I may be a *cad* in your opinion, but I'm no liar. I've said we are done for tonight. Turn around, Clarissa."

What he'd said was true. He'd been nothing but a gentleman, his man, Soames, nothing but a gentleman's gentleman. Still, he was The Disciplinarian, hired to transform her into a submissive wife. *By whatever means necessary.* He was a fool if he thought she'd cooperate in her own dubious training. And yet, she'd probably suffocate if she had to sleep in her tight corset...

"I give you my word," he repeated quietly.

She turned abruptly to present him with her back, holding herself ramrod straight.

He deftly went to work on the dozens of tiny buttons and loops of her dress, opening the gown to her waist. He kept his movements brisk, clinical, as if that would set her mind at ease. She shivered when he spread open the gown to give himself access to the laces of her corset, but again he was efficient and quick in his task, giving the ties just enough slack so that she could free herself after he left.

His job done, he stepped away from her. She turned to look at him, her arms crossed defensively across her chest as if she expected him to tear the gown off her.

"I will join you again for supper tomorrow evening," he said simply, giving her a quick bow before he turned and left the room.

Clarissa stared after him, speechless, and heard the key turn in the lock.

She wouldn't see him again until tomorrow night's meal? It was almost too impossible to believe! When were her lessons? When would he beat her?

This Disciplinarian was the most confusing man! Where she had expected coercion, he'd shown nothing but courtesy. Not force, but finesse. How could she defend herself against him when she didn't know what he was going to do? He hadn't behaved at all as she'd expected. She shivered, and it had nothing to do with the open back of her dress letting the cool air of the room onto her skin.

*There's a night rail in the armoire.*

Her breath caught. He was a fool if he thought she would shed her clothes, knowing there was no one to help her back into them tomorrow. She'd only allowed him to unbutton and unlace her in order to give herself some breathing room while she slept.

Still, curiosity got the better of her. She crossed the room to the armoire and threw open its doors. What she saw there made her gasp.

This was no serviceable piece of cotton nightwear.

The gown hanging there was a pale blue silk sheath in the Greek style—sleeveless, with a deep vee neck and an empire waist cinched with a dainty ribbon that tied just under the bust. The skirt flowed down from there in a gentle a-line shape to the ankles.

The gown was beautiful and delicate, but scandalous, too—it was slit high to the thigh on both sides.

She took it out and held it up for closer inspection. It was the loveliest thing she had ever seen.

She glanced toward the door and bit her lip. He had said he wouldn't be back until tomorrow evening, and he'd been as good as his word in everything he'd said so far. So he would never see her in this thin wisp of a garment, because she would be safely dressed once again in her many layers of proper clothing.

Why not indulge herself in this little luxury tonight?

She felt downright decadent as she slipped out of her clothes and into the cool silk. The luxurious material slid easily over her head and smoothed itself down around her body. There was something barbaric about being so very nearly naked. Gone were the constrictions of corset and protective layers of clothing. And gone with them, for a moment, were her inhibitions.

She twirled giddily around the room and caught sight of herself in the full-length looking glass set next to the armoire. She gasped at the reflection she saw there. The icy blue of the gown matched her eyes perfectly and flattered her figure as if it had been made for her. On a brazen whim, she tore at the pins in her hair and ran her fingers through it, freeing the long tresses until they tumbled around her shoulders and down her back.

Her breath caught. She looked like some glorious pagan goddess.

She should have regretted her action immediately. He had said there was no lady's maid in this place to help her, so there would be no one to put her hair to rights tomorrow. But instead of remorse, she felt exhilaration. Who cared, after all, if she looked like a banshee tomorrow? It would serve all these high-handed men right!

But tonight…

Tonight she stood in front of the mirror and admired herself for the first time in two years. Saw the young woman she had once been. Beautiful. Desirable. Happy. Before her father had coldly bartered her to make the best bargain he could on the marriage mart.

The gown flattered her figure outrageously and was truly beyond scandalous. Not only were her ankles showing, but as she turned this way and that, the gown swished and swirled to hide and reveal the delicate white skin of her calves and thighs. The caress of the silk bodice against her full breasts was making her nipples pucker, the effect blatantly obvious through the thin material.

She laughed in pure, outrageous delight. She was quite a temptation, if she did say so herself. Too bad she didn't have a man to tempt.

*A man like the terribly handsome Disciplinarian?*

She pushed that thought firmly from her mind and stayed at the mirror for several more minutes, before sighing and finally climbing into bed.

# Chapter Three

The smell of hot chocolate woke Clarissa.

She turned and stretched in the comfortable bed, snuggled deeper under the covers, and considered ignoring the tempting aroma.

Hot chocolate was a bad sign, after all. The only time that she allowed herself the sinful indulgence was when she had a particularly difficult day planned.

She sat up with a start, coming fully awake with the awful realization of the day that was actually in store for her.

*Your lessons will begin tomorrow.*

With a gasp, she looked around the room.

It was true. She was a prisoner of The Disciplinarian, locked up in one of his bedrooms. It hadn't been just a bad dream.

She jerked back the covers and felt herself blush scarlet. She had spent the night in the scandalous negligee he had provided! With a mortified cry, she pulled the covers up over her head and collapsed back onto the pillow, but the smell of the chocolate was too tempting to ignore.

She poked her head from under the damask spread and saw the serving tray at the side of her bed. Hot chocolate in a cup. A plate of delicately shirred eggs. Thin toast with a pot of butter.

Her stomach grumbled.

She sat up and looked around. The bedroom door was closed. Who had delivered the tray? Soames? The Disciplinarian himself? Had they seen her state of undress? As soon as she was finished with her meal, she would immediately dress again in her sensible clothes.

She propped the pillows behind her back and pulled the tray closer.

A sip of the delicious, rich chocolate helped to settle her nerves. The Disciplinarian had said he wouldn't be back until supper. For whatever reason, she believed him, so she felt she was safe for the moment.

She finished the chocolate before starting on the eggs, which were cooked to perfection. The toast was standing in a rack, to prevent it from getting soggy—a nice, elegant touch. She stared thoughtfully at the butter knife, but its blunt edge made her reject it as a potential weapon.

Besides, The Disciplinarian would surely check for it as soon as the tray was collected.

Once she had finished every crumb on the plate, she leaned back with a sigh. The meal had been delicious, the bed decadently comfy with its down-filled pillows and fine-woven sheets. So what was The Disciplinarian's strategy? To kill her with kindness? To lull her into a false sense of security before lowering the boom and beginning her painful *lessons*?

Whatever his plan, he wouldn't find a willing partner in her.

It was time to dress; time to gird herself against whatever the day might bring. She knew she'd feel more confident, protected even, once she had her corset and serviceable gray carriage gown back on. She glanced over at the chair by the dressing table and frowned. She could have sworn she'd left her gown and undergarments there last night.

She pushed aside the bedspread and stood up. She walked around to the foot of the bed, but her clothing was nowhere to be seen either on the rug or on the floor. In growing panic, she looked back toward the dressing table. Her hat, gloves and reticule were missing as well.

Unable to believe what her eyes were telling her, she flew to the armoire and threw open the doors, hoping against hope that Soames might have simply thought it was his duty to hang up her clothing when he'd come to deliver her breakfast.

The closet was bare.

She looked down in horror at the flimsy blue night rail that barely covered her body.

*The Disciplinarian had tricked her!*

She wanted to shout her outrage, no, she *would* shout her outrage, damn him! She flew to the door of her room and rattled the knob, then banged on the door with both fists. She shouted first for The Disciplinarian—using every unsavory name in her vocabulary—then, when her efforts went unanswered, she called stridently for Soames.

She yelled until she was hoarse, but no one came.

Finally exhausted, her rage spent, she dragged herself back to the bed and sat on the edge.

*So this is how it starts.*

He was deliberately putting her at a disadvantage. Making her feel vulnerable. Taking away even the false sense of comfort she might feel under the layers of her proper, protective clothing.

Or did he simply want to see her in this gown?

That thought gave her pause. He'd obviously wanted her to wear this. He had made such a point of mentioning the gown, made such a to-do of helping her unbutton and unlace herself last night, even if he had hidden his true motives behind a façade of trying to be helpful.

What a delicious fantasy to consider, even for a brief moment, that the darkly handsome Disciplinarian might think her attractive. She thought back to his muscled calves pressing intimately against her soft thighs in the carriage yesterday. Maybe that hadn't been an accident after all?

But no.

With no other weapon, she needed her anger to use against him. It was far safer to believe he had manipulated her into this gown to suit his own ends, and she knew she would discover exactly what those ends were at supper.

*Your lessons will begin tomorrow.*

How late had she slept? There was no clock in the room, another subtle strategy meant to disorient her, she was sure. She went to the window and threw up the sash. The sun was up; the birds were singing loudly. It looked to be mid-morning.

She would have hours to sit and dwell on The Disciplinarian's possible plans for her, to let her imagination run wild.

It was another way for him to strike fear into her.

Well, she wouldn't let him do it. She refused to dissolve into a quivering mass of nerves. She had to somehow take her mind off of what the day might bring. Her eyes went immediately to the bookshelves, where she scanned row after row, amazed once again at the broad range of subject matter, the interesting and diverse topics. Her index finger ran along the spines of the books and stopped at a vaguely familiar one: Jane Eyre, by a writer called Currer Bell.

She carried it to a far window, settled herself in the padded window seat, and opened the book.

Jared rode his horse hard, putting a good distance between himself and Rose Cottage. He knew he faced a great challenge in Clarissa Babcock, perhaps the greatest of his short career as The Disciplinarian, but he felt more certain of his strategy today. She had reacted well to his first two tests.

He'd held his breath this morning until Soames had come to his room with Clarissa's clothes. The fact that she'd taken the lure of the silk night rail told Jared she still had some sensual feelings buried beneath her hard exterior.

And the fact that she'd almost shouted down the house when she'd discovered her clothes were missing told him there was still enough passion left in her to stand up to her husband, once Jared had instructed her in how to do it.

Her lessons would begin this evening, but first Jared needed to visit the village to buy a few items he would use in her tutorial.

He spurred his horse onward.

A fly buzzing around her nose woke Clarissa from a light sleep. Her eyes fluttered open, and she was surprised to find she had been dozing in the comfortable window seat, the book lying open against her chest, the warm sun streaming in through the open window.

She sat up and could smell the heady scent of roses wafting up from the garden below. It really was an idyllic setting here, so peaceful, so pretty. Such a strange location for The Disciplinarian's diabolical *lessons*.

And yet, despite the gentleman he seemed, she believed his reputation was earned. His voice, the way he lowered it into a deceptively dangerous tone, that smooth, rich register, was a silken weapon he had used on her in the carriage and again last night when he'd demanded she turn over the dinner knife. There was no violence in his voice, but no room for argument either.

She shivered despite the warmth of the room. The Disciplinarian would have other weapons besides his voice at his disposal. And it was those weapons that she feared when he came to supper this evening.

She looked back out the window and saw that the sun was close to setting. He would be here soon. She scrambled from the window seat, and grabbed the book before it could drop to the floor.

Jared tucked the small strongbox under his arm and led Soames with the dinner tray to Clarissa's room. He knocked loudly on her door, took the key from his pocket and unlocked the lock.

The door swung inward, but Jared didn't immediately enter. He half expected Clarissa to leap out and hit him with something.

She wouldn't have been the first female to try it.

Instead, he saw her at the far end of the room by the window, holding a book across her chest as if it would offer her some sort of protection against him. He took a step into the room, followed closely by the servant. He heard the rumble of the tea tray as Soames trundled across to the table, but Jared only had eyes for Clarissa.

She was a vision in the pale blue gown with her long dark hair cascading freely in waves around her shoulders. If he had thought yesterday that she could be pretty, he'd been dead wrong. She was downright stunning. In fact, if he didn't know she'd been securely locked in this room for the last twenty-four hours, he'd swear this was a different woman entirely.

He tried to keep his expression neutral, but couldn't stop his eyes from sweeping her from head to toe. The gown fit her body to perfection, accentuating her curves and flattering the line of her hips. The choice had been a lucky guess on his part, but he sincerely hoped it had done the work he'd intended it to do.

He cursed silently when he saw that she'd noticed his intimate inspection. She dropped her book, flew to the bed and dragged off the damask comforter, draping it around her shoulders and clutching it tightly to her throat. Her eyes gazed in fear at the small chest he carried under his arm. He put the box carefully down next to his dinner chair.

Soames was oblivious to their silent interchange, busying himself with laying out the dinner places. Once he was finished, he bowed himself out of the room. Jared watched him go, then turned back to Clarissa. "Come," he said in his best Disciplinarian voice, holding out his hand.

When she made no move toward the table, he dropped the commanding tone and tried to give her a reassuring smile. "Come, Clarissa. It's just supper."

She did move then, but slowly, as if she still didn't trust that he only wanted to feed her. He moved around the table to pull out her chair, and he held it while she sat down awkwardly, still wrapped in the thick bedspread.

He poured them both some wine, and again served the dinner. Tonight it was stew in a bowl, and she only had a spoon to eat it with. His eyebrow went up wryly when her hand poked out from the coverlet to pick up the round utensil, but she didn't rise to the bait.

Dinner was a mostly silent affair. He knew she was terrified, and with just cause: he had told her that her lessons would begin tonight and so they would.

After one hour was up, Soames returned to clear the table.

After he'd gone, Jared poured himself another glass of wine, downed it in one go, and refilled both his glass and hers. Clarissa sat rigid, her eyes trained on the table.

He searched for some neutral ground on which to begin. "What book were you reading?"

She shrugged. "A novel called Jane Eyre."

"Ah, yes," he said. "Currer Bell. There are those who believe the name is a pseudonym, and the author is really a woman."

That got her attention. "A woman? You would have a book by a woman in your library?" She seemed sincerely surprised.

"Of course," he said. "I own many books, in this room, as well as in my study downstairs."

She was silent for a long time. "I don't understand you." She waved a hand vaguely at the room—at the bed, the books, the dinner table. "I don't understand any of this."

That was fine with Jared. He *wanted* her off balance, had planned this last twenty-four hours to ensure it. Her comment was the opening he needed.

"You don't need to be afraid of me, Clarissa."

He saw her swallow, hesitate, and then her chin came up a notch. "I'm not afraid of you," she answered, low. "I hate you."

But he could see by the look in her eyes that neither statement was absolutely true. "You don't hate me," he said. "I haven't harmed you. I haven't starved you. In point of fact, I'm here to help you."

Her eyebrows flew up at that. "You're The Disciplinarian. "You're here to—"

"—instruct you, yes. Men send their wives to me to teach them a lesson. And I do." He shrugged. "But perhaps not exactly the lesson their husbands expect."

She made a small scoffing sound.

"What I teach women," Jared continued, "is how to control their husbands. Subtly. I help women learn to exercise what limited freedom they have within the strictures of the modern marriage state. To enjoy what they can inside the tight bonds of matrimony."

"What?" Clarissa's confusion was now clearly written on her face. She didn't *want* to believe him. It was not what she'd expected. But then, it wasn't what any of the women he'd instructed expected. "Are you saying you—you don't hate women? You *help* them?"

"Yes. Usually, my lessons are very straightforward. But you are a special case, Clarissa. The first thing you must learn is that your husband is a dangerous man. The look in his eye yesterday is one I have seen before. That look can lead to murder. It's why even when your husband changed the rules of our agreement yesterday I couldn't turn my back and leave you with him."

"He changed the rules?"

"Yes. Your husband wants more than just a biddable wife—he wants an heir."

He saw her shift in her seat. "I know that," she said softly.

"But you may not know that your husband blames *you* for the lack of success these last two years."

Her eyebrows went up at that piece of information. "What?"

Jared nodded. "He thinks it's due to your... uncooperativeness in the bedroom. He's asked me to make you, well... more *receptive* to his attentions."

Clarissa shot up out of her chair, the bedspread falling unheeded from her shoulders. "Bastard!" she shouted, though for a moment Jared wasn't sure whether she was referring to him or her own husband. "And you *agreed?*"

"Sit down, Clarissa," he said calmly. "I'm on your side. Remember that."

He saw her fists clench and her chest heave in fury, but he turned placidly to reach for his glass of wine. Best not to stare at her breasts straining against the thin silk of her gown, no matter how much he was tempted.

"Please. Sit," he said again. "Let's figure out a way to deal with this."

She sat abruptly, though her breathing didn't calm any.

"Good," he said with a businesslike nod. "Now. Talk to me. Was there ever any physical attraction between you?"

She gasped. "I beg your pardon!"

He stared at her, noting how her eyes dilated with anger, how her back straightened in outrage at the question. "Perhaps at the beginning," he prompted, "when he was courting you?"

The look on her face gave him his answer.

"Courting? My marriage was a bargain struck between my father and my husband, an arrangement that suited all concerned. Except, perhaps, myself."

"I see." So Jared would not have long-forgotten desire to work with, since she and Charles Babcock obviously never had that spark of sexual heat between them.

"Basic physical satisfaction, then? Does your husband take time to give you pleasure during your marital relations?"

She looked at him blankly. "Pleasure? His sweating, heaving body should give me pleasure?"

Jared blinked, giving nothing away. So. She had never experienced a woman's pleasure. He knew very well that in this day and age love had little to do with marriage. Unions were made for social connections, business deals, political advancement, to pay off debt—there were a host of reasons.

Still, he despised the men who made their women miserable and bitter, when with just a little effort it didn't have to be that way.

"Clarissa," he began. "These are the cold, hard facts we're faced with: a wife is the property of her husband. By law, he can do with her what he will. Your husband wants an heir, and he believes your... frigidity is preventing it. It doesn't matter that he may be as much at fault, or more, as you yourself. He wants me to warm you up to the sexual act so that he can plant his seed in you and be done with his duty.

"You have two choices. You can either allow me to tutor you, to instruct you in ways you can enjoy your husband's attentions and ideally give him his precious heir, or you can go on as you have been, risking your husband's wrath, his fists, and possibly worse."

He held his breath as he waited for her answer. He'd never feared a woman's response as much as he feared Clarissa Babcock's, because he knew her choice meant life or death.

And he prayed that she realized it.

## Chapter Four

*Life or death.*

The Disciplinarian had no qualms about pointing out what he thought were Charles's intentions where she was concerned: give him an heir or suffer the consequences.

And Clarissa could easily envision 'the consequences'. She'd been dealing with them for these last two years. "I hate my husband," she said after a long moment.

"Unfortunately, that changes nothing," The Disciplinarian answered quietly. "This is your lot in life, but you can choose to take control of it, rather than become a victim of it."

"I'll never learn to enjoy his attentions!"

"Yes, you will. I'll show you how," he vowed.

She knew she had no real choice, but she had to come to terms with it. After several moments of silent debate, she heaved a great sigh. "So be it."

"Then let's begin your lessons."

She swallowed nervously as he came around the dinner table and held out his hand. What would he do to her? How did he possibly think he could teach her to 'enjoy' Charles's conjugal attentions?

"Clarissa…"

He was using his Disciplinarian voice again. That low, sweet, command-wrapped-in-a-velvet-glove. He wanted her to take his hand, to symbolically give herself over to his instruction. She started to shake violently.

"Clarissa…" he said again. This time, though, it sounded more like sympathy, or reassurance. "You will enjoy my lessons. I swear it."

She blinked back her tears. She wouldn't cry, *she wouldn't!* Terrified as she was, there was one small part of her that believed him, that needed desperately to trust that he'd told her the truth.

That he *helped* women, not hurt them.

He leaned over the table, and retrieved her untouched glass of wine. "Here," he said, placing it near her hand. "Drink this if you think it will help."

She grabbed for the goblet and downed the contents in three deep swallows.

And then his hand came out again, silently insistent. Patiently waiting for her consent.

She couldn't look at him as she put her hand in his.

"Good girl," he approved, pulling her gently to her feet.

She was immediately reminded that the bedspread had fallen from her shoulders earlier, and that she was nearly naked in this thin slip of a nightgown. But he ignored her state of undress as he turned and led her across the room to the bed. *Oh God, the lessons would be in bed!* How was she ever going to deal with this?

"Wait here," he ordered quietly, then went about the room dousing the gas lights. He took two thick, pillared candles from the fireplace mantel, placed one on each side of the bed's headboard, and lit them with a match he took from his pocket.

The room was now bathed in shadow, the candles throwing only enough light to illuminate the wide bed.

Clarissa watched as he retrieved the small strongbox from the floor next to his dinner chair and brought it across the room to lay it on the dressing table next to the bed. She swallowed hard. The tools of his trade were in there, the weapons he would use on her.

"I want you to lie down on the bed," he ordered in his smooth, rich voice.

Outright panic gripped her at those bald words. "I can't do this," she gasped. "I can't!"

He caught her chin in his hand and forced her to look up at him. His eyes were calm, his face relaxed. He certainly didn't look like a sadistic monster. Still, she could literally taste her own fear.

"You can do it, and you will," he assured her quietly. *"I won't hurt you."*

She was paralyzed, yet she knew she had to make a choice.

"Either you trust me, or you trust your future to him," The Disciplinarian said, as if he had read her mind.

Clarissa's knees almost buckled at that. She swallowed hard, but she knew her answer. She sat down on the edge of the bed.

"Good girl," The Disciplinarian approved.

He was silent for a long moment, which gave Clarissa time to catch her breath and come to terms with the decision she had just made. She had yielded to him, placed herself in his power. When she finally found the courage to look up at him, he was watching her carefully.

"Move to the center of the bed and lie on your back."

There it was again, that seductive command-that-must-be-obeyed. She wondered briefly whether his success as The Disciplinarian had as much to do with women falling under the spell of his lush voice as with his actual instructions.

She scooted to the center of the bed and lay on her back, rigid.

She heard a creak of metal and turned her head to see The Disciplinarian opening the lid of his strongbox to draw something out. In the shadows she couldn't quite make out what it was. Then he turned toward her, and the mattress sagged as he sat at the edge of the bed.

He held a silk scarf in his hands.

"I'm going to blindfold you," he said quietly. "Not to make you terrified of what I'm about to do, but in order to take away your sight so that your sense of touch becomes primary. Touch is a very potent aphrodisiac."

"Aphro—what?"

"Trust me," he said instead. "Lift your head."

Her mouth went dry, but she did as he ordered. He wrapped the black silk around her eyes and tied it behind her head, shutting out everything in the room, even the smallest trace of light.

"Now," he instructed. "Spread your arms out on the bed, shoulder height, palms up."

Amazing how her sense of hearing suddenly seemed more acute now that she couldn't see. And how his voice took on an even deeper, richer resonance.

She did as he asked.

"Good. Now spread your legs as wide as you can."

"*What?*" She tried to sit up at that, but before she could move, his hands were on her shoulders, his mouth next to her ear.

"Calm, Clarissa, be calm. If you give me control, I promise I will give you a pleasure you've never experienced. If it would help, I can tie you to the bed to give you no choice in this, but I think you are strong enough, and courageous enough, to trust me. Are you?"

The challenge was there. She had agreed to these *lessons*, and now he was daring her to go wherever he led her in them. Perhaps she *should* ask him to tie her down, maybe knowing she had no choice would free her from her instinct to fight him at every turn.

No. He had given her freedom of choice, knowing how important it was, and how little of it she had.

She spread her legs.

He was silent for an endless minute, and she would have given anything to see the look on his face. Surprise? Triumph?

She felt him rise from the bed. A moment later, the squeak of the strongbox told her he was taking something else from it. What weapon would it be this time?

No, that wasn't fair. A silk scarf wasn't exactly a weapon, unless you considered that it would allow you to assault the other senses.

"Clarissa." He was back by the side of her bed. "I want you to relax, to let go of everything except your sense of touch. Concentrate, and tell me how this feels."

She waited with bated breath, arms outstretched, legs spread-eagle, entirely vulnerable to whatever he had planned for her. And to her great surprise, she felt something soft brush against her cheek.

She jerked her head to the side. "What is it?"

"You tell me," he challenged quietly. "Describe it."

It felt soft, wide, round almost, with—

"Out loud," he ordered.

"Smooth, caressing. A feather maybe, but it's too big, too wide, and it has, um, tendrils, I think. I can feel something trailing behind as you're running it down my face."

"Good," he approved. "Did you know that the skin is the largest organ of the human body?"

"I didn't know skin was considered an organ," she admitted.

"The biggest sensory organ we have," he said, running whatever it was down past her jaw and along the side of her neck. She gasped at the feather light touch, and actually shivered.

"You have a lovely neck, Clarissa. A graceful, white, swan's neck."

"Charles thinks my neck is too long," she said, almost under her breath.

"Did you know the neck is one of a woman's erogenous zones?" he said, ignoring her comment.

She tried to frown, but the movement of the feather, or whatever it was, felt too good against her skin. "I don't understand your words. Aphrodisiac? Erogenous zones?"

"Pleasure points," he explained. "Sensitive spots. Some women are very sensitive along their neck." He dragged the feather slowly down to the hollow near her collarbone. "And here as well. How does this feel?"

It felt incredible. With only her sense of touch to rely on, her nerve endings were focused with rapt concentration on the soft brush of his strokes.

"Talk to me, Clarissa."

How to put the intense sensation into words? "It feels… nice," she said lamely.

The feather moved from her collarbone to trail slowly along the outside of her arm. It stopped to flutter over her palm.

"And this?" Back and forth, back and forth, The Disciplinarian dragged the feather across her outstretched palm.

She was tempted to close her fingers around it to finally determine what this strange weapon was, but its soft, rhythmic motion was making her palm tingle, and she was afraid to do anything that might ruin the heightened sensation.

"Good," she said, again at a loss for a better word.

"Hmm," The Disciplinarian murmured low. "Obviously your palm is a pleasure point. How about here?"

He dragged the feather to the inside of her wrist.

Oh yes, that was good, too, but not quite as pleasurable as her palm. He seemed to know it, and moved slowly on.

"Here?"

She gave a small gasp as the feather fluttered along the inside of her elbow. She'd never known she was so sensitive there. The subtle pressure of The Disciplinarian's motion made her want to squirm, but only because she wanted something more...more pressure, more friction, more *attention* there. She made a frustrated little sound.

"Another pleasure point," The Disciplinarian said, and Clarissa could hear the interest in his deep, rich voice. "You are a very sensual woman, Clarissa. Tactile. Physical. It is a beautiful quality."

His voice rolled over her like a soft caress. She felt languid, yet at the same time finely-tuned, her senses heightened, waiting for whatever he'd do next.

And what he did next was scandalous in the extreme.

She felt the path of the feather as it made its way from the inside of her elbow to glide along her upper arm. He never slowed the route of his weapon as it left her arm to run up the swell of her breast. She sucked in a breath as he circled the soft mound, rising higher and higher to the very crest. Then the feather ran across the thin silk of her nightgown to her other breast, and he began a slow, back and forth motion from one to the other, varying his pressure, dragging the feather harder, then softer, over both her nipples, making them rise to attention.

"Beautiful," he breathed.

Her hands fisted, and her breathing came in deep gasps, but she didn't ask him to stop. The rise and fall of her chest strained the silk against her sensitive buds and increased the luscious friction.

"How does that feel?" he asked.

How did it *feel*? It was indecent, immoral, wicked, and she never wanted it to end. But she couldn't trust herself to say any of that to him, could only pant helplessly at the exquisite sensation.

Too soon the feather left her breasts to run slowly down the outside of her torso, past her waist, and along the outside of her leg, which was bare where it peeked out from the side slit of her nightgown. With her legs spread-eagled, his feather had no trouble rounding the sole of her foot and beginning a path up the inside of her calf. Luckily, the gown covered her there, but dear Lord, he was going to go all the way up!

She gasped. *"Please…"*

But the feather never paused, and before she'd finished speaking, it had traced a path up her inner thigh and reached its goal: her very woman's center.

Clarissa could barely breathe, paralyzed with thoughts of what he was going to do now. He too, seemed to hesitate, but a moment later the feather began a slow caress against her, stroking its softness against her own softness, up and down the length of her from the top of her tight curls all the way down between her legs to where her bottom made contact with the bed. The feather was separated from her skin by only the thinnest layer of silk, and up and down it went, setting a rhythm that seemed to call to something deep inside of her. She couldn't, she *wouldn't* respond, damn it, but her traitorous body seemed to have a mind of its own as it arched for more contact with The Disciplinarian's seductive weapon.

She heard him suck in a breath. "My God, Clarissa. You humble a man with your uninhibited responses."

But instead of giving her what she wanted, what her body was clamoring for, he drew the feather away.

With the sensual spell broken, shame hit her like a fist. What a wanton she'd been! What liberties she'd allowed him! She should be disgusted with herself.

Yet she couldn't be, because she'd never, ever felt this way before.

Decadent. Dissolute. Debauched. And still wanting more.

"Clarissa…" he breathed. "Slide your hands up above your head."

He didn't sound disgusted with her. In fact, she could swear that his own breathing had quickened. What did he intend with this new decree? She hesitated, and then slowly slid her arms along the mattress, up and over her head.

He gripped both wrists tightly with one hand and pinned them down against the bed. "Good," he said, low. "Now, tell me. Did you enjoy what I just did to you? How did it feel? Be honest."

She swallowed. She didn't like being vulnerable, not physically or emotionally. She usually hid herself behind a wall of indifference; it was how she'd protected herself from Charles these last two years. "It felt incredible," she heard herself admit.

"Good," he said again, "because now we're going to start your next lesson. I'm going to retrace the path I just took… this time with my fingers."

He had her wrists firmly locked above her head in a powerful grip, and this time she actually *did* cede control to him, offering only a token struggle. How scandalously helpless it made her feel, to be entirely at his mercy!

"Relax," he instructed. "Concentrate on how this feels."

His fingertips began their journey along the side of her face, caressing her cheek. His fingers were feather light, almost as ephemeral as his previous weapon had been, but she was keenly aware that he was touching her, feeling her, his skin against her skin in intimate contact.

Shocking. Shockingly powerful. And shockingly pleasurable.

The pads of his fingertips glided down her neck, and she couldn't stop her quick intake of breath. The feeling was multiplied four-fold, since each of his individual fingers seemed eager to trace its mark on her.

It was worse when he reached the hollow of her neck. The sensitive indentation by her collarbone was the target of all his digits, and he lingered there in particular with his index finger, setting a slow, deliberate rhythm, seemingly intent on driving her to distraction.

When she began to squirm from the sheer pleasure of it, he ran his fingertips slowly up her arm to where he held her wrists captive. He raked his fingernails lightly over the palms of her hands. She gasped at the sensation and opened her hands wide, offering him more area, tacitly pleading for him to continue. Little shivers of delight radiated out from her palm and ran down along her arms and even farther down her body.

He indulged her for a delicious minute, then his fingers glided down along her forearm to the inside of her elbow and she thought she'd come up off the bed when he stroked her there. Back and forth he grazed her sensitive skin, and she could swear she almost felt his mouth on her, his hot breath, or maybe it was just because he was breathing so heavily.

And so was she.

His fingers moved on deliberately along her upper arm and stopped when they made contact with the neckline of her gown. But only for a moment. Then his bold hand slid across the silk to the base of her breast.

She gasped sharply, but that only served to make her breasts strain against the thin material. It seemed to be the only impetus he needed. She felt one finger start to circle her as the feather had, beginning at the base but going slowly higher, boldly tracing her soft mound until he reached the crest.

And paused.

Her breath was coming in short pants now, waiting for his next move, wanting it and fearing it at the same time.

She felt his fingertip settle on her nipple and was shocked to feel that she was already fully erect and straining for his touch. He slowly dragged the tips of his four fingers over the sensitive bud. She had to grind her teeth to keep from screaming out her pleasure, but she couldn't seem to control her body, which writhed and bucked under his hands.

"Don't stop yourself, Clarissa," he said, his voice sounding oddly strained. "Tell me how this feels."

"No... no," she moaned, too mortified to admit the sinful sensations, head thrashing between her upstretched arms.

His hand abruptly left her breast and she did cry out then, and it was from the loss of his touch. But his roaming fingers were already busy working their way down her side, to slide scandalously along the outside of her naked thigh, down her calf, around the sole of her foot, to begin the journey up the inside of her leg.

Good God, he really *was* going to retrace the path of the feather!

She considered fighting him then, clamping her legs together to deny him access, but his hand was already at her knee, halfway to its goal. Time seemed to stop for her at that moment as several things became clear. Here in the dark, in this unknown place, where this stranger was taking such scandalous liberties with her body, she suddenly wanted to experience everything he offered. She'd felt nothing but pleasure at his hands, a pleasure she knew she'd never feel with Charles. Since her husband was the one who'd turned her over to this man, a stranger she would never see again in her life, surely no one could blame her if she took what pleasure she could here, to keep with her through all the long, cold nights to come.

She let out a long breath.

"Yes. That's it, Clarissa," The Disciplinarian approved. "Let go of everything else and just *feel*."

What she felt when his hot hand came to rest on her soft curls was simply indescribable, almost beyond her capacity to absorb it. Her body was alive, every inch of skin conditioned by this man over the last few minutes to be receptive to his touch. Eager for it. Straining for it. When his hand began to move, she cried out at the sheer intensity of it and spread her legs wider.

"My God, Clarissa..." She heard his deep voice hitch in his throat.

He anchored the heel of his palm in her curls and dragged his four fingers along the length of her, stroking her with a curling rhythm over and over, driving her wild, pulling up a handful of silk with his every motion. Her cries of pleasure matched the movement of his fingers, five strokes, six strokes, until suddenly he paused.

Delirious with passion, she only then realized that in another moment the thin barrier of silk would be gone altogether and he would have full access to her most intimate space.

He slowly pulled the bunched material of her gown up onto her stomach, leaving her entirely exposed to him. She opened her mouth to speak—though what she wanted to say she had no idea—but then his fingers were threading their way through her tight curls to explore what was underneath, and everything else left her mind.

Not even in her wildest dreams did she imagine that a man could do what The Disciplinarian was doing to her.

He spread her gently and slid his index finger along the full length of her, sliding along her inner lips and up to circle around her sensitive bud. The blood rushed to her head at the bold intimacy of the act, but she barely had time to be aware of how wet she was becoming before he continued with his motion, stroking and exploring her.

"You are so beautiful in your passion, Clarissa, so responsive. It takes my breath away."

His agile finger continued to acquaint itself with her body, while at the same time accustoming her to his touch, teaching her to trust it. To trust him. She began to respond to the subtle but insistent pressure of his finger, to push up against it, to arch her body in pleasure when he stroked a particularly sensitive spot. The feelings were incredible, and yet she felt herself straining for something else. Something more.

She thought she could hear his breathing speed up, and feel his finger start to shake, yet when he spoke his voice was very definitely in control.

"Your first lesson taught you the erotic power of touch. This lesson will end by teaching you a woman's pleasure. Are you ready for that lesson, Clarissa?"

She frowned. A woman's pleasure? How much more sensation could she possibly bear? "Everything you've done tonight has brought me pleasure," she said honestly.

"But not the *ultimate* pleasure," he replied.

She paused. Could this 'ultimate pleasure' be the 'more' she was craving? Could there be some sort of erotic logic to all this?

She swallowed hard. Dare she risk surrendering to a pleasure she might never be able to experience again in her life? But on the other hand, could she risk passing up an opportunity she might never have again?

"Teach me," she said softly.

"Sweet Clarissa," he said in that rich, honeyed caress of a voice. "Trust me completely in this. Give yourself to me and experience what it is to be a woman."

The controlled urgency in his voice frightened her a little, but his words were so sinfully seductive that she shivered with anticipation. He still had her wrists restrained above her head, pinned to the mattress with one of his hands, so there would be no fighting him, no resisting this now that she'd made her decision.

She would trust him completely, and give herself to him as he'd asked.

His fingers resumed their intimate exploration. This time she could feel his thumb and middle finger spreading her wide, opening her up to his inspection. Slowly he circled her with his index finger, sliding along her secret lips and up to stroke her tiny bud. All this he had done before, and Clarissa relaxed into the rhythm of his touch, the familiarity of it. She could feel herself getting wetter, responding to his caress, shifting and arching her hips so that his fingers stroked her right where she wanted them.

"Yes," he breathed. "Take control. Take your pleasure."

Encouraged, she arched herself up more fully against his fingers, wanting firmer contract with him. And that was the moment he sank two fingers deep inside her, eased by her slick wetness and her accommodating position.

She cried out in surprise and shock.

"This is for you, Clarissa. All for you. Just enjoy it."

His fingers stroked slowly in and out of her, stretching her, spreading her, sliding into her welcoming wetness. The intimate invasion was more erotic than anything she could have dreamed, and for the first time in her life it made her wonder what it would be like to welcome a man into her body, not just be grimly forced to accept it as part of her duty as a wife.

She fantasized about The Disciplinarian's male member, how it would feel where his fingers were now. If it would give her the same pleasure. With that image in her mind, she moved in response to the slow stroking motion, taking his fingers deeper into her body, shifting her hips this way and that so she could feel him stroking her from the inside.

Oh, this was good. Very, very good. She couldn't hold back a small moan.

Immediately she felt his thumb come around to start stroking her little bud in time to match the motion of his fingers. Her pleasure instantly doubled. Impaled by his magic fingers and at the mercy of his insistent thumb, she felt her breath speed up, and that rush of blood again to her brain. She began to squirm under his hand.

"That's it, Clarissa. Just let go and give yourself over to the pleasure."

As if she needed one more point of stimulation to convince her, she felt his fingers hook slightly inside of her to stroke a new inner spot. The pressure of his thumb on her bud increased, and she was caught suddenly in an escalating tension, a rising tide of pressure, forcing her up toward some unknown point.

"Ah... ah... *ah!*" It crested violently, causing her body to convulse in wave after wave of incredible pleasure. She felt herself contracting fiercely around his fingers, and he rotated his hand, feeding her pleasure. She nearly came up off the bed with the intensity of the aftershocks he caused with that intimate motion. She gasped and shook, and finally collapsed in an exhausted heap in the center of the bed, desperately dragging air into her lungs.

He slowly removed his fingers and drew her gown back down to cover her. Above the ringing in her ears, she heard him whisper, "You are beautiful in your passion, Clarissa. Now you must count to thirty."

"Wha—what?" she gasped, still breathless.

"While you lay there, count to the number thirty," he said again.

"Slowly."

She had no idea of the reason behind his strange request, but she did as he requested. Then she paused and waited, listening for him in the room.

All she heard was silence.

She waited a long minute more, then dared to remove the silk scarf covering her eyes. The Disciplinarian was not in the room. She glanced over to her bedside table. His small metal strongbox was also gone.

He'd left her without saying a word.

As she looked in disbelief around the room, she saw that he had left her a token of his visit. On the pillow of the bed was a peacock feather.

And she'd lay odds it was one plucked from her own hat.

# Chapter Five

Jared paced furiously in his room.

Back and forth, back and forth he walked, until he lost count of his steps and threatened to wear a path into his rug.

He had only one thing on his mind.

Clarissa Babcock.

And how desperately he wanted her.

A moment ago, he'd had to call on every last ounce of his control as The Disciplinarian to force himself to leave her. But oh, how he'd longed to take her in his arms after feeling her powerful climax, tear the silk from her eyes and revel in the sated look on her face. That newfound look of awareness. And to know with a basic male satisfaction that *he* had been the one to put it there.

Even now he longed to rush back to her room, tear off her nightgown and show her with his own body how good she could truly feel.

He wanted it so badly he was in physical pain. His cock was straining against his trousers—protesting, frustrated, demanding attention. He actually considered throwing himself onto his bed and grinding himself into the pillow, imagining it was Clarissa's soft body beneath him.

Never in his life had he met a woman with such uninhibited passion, such unrestrained abandon. Many times during her lesson, Jared's hands had shook and his mouth had gone dry from the sheer force of the desire she'd aroused in him. It was inconceivable that Charles Babcock didn't know what a prize he had in his wife.

Jared had always been able to keep the women who were sent to him at arm's length, to treat them merely as students, despite the times—and there had been several—when they'd offered to show their gratitude to him for the lessons he'd taught them. But he'd always believed his satisfaction came from showing them how to deal with the unbearable situations in their lives.

From being able to save them from the same fate as his sister.

He should think of Clarissa also as a student, albeit of a different kind. The carnal kind. He should wash her scent off his hands right now and resolve to treat her with the same casual indifference he treated all those other women. Learn to be satisfied with the fact that he had helped her as he'd helped them.

He must look at this coldly. Analytically. He'd simply taught her a lesson tonight. She'd learned that she could enjoy the sexual act.

He brought his hand up to inhale her scent. His fingers were still slick with the evidence of her arousal, and he could still remember the incredible sensation of sliding them deep inside her.

The memory of how she'd taken him, moved instinctively beneath his hand, and experienced sexual pleasure for the very first time made him shudder with his own frustrated passion. He'd felt her body clutch at his fingers, literally tremble and shudder beneath his touch. His head spun with the sense of power it gave him, and he inhaled her scent again. He knew that only one thing would truly satisfy him, and that was to bury his face in this essence, her very core, and taste her sweetness firsthand. His blood raced at the thought of it.

Bloody hell, he was out of his mind!

He shouldn't be thinking about how beautiful she'd looked when he walked into her room tonight, or admiring her courage in letting him instruct her in the most basic of lessons. He didn't want to think about her intelligence, or the way they had conversed last night over dinner on everything from politics to religion. Better to attribute this burning desire for her to basic lust, because he knew it could never be anything more than that. She was married, and he could never have more of her than what she would give him this weekend.

*What she would give him...*

Or what *he* could give *her*?

He halted abruptly in his pacing. He had taught Clarissa tonight that she could experience sexual pleasure. He had intended tomorrow night to go one step further and teach her how to take control when her husband made sexual demands so she could at least insure her own satisfaction during the act. He had two particular sexual positions in mind that she could use to guarantee it. That had been his plan, but now...

Charles Babcock cared not one whit about Clarissa's pleasure, but Jared found *he* cared about it a great deal. Another lesson came to mind, a much more pleasant one. One designed to teach her *just how much* she could enjoy the sexual act. Not a lesson in how she could take control, but a lesson in ceding control. Jared wanted to give her a climax even more earth-shattering than tonight's. If Clarissa were destined to a lifetime of serving her husband, wasn't it the least Jared could do? To give her a pleasure this weekend that she could remember the rest of her life?

He would do this first for *her*, and then he would teach her how to control her husband.

He groaned. Bloody hell, who was he fooling? He wanted to pleasure her for himself alone, to see the satisfaction on her face. He was treading on very dangerous ground here. She was a treasure, a temptation, and this was sheer torture for him. He *must* get himself under control!

With a snort of frustration, he threw himself into the wing chair next to his bed, unbuttoned his trousers, and took himself in hand. But by God, if he didn't imagine Clarissa's face in front of him at the moment of his release.

Clarissa tossed and turned in her bed. It had been hours since The Disciplinarian had left her.

What would she have seen in his eyes at the moment of her violent climax if she hadn't been blindfolded? Disgust at her wantonness? Shock at her eager and total abandon to a stranger's touch? Cynical amusement that she, a married woman, never knew pleasure like this existed?

Clearly he had been repulsed by her shameless behavior, since he had run off so quickly.

She'd been both embarrassed and excited during his lesson, encouraged by the patient tenderness of his instruction, actually wondering what it would be like to welcome a man—*this man*—into her body, while all the time he'd been appalled by her. She blinked back mortified tears.

*You are beautiful in your passion, Clarissa.*

If that were true, if he'd truly meant it, then why had he run away?

*You humble a man with your honest and uninhibited responses.*

*This is for you. All for you. Enjoy it.*

She'd trusted those words, let go of every inhibition and given herself over to his expert tutelage. What had she done wrong? Why had he left so suddenly?

Perhaps now that The Disciplinarian had proven he could 'warm her up' he felt that his job was done, his duty to Charles fulfilled. How ironic that The Disciplinarian might want nothing more to do with her, while she wanted nothing more than to have his hands on her again!

She buried her face in her pillow.

She didn't want to think about how attractive The Disciplinarian was, or about the intense pleasure she'd felt at his hands, or how much she desperately wished she had married a man like him instead of her own husband. The Disciplinarian was a kind man, a gentle man, one who actually seemed to respect her as a person.

If she thought she'd been miserable in her marriage before, now she realized just exactly how much was missing in it. This time she didn't even try to stop her tears when they came.

Jared hadn't slept.

His night instead had been filled with elaborate fantasies of all the things he wanted to do with Clarissa Babcock, and he had finally given up on sleep altogether when his body had presented him with another painful reminder of just how much it wanted her.

He knew none of his erotic scenarios would be fulfilled, except one. The one he'd planned for tonight. After tonight, after he'd tasted her and gotten her out of his system, he would concentrate on coldly instructing her on how to manage her husband.

First he'd need to visit the village again.

And then find some way to pass the endless hours until supper.

Clarissa practically jumped out of the window seat when the knock came on her door late in the afternoon.

The Disciplinarian was early! She hadn't expected him until supper, if at all. Her relief was overwhelming, but now she wondered just what it was she would face when he came through the door.

What did it mean that he had come? That there was another lesson to be learned? That he hadn't found her wild abandon of last night completely abhorrent? Or had he come simply to tell her that her lessons were finished?

The loud knock came again.

"Come," she called tentatively.

She was astonished to see the servant Soames enter, alone. He bowed at her, looking uncomfortable in the extreme.

"Pardon me, ma'am," he began, but then seemed at a loss for words.

"Yes?" Clarissa prompted, his discomfort adding to her own sense of foreboding.

"The master, er, the master wonders, well, whether you'd like a bath."

Clarissa blinked and felt the color rise in her cheeks. "A bath?"

Soames cleared his throat. "Yes, ma'am."

Clarissa's mind raced. Considering Soames' obvious discomfort, this was not a courtesy made available to every 'guest' of The Disciplinarian. But then, The Disciplinarian himself had told her that he had never 'instructed' anyone in quite the way he was instructing her. Was this bath a luxury or a necessity? What exactly did The Disciplinarian have planned for her tonight? And did Soames have some inkling of it, of what was truly going on between them?

Clarissa felt herself blush again, but she forced her mouth to open. If it meant that The Disciplinarian would be coming to her tonight, she knew her answer. "I'll take the bath."

"Very good, ma'am." Soames bowed and backed to the door. He was gone for only an instant, and then he and another man, one she'd never seen before, were carrying in a copper tub. They set it in front of the fireplace.

"My apologies, ma'am," Soames said, "but I'm not allowed to build a fire for you."

Clarissa bit her lip. Clearly fires were off-limits in case whatever reluctant student The Disciplinarian was currently 'instructing' decided to try and burn the house down.

"Quite all right, Soames. It's a warm day today."

Soames signaled the other servant, who quickly brought in a three-sided screen, and set it up next to the tub to keep in some of the heat while Clarissa bathed. Soames himself brought in an armload of towels, and the two men carried in bucket after bucket of hot water, which they quickly poured into the tub.

The whole ritual took less than ten minutes. Then the door was locked securely behind them, and Clarissa found herself alone in front of the steaming tub.

She slipped the nightgown over her head and climbed into the copper container, sinking into its warm depths. She was careful to drape her hair over the rim to keep it out of the water. She longed to wash it, but with no fire, it would never dry before The Disciplinarian's visit.

She scrubbed herself clean with the creamy lavender-scented soap, and then allowed herself to lean back for a self-indulgent soak.

She closed her eyes and allowed the wet heat to caress her body even as the steam curled her hair riotously. The heavy liquid turned her thoughts languid as well. Was there a particular reason The Disciplinarian needed her to be freshly washed tonight? Did this mean he had another particularly *intimate* lesson to teach her? Would he put his hands on her body again tonight?

She certainly hoped so. She ran her palms lightly over her breasts, skimming her nipples, remembering how the teasing pressure of The Disciplinarian's feather had caused them to pucker in reaction. And minutes later, how his fingers had scandalously followed, fingertips raking lightly across her already pebbled peaks. The memory sent a shiver of pleasure through her. She squeezed her legs tightly together, remembering how The Disciplinarian's expert fingers had made her feel there as well. How he'd entered her, explored her and then encouraged her passion until she'd exploded with pleasure. She let her own hand slip between her legs, feeling what he had felt, sliding a tentative finger inside herself.

The sensation was pleasant, but it wasn't the same. It only made her frustrated, agitated, and anxious for something more—more of his hands, more of his fingers, and, God help her, maybe even more than that.

Jared cursed himself for a fool.

There was no reason for him to be sitting here in his room, alternately shifting uncomfortably in his chair or launching himself out of it to anxiously pace the perimeter of the floor. No reason at all to wait, as time dragged endlessly by, for the moment he could go to Clarissa.

What was there to stop him, after all? He was The Disciplinarian. He was the one with the power here, the man in charge. He could go to her right now if he so wished!

He actually turned and took a step toward the door.

*No. Not yet. Can't go yet.*

He dragged an unsteady hand through his hair. There were rules to be followed, strict rules that he had set himself, for his protection as well as his students'. True, Clarissa's case was completely different to any 'instruction' he'd given before, but there were still rules. Rules of conduct. Rules of propriety. Yet that didn't stop him from wanting to bend those rules this time, bend them until they threatened to break.

He thrust a hand into his vest pocket and yanked out his watch.

Four in the afternoon. A whole five minutes later than the last time he'd looked.

*Bloody hell.* He threw himself back into his chair with a groan.

She had accepted the bath he had ordered Soames to offer her. With any luck, she wouldn't linger in the tub, but would instead hurry through her ablutions, as anxious as he was for their meeting tonight.

His fingers dug into the leather arm of his chair as a vision of Clarissa, naked in her tub, sprang into his mind. All creamy white skin and luxurious black hair. Full breasts and luscious quim.

What he wouldn't give right now to trade places with that bar of lavender soap she was using, to be able to run over every inch of her perfection, explore every nook and cranny of her body. All her intimate places.

The image made him groan aloud. Every nerve ending in his body screamed at him, urging… *demanding* that he rush to her room and offer his services as her personal bath servant. He gritted his teeth at the thought, and considered calling for Soames to tie him to his chair.

He was dangerously close to the edge of his control.

What the hell was wrong with him? He had no right to her. He wasn't her husband. He had been hired to be her *teacher*.

But that didn't stop this intense craving he felt for her.

He stood and pulled the watch from his pocket again. This waiting and wanting were killing him. The sooner he got her out of his system the better. After tonight, he would be able to get himself back under control, and calmly and impassively give her the lessons she'd been sent here to learn.

All he needed was a little taste of her to satisfy him.

At least he bloody well hoped so.

# Chapter Six

Clarissa still didn't know what to expect from The Disciplinarian, whether he wanted her fresh and clean for a new 'lesson' or whether the bath had simply been a courtesy before sending her home. She had to consider that, having done what he'd been paid to do, he may have merely felt she might want to rid herself of any remnant, any memory of their intimate behavior last night.

Instead, she found she wanted more of it.

She'd been perched anxiously on the edge of her bed for the last twenty minutes, trying to prepare herself for either scenario, when the knock came at her door. She heard the key scrape and turn in the lock.

She swallowed and stood as the door swung open. Soames entered with the dinner tray, followed closely by The Disciplinarian himself. She kept her eyes downcast, afraid of what she might read on his face, but ironically, her lowered gaze caught on the very thing that answered all her questions.

The Disciplinarian held his strongbox under his arm.

*There will be a lesson tonight.*

Clarissa let out a breath she didn't know she'd been holding. She risked a glance up to see that The Disciplinarian was staring at her, an odd expression in his eyes. They were unnaturally bright, and his face was a bit flushed, as if he'd just endured some strenuous exercise. Even his breathing was quick and shallow.

She closely searched his face. At least there was no trace of disgust in his eyes. He didn't appear to be revolted at her wanton behavior of last night.

He nodded at her curtly and gestured with a hand toward one of the chairs. She obeyed the unspoken command and crossed the room to the dinner table. As soon as she had been seated, he put his strongbox on the floor at her feet.

She swallowed and stared at the thing. She knew very well what it meant, what it would mean for her later, and despite the fact that this was what she wanted, a rush of nerves assailed her, causing her to grip the four-inch tall wooden pineapple carvings at the ends of her armrests and squeeze them anxiously.

The Disciplinarian stared at the gesture.

"That will be all, Soames."

The servant had been laying the places for dinner, but his head jerked up in obvious surprise at The Disciplinarian's words. "Sir?"

"*That will be all.* Leave us."

"But, sir, I haven't—"

"*Now*, Soames. Out."

Soames arched an eyebrow at The Disciplinarian's harsh tone, and Clarissa could have sworn she saw a look of concern cross the servant's face.

Whatever it was that was worrying the servant, he kept it to himself. "Yes, sir." He dutifully left the place settings unfinished, bowed shortly to them both, and backed from the room.

Clarissa looked uncertainly at The Disciplinarian. He came and knelt on the floor in front of her chair, turning it slightly to face him, and began to stroke one of the hands that clutched the armrest so tightly.

"Are you hungry, Clarissa?" he asked in his low, smooth voice.

She didn't know how he wanted her to answer that. He'd just sent Soames away before he'd had the chance to serve their dinner, but he was using his Disciplinarian voice, that sweet-as-honey tone that let her know this was somehow part of the *lesson.*

"Are you hungry, perhaps, for something other than food?"

Now she knew what to say. "*Yes.*"

She *was* hungry for another lesson.

He smiled, though the expression in his eyes was still oddly intense.

"I'm hungry, too," he admitted, his gaze running from her face down the length of her body.

The bold words made her shiver with excitement and a little fear. Last night he'd calmly and rationally explained her limited choices, the practical necessity of his lesson, and she'd reluctantly agreed to it. Although the things he did to her were wild—even beyond her imagining—she'd felt he'd always been in control. Tonight was different. Tonight he seemed possessed by some fevered need. She wanted his hands on her, but this intensity frightened her.

He seemed to sense her hesitation, because suddenly the fierce look in his eyes was gone.

"Don't fear me, Clarissa," he murmured, continuing to stroke her hand with his index finger and then slide to trace the contours of the pineapple carving. "Tell me, did you enjoy the things I did to you last night?"

She sucked in a quick breath. Any answer she made would clearly reveal her sexual naiveté, but he had probably already guessed that by her husband's complaints and her own artless physical response. She just nodded.

"And did you enjoy your woman's pleasure, your first...*climax*?"

Her eyes widened at his shocking language, the brash intimacy of speaking about such a private thing, but again, she nodded.

He smiled fully at her then, a sinful, seductive smile that actually took her breath away. "I'm glad you enjoyed it, because tonight I'm going to make you feel even better."

It's a good thing she was sitting down, because Clarissa felt the room abruptly start to spin. Her breath came in short gasps, her heart began to pound and her blood roared in her ears. *Better than last night?* Impossible!

He must have seen the look on her face because he leaned in closely toward her ear, and lowered his voice to a soft whisper. "Oh yes, Clarissa, it is possible."

That voice was a seduction in itself. Low, smooth, rich, it was almost a physical caress. The way he said her name, in three syllables, *Cla-ri-ssa*, on a slow, silky breath, was pure temptation. It pulled at something inside her, something that needed whatever he wanted to give her.

She had to stop herself from eagerly shouting '*Show me!*'

"Do you trust me?" he asked quietly.

She gripped the pineapple carvings again, but said, "Yes."

"Do you trust that I can please you?"

God help her, she *knew* he could! "Yes."

"Then let's begin."

She caught her breath as he reached for the lid of his small strongbox, and he stopped to look up at her, reassurance again in his eyes. "I want to do this, Clarissa. *I want to please you.* Tomorrow will be soon enough for you to learn the ways to control your husband when he demands his conjugal rights.

"Tonight I want to be all about your enjoyment. Last night I taught you that you can experience sexual pleasure. Tonight is for showing you just how *much* you can enjoy it, when a man will take the time to please a woman."

The look of frank honesty on his face left her speechless. He *cared* for her in some way, cared at least that her life after she left him would have some pleasant memories of her otherwise difficult marital obligations.

How could she refuse what he offered her? "All right," she breathed.

He just nodded, and reached inside the strongbox, drawing out another black silk scarf. She knew it was different than the one he had used on her last night because she had slept with that one under her pillow.

He slowly stood and walked behind her chair. She craned her neck to follow his movement, but he stopped her.

"Keep your eyes forward."

She held still as she heard him smooth out the silk. Then he held it out just inches in front of her face. "Remember, the blindfold is not meant to frighten you, but to free you. To let you *feel* things more powerfully." He draped it across her eyes and secured it behind her head, shutting out her vision entirely.

Her sense of hearing once again sharpened to compensate for her lack of sight, and every nerve ending in her skin came alive in anticipation of his touch.

He stayed behind her chair but placed his hands on her shoulders and then slowly ran them down the length of her bare arms. Her flesh tingled along the path he took, her body reacting eagerly to the warm, sensuous stroke. His fingers circled themselves tightly around her wrists. He whispered into her left ear. "Trust me."

In one smooth move, he tugged her wrists off the armrests and guided her arms to wrap around behind the chair. Clarissa felt her back arch and her breasts thrust against the thin silk of her gown in the awkward position.

"Lace your fingers together," he ordered in his Disciplinarian voice, and she intertwined her fingers behind the chair. "Good," he approved. "Now, whatever you do—whatever *I* do to you—don't let go of this grip."

Clarissa swallowed hard at those ominous words, so full of the promise of what she both hoped and feared. She heard The Disciplinarian move around to the front of her chair and she cocked her head to try and follow his movement. She nearly jumped when she felt his index finger on her left cheek.

"Relax, Clarissa. Just relax." The deep tone of his voice was as hypnotic as his finger as it stroked her cheek, then began a slow path down the side of her neck to slide back and forth along her collarbone, pausing to lightly dip into the sensitive hollow there.

He moved next to trace the skin at the vee neckline of her gown, running down one side and then back up the other, hesitating each time at the valley of her breasts, sending little shivers of delight through her. "That's right," he approved. "Just enjoy it. You are so sensual, so responsive to my touch. So honest in your reactions. Always believe that you are capable of—no, that you *deserve* equal satisfaction to a man."

His finger slid lower, across the silk of her gown to the slope of her breast. A second finger joined in then, leisurely heading for the crest, and Clarissa could feel her nipple tighten in anticipation. She was very aware that her position, with the pronounced arch of her back, was thrusting her breasts forward as if they were blatantly offering themselves to him.

It was an invitation she wanted him to accept.

She gasped in pleasure when he finally scraped his fingers across the hard pebbled tip, first one breast, and then across to the other. Her whole body seemed to clench in response to that stimulus, and she nearly came up out of the chair when his thumb and index finger began to squeeze and roll her nipple, encouraging it to get even harder.

She moaned.

She couldn't help herself. She'd never felt like this, never felt these sensations he seemed to evoke in her so easily. He had magic hands, thrilling hands, and she'd never wanted to be at the mercy of a man's hands as much as she wanted to be at the mercy of his.

She was breathing so hard she didn't notice that his fingers had paused at the ribbon of her empire waist...the ribbon tied just under her breasts.

She felt him tug on the ribbon and loosen the bow. Her gasp this time was one of shock as he slipped the wide straps of the gown off her shoulders and pulled the bodice down, exposing her breasts to him and effectively trapping her arms against her body.

It all happened so quickly that in the second it took her to consider opening her mouth to give voice to her sudden doubts, his own mouth had closed over one sensitive nipple and the protest died in her throat, replaced by a pleasure so intense, so powerful, that if she hadn't been restrained by the material of her own gown she would have disobeyed his command not to let go of her grip behind the chair in order to hold his head against her breast more tightly.

He alternated between lapping at her nipple with his hot tongue and sucking it into his mouth. The strong pull of his lips caused her stomach to clench and her legs to tremble, and sent a fire racing through her veins that reached down into her very woman's center. With his left hand he played with her other breast, teasing it, alternating his hands and his mouth between both breasts, even burying his face between the soft mounds.

"Beautiful," he breathed.

Clarissa wanted to feel embarrassment, or guilt, but this was too good, too powerful.

He explored her breasts with leisure, tracing every inch of her with his fingers or his lips or the velvet heat of his tongue. He worshipped her breasts and she reveled in the attention, amazed that a man could have such an interest in a woman while demanding nothing in the way of his own satisfaction.

Long minutes later, he pulled away from her.

"You smell of lavender and taste of heaven," he murmured, "but that's not the last taste I want of you, Clarissa."

She fully expected him to return to her breasts after a comment like that, and so she was completely caught off guard when he suddenly lifted her left leg to drape it over the armrest of her chair, hooking it firmly behind something. Clarissa tried to move, but she was caught by the pineapple carving at the end of the armrest. The same carving she had clutched so nervously a few minutes ago, the same one The Disciplinarian had stared at. Did he have this in mind even then?

He swung her other leg up and over the right armrest and Clarissa suddenly found herself awkwardly immobile, spread-eagled and vulnerable. *That's not the last taste I want of you...*

"Oh, no," she choked out. "No, no."

But The Disciplinarian had already reached behind her with his hands, and pulled her bottom forward to the very edge of the chair in order to give himself greater access to her. The angle forced Clarissa's head against the back of the chair, and she struggled to catch her breath.

"Please..."

"Better than last night, Clarissa. I promise. Relax and enjoy it."

The Disciplinarian's hands were already sliding up the insides of both her thighs. With one hand on each, he dragged the material of her gown with them, going higher, exposing her skin, letting her know exactly what he intended, until he finally reached his goal.

He tossed the gathered material up onto her stomach and out of his way, and Clarissa squeezed her eyes shut behind her blindfold, wondering, mortified, at what he was seeing, what he was thinking. What he was about to do.

"Perfect."

He spread the silken folds that hid her womanhood, and then slid one finger along her length. She jerked at the initial contact, but his touch was gentle, his finger slowly exploring her, sliding up and down, then circling her sensitive nub. He had done this last night, and once she put aside her fear of his *tasting* her, her body began to relax and respond to him much the way it had before, shuddering with pleasure and shaking with need. Wanting more.

"So beautiful," he whispered.

He slipped a finger into her. She gasped at the invasion, but she could feel how wet she was by how easily he moved inside her. He drew out some of that creamy essence to spread it around her, lubricating her so that his fingers glided slickly along every intimate inch of her, stroking her, caressing her.

She moaned with the sheer pleasure of it, letting go of any doubts, ceding him absolute control, giving herself over into his expert hands.

He gave a little moan himself at her willing surrender, and slipped a second finger inside her, while his thumb came around to circle her sensitive bud. The two sensations at once nearly sent her to that violent climax of last night, but, as if he knew, he abruptly stopped the motion of his hand. When her heart slowed its racing and she could breathe again, he started up the motion once more, this time locking his mouth onto her breast as well.

Clarissa was sure she would swoon from the pleasure this time. The three intensely intimate sensations threatened to swamp her, and she realized she *wanted* to drown in this wild decadence. She wanted to be caught in that spiral of pleasure that carried her up and broke her apart, but once again he stopped, as if alerted to how close she was to that pinnacle of passion by her gasping moans of pleasure.

Again, it was only when her breathing slowed and her pulse rate calmed that he resumed his attentions, his lips back at her breast, his right hand still stroking her.

Every time he started up again, it seemed he added another twist, another new physical sensation to his attentions. Each time he drove her higher, and more quickly, to that peak she wanted to reach.

But with his mouth pulling at her breast and his hand playing her so expertly, she didn't want to think, didn't want to concentrate on anything beyond what he was doing to her. And when she felt his thumb pressing hard against her little bud and his fingers curl inside her to stroke her as they had last night, she bore down on his hand, wanting even more contact, needing every new pleasure he could give her.

So it came as a stunning surprise when he abruptly shifted his thumb and covered her bud instead with his mouth, sucking on her, pulling strongly as he had at her breast, forcing her tighter against his lips with the pressure of his left hand behind her bottom, while still stroking her from the inside with the fingers of his right.

She gasped and then screamed, as her body convulsed in wave after wave of sharp, jolting pleasure. Stunning, earth-shattering, indescribable pleasure. On and on it went, endlessly, until she thought she'd die from it.

Then she was boneless, panting, every part of her body trembling in the aftermath of such a violent climax, but he was not done with her yet. He kept his mouth on her, gently sucking, lightly nipping, his tongue taking its time now in a languid exploration of her, his fingers twisting slowly inside her and making her body clench with dozens of tiny aftershocks.

It was too much. And yet she didn't want it to end.

He withdrew his fingers from her finally and replaced them with his tongue, the soft velvety feel of it running over her feminine opening and then probing deeply inside, tasting her as she'd feared, but for the life of her, she couldn't remember *why* she had feared it.

He drew back and her body actually felt the loss of his lips.

*"Open your mouth."*

Clarissa barely heard the softly spoken words, but she obediently parted her lips.

He slid his fingers, still covered with the evidence of her climax, into her mouth. In surprise, her lips closed around them.

"Taste, Clarissa. You are pure honey, heavenly nectar, absolute perfection. That is what a satisfied woman tastes like to a man."

# Chapter Seven

Jared had made a terrible mistake.

One taste of Clarissa Babcock had not satisfied him, and now he feared not even a lifetime of her would.

He stood leaning against his bedroom window, one forearm braced against the frame, staring out over the gently rolling hills of his estate. The picturesque view was bathed in early morning light, but he saw nothing of it. His mind was focused instead on last night.

*Clarissa.*

He'd been so sure that if he satisfied himself with a taste of her, then he could assuage this lust, this urgent longing, and get her out of his system

Instead, she'd haunted his night long after he'd left her. Even now he couldn't get her out of his mind.

He smiled, remembering how her nervous fiddling with the carved pineapples on her chair last night had given him a sudden idea, a wonderfully wicked idea, and how he'd been so impatient to try it out that he'd ordered Soames away before the man could even serve dinner, without so much as a thought for Clarissa's appetite.

She hadn't protested. In fact, after her initial hesitation she'd been downright eager, willing, accepting of whatever he did to her. Bloody hell, the sight of her with fingers laced tightly behind her chair and breasts thrust forward in blatant invitation had been so erotic that his cock had sprung instantly to attention. Rock-hard attention. Thank God he'd blindfolded her. She had no idea how powerfully she affected him, and the silk allowed him to hide that fact from her, ironically protecting them both.

He groaned.

He'd taken his time, done everything he could to please her last night. He had explored her perfect body without the barrier of her nightgown between his fingers and her luxurious skin, and it had been the most electrifying contact of his life.

And her climax! The intensity of it had shaken him as much as it had her. She'd been so spent, so sated by it that he'd actually had to carry her to her bed before he left her. And while he had obviously succeeded in his goal to give her a pleasure she would remember forever, it hadn't satisfied him so much as made him want to crawl into the bed next to her and see if he could do it again.

She was so sensual, so responsive, every man's fantasy woman, with a quim that tasted like sweet honey. He could have happily drowned in that honey last night.

He would never, ever forget the taste of her.

It had been an outrageous thing for him to do, sticking his fingers in her mouth like that, but far safer than what he'd actually wanted to do, which was to share the taste of her, mouth to mouth, tongue to tongue.

Even he knew that to kiss her would be disastrous, far too intimate, crossing a line from which he might not be able to step back. He was already much too close to that line.

❧⟨♥⟩❧

Clarissa didn't want to wake up. She was dreaming of a dark-haired man, blissfully wrapped in his strong arms, making slow, sweet love with him.

*"Beautiful."*

He was naked, his lean body warm and silky against her skin, gentle as he moved inside her.

*"Perfect."*

She felt him everywhere, his mouth on hers, his hands at her breasts, his rigid manhood surging into her, urging her up toward that elusive goal he called 'a woman's pleasure.' Except it was never elusive with him. He'd sent her to that peak and over its edge both times they'd been together.

*"So passionate."*

She was at the edge of that peak right now, and she arched her hips toward him, taking him deeper, increasing their contact, the sensations mounting until she felt that magic moment of climax. She wrapped her arms and legs around him as her body convulsed with the sheer pleasure, the pure power of it.

Moments later, heart still pounding, Clarissa reluctantly opened her eyes. She realized with surprise that she was indeed in bed, but her arms and legs were wrapped tightly around her pillow.

She frowned in confusion, looked at the empty room, and then almost laughed out loud. It seemed The Disciplinarian had created a monster—it appeared she didn't actually need him anymore, she only needed the *idea* of him to send her into paroxysms of pleasure.

That thought gave her pause. She might not need him, but oh, how she *wanted* him. He had shown her how beautiful the sexual act could be between a willing man and woman.

*Almost.*

They'd experienced every intimacy but the one she'd just played out with her pillow. He'd called her *beautiful,* her body *perfect,* her reactions *passionate.*

He'd even been moved enough by what they'd done to share the taste of her climax. She'd been utterly shocked at that, scandalized by such a thing, but he'd said she tasted like honey to him, like perfection. He was obviously as affected by their lessons as she was.

*Did he want her as desperately as she wanted him?*

Clarissa bit her lip. If The Disciplinarian truly wished to send her home with memories that would comfort her in the years to come, he would have to give her *himself* tonight. Nothing less would do.

Jared sent Soames into Clarissa's room with the dinner tray first and waited outside her door, pacing in measured steps, until he heard the clink of china as the servant set the table. He was determined to use anything at his disposal to delay facing her, to deflect this mad urge to rush in and take her in his arms.

Not even rationalizing the situation during the day had cooled his desire for her, so he had practiced schooling his features into a mask of calculated indifference in the hope that he could fool her, if not himself.

It should be second nature to him by now. He held all his students at arm's length, and always had.

But Clarissa was no ordinary student. And his feelings for her were anything but ordinary.

Too soon Soames reappeared at her door, his duties done. The servant shuffled off and Jared took a deep breath before entering Clarissa's room. She was already seated at the dinner table, and gave him a brilliant smile as he entered.

Her beautiful face, lit up in obvious welcome, was almost his undoing.

*She's married,* Jared reminded himself sternly, clenching his jaw in resolve.

He had no strongbox this evening, had no need of it for the lessons he'd planned, and he watched as Clarissa's eyes immediately noticed his empty arms and then shifted to his face in silent question.

He took a deep breath. *I must do this.*

"Come now, Clarissa," he said sharply. "I have no need of blindfolds or tools of seduction tonight. You will be leaving tomorrow. Tonight is for learning the cold, hard facts of how to deal with your husband."

He saw her flinch, as if his words were a physical blow, a painful reminder of something she'd rather not face. But face it she must, and he must show her how.

Last night had been pure fantasy, but tonight they had to deal with harsh reality. The thought left a bitter taste in his mouth. "Let's eat first," he said, sitting down at the table.

But neither one of them touched much of the food on their plates. Clarissa pushed her meat around for a while, and Jared had no appetite at all. Not for the food, nor for the instruction he was about to give her. After a few moments, he gave up the pretense of eating altogether and threw his fork onto his plate. Clarissa jumped at the clattering noise it made, while he leaned back in his chair. He forced himself to relax, to slow his breathing, to slide into his persona of The Disciplinarian.

There was nothing else to be done.

"You said your husband has hit you."

She paled visibly at his words. He hated himself for the cool, detached tone of his voice, but he needed to establish control here, to put a safe teacher-and-student distance between them.

"Don't," she said, a frown pulling down the corners of her mouth.

"We must," he responded matter-of-factly, steepling his fingers and regarding her closely. "It's why you're here, after all."

"Please—"

"Just answer the question," he interrupted, ignoring the plea in her voice. "The first day we met, you said your husband hit you."

She scowled at him then, a look he hadn't seen on her face since he'd first brought her to his house more than two days ago. Good. Anger was far easier for him to deal with than that dazzling, heart-wrenching smile she'd given him a moment ago.

"He hit me for the first time the day you picked me up." She ground out the words.

He knew what mortification it cost her to admit that. She was not the only woman in the world to marry for reasons of security or wealth or social advancement and then find herself in an unhappy marriage. God knew there would be no need for The Disciplinarian if that were the case.

Hers was an intolerable situation, but she must come to terms with it and find a way to deal with it, or else fear for her life every time her husband got angry.

Jared could help with that. He believed, given Charles Babcock's comments when he'd turned her over to him that Babcock's rage was fueled by his frustration over the lack of an heir.

He swallowed hard. "If you will let me, I can show you a way to restrain your husband's rage, to hopefully prevent the beatings, even turn his anger into an experience that you can enjoy."

"*Enjoy?*" she asked incredulously.

"Clarissa," he said slowly, "a husband has the right by law to strike his wife. We cannot change that. You are basically his property, his possession. But you can diffuse his anger and turn his punishment into your pleasure. I will show you how." He rose from his chair and held out his hand. "Come. Stand up."

"I will not!"

"This is your lesson for tonight, Clarissa. *Possibly the most valuable one I can teach you.* Now stand up."

She stared at him, and he wanted desperately to show his caring, his concern for her, but knew he couldn't. He had to continue the necessarily cold instruction of The Disciplinarian. *I'm trying to help you, sweet Clarissa.*

She stood uncertainly. "Why are you doing this?" she demanded, her voice nearly cracking. "Why are you being so cruel?"

The anguish in her voice brought him up short. He looked at her, opened his mouth, then closed it. Maybe if he confessed everything to her, she would understand his motivation in all this. He had never shared his story with any of his students, not even those who'd openly hated him and who never understood what he'd actually been doing for them.

"If I am being cruel, it's in order to be kind, Clarissa. My own sister, Amelia, was killed by her husband, beaten to death in a domestic rage. It is the reason I became The Disciplinarian, to make sure it would never happen to another woman, if I could possibly prevent it."

Clarissa just stared and said nothing, taking in what he'd said.

"Clarissa, husbands send me their difficult wives to 'instruct' them in how to be more biddable, and I do *teach* them, but not exactly the lessons their husbands expect. I told you once before that I *help* women, not *hurt* them. I empower women by showing them how to control their men.

"It's never been about sex, I've only taught them ways to manipulate. But your case is different. You don't ever have to practice this lesson I'm about to give you, but won't you at least let me show you one way to deflect your husband's anger when he threatens to strike you?"

He could see the battle in Clarissa's eyes, the way she struggled against the wretched unfairness of her situation. But reason won out, as he'd hoped it would, and she grudgingly nodded her agreement.

"Good. Now, when your husband rages and you believe he may strike you, say to him, 'I deserve to be punished, I know, but let me show you how *The Disciplinarian* prefers to punish a woman.' He won't be able to resist that challenge."

Her eyebrow reluctantly came up in question.

"Then say to him, 'Your bedroom or mine?' and watch how his anger begins to dissipate as his passion begins to build.'

"But I don't want his passion!" she protested.

"Yes, you do," Jared insisted. "You want to use his passion to fuel your own. I will show you how. Come with me."

He led her to the foot of the bed, where he sat down. "You must lead him here, like this. Make him sit at the edge of the bed. Then you must drape yourself across his knees, and offer up your bare bottom to the slap of his hand. Tell him to discipline you this way."

"*What?*" she cried, even as he maneuvered her across his lap and pulled up the silk of her gown to expose her smooth rear cheeks.

She struggled under the weight of his left arm as it pinned her down, while his right hand began a slow caressing of those delicate orbs. They were perfect and pink, full and lush under his fingers. Gorgeous. He felt his own breathing speed up, while he heard hers catch suddenly in her throat.

"Trust me," he soothed. "I won't hurt you."

She stopped squirming long enough for him to raise his hand and bring it down in a stinging slap, then another.

She shouted more in outrage than in pain, and tried to buck off his lap, but he held her down with his left arm while soothing her cheeks with his right hand.

"Instead of arching up like that, try grinding your hips down against my legs," he instructed. "The contact of your woman's center with the hard muscle of my thigh should be quite pleasurable for you."

She stilled completely at the shocking bluntness of his language, and though she was still breathing heavily he knew she was considering his words.

He drew his hand back and slapped her bottom again, then once more, gentler this time. He felt her press down hard against him and heard her gasp of surprise at the resulting sensation. She wiggled her hips experimentally for more contact, and he had to grit his teeth as his cock hardened automatically in response to her artless passion.

"Good," he forced out on a level breath. "And when that pressure isn't enough to satisfy you, open your legs slightly."

She balked at that. "*I will not!*" She struggled again, but he held her down using only enough pressure to keep her in place.

"Open your legs," he urged. "I want to show you exactly how pleasurable this punishment can be. Have I hurt you yet? Be honest."

"You haven't, but *he* surely will!"

"He won't. He'll be so stunned, so aroused that he'll forget all about your punishment. He wanted you 'warmed up' and no man can ask for warmer than this. I'll wager not even his mistress is this inviting. Now open for me."

She hesitated. After a moment, she parted her legs slightly.

His fingers strayed toward the invitation of her sex. He heard her gasp when his hand covered her there, parted her, played with her. Penetrated her.

"Take control," he encouraged. "Move your body so that you have more contact with my fingers, my hand. Insist on your pleasure. How does this feel?"

"So… intense." She said, panting. "Fingers… so deep."

He rotated his fingers inside her and she writhed beneath him, moaning loudly in pleasure. "Please… I can't—"

"Yes," he murmured. "You *can*." And to convince her, his left hand abandoned its hold on her back and slipped into the deep vee of her gown to play with one breast. He tugged the nipple to a taut peak, while with his right hand he tugged with a similar motion at the sensitive bud between her legs.

"Ah—*ah*," she cried, as he built the pressure, teasing and gently pulling, until she began to convulse violently beneath his fingers and finally went limp across his lap.

Bloody hell, she was so responsive. So ripe for his touch. So primed for passion. She was perfect, and he had made her that way.

It was going to kill him when she left tomorrow.

He pulled her gown back down to cover her slightly pinkened bottom, and helped her stand. He saw her legs threaten to buckle, so he swept her into his arms, and walked to the head of the bed, where he gently laid her down.

As her eyes fluttered open, he leaned over her and swept a wayward curl from her sated face. "You see? There is a way to enjoy your husband's punishment. Just remember these things: you must dictate the terms. And you must spread your legs—no man can resist a woman's sex when it's offered to him like that. Then take your pleasure from it."

He frowned.

"One last thing. What we just did is likely to inflame a man's passion. If your husband takes you afterwards, just remember that you have claimed your equal pleasure, on your terms."

He didn't like the way her eyes went instantly to his groin at those words. There was no blindfold tonight, no way for him to hide how powerfully she affected him. If possible, he seemed to grow even bigger under the blatant interest of her gaze. But there was still another lesson to teach her.

However, for that one he was going to need a glass of wine for courage.

He was about to turn and head back briefly to the dinner table when her hand suddenly snaked out to caress him.

He froze, paralyzed. He could only stand there as her fingers tightened around his cock. As her hand slid slowly up and down the length of him.

"*You* have not claimed your equal pleasure," she said in a tentative voice.

He gasped and caught her by the wrist to still her movements. He allowed no student to touch him. It was The Disciplinarian's Rule Number One, but then, no woman before had affected him as Clarissa had.

He *wanted* her touch. He longed for even more than that. But he could never have it.

*She's married.*

Still, he couldn't stop himself from grinding into her captive hand—just once—before pulling away.

To hell with the wine. He was going to need all his wits about him for this next lesson.

"Move over," he said. "I'm getting into bed with you."

# Chapter Eight

Clarissa held her breath as The Disciplinarian laid down next to her on the bed. She was on her back, afraid to move a muscle, afraid even to turn her head toward him for fear of breaking this fragile spell.

*He was in bed with her.*

She'd wanted this so desperately. What would he do now? What would he say? She could feel her pulse racing as she stared at the ceiling, waiting in eager anticipation for his next move.

"Do you ride, Clarissa?"

She blinked. Those were not exactly the passionate words she'd expected to come pouring from his mouth after she'd dared to touch him as she had.

After he'd held her wrist so tightly and thrust himself blatantly into her hand.

It was obvious that he wanted her as much as she wanted him, but it sounded now as if he were trying to make small talk. Polite conversation. How absurd. "Ride?" she asked. "A horse, do you mean?"

He, too, was lying on his back. "Yes."

She frowned. "Well, certainly. On occasion."

"Clarissa, a man rides astride."

She frowned again. "I know that."

"Do you know the differences in a horse's gait? Between a trot and a gallop, for instance?"

"Of course."

"Well, I'm going to teach you to have sexual relations in that same fashion. I'm going to show you how to guarantee your pleasure when your husband demands his marital rights."

Clarissa gasped in shock. What was he talking about? Was he going to take her from behind like some rutting animal? Or—

"Come and sit astride my hips."

"*What?*"

"Come and sit atop me, with your thighs straddling my hips, like a man straddles his horse."

She had to form the picture in her mind before she could respond. "You want me to—to *ride* you—like a man rides a horse? To sit on top of you and ride your male member?"

"Yes. This way you will be in control. You can dictate the pace, the position, the depth of penetration, and, as a result, your own pleasure."

Clarissa almost swooned at his words. Not only were they going to have sexual relations, but he was going to let her *control* it so that she would have the greatest pleasure possible! He was going to give her his body so that she could experience a woman's climax with a man. She wanted this so much, wanted it with *him*. She could feel herself getting wet in anticipation.

"Mount me, Clarissa."

It was an order from The Disciplinarian, delivered in that honeyed tone of command, but it was an order she willingly obeyed. She rolled onto her side and then rose up on her knees. His eyes were dark, intense, alert as he watched her approach. He held out his hand as she reached his side, in order to steady her while she lifted one leg over his body and settled it on the other side of his hips. She was astride him now, the side slits of her nightgown giving her thighs ample room to maneuver. She slowly lowered herself down onto his hips, boldly pulling the nightgown out of the way so that she could feel the material of his trousers directly against her naked flesh.

She was shocked at her own boldness. It was brazen, shameless. And terribly exciting.

He obviously thought so, too. She noticed that his pupils had dilated, his chest was rising and falling quickly, and another part of him had risen even more prominently than when she'd touched it a few moments ago.

She reached out her hand, eager now to acquaint herself with the instrument of her future pleasure.

He gasped as her fingers closed around him. "*No!* You are not allowed to touch me."

She frowned at that, since she had just touched him a moment ago and he'd certainly seemed to enjoy it. His hands suddenly came up to lock onto her hips, and he pulled her down hard against him, grinding her against his body. With her thighs spread wide as they were, the friction of the rough material of his trousers, coupled with the hard muscle of his sex beneath it, was so intense that it nearly sent her right over the edge. She moaned loudly at the unexpected pleasure of it, but her involuntary response made him stop cold.

Clarissa waited, panting, frustrated. She could easily have climaxed just by rubbing up against him like that. A few seconds more and it would have been all over for her. If she felt such excitement from just this simple contact with him, how would she possibly hold out for more than a moment when he was finally inside her?

*Inside her.*

Breaching her. Buried deep. Penetrating. Pleasuring her. She wanted that and she wanted it *now*. Her whole body shuddered in anticipation.

He obviously misunderstood her reaction.

"Clarissa, don't fear me," he rasped. His hands were still on her hips, but his grip on her abruptly relaxed. "I'm sorry for that."

"Sorry for what?"

He grimaced. "For getting carried away. For caring more in that instant about my own pleasure than yours. Forgive me. I'm just a man. A man who finds it very hard to resist such a beautiful, sensual woman."

She stared at him, her eyes widening in surprise. He truly thought her beautiful? *Sensual?* She rolled that amazing observation around in her head for a moment. What a difference from Charles, who barely even noticed her anymore, except to find fault. And who never showed more interest in her body than to attempt to plant his seed and be done with it.

She looked down at The Disciplinarian's intense face. She actually *felt* beautiful and sensual in his hands. His patient instruction these last three days had made her realize that a woman *could* feel desire in the hands of the right man, and not simply have to endure her marital obligation. The Disciplinarian's tender attentions had made her secure enough in this new-found knowledge to openly, and often very vocally, *express* her desire. The thought swelled her chest. "Don't apologize," she reassured him. "It was pleasurable for me as well."

The Disciplinarian groaned loudly and thrust his hips up against her. "Bloody hell, Clarissa, you have no idea what you do to me with your art-less honesty."

Clarissa frowned. What had she said to provoke that frustrated reaction? She'd just wanted him to know that she found him as sexually exciting as he seemed to find her. Considering what they were about to do, what was wrong with that? "My lesson—"

"Yes, yes, your *lesson*," The Disciplinarian quickly agreed, as if grasping at something that could calm him.

But being inside her surely wouldn't do that!

"Clarissa, would you fetch us both a glass of wine from the dinner table?"

Her eyebrows flew up at his words. "You want wine? *Now*?"

"Please."

Clarissa glanced at the table across the room, and then back at him, her eyebrows still raised in question. He nodded. Reluctantly, she dragged herself off him and slipped out of bed. She crossed the room and poured two glasses of wine.

"Better yet, bring over the whole bottle," The Disciplinarian urged.

She bit her lip. What was the reason for his sudden hesitation? He had called her beautiful, sensuous. His manhood was straining against his trousers at rock-hard attention. That meant he wanted her, didn't it? So why the wine? His passion should be all the drug he needed. It certainly was all the stimulation *she* needed!

"Come now. Bring it here," he said, obviously noticing the way she was lingering at the table.

She sighed and tucked the bottle of wine in the crook of her arm, and carried the two glasses across the room. He sat up in bed, propped several pillows behind his back, and took one of the glasses she offered, along with the bottle. She sat on the edge of the bed and watched in surprise as he quickly downed one glass and then a second.

"Right. Much better," he murmured under his breath, as if he were talking to himself. He put down the glass and looked at her. "Now then, where were we?"

His voice was too brisk, too brittle all of a sudden. Cool and efficient. Not the smooth, sensuous tone he'd been using just a few moments ago. And certainly not the voice a man would use to seduce a lover.

"My lesson," she prompted.

"Yes. Right. Your lesson." He eased himself back down flat onto the bed. "Well then, let's get to it, shall we?"

Clarissa paused, the glass of wine still untouched in her hand. *Let's get to it?* Where was the romance in that? Where was the sensuous spell he'd always woven around her in order to ease her fears and set the mood for such intimate instruction? *Let's get to it?* Good God, it sounded almost as if this were suddenly a distasteful *chore* for him!

She carefully put her glass down on the bedside table. "What's wrong?"

The Disciplinarian held out a hand to her. "Nothing is wrong. Now come, climb on top of me."

Clarissa stared at him for a moment longer, then took his hand. Maybe his attitude would change once she was straddling him again. He'd certainly been *interested* a moment ago, bucking up against her like that and pulling her down hard to grind against his body. *That* was the man she wanted—the one who was desperate for her, his desire overriding even the iron control of The Disciplinarian.

She would just have to figure out a way to make him lose that control.

He helped to guide her back on top of him, her thighs spread wide across him, but he positioned her slightly lower on his body this time, just at the tops of his legs, well away from his groin.

She saw him take several deep breaths, and actually close his eyes. His hands made their way again to her hips.

"Now," he said, his voice cool, all business. "Let's start with the trot. In this particular gait, the horse's motion alternates between one diagonal and the other, and, in fact, at one point all four legs are off the ground at once. Since the trot has that moment in mid-air, it is more comfortable for the rider and the horse to rise up and down on every *other* beat. A man will 'post' when his horse trots, rising up completely out of the saddle like this—" His hands tightened on her hips and he pushed her up off his body so that she was kneeling, her upper body straight, suspended above him. "And then on the off beat, he will come down into the saddle, like this." He slowly lowered her back down onto him.

"Now. When a woman has sexual relations with a man like this, she can use this *posting* technique to raise and lower herself on his cock. Up and down, just like on a horse, but riding a man's cock, as deeply or as shallowly as she likes, until she climaxes."

Despite herself, Clarissa blushed furiously at The Disciplinarian's dispassionate recital of so passionate an act. It seemed shocking, downright scandalous. Who could have thought up such a method?

But the thought of being so intimate with a man, with *this* man—a man so willing to pleasure a woman that he would surrender his body to her—made her breathless with excitement.

"With the gallop," The Disciplinarian continued, unaware of her wayward thoughts, "instead of an up-and-down movement, there is more of a rolling, undulating motion, to match the rhythm of the horse. Try it," he said. "Try rhythmically rotating your hips against me, back to front." His hands were still on her hips, and he guided her into a slow, rolling motion. "This way, with a man's cock inside you, you can feel it deeply, stroking you in different places as you slowly tilt your hips. You can control the rhythm and the position to make it as pleasurable for you as possible. You can even lean forward, or back, if that feels better."

Clarissa gave a little gasp. She could already tell this *gallop* was nicer than the *post,* since she could feel more contact with The Disciplinarian's body with this broader range of motion.

"There," he said, finally opening his eyes and looking up at her. "That's it. Do you understand both techniques?"

She nodded, and then took a deep breath. "Yes. I'm ready to try them."

The Disciplinarian went completely still. "What?"

"I'm ready to try them," she said, "to practice them, to see which one works best for me."

In fact, she couldn't wait to have him inside her. It's what she'd wanted since he'd climbed into bed with her.

The Disciplinarian sucked in a breath. "Clarissa, *that* was the lesson.

We're not going to... actually do... I have *never...*"

Clarissa looked at the outright panic on The Disciplinarian's face and understood everything in that moment. Understood that he had been very careful in how far they went in her sexual tutoring because he was attracted to her. Attracted enough to want to have her now, and resisting the urge with all his might, because above all else, he was a gentleman and an honorable man. Despite his desire, he would rein in his own needs because of his respect for her, and for the job he'd been hired to do. He would never cross that moral line.

His sense of duty and honor only increased Clarissa's admiration for him, but she was just as desperate as he was, although for an entirely different reason. She wanted it to be *his* face she saw, *his* body she felt in the future, even if it was her husband in her bed. She needed this memory of one perfect night to carry her through the rest of her life.

Looking down into the face of The Disciplinarian, she saw a noble man standing on moral ground, but it was shaky ground at best. She felt her own power suddenly, and realized he had done exactly what he'd said he would. *He had empowered her.* And now she was going to use her newfound control to take charge and demand exactly what she wanted.

She would show him how good a teacher he was.

With a smile, she reached for the buttons of his trousers.

Jared clenched his jaw so tightly that his teeth threatened to shatter. *What the bloody hell did she think she was she doing?* His hands were still on Clarissa's hips, but for the life of him he couldn't get them to move. He was frozen, unable to stop her deft fingers from easing the buttons of his trousers out of their fastenings, one after the other, until his cock sprung free of any constraint.

This was what he desperately wanted, and the thing he most desperately feared.

*"Please,"* he rasped. But even *he* didn't know what he was pleading for—for her to touch him or for her *not* to touch him?

His eyes rolled back into his head with pleasure as her soft hands closed around him, tentatively stroking, gently squeezing, making him harder than he'd ever thought possible. His cock felt enormous under her curious fingers, and he found himself thrusting against them for more contact, secretly thrilled that not even both her hands could cover the full length of him.

He had to find a way to stop this before things got completely out of control. Instead, he found himself letting out a strangled moan of pleasure as she ran the pad of her thumb over the sensitive tip of his erection.

*Bloody hell! I am The Disciplinarian. I am the one who should be in charge—*

She moved before he could finish the thought, inching above him, holding him steady as she positioned herself at the tip of his cock, and then taking him slowly into her body. He could feel how ready she was, hot and slick and wet, and it took every last ounce of his already tenuous control not to give himself over to the incredible sensation and thrust himself deeply up inside her. Instead, he held rigidly still, allowing her to take command, to dictate the pace, to use his body for her own pleasure.

It very nearly killed him.

She twisted and she wriggled, taking him deeper inch by agonizing inch, until his jaw ached from gritting his teeth, and he had to force himself to think about the upcoming harvest on the estate. The rose crop that was nearing the end of its season. Yesterday's foaling of Princess' filly—which he'd inadvertently named Clarissa.

*No, no! Think of anything* but *Clarissa!*

"Tell me, is this right?"

His eyes snapped open and he stared up at her in disbelief. Bloody hell, she'd taken nearly his full length inside of her and she was asking if she was doing it *right*?

*Don't even think about how incredibly right it is!*

"You're doing it right if it feels good to you," he managed to get out from behind his clenched teeth.

"Let me try this *posting* then." She raised herself nearly off him only to lower herself fully down again, slowly taking his cock back inside her body, more easily this time, and certainly deeper.

It was almost more than he could take. His fingers dug into her hips as he tried desperately to prevent her from moving.

*Harvest. Roses. Horses. Crops. Harvest—Yes, the back forty acres will have to be planted next year...*

"Hmm," she mused. "That's nice, but I'd like to try the other."

"The other?" he asked breathlessly.

"Yes. The gallop technique."

*The gallop.* Heaven help him!

She began to rock her hips slowly, following his previous instructions, undulating her body along the length of his cock. This was passion as he'd never experienced it. Every roll of her hips was a perfect stroke of pleasure for him. He was fully inside her, touching her in the most secret and intimate of places, his cock caressing her velvety inner flesh. He wanted to reach up and wrap his hands around her breasts, only managing to stay the desperate urge by sheer force of will. This wasn't about him. It was about *her*. He wanted Clarissa to be the one in control here, practicing her lesson, taking her pleasure. As long as she kept her movements slow and steady like this, he could almost convince himself that he was merely the instrument of her instruction, despite how hard he was fighting his own physical instincts.

*I may survive this after all...*

That tiny bud of confidence was short lived.

"Oh! *Oh!*"

As Clarissa leaned back slightly, both her movements and her breathing suddenly began to speed up. Jared intuitively knew she had found her rhythm, the perfect pace she could ride to her climax. She was *using* his body now, and when he heard her surprised little gasps of pleasure, he knew she wasn't far from her peak.

He felt the sweat break out on his brow as he fought against his own body's natural instinct to respond to her, to match her rhythm and join her in the familiar dance of release. Instead, his grip tightened on her hips and he urged her on toward that peak alone, whispering words of encouragement, bucking his hips so she could feel him more fully—and more deeply inside her—until she blindly grabbed fistfuls of his shirt with both hands, and rode him until she screamed out her climax.

It was only when Jared felt her body contracting violently around him, clutching his cock in wave after wave of pure bliss, that he could no longer resist his own release. He abruptly pulled her off of him so he could come in hard, jerking spurts of pleasure, ruining his shirt, but at least saving her from any risk of pregnancy.

And saving her from her husband's anger, because now she'd go back to him exactly as he'd demanded—*warmed up* and ready for an heir.

Jared had done his job, but the accomplishment left him cold. Empty inside. Clarissa would be leaving tomorrow. He'd taught her everything he could, but somehow it wasn't nearly enough.

He wanted more.

He wanted *her.*

# Chapter Nine

Jared was vaguely aware of Clarissa curling up into a tight ball—and deliberately turning away from him on the bed—as he struggled for breath in the aftermath of his climax. Bloody hell, he had embarrassed himself in front of her, spilling his seed all over his clothes, undoubtedly shocking her to her very toes.

He glanced grimly at her rigid back. It had been nearly the best sexual experience of his life, could only have been better if he had reached that sexual peak simultaneously with her and spent himself inside her luscious body. He wanted that more than he'd wanted anything in a very long time, wanted the thrill of taking them both to the height of passion, and then plunging with her into that shattering release, sharing that exquisite intimacy with her.

He had to stop himself from reaching out right now to take her in his arms.

*She's married.*

How pathetic he was. The notoriously strict Disciplinarian, undone by his own student.

*In love with his own student.*

With a silent curse, he tore at the buttons of his cuffs and then his shirt collar, pulled the ruined garment up and over his head, and tossed it onto the floor. It was only then that he realized that Clarissa was crying quietly next to him. He quickly stuffed his still partially erect cock back inside his trousers and hastily tried to right himself.

"Clarissa," he soothed, turning anxiously to stroke his fingertips down her bare arm. "I'm sorry if I was rough just then, but I couldn't risk your safety."

She curled into an even tighter ball and her sobbing grew louder.

"Sweet Clarissa, please don't cry," he begged. He wanted to comfort her, but kissing the soft skin beneath his fingertips, as he longed to do, would be disastrous. Pulling her into the crook of his arm to lay her head on his bare shoulder would be too intimate.

"Your husband—" he tried lamely.

*"I hate you!"*

He supposed it was no more than he deserved. He had crossed a line, made a serious error in judgment by allowing the lessons to reach such levels of intimacy. By allowing himself to fall in love with her.

"Clarissa, please look at me—"

*"Go away!"*

His breath caught at the fierceness of her tone, the dismissal, the finality in it. This was not the way he wanted things to end between them, but she was giving him no choice.

It was over. Her lessons, their time together, everything was over between them.

"Clarissa," he murmured, fighting to maintain his control. He quietly reached down to take her hand, brought it to his lips for a quick kiss, laid her palm over his heart for a brief instant, and then reluctantly let her hand drop. "I'm sorry. So very sorry."

She had gone quiet in that moment, and he held his breath. Waiting. For something, a signal from her, anything at all. But then she broke out into heartbreaking sobs, so he rose from the bed, grabbed his discarded shirt, and silently left the room.

Clarissa was inconsolable.

After The Disciplinarian had left her last night she hadn't slept at all, alternating between blind rage and abject despair.

*How dare he?* How dare he teach her about the sexual act, show her how wonderful it could be between a man and woman, excite a passion in her she never knew existed, and then expect her to placidly go back to her husband?

How dare he do all those intimate things to her, get to know her body better than she knew it herself, drive her to the pinnacle of pleasure again and again, and then allow her to leave as if he didn't care one whit about her?

He'd called her beautiful, sensual. His body had responded to hers in the most basic way. And yet he'd restrained himself last night, denying her that ultimate sharing of man and woman, the pleasure she felt sure a joint climax would bring.

Denying her the one memory she had hoped to carry with her forever.

Despite her best efforts last night to use her body to tempt him, he had still managed to stay in control, simply giving her a *lesson,* while she was completely out of control, head over heels in love with him.

How pathetic she was.

She'd tossed and turned all night, crying until she had no tears left, dreading what she knew the dawn would bring: the trip home to a man she despised.

When Soames had slipped silently into the room this morning with her breakfast tray, she'd pretended to be asleep. But the familiar smell of the hot chocolate wafting from the tray he'd left behind burned itself into her memory, and she knew it would forever remind her of this weekend with The Disciplinarian, the pleasure he'd given her and the heartbreak he was leaving her with.

Although she could have sworn she had none left, she'd felt a tear in her eye.

Then she'd noticed that not only had Soames brought her meal, he'd also brought her clothes, which he'd laid neatly across the back of the chair at the dressing table. Her reticule, gloves and hat were there as well.

*Her hat.*

One look at the peacock feathers stuck jauntily in its brim brought back memories of The Disciplinarian's first lesson, and another tear to her eye. How was she ever to endure this?

*She didn't even know the* name *of the man she loved.*

It was simply too much to be borne, but bear it she must, since The Disciplinarian had given her no indication that he wanted anything else but to send her home to her husband today. For a moment last night, when he'd kissed her hand and laid it so gently over his heart, she'd held her breath, waiting, hoping, but he'd said nothing except *I'm sorry.*

With a final choked cry, she slipped her hand under her pillow and withdrew the two black silk scarves The Disciplinarian had used during her first two lessons. She had hidden them there after each session, holding the memories they represented equally close to her. Now she sat up in bed and folded them again and again, until they were nothing but two tiny squares, small enough to fit into her reticule, and innocent enough not to attract notice. She would keep these with her always.

With a heavy heart, she silently ate her meal, stripped off her nightgown, performed her morning ablutions, and struggled as best she could into her stockings and corset, her undergarments and traveling gown.

Then, as if on cue, there was a sharp rap at her door, and The Disciplinarian entered.

He stood tall and elegant in his dark blue morning coat, black trousers and shiny black boots, obviously dressed for travel. She thought back to her first sight of him when Charles had introduced him. She had looked at him in sheer terror then, but it was not fear she felt now. It was sheer misery.

"I come to offer my services as lady's maid," he said, eyeing her dress.

Dare she let him help her? Would he be able to tell how her body longed for his touch if she let him so near? She had no choice, really. Without his help she couldn't finish dressing, and she could hardly go home with her corset unlaced and the buttons of her gown undone.

She silently turned her back to him.

He crossed the room and stopped behind her. Clarissa could feel the heat of his body just inches away and longed to lean back against him, but she held herself rigidly straight. His fingers deftly began to tighten her laces, but even that small contact sent a shiver of desire through her, and she felt her body tremble.

His hands paused. "Are you all right?"

"Your... your fingers are cold," she lied.

He hesitated, and then blew on his hands to warm them, quickly finishing up with her corset and turning his attention to the buttons of her gown. He was done too soon, and Clarissa mourned the loss of his touch.

"Ready?" he asked.

She glanced down at the bed. The memories of all he had done there to her came rushing back. *I'll* never *be ready to leave you. To go back to Charles!*

"Yes," she said quietly.

He gestured to the door with his hand, and she gathered up her reticule, gloves and hat, and followed him as he led her to where his carriage stood waiting on the cobblestone drive. Her feet calmly carried her forward even as her mind screamed for her to dig in her heels and refuse to go.

But all she could do was hold onto her dignity. It was the only thing she seemed to have any control over.

Soames was standing beside the carriage, and opened the coach door as she approached. The Disciplinarian handed her up, climbed in himself, dropped onto the bench seat across from her, knocked on the carriage roof, and off they started.

And so it was over. The most life-altering weekend of her existence had come to this quick and insignificant end.

They rode in strained silence for almost two hours, until The Disciplinarian finally cocked his head and asked, "Will you be all right?"

The look on his face and the concern in his voice triggered something in her, broke the dam she'd been struggling to build around her emotions. *The hell with dignity!* If she was destined to go back to Charles, she would at least give The Disciplinarian a piece of her mind, let him know just how angry she was.

*"How could you do this to me?"*

"Clarissa—"

"How could you show me how beautiful the sexual act can be between a man and woman, and then expect me to go back to my husband!"

She saw a troubled crease appear on his forehead. "Clarissa, my lessons have been..." The Disciplinarian swallowed hard. "Let's just say I've been *conditioning* you this weekend, so that you can respond to certain stimuli, enjoy marital relations with your husband, take control when he makes his demands. I've tried to help you."

She stared at him, furious at both his facile explanation and his sanctimonious tone.

"Damn you! You *haven't* helped me! Before I met you, I never knew about a 'woman's pleasure,' or that my body could react so—so *incredibly* to a man's touch. Marital relations were simply something I endured, but never *enjoyed*. And now, because of you, I'm doomed to know that I will never experience pleasure like that again. *It would have been better if I never knew what I'd been missing!*"

He looked surprised and horrified at her words. "No, no, Clarissa, don't say that. I've shown you a way to stay alive, to escape your husband's wrath. You are a sensuous woman, one who could experience sexual pleasure no matter who your partner is."

"*No matter who my partner is?*" Clarissa's fury knew no bounds now. "It's not *sexual pleasure* I love," she cried shrilly, wanting to curse him for an idiot, "it's *you!*"

The shocking words hung in the air between them.

Jared stared at her, forgetting to breathe. Had she just said she *loved* him? He looked quickly around the swaying carriage, trying to figure out if this was some cruel dream. He actually reached out to touch the door handle. Solid. Cold. *Real.*

No dream.

He looked back at Clarissa. There was a stunned expression on her pale face, her body frozen as if waiting in terror for his reaction to her stunning revelation.

*She loves me!*

His heart swelled in his chest. He went down on his knees on the carriage floor between their two bench seats, took her face between his hands, and kissed her full on the mouth. He dragged his lips across hers until her body abruptly unfroze from its rigid set, and she flung her arms wildly around his neck. And he kept kissing her until her mouth opened to his and he thrust his tongue home, claiming her mouth, claiming *her*, finally giving her what he'd wanted to for so long.

The *man* behind The Disciplinarian.

"I love you," he whispered, pulling away only long enough to get the frenzied words out, then swooping back for another kiss. "*I love you, Clarissa.*"

She was crying now—tears of happiness, he hoped—but he couldn't seem to stop himself. His lips had a mind of their own and they wanted to touch her everywhere—her eyelids, her nose, the tempting lobes of her ears. He cursed the high collar of her traveling gown because his lips wanted access to her perfect neck, that long, graceful swan's neck. He groaned with the wanting of it.

"Wait... please... " she gasped.

Her protest was feeble, but it was the dash of cold water he needed. He sat back on his haunches, struggling to catch his own breath, realizing the enormity of what had just happened here.

*She loved him!* And he loved her. He wanted to shout his joy to the world. As it was, he couldn't seem to wipe this silly grin off his face. He took her hand in his and kissed each of her fingertips, unable to stop himself, unwilling to break this new, emotional contact between them. "Let me turn the carriage around."

She looked at him, her eyes widening.

"We're already at the outskirts of London," he pointed out. "Let me give the order to the coachman to turn the carriage around."

She gasped. "What are you saying? That you want me to stay with you, to—to live with you? Forever?"

He almost laughed at the look of surprise on her face. "Yes, sweet Clarissa. That's exactly what I'm saying. I love you. I can't let you go back to that brute of a husband."

*Husband.*

The word suddenly lay like a chasm between them.

"Charles..." she murmured, as if just now fully understanding what Jared was saying. "You want me to leave Charles and run away with you."

Jared paused, his happiness dissipating slightly. Why was she hesitating? Surely she didn't want to risk her life by going back to her odious husband.

But the longer she paused, the clearer the situation became. He had no right to encourage her to wifely desertion, even to desert a man like Charles Babcock. While Jared could offer her his heart and his home, he couldn't give her his name in marriage—merely a lifetime spent in the shame of adultery. Divorce could only be decreed by an act of Parliament, and even then only if Charles Babcock agreed to it, which was highly doubtful because of the social embarrassment it entailed. Any property or dowry she had brought to her marriage legally belonged to her husband now, so if she left him she would have nothing.

Suddenly, *love* didn't seem a fair enough trade for all of that.

But wasn't her *life* worth it?

"Clarissa, I know this is a difficult decision—"

"It's not that," she insisted, frowning.

"We can petition Charles for a divorce, but if he doesn't agree, I may never be able to marry you."

"It wouldn't matter. I love you."

"If you run away with me you'd be disowned by your family, disgraced in the eyes of Society."

"I don't care about that!"

"What is it then?"

She took a deep breath. "You don't know Charles. He would be furious. He'd come after us—"

Jared squeezed her hand reassuringly. "Impossible. I've always kept The Disciplinarian's identity and whereabouts a secret. No one could—"

"Charles would find out somehow, hire people to track us down," she insisted. "He'd be incensed at being cuckolded. He might even try to kill you in his rage. I can't take that chance!"

"I'm quite capable of defending myself," Jared assured her quietly.

"You can't be certain of that. You've never seen the extent of Charles's fury."

Jared let out a breath. "All right, then we'll leave the country—"

"No! I could never ask you to give up your home, your life."

"*You* are my life now." He stared at her, unable to believe where the conversation was headed, beginning to see her slip through his fingers

She held up her hand, as if to stifle any further protest from him. "No, I must go back to Charles."

"Clarissa—" Jared felt like he'd just been punched in the gut. How could he possibly have gone from the heights to the depths—found love and then lost it—in the space of just three minutes? He didn't know what to say, what he could do to convince her. He wanted to protect her by keeping her with him, while she believed she was protecting him by going back to her husband. The irony of the situation wasn't lost on him, but no matter how he tried to rationalize it, in the end he kept coming back to the same question.

What rights did he have here? This was her life, her choice. Her decision was final. And yet he couldn't stop himself from one last attempt. "Are you certain this is what you want to do?"

"Not *want*," she said quietly, "It's what I *must* do. Please don't think me a coward for choosing this way. I really believe it's best for the both of us."

"It's not best for you," he sighed. "And it's certainly not best for me."

"Nonetheless," she said, "it's my decision."

He stared deeply into her eyes and then nodded his acceptance, brushing his index finger down the side of her soft cheek. "I'd never think you a coward, Clarissa," he murmured. "In fact, I've never met a braver woman." He was still on his knees at her feet, and he slipped his hand behind her neck to pull her head down toward him for a kiss.

It was a long, lingering kiss—a slow, seductive savoring of every inch of her lips. He wanted to remember this taste of her forever, the satiny texture of her mouth, the lush fullness of it against his lips. Smooth. Soft. Responsive.

And he wanted to leave her with something to remember him by, a final lesson, that of the perfect kiss—the profound vulnerability, the openness and trust, the mutual sharing, by two people who love each other.

One perfect kiss to last them a lifetime.

When it was over, he reached under his bench seat and pulled out a single white rose. "Something to remember our time by," he said. "I picked it this morning from my garden."

She took it from his hand and clutched it tightly to her heart.

*"Whoa, boys! Whoa, now!"*

The coachman's muffled command slowed the horses, and Jared glanced out the carriage window to see that they were pulling to a stop outside Clarissa's townhouse. Reluctantly, he pulled himself up off his knees and sat back on his bench seat. But he made no move toward the carriage door.

"Tell me your name," Clarissa said suddenly. "Please. If I am to spend the rest of my life with a man I hate, at least let me know the name of the man I love!"

Jared shook his head slowly. "No, Clarissa. If we are to part here forever, it's better that you just forget me."

She gasped. "I will *never* forget you! I'm counting on the memory of you to get me through those—those *times* with Charles! It will be *you* I'm thinking of when *he's* inside me."

Bloody hell, this was killing him. His stomach was tying itself in knots just thinking about Clarissa at the hands of Charles Babcock, even if the man *did* have legal rights to her. He shook his head again. "No. I will not tell you my name. It's best that you never know it. I'd never endanger you by risking that you might call out my name during those—*times*—and suffer your husband's consequences."

"I don't want things to end like this between us," she cried, a tear slipping out of the corner of her eye.

He leaned forward, his thumb brushing away the emotional droplet. "I don't want things to end between us either, Clarissa, but I understand and accept your decision." He laid a hand on the coach door latch. "Come. It's time. You don't want your servants wondering about a strange carriage loitering outside your door."

He saw her throw an anxious glance out the window toward her house. She stared at it for a full minute, but eventually nodded and determinedly gathered up her hat and gloves. She clutched the rose he'd given her tightly in her hand, and looked back at him.

"Kiss me once more. For courage," she whispered.

That plea almost broke his heart. And his resolve. Neither one of them had an easy choice in this tragic situation, and he was so damnably close to shouting an order to his coachman to just take them both away from here that he had to force himself to lean toward her for the requested kiss. He struggled to put everything he felt into that kiss—his love, his regret, his very heart and soul—everything he felt but couldn't say.

When it ended, she smiled up at him, her love shining in her eyes, and he knew she'd understood. She put her hand on the door latch.

He abruptly put his hand over hers to make her pause. "Promise me one thing, Clarissa. I've tried to the best of my ability to teach you how to deal with your husband. Promise me that you'll be brave enough and clever enough and strong enough to deal with him. *Please.* I couldn't bear it if he—if you—"

She put a gentle finger to his lips. "It's all right," she soothed. "I will be all right."

"You can't promise that," he said, shaking his head. He reached into his vest pocket and pulled out a card. "Take this. Please. It's the name and direction of my solicitor here in London. If things ever get too dangerous with Charles, if you ever feel you need help, this man can be trusted to get you away quickly. He will bring you to me."

She nodded, took the card, and gave him a last, lingering look. "I love you," she breathed.

"And I love you," he vowed. He didn't stop her this time as she pushed down the lever, opened the door, and stepped out of the carriage.

Out of his life.

Clarissa blinked as the midday sun blinded her for a moment. She dared not look back at the coach as she made her way down the walkway to her house, feeling oddly self-conscious as she knocked on her own front door. It was only when the door swung open that she heard the carriage begin to pull away, but when she stole a final glance at it, she saw that the shade had already been pulled down over the window as it moved off into the street.

With a resigned sigh, she turned back to her door.

# *Chapter Ten*

It was curious to see the reaction of Hawkins, the butler, as he opened the door to find her standing there.

He greeted her first with his usual butler face, the carefully blank, slightly snooty expression that Charles had deemed appropriate for servants in the Babcock household. But once Hawkins realized who was at the door, his expression changed to one of obvious shock, which turned quickly to relief.

"Oh, thank the lord! Come in, come in, milady," he whispered urgently, offering his hand to help her across the threshold, and quickly closing the door behind her. "Poor Alys and me have been worried right sick, we have, over what might have happened to you—" He stopped suddenly, a look of mortification coming over his face at the profound breach of protocol. It was simply not done for a servant to be addressing the lady of the house with such familiarity, even if he *had* feared for the lady's safety. He looked down at the floor.

Rather than be affronted, Clarissa was touched by the butler's show of emotion. It was a sad irony that she should get more affection from her servant than from her own husband.

She laid a gentle hand on the butler's arm. "I appreciate your concern, Hawkins. As you can see, I am returned unharmed. Please tell Alys I'll come up to my room in a moment. Where is my husband?"

At the mention of Charles, Hawkins's face fell back into its blank expression. "He's in the library, milady."

"Alone?"

"Yes, milady."

"Thank you, Hawkins."

Clarissa took a deep breath and started across the foyer. Every nerve in her body was protesting this confrontation, every muscle objecting as she struggled to put one foot in front of the other. Fear and resignation warred inside her, and she had to keep reminding herself that it had been *her* decision to do this. To come home to the husband she hated, in order to protect the man she loved. Her hand actually shook as she knocked once on the library door, and then pushed it open.

Charles looked up from behind his desk. "So," he said, putting down his newspaper and cigar. "You are returned."

Clarissa took a step into the room. "Yes."

He stared at her for a long minute. "Well? Did The Disciplinarian do his job? Did he *warm you up* for me?"

Clarissa had tried to prepare herself for just this question, but the bald brutality of it, the coldness in Charles's voice, contrasted so painfully with the warmth of The Disciplinarian—his gentleness, his tenderness—that unbidden tears sprang to her eyes.

"Humiliated you, did he?" Charles said, misinterpreting the glistening in her eyes. "Good. You needed to be shown your place. And I will make damn sure you know it this evening. Now be gone with you."

She paled at the threatening promise in his remark and made her escape up the stairs to her room.

"You look quite nice, milady," Alys said with a frown as she fluffed a ruffle on Clarissa's pink nightgown and straightened the matching robe.

Clarissa sighed. She couldn't blame her maid for the confusion she heard in her voice; Clarissa had never bothered to *dress* for bed before. All of the servants were well aware of the strained relationship between their master and mistress.

But Clarissa was hoping that if she looked *willing* tonight, Charles would go easier on her, might overlook the fact that her body might not be quite as *warmed up* as he expected. Perhaps he'd be quick to do his duty, and then leave her to her misery. Unfortunately, the most enticing thing in her wardrobe had been this high-necked, long-sleeved pink cotton gown. Even with all the buttons at the neckline undone, her skin was only exposed to her collarbone.

Before her visit to The Disciplinarian, she'd never considered that clothing could so excite a man. Why hadn't she thought to ask The Disciplinarian to let her take home the scandalous blue gown she'd worn at his house? The mere sight of her dressed in it would probably have been enough to send Charles halfway to his goal before he'd even touched her.

Yet wearing the blue gown would have been horrible, a sacrilege, almost. She could never endure the pain of Charles's hands while wearing the same gown in which she'd experienced the pleasure of The Disciplinarian's.

She should have gone out this afternoon to purchase something suitable, but she hadn't really *wanted* anything suitable. Tonight was not an evening she was looking forward to.

"Milady—"

Clarissa saw the look of concern on her maid's face. After the relief of Clarissa's safe return, there had been a palpable tension in the air all day, and the entire household seemed to be walking on eggshells, Clarissa included. Everyone except Charles, that was.

She patted her maid's shoulder. "It's all right, Alys. I will be all right." How ironic that it fell to her, the very person in the most jeopardy, to reassure everyone else of her safety. Alys, Hawkins, even The Disciplinarian. Reassure them all, when she was hardly certain of it herself.

A loud knock at the door made both women jump.

Clarissa swallowed hard, but there was no need for a response. Charles simply threw open the door, his gaze taking in the two women.

"Out," he ordered, his eyes settling on Alys.

The maid threw Clarissa a worried look, gave a quick curtsy to Charles, and scurried from the room.

Clarissa swallowed again. Charles was in his dressing gown, and she could see his thin, bare, hairy legs peeking through the join of his gown with each stride he took toward her. He was obviously naked underneath.

She thought back to The Disciplinarian's words in the carriage earlier today. *'I've conditioned you so that you can respond to certain stimuli.'* Looking at the ferocious expression on Charles's face, she knew in her heart she'd never be able to respond to him. Despair flooded her, and she felt a moment of true panic.

"What's this?" Charles demanded, looking at her attire. "Is this the best you can do?"

"Charles—"

"Take off that damned robe."

She hesitated, and then slipped the robe from her shoulders, letting it fall to the floor.

"You call this warmed up?" he sneered. "You're dressed like a damned nun!"

Despite his scathing tone, Clarissa could see that Charles was aroused, that he'd probably been thinking about all the wicked things The Disciplinarian might have done to her.

At this rate it wouldn't be long before he'd be forcing himself inside her. She had to act now.

"Charles—"

"Take off your gown."

"Charles, wait a moment—"

"I gave you an order!" he shouted. "I am your Disciplinarian tonight, and you will obey me." He roughly hooked both hands into the open material at her neck and tore the cotton gown to her waist. "Now take it off!"

Clarissa gasped at the violence of his action. She was quickly losing her chance to exercise any control over this situation, especially if Charles was determined to play the part of The Disciplinarian in order to dominate her. She *must* find an opportunity to take charge, but it was never best to confront Charles directly. It only fueled his anger. She nervously slipped the gown over her hips to let it pool at her feet.

He grabbed for her immediately, pawing one breast with his left hand, while rooting around between her thighs with his right.

"Charles," she begged. "Wait. I have an idea—"

But instead of piquing his interest, her words only seemed to infuriate him.

"Bitch!" he roared, pulling away from her. "It's always *wait, wait, wait* with you! Did you learn nothing while you were away?"

His face turned red with rage, and he raised a hand to strike her. Instinctively, Clarissa reached out to stop it, both her hands wrapping around his wrist, mere inches from her face. They stood there for a moment just staring at each other—Charles, obviously disbelieving what she'd just done.

Clarissa herself was stunned at her daring. Her breath came in shallow pants, and her mind raced frantically. This was what The Disciplinarian had prepared her for, and she opened her mouth to say the words he had taught her. *'I deserve to be punished, I know, but let me show you how The Disciplinarian prefers to punish a woman.'* The words were meant to deflect Charles's anger into sexual energy, thus sparing her his fists. She intended to say the words, truly she did, but one look at Charles's face changed her mind about submitting to this hateful man.

She wanted to control him instead.

So what came out of her mouth instead was, "*You will never hit me again.*"

It was her attempt to startle Charles, to silence him momentarily into at least listening to her proposal—that she tie him down and ride him like The Disciplinarian had taught her. The shocking suggestion would hopefully titillate Charles enough to let her take control.

But it had the opposite effect. If he had been red with rage a moment ago, he now turned purple with his fury.

"Stubborn, willful, headstrong bitch! I'll hit you if it pleases me. Why, I'll damn well throttle you with my bare hands, if I want!"

And indeed, his fingers reached for her neck. Clarissa fought him mightily, trying to pull his hands away from her throat while kicking him as hard as she could in his shins. They fell onto the bed together, a tangled mass, Clarissa still flailing at him.

As they struggled, an odd look came over Charles's face. He looked surprised, then annoyed, and finally, frightened. His grip on her loosened, letting go altogether as he clutched his chest and started gasping desperately for air. His face, already purple with rage, now took on a sickly tinge, fading to an ashy white. He glared at her accusingly but couldn't manage to speak.

Clarissa herself was dragging in great lungfuls of air, coughing and massaging her injured throat. She saw Charles collapse onto his back on the bed, making odd gurgling noises before finally quieting. His eyes were open, but Clarissa was afraid to approach him, afraid to press her luck. She said a fervent, silent prayer of thanks for her near escape.

It was only after several moments had passed that she finally realized Charles would never, ever threaten her again.

He was dead.

# Chapter Eleven

The next week was a nightmare for Clarissa. The doctor had come and ruled Charles's death to be simple heart failure, but Clarissa had been terrified during his visit, fearing that the physician might catch a glimpse of her darkly bruised throat beneath the high neck of her gown and suspect some foul play on her part.

To her immense relief, the doctor had simply expressed his condolences on the loss of her husband, and gone off to file his report.

After that, Clarissa had forced herself to play the dutiful widow, dealing with Charles's burial and then his unfinished business affairs, even though her mind had been focused on another man entirely.

At the end of the week, with her emotions stretched to the breaking point, she locked herself in her bedroom and frantically ransacked her dresser drawer to find the card she'd hidden there deep beneath her clothing.

The card The Disciplinarian had given her.

*If things ever get too dangerous... If you ever feel you need help...*

Those were the reasons The Disciplinarian had left her this card. But things weren't dangerous for her any longer. She didn't need help, but she needed *him.*

She stared at the name of the solicitor. Was it fair of her to try and get in touch with The Disciplinarian now, simply because she was free? She had rejected him in the carriage, chosen to go back to her husband, but the decision had been motivated by her love for him, as surely as his offer to take her away had been motivated by his love for her.

Still, she felt guilty, undeserving.

What must he think of her?

A sudden idea popped into her head and she crossed the room to sit at her desk. She pulled out a sheet of stationery and a pen, and began to write.

Yes, this was the only fair thing to do. She would simply inform The Disciplinarian of the death of her husband, but not ask him outright to come to her.

She would let *him* decide their future.

# Chapter Twelve

*One year later.*

Clarissa glanced at the calling card her maid Alys had brought up to her room.

*Jared Ashworth.*

It was a name she didn't recognize, and wouldn't deign to recognize today of all days—her first day out of mourning.

This Jared Ashworth was probably someone to whom Charles had owed money—a gambling debt perhaps, or the landlord of his mistress' flat come for payment of back rent. Obviously it was someone who couldn't wait one minute beyond the required year after Charles's death to come collecting. Well, she wouldn't have it. There was only one man she wanted to see, and that was the one man she'd likely never see again.

The Disciplinarian.

She had sent her trusted butler Hawkins to deliver her note to The Disciplinarian's London solicitor, but the only response she had received had been a formal note of condolence. She had placed her future in The Disciplinarian's hands, but it was obvious he didn't want her.

Even now, almost a year later, she had to force away a tear of regret. She had been a coward to let him go, to give up love in favor of a twisted logic that judged going back to Charles the only sure way to protect The Disciplinarian. This cruel fate was of her own doing; this life of grief was the one she deserved.

She knew her mourning clothes represented more than just the loss of a husband.

Technically, she could give up her dark gowns today and rejoin the world, but by habit she'd dressed in black anyway. It matched both her mood and her motivation. There was nothing for her to look forward to, no reason for hope.

With a profound sigh, she tossed Jared Ashworth's card onto her dresser and picked up her hairbrush.

Alys came back into her bedroom carrying a vase of fresh flowers, and set them at the edge of Clarissa's dressing table, humming while she arranged them into a plump display in the crystal bowl.

Clarissa turned, intending to tell her maid to have Hawkins get rid of their unknown visitor downstairs, but she took one look at the bouquet of beautiful white roses and felt herself turn the same shade as the delicate blooms.

*"Where did you get those?"*

The maid jumped a little at her harsh tone and turned toward her. "Milady?"

"I said, where did you get those roses?" Clarissa almost shouted the question, then forced herself to take several deep breaths, trying to get herself back under control. She couldn't bear to be reminded of The Disciplinarian today. Didn't want to think of identical petals from the single rose he'd given her their last time together, now pressed between the pages of a book she kept under her pillow. Along with two black silk scarves.

She carefully put the hairbrush down on her dresser. "Get rid of them," she told her maid with a forced calm. "Get them out of my sight."

"But the gentleman—" Alys sputtered, obviously confused by Clarissa's violent reaction.

"What gentleman?"

"The gentleman who brought them... The one downstairs in the sitting room... He insisted I bring them up to you."

*"What?"* Clarissa stood so quickly that her dressing chair toppled over behind her.

Alys was looking distinctly worried now. She waved an uncertain hand at the flowers. "The Ashworth roses, milady..."

"The *Ashworth* roses?"

These were the same roses that adorned the coat of arms on his carriage! Could it be possible that The Disciplinarian was downstairs in her sitting room right now? The thought robbed her of breath. She said a desperate prayer, and then she was running out of the room, barely hearing her maid's frantic call. "Milady, your *hair!*"

But there was no time to waste on formalities. Who cared if her hair was curling wildly about her shoulders instead of tamed into a proper bun? Especially considering the utterly *improper* states The Disciplinarian had seen her in!

She flew down the staircase, her feet barely touching the wooden risers, ignoring the look of surprise from Hawkins at her unladylike haste. She crossed the foyer and paused for a hairsbreadth at the door to the sitting room as a terrifying thought occurred to her.

*Oh, God, what if it isn't him?*

She felt the familiar constriction around her heart but forced the pain away. *Jared Ashworth.* Was that his name, truly? Was that the name she'd so desperately tried to get out of him that last day in the carriage? And why had he come today, not a year ago?

*Jared Ashworth.*

If he was really in her sitting room she would never, ever let him go again. If he still loved her.

*Please let it be him.*

She took a deep breath and pushed open the double doors.

He stood at the far end of the room, one arm braced on the fireplace mantel, tall and elegant in his grey morning coat, paisley waistcoat, black trousers and polished black boots. He was all that she could ever want, with his shining black hair and beautiful blue eyes.

But she couldn't read the look in those eyes as he turned toward her, didn't know whether to run and throw herself into his arms or to bitterly admit that things would never again be the same between them.

She had to force herself to breathe.

*I will not ruin this chance!*

"Black doesn't suit you, Clarissa," he said, eyeing her dress.

It was the opening she needed. "I'll never wear black again if it displeases you," she said carefully. "Would *blue* be more to your liking?"

Her bold words set off a momentary flare of heat in his eyes at her reference to the nightgown she had worn while in his house.

Clarissa's heart soared at the sight, and that heat from his eyes warmed her skin right through. *He still wants me!*

"Blue becomes you very well," he said low, moving slowly toward her. "As I think you know."

They met at the sofa, and stood there staring at each other.

"I wanted desperately for The Disciplinarian to come to me after Charles's death," she whispered, her heart in her eyes.

"There is no more Disciplinarian," he answered gruffly. "Not since that day we parted. There have been no lessons, *no other women,* since you."

The words sent a thrill through her, but she frowned. "If that's the truth, why didn't you come to me?"

He gave her a wry smile. "I did it for you, Clarissa. If you've learned anything about me at all, you know that I'm a gentleman. I've waited the requisite year after Charles's death not only out of respect for you and for propriety's sake, but also to give you time to decide how you truly feel about me. It nearly killed me to stay away, but in truth, I didn't know if you would still want me."

"*Not want you?*" she said, confused.

"I have something to tell you and you must listen carefully." He took a deep breath. "I'm not the nobleman I pretend to be. My coach with its elaborate coat of arms? That was mere show so that men would be more comfortable sending their wives to me, believing I was a gentleman like them. In truth, I'm nothing but a gentleman farmer. My life is in the country, far from the excitement and sophistication of Town. I have no rank or special privileges. My wife would not be called *milady*, as you are now, but merely Mrs. Ashworth."

*Mrs. Ashworth.* Clarissa couldn't think of a more beautiful name. *Clarissa Ashworth.* She closed her eyes at the dreamy possibility.

He took her by the shoulders and shook her gently. "Listen to me. You are a wealthy widow now, Clarissa, a woman finally in charge of her own life. You could do far better than to settle for me. My feelings for you are the same as the day we parted—*I love you*—but I've come here today to ask what it is that *you* want."

Clarissa didn't even hesitate. The lesson he had taught her came rushing back to her. *Take charge. Take control to ensure you get what you need.* That advice applied to so many things.

She turned to walk to the sitting room doors, pulled them closed with a stout thud, and locked them with a firm twist of the key. Then she came back to the sofa where he stood, grabbed him by the lapels of his morning coat, stood on her tiptoes and kissed him full on the mouth.

It seemed to be all the answer he needed. With a low moan, he swept her into his embrace and plundered her mouth. She took everything he offered and gave it right back to him in equal measure.

When the kiss ended, he hissed, *"Marry me, Clarissa."*

She almost laughed up into his face, so great was her happiness. "Yes, yes, yes!" she cried. "I want that more than anything in the world. But first…" With her grip still on his lapels, she roughly pushed him back onto the cushions of the sofa.

He sat down with a hard thump and looked up at her in surprise.

"There is one more thing I want."

"Anything," he agreed with a look of confusion.

"Close your eyes."

"Pardon?"

"Rest your head on the back of the sofa and close your eyes," she instructed. "Then put your hands down at your sides, flat on the sofa cushion, and don't move them, whatever you do. Or, should I say, don't move them *no matter what I do to you.*"

He looked at her through narrowed eyes. "Those are Disciplinarian words. What do you intend, Clarissa?"

She gave him a pointed look. "I want that lesson you denied me a year ago. That *ultimate* lesson."

"Here? *Now?*" he said incredulously. She saw him throw a glance at the sitting room doors, but the key was safely in her skirt pocket. They would not be disturbed.

"Here," she agreed. "Now." Then she smiled at him wickedly. "To seal our marital agreement."

"Clarissa..." Despite his hesitation, she could gauge his obvious interest by the tightening of his trousers.

"Close your eyes," she ordered. "*I'm* the one in charge today."

He swallowed, but obeyed her instructions and laid his head on the back of the sofa, closing his eyes. His hands were in tight fists at his sides, but she saw him force them open, laying them flat on the sofa cushion.

"Good," she approved in what she hoped was that slow, silky tone he'd so often used with her. "Now don't move."

She had intended simply to unbutton his trousers and climb onto his lap, but she paused for a moment once she'd kicked off her black kid slippers. What a temptation he was, sitting there like that, entirely at her mercy. As she watched, his cock actually grew bigger beneath her gaze, as if in anticipation of what was to come.

What power she felt over him!

His breathing sped up as she reached deliberately for the buttons of his trousers and opened the fastenings one by one. She reached inside the material to draw him out and he groaned as her fingers closed over him.

"*Bloody hell*, Clarissa..."

What a beautiful cock he had. Clarissa fell to her knees in front of him to examine it more closely. She marveled at the smooth, hard shaft, the sensitive tip. The soft, silky skin that covered the powerful muscle beneath. He seemed far too big to fit inside her. Why, even using both her hands, she still couldn't contain the length of him. She curved her fingers beneath him to cup his balls and he nearly came up off the sofa.

"*Have mercy*, Clarissa!"

He'd shown *her* no mercy while driving her to the heights of passion. She wanted to give him a taste of that raw pleasure, so she took his shaft into her mouth.

"*Ah, God, no, no!*" His body bucked up, forcing his cock deeper down her throat. Clarissa had never done this before and the feel of him so far inside her was a shock. Was it wrong? Was that why he was protesting? She'd simply wanted to make him feel as incredible as he'd made her feel when his lips had been on her. She quickly removed her mouth, but couldn't resist running her tongue up his thick shaft, and sucking the tip of it—just a little—into her mouth.

It was simply too much of a temptation.

He was gasping for air now, dragging great lungfuls of it into his chest, and his hands had again clenched into tight fists at his sides. "Clarissa, climb on top of me for pity's sake!" he begged. "I can't stand much more of this sweet torture."

Ah, so he *had* been enjoying it.

With a satisfied smile she gave the tip of his cock a final kiss. It jerked of its own accord, responding eagerly to that caress, and The Disciplinarian groaned again.

She stood up and reached under her skirt, pulling recklessly at the ribbon tie of her drawers and sliding them quickly down her legs. She kicked them away and slowly raised her gown as far as her knees, then climbed onto the sofa and straddled his lap. She reached down to guide his cock to the opening of her body.

He gasped as she settled there, poised to take him into her woman's center, into her very heart and soul. She rubbed the tip of him along her cleft, letting him feel how wet she was, how very much she wanted this.

"Good God, Clarissa, I pray that I don't expire before I can give you what you want!"

She never doubted him. It was pure heaven to feel him sliding into her as she pushed down hard, feeling herself stretching to accommodate every masculine inch of him. He was an active participant in this lover's quest, forcing himself up to meet her downward plunge, both of them in a desperate effort to fuse their bodies together.

And when he was buried inside her to the hilt, she began to rock. It was exactly as he had instructed her—she chose the *gallop* technique over the *post*—and she felt caught in that silken web of pleasure almost instantly. He was very deep inside her, and she could feel his hard muscle stroking her intimately as she rolled her hips. She knew she wouldn't last long in this incredible position, but she was counting on the fact that he wouldn't either, a hope that was rewarded when he began to buck and pant and match her rhythm as if they'd been practicing this motion forever.

"*Now,* Clarissa," he gasped. "Come with me *now.* Together!"

He let out a fierce growl, and she felt his body contract, jerking inside her. It triggered a corresponding response in her own body, that familiar shattering release, the letting-go of all control even as her body gripped him, clutched at him, milked him as he filled her with his hot seed.

A long time later, she came back to her senses and realized she must have collapsed against his chest after their climax. He had his arms around her, running his fingers through her hair and stroking down her back. She could still feel him inside her.

"*Vixen,*" he accused. "You learned that particular lesson too well."

"I had a good teacher," she reminded him.

He hugged her tight. "I love you, Clarissa," he murmured. "How soon can we wed?"

"Take me to the nearest registry office," she replied happily. "I don't think

I can wait while the banns are read in church!" Then she buried her head self-consciously in his neck. "And considering what we've just done..." "The registry office it is," he agreed. "But don't ever be sorry for what we've done. I love you, Clarissa."

"And I love you, *Jared Ashworth*," she sighed, letting his name roll deliciously off her tongue. "And if there should ever come a day when you find yourself missing your old profession, I give you permission to discipline me any time!"

## *About the Author:*

*Leigh Court lives in Southern California with her husband. This is her first Red Sage novella, and she'd love to hear from her readers! You can contact her at* hadleighcourt@verizon.net *or* www.hadleighcourt. com.

# Men you've been dreaming about!

## Secrets

*Satisfy your desire for more.*

eel the wild adventure, fierce passion and the power of love in every **Secrets** Collection story. Red Sage Publishing's romance authors create richly crafted, sexy, sensual, novella-length stories. Each one is just the right length for reading after a long and hectic day.

Each volume in the **Secrets** Collection has four diverse, ultra-sexy, romantic novellas brimming with adventure, passion and love. More adventurous tales for the adventurous reader. The **Secrets** Collection are a glorious mix of romance genre; numerous historical settings, contemporary, paranormal, science fiction and suspense. We are always looking for new adventures.

Reader response to the **Secrets** volumes has been great! Here's just a small sample:

*"I loved the variety of settings. Four completely wonderful time periods, give you four completely wonderful reads."*

*"Each story was a page-turning tale I hated to put down."*

*"I love **Secrets**! When is the next volume coming out? This one was Hot! Loved the heroes!"*

**Secrets** have won raves and awards. We could go on, but why don't you find out for yourself—order your set of **Secrets** today! See the back for details.

# Secrets, Volume 1

## Listen to what reviewers say:

"These stories take you beyond romance into the realm of erotica. I found *Secrets* absolutely delicious."

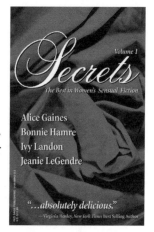

—Virginia Henley,
*New York Times* Best Selling Author

"*Secrets* is a collection of novellas for the daring, adventurous woman who's not afraid to give her fantasies free reign."
—Kathe Robin, *Romantic Times* Magazine

"…In fact, the men featured in all the stories are terrific, they all want to please and pleasure their women. If you like erotic romance you will love *Secrets*."

—*Romantic Readers* Review

## In *Secrets, Volume 1* you'll find:

*A Lady's Quest* by Bonnie Hamre
Widowed Lady Antonia Blair-Sutworth searches for a lover to save her from the handsome Duke of Sutherland. The "auditions" may be shocking but utterly tantalizing.

*The Spinner's Dream* by Alice Gaines
A seductive fantasy that leaves every woman wishing for her own private love slave, desperate and running for his life.

*The Proposal* by Ivy Landon
This tale is a walk on the wild side of love. *The Proposal* will taunt you, tease you, and shock you. A contemporary erotica for the adventurous woman.

*The Gift* by Jeanie LeGendre
Immerse yourself in this historic tale of exotic seduction, bondage and a concubine's surrender to the Sultan's desire. Can Alessandra live the life and give the gift the Sultan demands of her?

# Secrets, Volume 2

## Listen to what reviewers say:

"*Secrets* offers four novellas of sensual delight; each beautifully written with intense feeling and dedication to character development. For those seeking stories with heightened intimacy, look no further."

—Kathee Card, *Romancing the Web*

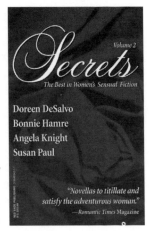

"Such a welcome diversity in styles and genres. Rich characterization in sensual tales. An exciting read that's sure to titillate the senses."

—Cheryl Ann Porter

"*Secrets 2* left me breathless. Sensual satisfaction guaranteed...times four!"

—Virginia Henley, *New York Times* Best Selling Author

## In *Secrets, Volume 2* you'll find:

*Surrogate Lover* by Doreen DeSalvo

Adrian Ross is a surrogate sex therapist who has all the answers and control. He thought he'd seen and done it all, but he'd never met Sarah.

*Snowbound* by Bonnie Hamre

A delicious, sensuous regency tale. The marriage-shy Earl of Howden is teased and tortured by his own desires and finds there is a woman who can equal his overpowering sensuality.

*Roarke's Prisoner* by Angela Knight

Elise, a starship captain, remembers the eager animal submission she'd known before at her captor's hands and refuses to become his toy again. However, she has no idea of the delights he's planned for her this time.

*Savage Garden* by Susan Paul

Raine's been captured by a mysterious and dangerous revolutionary leader in Mexico. At first her only concern is survival, but she quickly finds lush erotic nights in her captor's arms.

## Winner of the Fallot Literary Award for Fiction!

# Secrets, Volume 3

## Listen to what reviewers say:

"*Secrets, Volume 3*, leaves the reader breathless. A delicious confection of sensuous treats awaits the reader on each turn of the page!"

—Kathee Card, *Romancing the Web*

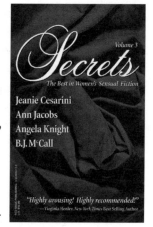

"From the FBI to Police Dectective to Vampires to a Medieval Warlord home from the Crusade—*Secrets 3* is simply the best!"

—Susan Paul, award winning author

"An unabashed celebration of sex. Highly arousing! Highly recommended!"

—Virginia Henley, *New York Times* Best Selling Author

## In *Secrets, Volume 3* you'll find:

*The Spy Who Loved Me* by Jeanie Cesarini

Undercover FBI agent Paige Ellison's sexual appetites rise to new levels when she works with leading man Christopher Sharp, the cunning agent who uses all his training to capture her body and heart.

*The Barbarian* by Ann Jacobs

Lady Brianna vows not to surrender to the barbaric Giles, Earl of Harrow. He must use sexual arts learned in the infidels' harem to conquer his bride. A word of caution—this is not for the faint of heart.

*Blood and Kisses* by Angela Knight

A vampire assassin is after Beryl St. Cloud. Her only hope lies with Decker, another vampire and ex-mercenary. Broke, she offers herself as payment for his services. Will his seductive powers take her very soul?

*Love Undercover* by B.J. McCall

Amanda Forbes is the bait in a strip joint sting operation. While she performs, fellow detective "Cowboy" Cooper gets to watch. Though he excites her, she must fight the temptation to surrender to the passion.

## Winner of the 1997 Under the Covers Readers Favorite Award

# Secrets, Volume 4

## Listen to what reviewers say:

"Provocative...seductive...a must read!"

—*Romantic Times* Magazine

"These are the kind of stories that romance readers that 'want a little more' have been looking for all their lives...."

—*Affaire de Coeur* Magazine

"*Secrets, Volume 4*, has something to satisfy every erotic fantasy... simply sexational!"

—Virginia Henley, *New York Times* Best Selling Author

## In *Secrets, Volume 4* you'll find:

*An Act of Love* by Jeanie Cesarini

Shelby Moran's past left her terrified of sex. International film star Jason Gage must gently coach the young starlet in the ways of love. He wants more than an act—he wants Shelby to feel true passion in his arms.

*Enslaved* by Desirée Lindsey

Lord Nicholas Summer's air of danger, dark passions, and irresistible charm have brought Lady Crystal's long-hidden desires to the surface. Will he be able to give her the one thing she desires before it's too late?

*The Bodyguard* by Betsy Morgan and Susan Paul

Kaki York is a bodyguard, but watching the wild, erotic romps of her client's sexual conquests on the security cameras is getting to her—and her partner, the ruggedly handsome James Kulick. Can she resist his insistent desire to have her?

*The Love Slave* by Emma Holly

A woman's ultimate fantasy. For one year, Princess Lily will be attended to by three delicious men of her choice. While she delights in playing with the first two, it's the reluctant Grae, with his powerful chest, black eyes and hair, that stirs her desires.

# Secrets, Volume 5

## Listen to what reviewers say:

"Hot, hot, hot! Not for the faint-hearted!"

*—Romantic Times* Magazine

"As you make your way through the stories, you will find yourself becoming hotter and hotter. *Secrets* just keeps getting better and better."

*—Affaire de Coeur* Magazine

"*Secrets 5* is a collage of lucious sensuality. Any woman who reads *Secrets* is in for an awakening!"

—Virginia Henley, *New York Times* Best Selling Author

## In *Secrets, Volume 5* you'll find:

*Beneath Two Moons* by Sandy Fraser

Ready for a very wild romp? Step into the future and find Conor, rough and masculine like frontiermen of old, on the prowl for a new conquest. In his sights, Dr. Eva Kelsey. She got away once before, but this time Conor makes sure she begs for more.

*Insatiable* by Chevon Gael

Marcus Remington photographs beautiful models for a living, but it's Ashlyn Fraser, a young corporate exec having some glamour shots done, who has stolen his heart. It's up to Marcus to help her discover her inner sexual self.

*Strictly Business* by Shannon Hollis

Elizabeth Forrester knows it's tough enough for a woman to make it to the top in the corporate world. Garrett Hill, the most beautiful man in Silicon Valley, has to come along to stir up her wildest fantasies. Dare she give in to both their desires?

*Alias Smith and Jones* by B.J. McCall

Meredith Collins finds herself stranded overnight at the airport. A handsome stranger by the name of Smith offers her sanctuaty for the evening and she finds those mesmerizing, green-flecked eyes hard to resist. Are they to be just two ships passing in the night?

# Secrets, Volume 6

## Listen to what reviewers say:

"Red Sage was the first and remains the leader of Women's Erotic Romance Fiction Collections!"

—*Romantic Times* Magazine

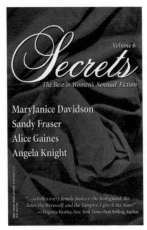

"*Secrets, Volume 6*, is the best of *Secrets* yet. ...four of the most erotic stories in one volume than this reader has yet to see anywhere else. ...These stories are full of erotica at its best and you'll definitely want to keep it handy for lots of re-reading!"

—*Affaire de Coeur* Magazine

"*Secrets 6* satisfies every female fantasy: the Bodyguard, the Tutor, the Werewolf, and the Vampire. I give it Six Stars!"

—Virginia Henley, *New York Times* Best Selling Author

## In *Secrets, Volume 6* you'll find:

*Flint's Fuse* by Sandy Fraser

Dana Madison's father has her "kidnapped" for her own safety. Flint, the tall, dark and dangerous mercenary, is hired for the job. But just which one is the prisoner—Dana will try *anything* to get away.

*Love's Prisoner* by MaryJanice Davidson

Trapped in an elevator, Jeannie Lawrence experienced unwilling rapture at Michael Windham's hands. She never expected the devilishly handsome man to show back up in her life—or turn out to be a werewolf!

*The Education of Miss Felicity Wells* by Alice Gaines

Felicity Wells wants to be sure she'll satisfy her soon-to-be husband but she needs a teacher. Dr. Marcus Slade, an experienced lover, agrees to take her on as a student, but can he stop short of taking her completely?

*A Candidate for the Kiss* by Angela Knight

Working on a story, reporter Dana Ivory stumbles onto a more amazing one—a sexy, secret agent who happens to be a vampire. She wants her story but Gabriel Archer wants more from her than just sex and blood.

# Secrets, Volume 7

## Listen to what reviewers say:

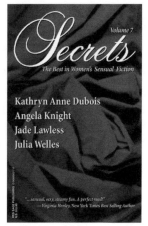

"Get out your asbestos gloves — *Secrets Volume 7* is…extremely hot, true erotic romance…passionate and titillating. There's nothing quite like baring your secrets!"
—*Romantic Times* Magazine

"…sensual, sexy, steamy fun. A perfect read!"
—Virginia Henley,
*New York Times* Best Selling Author

"Intensely provocative and disarmingly romantic, *Secrets*, *Volume 7*, is a romance reader's paradise that will take you beyond your wildest dreams!"
—Ballston Book House Review

## In *Secrets, Volume 7* you'll find:

*Amelia's Innocence* by Julia Welles

Amelia didn't know her father bet her in a card game with Captain Quentin Hawke, so honor demands a compromise—three days of erotic foreplay, leaving her virginity and future intact.

*The Woman of His Dreams* by Jade Lawless

From the day artist Gray Avonaco moves in next door, Joanna Morgan is plagued by provocative dreams. But what she believes is unrequited lust, Gray sees as another chance to be with the woman he loves. He must persuade her that even death can't stop true love.

*Surrender* by Kathryn Anne Dubois

Free-spirited Lady Johanna wants no part of the binding strictures society imposes with her marriage to the powerful Duke. She doesn't know the dark Duke wants sensual adventure, and sexual satisfaction.

*Kissing the Hunter* by Angela Knight

Navy Seal Logan McLean hunts the vampires who murdered his wife. Virginia Hart is a sexy vampire searching for her lost soul-mate only to find him in a man determined to kill her. She must convince him all vampires aren't created equally.

**Winner of the Venus Book Club**
**Best Book of the Year**

# Secrets, Volume 8

## Listen to what reviewers say:

"*Secrets, Volume 8*, is an amazing compilation of sexy stories covering a wide range of subjects, all designed to titillate the senses. …you'll find something for everybody in this latest version of *Secrets*."

—*Affaire de Coeur* Magazine

"*Secrets Volume 8*, is simply sensational!"

—Virginia Henley, *New York Times* Best Selling Author

"These delectable stories will have you turning the pages long into the night. Passionate, provocative and perfect for setting the mood…."

—*Escape to Romance* Reviews

## In *Secrets, Volume 8* you'll find:

*Taming Kate* by Jeanie Cesarini

Kathryn Roman inherits a legal brothel. Little does this city girl know the town of Love, Nevada wants her to be their new madam so they've charged Trey Holliday, one very dominant cowboy, with taming her.

*Jared's Wolf* by MaryJanice Davidson

Jared Rocke will do anything to avenge his sister's death, but ends up attracted to Moira Wolfbauer, the she-wolf sworn to protect her pack. Joining forces to stop a killer, they learn love defies all boundaries.

*My Champion, My Lover* by Alice Gaines

Celeste Broder is a woman committed for having a sexy appetite. Mayor Robert Albright may be her champion—if she can convince him her freedom will mean a chance to indulge their appetites together.

*Kiss or Kill* by Liz Maverick

In this post-apocalyptic world, Camille Kazinsky's military career rides on her ability to make a choice—whether the robo called Meat should live or die. Meat's future depends on proving he's human enough to live, man enough…to makes her feel like a woman.

### Winner of the Venus Book Club Best Book of the Year

# Secrets, Volume 9

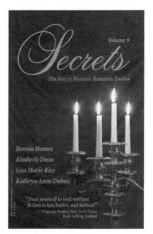

## Listen to what reviewers say:

"Everyone should expect only the most erotic stories in a *Secrets* book. ...if you like your stories full of hot sexual scenes, then this is for you!"

> —Donna Doyle Romance Reviews

"*SECRETS 9*...is sinfully delicious, highly arousing, and hotter than hot as the pages practically burn up as you turn them."

> —Suzanne Coleburn, Reader To Reader
> Reviews/Belles & Beaux of Romance

"Treat yourself to well-written fictionthat's hot, hotter, and hottest!"

> —Virginia Henley, *New York Times* Best Selling Author

## In *Secrets, Volume 9* you'll find:

*Wild For You* by Kathryn Anne Dubois

When college intern, Georgie, gets captured by a Congo wildman, she discovers this specimen of male virility has never seen a woman. The research possibilities are endless!

*Wanted* by Kimberly Dean

FBI Special Agent Jeff Reno wants Danielle Carver. There's her body, brains—and that charge of treason on her head. Dani goes on the run, but the sexy Fed is hot on her trail.

*Secluded* by Lisa Marie Rice

Nicholas Lee's wealth and power came with a price—his enemies will kill anyone he loves. When Isabelle steals his heart, Nicholas secludes her in his palace for a lifetime of desire in only a few days.

*Flights of Fantasy* by Bonnie Hamre

Chloe taught others to see the realities of life but she's never shared the intimate world of her sensual yearnings. Given the chance, will she be woman enough to fulfill her most secret erotic fantasy?

# Secrets, Volume 10

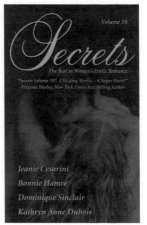

## Listen to what reviewers say:

"*Secrets Volume 10*, an erotic dance through medieval castles, sultan's palaces, the English countryside and expensive hotel suites, explodes with passion-filled pages."

—*Romantic Times BOOKclub*

"Having read the previous nine volumes, this one fulfills the expectations of what is expected in a *Secrets* book: romance and eroticism at its best!!"

—*Fallen Angel Reviews*

"All are hot steamy romances so if you enjoy erotica romance, you are sure to enjoy *Secrets, Volume 10*. All this reviewer can say is WOW!!"

—*The Best Reviews*

## In *Secrets, Volume 10* you'll find:

*Private Eyes* by Dominique Sinclair

When a mystery man captivates P.I. Nicolla Black during a stakeout, she discovers her no-seduction rule bending under the pressure of long denied passion. She agrees to the seduction, but he demands her total surrender.

*The Ruination of Lady Jane* by Bonnie Hamre

To avoid her upcoming marriage, Lady Jane Ponsonby-Maitland flees into the arms of Havyn Attercliffe. She begs him to ruin her rather than turn her over to her odious fiancé.

*Code Name: Kiss* by Jeanie Cesarini

Agent Lily Justiss is on a mission to defend her country against terrorists that requires giving up her virginity as a sex slave. As her master takes her body, desire for her commanding officer Seth Blackthorn fuels her mind.

*The Sacrifice* by Kathryn Anne Dubois

Lady Anastasia Bedovier is days from taking her vows as a Nun. Before she denies her sensuality forever, she wants to experience pleasure. Count Maxwell is the perfect man to initiate her into erotic delight.

# Secrets, Volume 11

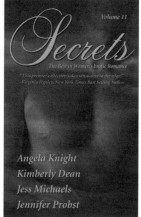

## Listen to what reviewers say:

"*Secrets Volume 11* delivers once again with storylines that include erotic masquerades, ancient curses, modern-day betrayal and a prince charming looking for a kiss." **4 Stars**

*—Romantic Times BOOKclub*

"Indulge yourself with this erotic treat and join the thousands of readers who just can't get enough. Be forewarned that *Secrets 11* will whet your appetite for more, but will offer you the ultimate in pleasurable erotic literature."

*—Ballston Book House Review*

"*Secrets 11* quite honestly is my favorite anthology from Red Sage so far."

*—The Best Reviews*

## In *Secrets, Volume 11* you'll find:

*Masquerade* by Jennifer Probst

Hailey Ashton is determined to free herself from her sexual restrictions. Four nights of erotic pleasures without revealing her identity. A chance to explore her secret desires without the fear of unmasking.

*Ancient Pleasures* by Jess Michaels

Isabella Winslow is obsessed with finding out what caused her late husband's death, but trapped in an Egyptian concubine's tomb with a sexy American raider, succumbing to the mummy's sensual curse takes over.

*Manhunt* by Kimberly Dean

Framed for murder, Michael Tucker takes Taryn Swanson hostage—the one woman who can clear him. Despite the evidence against him, the attraction between them is strong. Tucker resorts to unconventional, yet effective methods of persuasion to change the sexy ADA's mind.

*Wake Me* by Angela Knight

Chloe Hart received a sexy painting of a sleeping knight. Radolf of Varik has been trapped for centuries in the painting since, cursed by a witch. His only hope is to visit the dreams of women and make one of them fall in love with him so she can free him with a kiss.

# Secrets, Volume 12

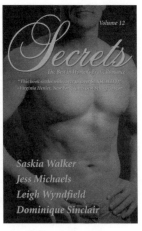

## Listen to what reviewers say:

"*Secrets Volume 12*, turns on the heat with a seductive encounter inside a bookstore, a temple of naughty and sensual delight, a galactic inferno that thaws ice, and a lightening storm that lights up the English shoreline. Tales of looking for love in all the right places with a heat rating out the charts." **4½ Stars**

*—Romantic Times BOOKclub*

"I really liked these stories.You want great escapism? Read *Secrets, Volume 12.*"

*—Romance Reviews*

## In *Secrets, Volume 12* you'll find:

*Good Girl Gone Bad* by Dominique Sinclair

Reagan's dreams are finally within reach. Setting out to do research for an article, nothing could have prepared her for Luke, or his offer to teach her everything she needs to know about sex. Licentious pleasures, forbidden desires… inspiring the best writing she's ever done.

*Aphrodite's Passion* by Jess Michaels

When Selena flees Victorian London before her evil stepchildren can institutionalize her for hysteria, Gavin is asked to bring her back home. But when he finds her living on the island of Cyprus, his need to have her begins to block out every other impulse.

*White Heat* by Leigh Wyndfield

Raine is hiding in an icehouse in the middle of nowhere from one of the scariest men in the universes. Walker escaped from a burning prison. Imagine their surprise when they find out they have the same man to blame for their miseries. Passion, revenge and love are in their future.

*Summer Lightning* by Saskia Walker

Sculptress Sally is enjoying an idyllic getaway on a secluded cove when she spots a gorgeous man walking naked on the beach. When Julian finds an attractive woman shacked up in his cove, he has to check her out. But what will he do when he finds she's secretly been using him as a model?

# Secrets, Volume 13

## Listen to what reviewers say:

"In *Secrets Volume 13*, the temperature gets turned up a few notches with a mistaken personal ad, shape-shifters destined to love, a hot Regency lord and his lady, as well as a bodyguard protecting his woman. Emotions and flames blaze high in Red Sage's latest foray into the sensual and delightful art of love." **4½ Stars**

*—Romantic Times BOOKclub*

"The sex is still so hot the pages nearly ignite! Read *Secrets, Volume 13*!"

*—Romance Reviews*

## In *Secrets, Volume 13* you'll find:

*Out of Control* by Rachelle Chase

Astrid's world revolves around her business and she's hoping to pick up wealthy Erik Santos as a client. Only he's hoping to pick up something entirely different. Will she give in to the seductive pull of his proposition?

*Hawkmoor* by Amber Green

Shape-shifters answer to Darien as he acts in the name of the long-missing Lady Hawkmoor, their hereditary ruler. When she unexpectedly surfaces, Darien must deal with a scrappy individual whose wary eyes hold the other half of his soul, but who has the power to destroy his world.

*Lessons in Pleasure* by Charlotte Featherstone

A wicked bargain has Lily vowing never to yield to the demands of the rake she once loved and lost. Unfortunately, Damian, the Earl of St. Croix, or Saint as he is infamously known, will not take 'no' for an answer.

*In the Heat of the Night* by Calista Fox

Haunted by a century-old curse, Molina fears she won't live to see her thirtieth birthday. Nick, her former bodyguard, is hired back into service to protect her from the fatal accidents that plague her family. But *In the Heat of the Night*, will his passion and love for her be enough to convince Molina they have a future together?

# Secrets, Volume 14

## Listen to what reviewers say:

"*Secrets Volume 14* will excite readers with its diverse selection of delectable sexy tales ranging from a fourteenth century love story to a sci-fi rebel who falls for a irresistible research scientist to a trio of determined vampires who battle for the same woman to a virgin sacrifice who falls in love with a beast. A cornucopia of pure delight!" **4½ Stars**
— *Romantic Times BOOKclub*

"This book contains four erotic tales sure to keep readers up long into the night."

— *Romance Junkies*

## In *Secrets, Volume 14* you'll find:

*Soul Kisses* by Angela Knight

Beth's been kidnapped by Joaquin Ramirez, a sadistic vampire. Handsome vampire cousins, Morgan and Garret Axton, come to her rescue. Can she find happiness with two vampires?

*Temptation in Time* by Alexa Aames

Ariana escaped the Middle Ages after stealing a kiss of magic from sexy sorcerer, Marcus de Grey. When he brings her back, they begin a battle of wills and a sexual odyssey that could spell disaster for them both.

*Ailis and the Beast* by Jennifer Barlowe

When Ailis agreed to be her village's sacrifice to the mysterious Beast she was prepared to sacrifice her virtue, and possibly her life. But some things aren't what they seem. Ailis and the Beast are about to discover the greatest sacrifice may be the human heart.

*Night Heat* by Leigh Wynfield

When Rip Bowhite leads a revolt on the prison planet, he ends up struggling to survive against monsters that rule the night. Jemma, the prison's Healer, won't allow herself to be distracted by the instant attraction she feels for Rip. As the stakes are raised and death draws near, love seems doomed in the heat of the night.

# Secrets, Volume 15

## Listen to what reviewers say:

"*Secrets Volume 15* blends humor, tension and steamy romance in its newest collection that sizzles with passion between unlikely pairs—a male chauvinist columnist and a librarian turned erotica author; a handsome werewolf and his resisting mate; an unfulfilled woman and a sexy police officer and a Victorian wife who learns discipline can be fun. Readers will revel in this delicious assortment of thrilling tales." **4 Stars**
—*Romantic Times BOOKclub*

"This book contains four tales by some of today's hottest authors that will tease your senses and intrigue your mind."
—*Romance Junkies*

## In *Secrets, Volume 15* you'll find:

*Simon Says* by Jane Thompson

Simon Campbell is a newspaper columnist who panders to male fantasies. Georgina Kennedy is a respectable librarian. On the surface, these two have nothing in common... but don't judge a book by its cover.

*Bite of the Wolf* by Cynthia Eden

Gareth Morlet, alpha werewolf, has finally found his mate. All he has to do is convince Trinity to join with him, to give in to the pleasure of a werewolf's mating, and then she will be his... forever.

*Falling for Trouble* by Saskia Walker

With 48 hours to clear her brother's name, Sonia Harmond finds help from irresistible bad boy, Oliver Eaglestone. When the erotic tension between them hits fever pitch, securing evidence to thwart an international arms dealer isn't the only danger they face.

*The Disciplinarian* by Leigh Court

Headstrong Clarissa Babcock is sent to the shadowy legend known as The Disciplinarian for instruction in proper wifely obedience. Jared Ashworth uses the tools of seduction to show her how to control a demanding husband, but her beauty, spirit, and uninhibited passion make Jared hunger to keep her—and their darkly erotic nights—all for himself!

# The Forever Kiss
## by Angela Knight

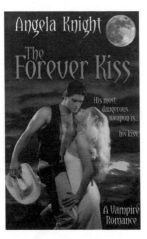

### Listen to what reviewers say:

"*The Forever Kiss* flows well with good characters and an interesting plot. ... If you enjoy vampires and a lot of hot sex, you are sure to enjoy *The Forever Kiss*."

—*The Best Reviews*

"Battling vampires, a protective ghost and the ever present battle of good and evil keep excellent pace with the erotic delights in Angela Knight's *The Forever Kiss*—a book that absolutely bites with refreshing paranormal humor." **4½ Stars, Top Pick**

—*Romantic Times BOOKclub*

"I found *The Forever Kiss* to be an exceptionally written, refreshing book. ... I really enjoyed this book by Angela Knight. ... 5 angels!"

—*Fallen Angel Reviews*

"*The Forever Kiss* is the first single title released from Red Sage and if this is any indication of what we can expect, it won't be the last. ... The love scenes are hot enough to give a vampire a sunburn and the fight scenes will have you cheering for the good guys."

—*Really Bad Barb Reviews*

### In *The Forever Kiss*:

For years, Valerie Chase has been haunted by dreams of a Texas Ranger she knows only as "Cowboy." As a child, he rescued her from the nightmare vampires who murdered her parents. As an adult, she still dreams of him—but now he's her seductive lover in nights of erotic pleasure.

Yet "Cowboy" is more than a dream—he's the real Cade McKinnon—and a vampire! For years, he's protected Valerie from Edward Ridgemont, the sadistic vampire who turned him. Now, Ridgmont wants Valerie for his own and Cade is the only one who can protect her.

When Val finds herself abducted by her handsome dream man, she's appalled to discover he's one of the vampires she fears. Now, caught in a web of fear and passion, she and Cade must learn to trust each other, even as an immortal monster stalks their every move.

Their only hope of survival is...*The Forever Kiss*.

**Romantic Times Best Erotic Novel of the Year**

# Finally, the men you've been dreaming about!

## Give the Gift of Spicy Romantic Fiction

Don't want to wait? You can place a retail price ($12.99) order for any of the *Secrets* volumes from the following:

① **Waldenbooks and Borders Stores**

② **Amazon.com** or **BarnesandNoble.com**

③ **Book Clearinghouse (800-431-1579)**

④ **Romantic Times Magazine**
Books by Mail (718-237-1097)

⑤ Special order at other bookstores.
Bookstores: Please contact Baker & Taylor Distributors, Ingram Book Distributor, or Red Sage Publishing for bookstore sales.

## Order by title or ISBN #:

**Vol. 1:** 0-9648942-0-3

**Vol. 2:** 0-9648942-1-1

**Vol. 3:** 0-9648942-2-X

**Vol. 4:** 0-9648942-4-6

**Vol. 5:** 0-9648942-5-4

**Vol. 6:** 0-9648942-6-2

**Vol. 7:** 0-9648942-7-0

**Vol. 8:** 0-9648942-8-9

**Vol. 9:** 0-9648942-9-7

**Vol. 10:** 0-9754516-0-X

**Vol. 11:** 0-9754516-1-8

**Vol. 12:** 0-9754516-2-6

**Vol. 13:** 0-9754516-3-4

**Vol. 14:** 0-9754516-4-2

**Vol. 15:** 0-9754516-5-0

**The Forever Kiss:** 0-9648942-3-8 ($14.00)

# It's not just reviewers raving about *Secrets*. See what readers have to say:

"When are you coming out with a new Volume? I want a new one next month!" via email from a reader.

"I loved the hot, wet sex without vulgar words being used to make it exciting." after *Volume 1*

"I loved the blend of sensuality and sexual intensity—HOT!" after *Volume 2*

"The best thing about *Secrets* is they're hot and brief! The least thing is you do not have enough of them!" after *Volume 3*

"I have been extreamly satisfied with *Secrets*, keep up the good writing." after *Volume 4*

"Stories have plot and characters to support the erotica. They would be good strong stories without the heat." after *Volume 5*

"*Secrets* really knows how to push the envelop better than anyone else." after *Volume 6*

"These are the best sensual stories I have ever read!" after *Volume 7*

"I love, love, love the *Secrets* stories. I now have all of them, please have more books come out each year." after *Volume 8*

"These are the perfect sensual romance stories!" after *Volume 9*

"What I love about *Secrets Volume 10* is how I couldn't put it down!" after *Volume 10*

"All of the *Secrets* volumes are terrific! I have read all of them up to *Secrets Volume 11*. Please keep them coming! I will read every one you make!" after *Volume 11*